UNLANGUAGE

UNLANGUAGE

MICHAEL CISCO

ERASERHEAD PRESS
PORTLAND, OREGON

ERASERHEAD PRESS
P.O. BOX 10065
PORTLAND, OR 97296

www.eraserheadpress.com
facebook/eraserheadpress

ISBN: 978-1-62105-266-1
Copyright © 2018 by Michael Cisco
Cover art copyright © 2018 Matthew Revert

Printed in the USA.

WHITE SPACES BLACK LETTERS

This stretch of my way is not romantic or unromantic. Engulfed suddenly in shadow. It's densely crowded with black figures crossing and uncrossing my path, silhouetted against the white light on the shadow's far border up ahead of me, and when I emerge I find a book pressed into my hands—this book. Yes, with these words, not one missing, not one added. It's an easy enough thing to check, see, since they're the first words.

INSIDE THE FRONT COVER

Inside the front cover there is a table which records the illegible names of the students who have used this workbook before. An adjacent column lists dates of possession in sequence, specifically dates of acquisition. There are no dates of return.

INTRODUCTION

The language which is the subject of this work book has been given any number of valid names. In this work book, we will usually refer to our subject as **unlanguage of unknowing**. There will be exceptions to this policy, however, because the student must not become too attached to any one name, nor is it of any benefit to leave the student in ignorance of the others, which include: lingua obscura, enigmatica, oraculo, youming yuyan (language of the quiet depths), lugha al lughz (language of riddles), bhasa sammudha (bewildering language), confusion, phantasmagoria, parabolica, eavesdropia. The language that dies, of perennial leavetaking. Language that is the closest of all to what is outside of it. You will learn this unlanguage. As everyone does, sooner or later.

> *A long, thick rope of fluid, which ran down my leg a couple inches before it congealed. The scab covering half my knee must have torn loose along the bottom sometime, sometime early on, when I was walking out here, with all the flexing and unflexing of the joint, and this stuff leaked out. Leaked out, and hardened.*
>
> *I kneel on a tuft of grass, pull up my pant leg, and examine. A hot stalagmite or tite I can never remember, the downhanging kind. I touch the scab. It's dry, and hot underneath. I brush the surface lightly; press, and very slightly roll it under my finger. Brown-orange and custardy grey. Some hair matted into it, too. I could tear it off, but it's the only thing stopping up the crack in the scab.*

My body made this nameless thing. Made it, without my being at all aware.

There are graduated contours of roughened white skin all around the scab like surf around an island, viewed from above. These white outlines mark the contraction of the wound as the skin repairs itself. If I tore off my scab, my body would manufacture another. It has to. The action is blind.

This special language slides over everything and grips nothing, not even like water, not even like time or air. It's a dimension. It sleeps. God doesn't use it, and neither does humanity. Unlike other languages, this one does not seem to require a user; unlanguage uses itself. One studies this divinatory language to hear what it says, not what it is used to say. One does not consecrate oneself to the study of this language to inquire after the location of toilets and train stations, to transact <u>business</u>, or to decipher ancient inscriptions. This unlanguage is neither dead, because it continues, nor alive, because it is never used. Therefore, it is an undead language. It came into the world unnoticed and unbaptized. There is no way it can die, and no life for it.

Unlanguage only superficially resembles occult jargon. Occultism never imparts anything new.

It's sunset—a bluff over the ocean. The sky streaked with bands of dark orange, brown, vivid yellow—the Second Person, just a silhouette, close by, with wind-ruffled hair and an open collar. He comes up to me. The wind rattles in my ears, the surf sloshes monotonously—for one instant it's all too clear, the opposite of that murkiness turned inside out and become annihilating clarity I am barely able to experience. The Second Person looks around; suddenly everything seems to return to normal.

This is a memory. I'm here, in the present, remembering this, which took place in the past, but I still use the present when I describe it, because I wish I could go back to that moment, before I found this work book and doomed myself by reading it. My experience of remembering, and your vivid imagining of this scene, are not so easily told apart.

Remember, this is your story, or it will be. These words have been waiting here for you and you have only just caught up with them. This is a warning. If you read on, you read on against this warning.

"Enjoy your walk?" he asks.

"Fine," I say, straightening up, letting my pant cuff fall.

"Your leg all right?"

"Sure."

He's waiting. I notice he has crossed the fingers of his left hand.

"Starting out I felt great. I went full on NM right away, and then I went light."

NM stands for Negative Machine, a mental state of relentless advance with no secondary purpose, no secondary anything. You smash through every obstacle, like a freight train. You can't, of course, but the idea summons all of your villainous tenacity. Going light, by that I mean the wind, the exertion, the brilliancy of the bygone day, seemed to knock everything out of my head and leave it ringing like an empty wineglass, and to knock the hours out of the day.

"It was like I was hearing the Wolves chanting me on."

The Wolves were a group of doomed ascetics; the Second Person had been one once. They lived in a cabin in the woods, mummies blearily gazing down from the rafters and burrows dug under the ground, and they ran miles every day. Miles and miles. Every day. Miles and miles. Chanting into dawn and into dusk. It made them hard as ice. Males and females, mixed. If any of them wanted to fuck they had to do it in front of the group and they had to do it in Negative Machine.

The wind whips the sky into a chaos of white rags, as if he emerges out of this, or is that me?

"It's time you learned unlanguage," the silhouette says, handing me this book.

He learned it from his teacher, a louring figure who overshadows our every encounter like a sinister island on the horizon. I don't know what his work book said. Always there on the horizon, his teacher, like the living incarnation of monster island.

Normal grammar and rhetoric maintain that there is a level of minimal significance, beyond which there is nothing more to be gained by breaking down sounds or signs any further. The rhetorically atomic level is not attained by subtraction alone, but by addition also of the logical operator "atomic," which presents an obvious problem. A sign or sound alone may be atomic, but, with addition of the operator "atomic," that sign or sound is now two, therefore subject to at least one more decomposition, therefore no longer atomic. This problem does not arise where the periodic elements of matter are concerned because the designation "atomic" belongs to the order of rhetoric, which is distinct and different from the periodic order. However, where the thing designated is itself rhetorical, the order of the operator is the same and the contradiction arises, as two elements of a common order are combined by the process meant to isolate them, plainly demonstrating that decomposition is continuous, rather than punctuated, and that it is not composition in reverse, but rather altogether another mode of composition. Phantasmagorigrammar decomposes normal grammar, producing meaning as it is released and unbound, not as it is limited and directed.

Science, and any objective discipline for that matter, wants univocality, which means it wants to produce meaning with maximum generality. Polyvocality is an alternative to univocality, but not its opposite; avocality, which is the utterance of exactly no one—no person at all, speaking— is the thing that stands equally opposed to both. Avocality is impossible and is the mode of impossible expressions, which take the form of apparitions in the interstices of univocal or polyvocal expressions. Whoever employs the avocality is calling speculatively, as if adopting a point of view that is unattainable by any real speaker; avocal expression is an unverifiable approximation made possible by the decomposition or inversion of univocal or polyvocal expressions. Very often a univocal saying will rule out certain possibilities; these cancelled possibilities may take the form of an anti-coherent, tacit alternative. The one who speaks avocally strives to achieve an impossible perspective, in the hope that, the experiment succeeding by pure luck, the person, body and soul, of the speaker will actually undergo translation into that impossible life, will actually achieve literal transformation. A change in one's lexical parts. The change may be fleeting, the thing of an instant, but there are some who believe that what can be seen and remembered as a consequence of even a single successful experiment of this kind will improve the odds of later trials, and that what may not be possible at a stroke may be achieved gradually by compounding increments. The compilers of this work book hope that it will make the benefit of such experiments available to the student.

Put another way, the student who learns unlanguage will know how to hear and how to use the voice or voices that so many writers have testified "spoke through" them. What is said by a voice or voices of this kind must be relayed; like the story of the Ancient Mariner, it compels the recipient to speak or record it, and so unlanguage is sometimes referred to as "mustlanguage."

Unlanguage is already present in all languages. It translates English into English, Spanish into Spanish, Greek into Greek. Unlanguage has a family line and a history of its own, alone equally related to every other language. Alone of all languages, it is in this one only that mysteries can be communicated without they cease to be mysteries. Unlanguage takes by giving, gives by taking away, and, in this course, you will become adjusted to its restless and irregular grammar.

The course is divided into units, each of which will explain an aspect of grammar; each unit includes a reading, and space has been provided for the completion of exercises and for student notes.

NOTES

At the end of a relentlessly long drive—nearly to the end of the line—the building, rambling and drab—pale lights in only a few of its many windows—silence of ceaselessly whirring air vents—tall, narrow white corridors of institutional plainness and squareness— pipes below the ceiling—paint peeling on the walls becoming pink and inflamed—wan fluorescent lights in trays—thin, sour odor of decomposing flesh—a metal door like the rest, with its thick integument of blue paint and an arrow slit. The school is not elegant; it's like a gas station.

The classroom. Everyone else is carrying the book from the shadow, too. Only half the lights are working, all at the back. The light shines past us and I am looking into my own shadow; the front of the class is a black cloud. A smudge of white dimly glowing in the murk in front of me. It's like gazing down into the sea, or into night from a high crag.

From somewhere inside that cloud, from time to time, a lamp appears and its glow is swept along a word written in shaky letters on the white board. The hand that holds the lamp is almost hidden in the shadow of its lid. The cloud is incense smoke. The wisp of incense smoke folds, elongates, turns, passes steadily out of sight with a mechanically even movement. The index finger points.

The voice—the teacher is at the head of the class, over toward the right, and keeps retreating into what appears to be a tent, or canvas booth. Like an isolation tent. He seems never to leave. Perhaps the hand I see is not his, but a helper's? An iris adjusted to the gloom will discern a pair of faint lights side by side, now up near the peak of the tent, now high on the wall by the board, now on the floor beside the tent. They never stray far from the teacher, and no amount of careful watching will ever catch them moving. The teacher faces the front, like the rest of us, and his voice is projected forward in waves that the board drives back, back over the teacher, back toward us. The other students are shadows, like me. We're all anonymous silhouettes. Some bend with a sound of frenetic scratching that I hope is only the noise of pen nibs, others are so still they might be props.

Forever I've been haunted by the idea that language is after life and we speak read and write ghosts. I ask myself what do I want here. But that I want something, and expect to get it, is not something that I need to ask.

The teacher draws breath rheumatically, and from his lungs comes the sound of wind whistling in the bare branches of trackless woods. He speaks, and from the floor at his feet comes the sound of splattering blood.

UNIT ONE
PARABLES

Unlanguage is sometimes known by the name, parabola. This registers both the unsurpassed affinity it has for the parable, and the parabolic lexical contour of meaning to which it lends itself. Meaning is parabolic where it has curvature, and specifically, a curvature that originates away from, then bends towards, and thereafter away from, but not in the same away from out from which it originated. Thus, parabolic meaning comes from anywhere and anywhen in a temporary or provisional deviation towards intelligibility, and then "snaps back" when the reciprocal pressure of counter-intelligibility reacts on it. That the approach is a curve shows it to be a deviation, since what is intended lies in the linear path.

The grammar of unlanguage is parabolic in structure. Every inflection in unlanguage can be decomposed into at least two simultaneous correlative counterinflections whose divergence forms the parabolic inflection.

A: Define "parable."
B: A bad story that doesn't go anywhere.
A: And if the story is bad, and doesn't go anywhere, why tell it?
B: Eh, the world needs bad stories too, I guess.

The parable is a story that bears an inscrutable relation to the need for it. The meaning of whatever calls upon parables to articulate itself can never be found within any parable but is interparabolic, and hence can only be found among the parables like the disembodied countertenor that no one sings but which arises on its own recognizance from the coupled overtones of the chanting monks. The axiom that all parables are by definition necessary is true. The parable is not fathomed except insofar as its necessity is determined. The readings in this book will all be parables. These readings are each subparables of the main parable, which is the whole, while some subparables will contain sub-subparables.

INTERROGATIVES

The teacher was the First Person. That is, for the Second Person, it all started with the teacher. Following the teacher, he became the Second Person. Following him, following the teacher, I become the Third Person. It's a mistake for me to go on saying "I." Too bad I can't seem to avoid it. Perhaps he will learn to say "he" when I mean "I."

The Second Person waves his crossed fingers against the sky and the ocean and says, "I'm going to say something I want you to repeat. Don't think about it, just say it back to me the moment you hear it. Ready?"

I nod.

After a moment, he says, "Ss'chess dafwo iaeiien an'net."

I repeat the words as he instructed, and yet what I hear myself saying is: "Maswoi on'na ajz monhrlm ..."

"See?" the silhouette says.

I was sure I was merely repeating what he had said, and actually the rhythm of the phrase I uttered was the same. The meaning, too, was the same, I think. I don't really know what they meant, only that they were portentous words.

The crazy idea reaches me—and this has to be his point - that the meaning switches its garments of sound and writing to keep on hiding, like an animal, slinking from one bit of cover to another.

Interrogatives are formed by introducing question-words and/or augments, which take the form of dispondees, dochmiacs, or ionics minores. Each particle includes the spondee, which is the form of the verb "to be."

Unlanguage employs a variety of particles so great that it defies complete enumeration, unless perhaps it could be said to equal the number of possible monosyllables, as they nearly always are simple words. Clouds of these particles coalesce around sentences in unlanguage, minutely inflecting the meaning of the words with unsurpassable subtlety. As there are few rules for the use of these particles, students will have to address themselves carefully to mood, tone, and above all to the cultivation of unwonted precision in articulation, in order to learn their use and to interpret them skillfully.

> *Wind tosses the locks of the silhouette. We go inside, through the glass door I can still see the colorless dim white daylight, the waves. I'm a silhouette too. I feel it. He breaks off a piece from an incense stick and lights it. The flame, the abrupt red hollow of his hand, the butter flame at the end of the stick. He blows it out. An ember floats there, a red ring. He holds the unlit end of the stick in his mouth, just like a cigarette, and the silhouettes of the smoke lift and twine against the window. His breath drives the smoke forward at intervals.*
>
> *As I recall, the silhouettes in that dark bend leapt, many of them did. They flashed by me like bevies of ballet dancers quietly hastening to their marks in the black interval before the curtain rises. I heard their feet scrape, and breathing. Like a dance to a memorized piece of music. As I remember, sometimes one would leap very high, very slow. A slow bound. I saw, now that I remember it, upside-down figures and faces in the brilliant white gaps between the silhouettes. The whiteness came from the light on the border before me. The border isn't exactly before me, that's not it exactly, the border is on my path. Addressing itself to my path, and not directly to me, keeping its distance, it also keeps the meter. All the same, it is on my path: the path that is specifically mine, not just the one that happens to be mine just now as I'm taking it, I suppose it is my destined light border. I think that's what I must have fallen over when I hurt my knee. My pant leg has a damp spot—bleeding again.*

In unlanguage, an unusually large proportion of utterance in general consists of questions, a fact that cannot be entirely attributed to the practice of responding to questions likewise in the interrogative, answering questions with questions, in other words. Below are listed some of the more common questions. Translate them in the space provided. Do **not** refer to the later units in this work book. You should find that you are already competent to do this exercise.

Do **not** continue to the next unit until you have completed this exercise to your instructor's satisfaction. Whether the exercise is completed orally or in writing, be careful to speak or to write **indistinctly**.

COMMON QUESTIONS

Who are you?

Have we met before?

What is your name?

What do you want?

Why did you bring me here?

Are you there?

Are you ever coming back?

Why can't I see you?

What are you saying?

What was that again?

Are you smiling?

Do I have to take these?

Why did you abandon me?

What is this?

Are there side effects?

Will I get what I want?

What is going to happen next?

When will I be released?

Have you forgotten your promise?

UNIT ONE READING

A person, not yet identified, somehow comes into possession of a work book, the ordinary appearance of which belies its entirely bizarre approach to English grammar—if it is English. Studying this work book, entirely alone and unprompted by any external force, this person, not yet identified, acquires the First Person, the power to say "I." I believe this is I destiny, unlocked by this work book, which has fallen into I hands by design.

The First Person sat in the corner, so that he was supported both against his back and sides, and then his head lolled back and he began. The mouth drooped and his flesh slackened. The eyes rolled and the lids stopped. The body spread. He went gray, and a horrible stink poured out of all his openings, like a breath he'd been holding. The stomach distended even as the limbs deflated, and it was nightmarish, the way all of him settled and lowered. Animated curlicues slithered just under his skin, as if someone were drawing on him with an invisible marker. Black liquid welled up his throat and stopped short of spilling, so there was a gleaming, mirrorlike black pool there inside his jaws. The hands lay limply to either side of him, palms up, like dried corn husks. There was no finding those two will o' the wisps anywhere.

When I was initiated, my notebook was marked with a special symbol. We all received one, although each was different. We were told that the symbol would act as our eyes during the visions. Now I had to hold my symbol before the eyes of the corpse, which were just grey pits, to see what it was seeing.

The interior corner of a futuristic train car. Everything white, with dark blue upholstered chairs and carpeting. The windows are large, taking up most of the sides; each must be twenty feet across; with rounded corners, thick rubber seals. Two buttery yellow gleams shine greasily on the wall of the car, up where it folds into the ceiling. Still in its state of suspended decay, the corpse sits in a corner seat by the window. The train glides so smoothly that not so much as a hair on the corpse's head moves, now almost doubled back on the neck, and resting on a luxuriously padded headrest.

Outside the window, a white desert. Dotted with crags. Blue shadows. A rime of frost. Not untouched by human feet, but by very few human feet. They lived or passed through here and their leavings were only the simplest contrivances, really only pieces of the desert gingerly rigged up into altered combinations that all but return to the desert. Crumbling them back into pieces is the work of an instant, the same work that is everywhere being done, at every moment. The same work that impels this silent train, but then how would I know that?

The sensation is like being tipped forward. Our course is level, though, so I must be wrong. But some interpretations are so basic, like the recognition of the physical effects of hunger or anger, and balance, too, that it doesn't make sense to question them. I'm not imagining the sensation. I know that, because I'm not getting tired.

The other passengers are distinct shadows, almost perfectly opaque, three dimensional. As one turns its head, rays of brilliant, starlike light, cool and pale, flash from the other side. It's as if they were all silhouetted against the sun. They're active, going from chair to chair, passing through each other in tangles of outlined limbs.

Forward, there's a wide open door, like the side door of a boxcar, a white, faintly scintillating square in the dark. That part of the car—or is it another car?—is not lit. Shadows of what seem to be slender boys are gathered there, climbing from a secret hatchway in the floor, looking out the door with a kind of electric excitement - many of them appear to have their hands clasped up against their chests, under their chins, like swimmers who've momentarily emerged from a pool to wait shivering for the next plunge, and the white square is crossed and recrossed by the narrow rods of their arms as they jostle each other. Suddenly one leaps high through the square, the outer light reflected from the shadow body traverses the entire car in a soft pulse. Other boys hop in place and throw their hands up jubilantly.

All this is silent, although I can hear the corpse gurgling and creaking, the whir of the air conditioners, and the hum of the rails. The dining car. There's a pile of books on the table and I take one at random, thin and spread out and supple like a school work book. I take up the book of unlanguage and turn its pages. "Are you smiling? Why did you leave me?" Then I see "Everything white, with dark blue upholstered chairs and carpeting. The windows are large—"

I turn back to look at him, and I end up looking directly into his mouth, and I'm standing on the shore of a still lake, a black lake, on a pitch black night. Eerie invisible suspense.

UNIT TWO
ORTHOGRAPHY

The teacher—every now and then with a rasp of static the face blurs shivering over his crystal skull; lights traverse his features as if he were driving at night. I can visualize him, although the Second Person never described his appearance; the long white hair that descends to the shoulders like a wide hood, the head craning forward, the chalky face and glassy eyes that squint and stare, the down-turned shark's mouth, the white shirt, the hands resting at arms' length on the edges of the table. Those two patches of light side by side gaze up at him from the table top, or the wall behind him, or the ceiling above him. He drones, and at intervals his hoarse voice catches; there's a soft hiccup, and a few spoonfulls of his own blood drip from his lips and run down his chin. The white shirt is splattered with red. He doesn't react; this is normal. He used to wipe it away, but there was no end. One hand lifts and he points to nothing; he's always pointing. His teeth turn to glittering silver mackerels. Bloody foam catches in between them.

My memories may have some order of their own, but to me, their order will have to be relative to whenever I am now. I don't remember these things in order; now I remember something that happened recently, and now I remember something that happened a very long while before. Perhaps I would have to remember everything, every time, in order to keep them in the order in which they occurred; memory is probably more useful the way it is, because I can jump unmoored from one moment to another. The price for this is strictness of order; there will be a succession, but not a strict one. But, each memory does come with a mark that I can feel but not point to, telling me roughly how old a memory it is.

The use of any method of writing is a gambit, the purpose of which is to capture or seduce unlanguage to endue the writing with itself. One of the many unusual attributes of unlanguage is that it has no writing system of its own. Any formal approach to writing is equally inappropriate to it, because unlanguage is strictly bound to be loosely bound to form, and, like a captured soldier, must make every effort to escape. Regularity is easily evaded.

Therefore, the written form of unlanguage may only be borrowed; unlanguage is most likely to be caught in irregular writing. Hieroglyphic or otherwise ideographic signs will have to be broken down into basic radicals, and new signs assembled out of these radicals. Writers using alphabets and abjads must adopt foreign signs to indicate unusual sounds, to reverse customary scanning orientation, and to combine letters to form talismanic pictograms. Such interpolations and rearrangements will not often be necessary, however, because unlanguage of unknowing inheres in what is most common; as a hybrid, it can have no real affinity for any one language or language type.

I don't have much luck holding the memory stable; the setting, place and instant, keep changing. We meet back in the brown and orange 1970's from whatever second we find ourselves in. The Wolves went their separate ways long ago, unless they haven't found each other yet. The Second Person tells me about it: chanting into dawn and dusk, their heads thrusting up and down like pistons in an engine. Chill air in the hour before dawn, their misting breath rose up around them like engine smoke, a wreath-headed killer, each one, and the Second Person was a wreath-headed killer once, and still is. I must remember that. The Second Person is also A First Person. They slept on the floor, looking up into the faces of the mummies; this was part of some procedure they never really ironed out or gave a formal designation, although they usually described it as "mirroring," and just couldn't find the right qualifying term. The mummies were considered active members, albeit of a different degree.

The ocean, the high sky are plummeting away from us. The trees close in, then ruins and cemeteries, silhouettes that look like young boys and girls trot across my field of vision, then the blue town and blue streets, palely glowing in the dusk before the imposition of the streetlights. Crowds of children crossing at the crosswalk, all shadows, and adult shadows in the streets, and we, or is it just me now, flying past unseen like witches. Through the windowpanes of the houses going by I see prismatic dining room lights crisply blazing like cyphers, and figures carrying plates of food, fragments of briefly glimpsed gestures as each butter yellow window is swept away into the blue and the black.

Despite this lack of systematic affinity, unlanguage of unknowing does, however, seem to express unsystematic and inconstant preferences, or what could be called "taste," or even "interest." At times it favors artificial writing systems, such as the beautiful letters of the Beitha Kukju alphabet, or the Litterae Ignota created by Hildegard of Bingen for the partially disintegrated Latin in which she related her visions. Unlanguage perversely absents itself most reliably from occultists' codes, such as John Dee's Enochian alphabet; the mystery evaporates that much more rapidly the greater the hermetical character of its initial appeal to the reader.

This work book will present confusion in a writing system familiar to the student. Interpolated new characters and new arrangements of radicals will be kept to a minimum, and in many cases the student must determine meaning without the assistance of glosses or prompts—only some of the permutations in this book will be marked. Students should not assume that abnormal spelling or punctuation, when present, are always typographical errors. Certain of these errors are deliberate, even if they remain errors, like the flaw in the carpet. Other passages that are to all appearances conventional will, to the skillfull reader, reveal that other language vrery plainly.

Be careful to substitute diacritical marks for the more frequently-used letters. This makes it impossible for anyone to learn phantasmagoria without hearing it.

You always keep something back. Outside, the clouds walk by on kinky lightning legs like browsing insects. Their vague bodies blend together to make a watercolor roof. I'm with the Second Person again and some others as well, in a kind of a Japanese house, the open kind. The last moment of dusk is just outside, like the wall of an aquarium. I don't recognize the one who seems to officiate, or teach. As she speaks the top of her head fizzes and a jet of ectoplasmic fire bursts out. She's got it balanced there on top of her head like a candle flame, goes on talking apparently not having noticed it. The flame is luminous without seeming to shed light; the wavering shadows it casts don't correspond to objects in the room. The hand of the Second Person squeezes my shoulder and he points with crossed fingers, drawing my attention. There are things around her head, they spin, they float in the air. I see one of them; it comes out of the shadow behind her head, looks like a marble, striped with ribbons of yellow and orange. There's a red, eyelike dot there toward the underside—it's Jupiter. And that little red one up there, just coming into view, that's Mars. The solar system is orbiting her head—Person Zero—she's God, don't you get it she's God.

When writing unlanguage, students are encouraged to exhibit resourcefulness and independence. It should be drawn in a manner adapted, even with respect to its lesser details, to the particularities of the semantic occasion. The truly advanced student will learn to listen to unlanguage itself, and to give it the form it most "desires." Simultaneously, each passage must also represent unlanguage itself in its entireity. The instructor will add his judgement to the student's in the assessment period.

Do not use your judgement. Allow the characters to take shape randomly. The result will be the aleatory scrawl of the true diviner.

Read, translate, and transliterate the following passage into a jumbling of at least **three** different writing systems. Do not refer to later units in this work book.

UNIT TWO READING

After the work book was discovered, its unidentified possessor evidently became homeless and wandered for years. Despite all manner of accidents and repeated incarcerations in county jails but never any psychiatric institutions, this person never lost this work book, this very copy of this work book, which even identified itself as such in writing, in these very words. This person, who clung to this work book so fiercely that it proved to be the only possession that was not lost or taken away, is currently reading these words, which can only be read by the one who is once and for all destined to read them, the one about whom I speaks.

A word about the teacher's qualifications:

A kind of chapel, created by making alterations to an ordinary house. The ceiling was removed, and the upper story converted to an open space, giving the room something of the appearance of the bottom of a huge elevator shaft. A drapery hangs from the height and screens one end of the room. The only light comes from a few unshuttered windows on one side, shining in a corner just next to the drapery.

Behind the drapery, the walls are covered in black hangings and the floor is painted red. There's a simple wooden dais in the center of the cordoned area. On the dais is a white wooden chair with wide, flat arms, and a red cushion. A man in a white suit and large sunglasses slumps in the chair, drooping to one side, his right arm curled against his chest and a heavy black pistol slid into his lap. The right temple. The left side of the skull is blown out. A splatter of dried blood, bone fragments, and lumps of brain, now grey, shrivelled and dried, marks the spray line on the chair, the dais, the floor, and the dark hangings.

In front of the drapery, and over to the side where dim sunlight filters in, there is a long table, wooden top on a folding metal frame, the kind schools use. On this table there is a large metal punchbowl filled with shards of glass. Next to it, on the right, stand stacks of glasses one inside another, and a hammer. To the left of the bowl is a massive stone mortar, the heavy pestle lying by its base. The mortar is filled with a shining powder of finely ground glass. There is another punchbowl, filmed with the residue of evaporated water, and beside this are numerous small brown bottles marked "aspirin" and "morphine," all empty.

Although in shadow, the rest of the room, which is the larger of its two halves, is not entirely dark, because the walls are an even, white, undecorated plaster. There is nothing here except for a thick, irregular carpet, mottled and uneven. Broad streaks of blood spread thin, and dark splashes mar the uniform whiteness of the plaster to a distance about two feet off the floor. Bodies sprawl all over the floor. Men and women alike, all wearing the same white shirts. Their rigid mouths gape open, blood all over their faces, their hands clutch paper cups filled with a residue of sweetened water and finely ground glass. Their hands clutch their own throats. Their hands clutch at each other, their bodies are woven and tangled together, and mired in their own congealed blood.

Now one of them, the First Person, rises, tilting forward in a slow hydraulic movement, the stiff, befouled face flashes across a stray beam of light.

The shadowed figure is struggling to rise to its feet. It clutches the projecting edge of the table with its left hand. The frayed head lifts. The body rises. It stands.

This is really happening. A man who is dead stands upright. A suicide. He looks.

A distending stripe of vomited blood blackens the white shirt from the chin to the waist, and the back of the pants where the anus gushed blood. The staring white face is already turning pink at the ears, the nostrils. The eyes swivel, darting from body to body. His breath bursts, resounding in the murderous stillness of the room. Full understanding floods the eyes. Grief and terror wrench the features, understanding brims and drips from the eyes, the hands grope blindly above dead friends. Full of trust, they had each taken a cup. Suffused in the splendor of that perfectly full trust, each drank.

In memory, your future teacher sees again their uncertain, searching eyes. The blood had boiled out from their mouths even before they lowered their cups, and hands gripped throats stopped with a bolus of glass, to ease down the bolus of glass. Some vomited the sparkling water, which was too quickly followed by the dark gusher. There was the puzzled, fading eye ... painkiller, and aspirin to thin the blood and aid in its escape ... death, dying, but no pain, numbness ... numb alcoholic death ... the wondering look in the face as inner lacerations they could not feel ... in their bodies' numbed interiors ... gazing with dimming eyes, with stupefied fascination, with dwindling understanding, at each others' bloody jaws, red chins, red teeth ... the cups still in the slackening fingers ... and then, on the floor, feebly writhing, drugged swimming ... Their faces are already freckled with decay. Decay is changing the shapes of the blood on the floor.

Two quick sobs. Then, bleats of horror. Gouts of blood spill from the contorted lips and run down the chin. Hands feeling the softening face, the body.

Now he's trying to get away, in a panic, outside, the room inside and all its corpses, the body of the leader in his chair. Like a child who has soiled himself he walks stiff legged down the overgrown median strip down the center of a busy highway. Trucks buses and cars dash by relentlessly. Their wind batters him, nearly knocking him down. On overpasses, in parking lots overlooking the freeway, cars and cabs of big rig trucks stare at him with headlights like enraged, burning eyes. They turn to follow him as he goes, like the heads of buried giants. His shirt hangs out and his pant legs are split open to the knees. He's covered in his own blood and the glare of oncoming traffic. Stunning waves of traffic force crash over him and he has to drag his feet forward like he's waist-deep in a slough.

Following the bend, somehow getting across, getting to the slope that overlooks the basin, eruption of the city under brown haze, dusk blue sky and a flat, sullied-looking moon, and he up to his waist in brush with the cataract of the freeway raging behind him staring out at it like a man staring into the bottom of his nightmare.

UNIT THREE
NEGATIVE VOICE

The ineffable is language at the moment of death, when death may just as likely be in the past as in the future. Some languages are considered living and others dead, but unlanguage of unknowing is undead, which is the first negation. Negation curses. It shows what is not there, for example, when one says, "there is no cat," the other thinks of the cat; when one says, "your friend is dead," the other thinks of the friend; when one says, "I sentence you to death," the other thinks of the world without the self. The latter example is a special case, because the other is actually trying to subtract the self from the self in conceiving of its own absence.

The Second Person is explaining. We're alone, in the Japanese house. Outside, it's the blue hour before dawn. There is a body on the floor. She may be dead or asleep. The Second Person has been talking all night and I've been listening in and out. Three shadows appear beside his silhouette, one on top of the other, three pom poms hanging in space. One by one, in quick succession, they streak into his outline with a little chirp or sob. The Second Person doesn't seem to notice. He goes on and on, without effort, without trying to make me understand, as if I weren't there and he were talking to himself, or thinking out loud.

Look around. All of space? Your bedroom. Raise your head. Look around yourself, like God. See all of space. Just your bedroom. The sweet kind of energy, like the lights that show you where the road is in the dark, and you go on smooth and fast and easy light to light, and no car, no effort, whir only, whir after. Comet.

In phantasmagoria, there are distinct grammatical voices for the living self and for the unliving self that is the ghost the former self subtracts in conceiving of its own death, and one may speak or write as either.

The latter, subtracted, self employs the active voice and the negative personal pronoun or a term in antinominative case; this combination is called simply "dead voice." Using dead voice, one would say, "not-I visited the country," because the one who speaks is an image the speaker invents to speak of the self as if it were dead.

The subtracting self, on the other hand, employs the passive voice with the negative reflexive personal pronoun or a term in antinominative case; this combination is called "negative machine." Using negative machine, one would say "the country was visited not by myself," because the one who speaks is referring interlocutors to an image of the self as dead, while the speaker is not dead.

As the distinction between dead voice and negative machine is easily missed, it bears repeating that, in the former case, the speaker is the image of the dead speaker, while in the latter case the speaker is the one who creates and steps behind such an image.

Translate the following into eavesdropia as per the instructions in Unit Two.

UNIT THREE READING

The First Person looking around. Horrified. It all unfolds with the implacability of a ritual whose meaning is impossible to mistake, brutally overwhelming his frenzied refusals and forcing him to see and accept, indifferent to the torture it is already allowing, zeroing in on him, him, him. This is plainly wrong, the wrong thing is happening. They were all meant to die. They all did. All, all, all.

He fell with the rest of them, but he fell on his hand. He rolled in his death agony over and over on his hand, inadvertently tangling up his fingers, so he died with his fingers crossed.

If it is a mistake, why is he terrorized by the idea the ritual has taken its intended course?

By including mistakes, the ritual immunizes itself against them. What sends him fleeing out the door and to the street is in part the realization that he is the victim of the second part of the ritual, being sentenced to death and to living. He feels the horror of being chosen.

The wanderer was not an innocent and was not always persecuted for no good reason. Anyone who wanders in spirit lacks a place, and such outsiders can never expect justice. For them, it is mercy or nothing, they have no choice but to trust, while a person with a place trusts the place and so has the advantage of dispensing with other trust, provided that place and that person remain attached to each other.

This is your teacher. He sits at the front of the classroom inside his tent, his back to the students, and teaches the lesson, now and then emerging in black incense to sweep the meager light of his small, toylike lamp along some words he wrote in the dark. His students can smell the decay, and the iron scent of blood that dribbles from his lips at intervals, to patter on the floor of blackened steel tiles.

Anyone who dares to teach others unlanguage is cursed. This is why the students trust the teacher; he has every reason not to teach this language. The students form a cult around the teacher, and he becomes the cult leader. He is driven to school in a big black mark three Lincoln Continental with tinted windows and a curtained rear, there are sturdy rings set with manly square stones on his long angular fingers, and he wears enormous brown sunglasses that give him an insect's exaggerated stare. Every now and then, as he speaks, there's a catch in his throat, he gulps, and some blood spills from his downturned mouth. It runs down his chin and the front of his white shirt. He continues to speak, obliviously. He teaches, and then goes back to death. Back to the grave. Later, angels sing you into a delirious vision of knowledge unlearned and meaningless, terrifying comforts, lacerating intensities.

His narratives are nothing but isolated rooms in a house with no halls, nothing but secret passages. A house that can't be lived in, because it has only secret passages. The occupant can only be the fugitive, the escaped slave hiding from the rapist, or a hidden hostage: a missing piece who circulates in secret passages that keep him or her missing. The missing piece prefers being missing and wants to stop being missing: not by being found, but by waiting to be forgotten. No longer missed, and so no longer a piece of someone else's contrivance. That contrivance as something which could only exist with all of its pieces might cease to exist as it forgets what it's missing. The missing one outlives what misses.

NOTES

Carbon wants to find its way into organic compounds—trying to stop life is like trying to have water that can't boil—the infant learning to speak is the ghost of all children—universes grow inside each other like ripples—there are universes inside and outside ours and the time in ours is their eternity and vice-versa, the whole backdrop or surrounding is a durationless neuter level—there has always been life, there has always been death, each unniverse exactly the same—no, but infinite in number so infinite this, infinite undead minds, a mind that holds the living idea of death is undead, infinite undead universes, who's to say some minds aren't—the pattern is microuniverses you disappear if you keep climbing—unlanguage: communiques from the Forbidden City, passing over the wall, announced with quaint and laughable pageantry, but then something unsettling steals into your soul when you ask yourself who wrote it—or what?

An arrow thunks into the wall. Came through the window. Look out the window. Nothing but trees. A note wrapped around the shaft. Read it. Eerie, simple and yet unintelligible. Who wrote this? Look again out the window. Trees. Did they write it?

UNIT FOUR
NEGATIVE PARTICLES

Unlanguage is filled with un's and other unwords, particles, suffixes, prefixes, augments, and detentes, which, when used skillfully, can establish degrees of negation with supreme precision. In some cases, for example, when a question is answered with the word "no," the word is plainly an adjective modifying the verb to be. There is something, or nothing is, but not that. In other cases, the same "no" is an act of refusal or disagreement by the speaker, and directly modifies no thing. The first of these uses of "no" is the "no of absence," while the second variety is called the "no of refusal," or occasionally the "demurritative no."

The absolute is impossible to limit, so that even the concept of the absolute, being a concept and therefore possessing limits, necessarily must misrepresent it. To posit it, one must resort to negative positing. The concept of limitlessness is not limitless. So it is impossible to speak the absolute, but only to speak about it, which is necessary, since the absolute is undetectable by the senses and can only be intuited rationally in speech, and therefore can only be discovered in reasoning in speech. Since not everyone reasons this way, and since the absolute is supposed by many to be of paramount importance because it is the foundation of all things, it is necessary to talk about the absolute, even though simply to speak of the absolute, using only positive terms, is to negate it by limitation just the same.

A haggard silhouette, walking all over town, street to street, with doom beating at his back. Beating with light, familiar strokes. As if walking could escape him from doom. He only imagines the strokes fall on his back, and the realization that this is only a consoling bit of whimsy he holds at arms' length, already half made, but he can manage to avoid acknowledging it a while longer and squeeze a little more relief out of walking. But doom is all around him. There it is. The pursuing phantom a few steps behind unveils the rest of itself and stands naked his surroundings, the street, the sky, his body. Gradually now, the effort of continuing to walk is making subtractions from his continuing to talk, to interject, to brood, as intended. Petering out. The dread is not of death or like the fear of growing old, somehow magnified. It's the prey's fear. Terror of being stalked. His stride falters and he stops. An old woman sweeping her front steps throws him a daring look. The whole steaming world conspires. Lights in pairs, always watching. When the moment comes, he expects he will see the baleful lights inside a couple of human eyes, and accept in an instant that this is the face unlanguage finally selected for his executioner.

Unlanguage of unknowing expresses the absolute completely, by taking back even as it gives. This is why negation is the essence of this language, which is sometimes known as the cursed language, the language of doom.

Where the negative is a simple nothing, like the absence of a fish from a flock of sheep, it is called the "unrelated negative." Having nothing to do with each other, at least as far as the activity of shepherds is concerned, does not become a subtle relationship between fish and sheep. In other circumstances, the negative is simply everything; for example, the goodness of the God of the Christians, or His love or wisdom, etc., is attributed to Him even as it is insisted that He is absolute and therefore cannot be limited by any concept. This is not a stupid contradiction because the goodness attributed to God is maximal; the superlative, which expands the concept to exceed the mind's ability to encompass it, is therefore a kind of negation which identifies the point beyond which there is nothing further, no more. This is called the "unsurpassed negation." The child who wants to express the enormity of something will spread its arms as far as it can, and then fall over.

Identify all the different varieties of negation in the following passage.

UNIT FOUR READING

The wandering student of the work book abandoned the life the wandering student had made. Decay is the door to new life. The matter of life conjugates and declines. With steely passivity the student watched as everything that had been life disintegrated, not lifting a finger to prevent the disappearance of a career, a home, the dispersal of carefully collected and preserved property, the evaporation of love and fellowship. It was a little like standing on a prominence looking back on the rubble of a home town reduced to smoking ruins and blanketed in corpses that can't be told apart, then turning to enter a new day of isolation, poverty, want, exile, shame that's inescapable because it has nothing to do with the faltering of any merit, a fatal and maybe impregnable language barrier has risen. All the same, the student allows it all to die, making not even a fruitless effort. He will wander homeless through the world and suffer, but he will at least be spared the humiliation of confinement to a psychiatric hospital, which never befalls him.

The First Person, the teacher, is brought in by four students carrying him in a litter, which is a swivelling desk chair supported on a couple of wooden posts actually, and the teacher himself is a corpse. The students convey him to one corner of the spacious, windowless classroom with walls of bare cinderblock and tip him onto the floor by a bunch of cardboard boxes. The teacher's corpse falls in a seated position, sprawling against the boxes, head a little lolled back, one hand resting on the floor. The legs are bent and sideways. His lips have shrivelled away to nothing and his open mouth is a black sharpness in his face, clean-cut as a hole punched in a paper cone. The whole body has a slack, deflated look; the flesh sags and seems to be hardening into soap.

The bell on the wall rings shrilly, on and on.

As class begins, his frame swells with a soft, liquid pulsation. The sunken eyes rise up beneath the sagging eyelids. The lips unwither, the body fills out. Coruscations burst from the mirror ball scattering little flechettes of light all around the room, the lamps snap on and off and the music pounds. A stir lifts from the floor hands with fingers like empty seed pods. The teacher is hideously reviving from the outside in; his eyes stare fixedly into space as he endures the horrible indignity of being a living rind around a still heart, slack lungs, sour corroding entrails. He gulps, and a black jet of rotten blood drapes across his chin. The sallow eyes whiten. He sweats out a vinegar smell. The dry skin pleached up in stiff furrows is bathed in a humid warmth, as though someone were breathing on him to polish and warm him up; the rigidity of the flesh sinks, the tissues become supple, the mustard body pinks and the ears stand at attention. The teacher wriggles, eyes still off in the distance, not fixed with the drunken inertness of death but alert and fierce with will to endure the ordeal. He gulps again, and now the blood that splashes over the lips is scarlet, with the scent of live action; under the plain white shirt, the ribcage expands and contracts convulsively, as if each dislocated rib moved independently of the others.

An iris adjusted to the gloom will not fail to notice the gradual opening of a pair of dim lights, side by side, on the wall above the teacher's body.

Students hurry forward to help the teacher to his chair, and a wooden screen ornamented with images of shivery-outlined half human monsters revelling in sodomy is quickly produced to shield him. The music stops as his voice begins, resuming the lesson. He tells us to listen. The listener will hear the glass throated voices of the dead in paradise filling the air with calls. They sing. They don't sing softly. They sing hard. They never sing. There are resounding cries, like warnings and announcements of disaster. Sentences are passed, curses and blessings. The language they use is not primal, not antique. It is a murmur, too, the ghostly aftersounds of myriad voices that talk meaningful nonsense.

What do I want here? The question presses itself on me with tiresome insistence, and whenever it comes again I have to stop what I'm doing and wring out my brains until I find a new answer. Is this alcohol of death and rot the masquerade of that other language I've heard about? The language of dream and immortality, that bestows happiness and eternal life on those who learn it?

Most of the rooms are occupied. In the halls and stairwells, if we stand still a moment, we can hear the muffled boom of voices behind locked doors. The spirits are always scurrying from room to room using the secret passages, untalking unlanguage to themselves, unechoing it back to itself, too, compulsively talking in their death, revealing the nonexistence of secrets. Their blind gaze traverses lust-maddened students rutting on the bathroom floor the way an avid stargazer watches for meteors. With absentminded clairvoyance they can catch glimpses of the teacher's abandoned, solitary body in a frame of silver fires, his head turned away. It turns back—a spectral head with a gaping mouth—a buzzing voice tears loose from his face and evaporates. The dead speak as the dead, not as revived people. The rooms here are occupied by corpses. They lie on the tops of evenly-spaced desks, destirring the motionless air with their unbreath.

The teacher is both honored and treated callously. He is not paid. Knowing unlanguage is not forbidden; that is neither here nor there. But unlanguage can only be taught to others under a condemnation that can never be appealed, and this is why the teacher is entitled both to respect for his sacrifice, and to disdain for his crime against what he teaches. It is that which imposes the curse, unlanguage itself, which is not death or the return from death, but a warlock ban of forsakenness that manifests itself in impotence, hopelessness, and wandering.

UNIT FIVE
VOID NOUNS

Each noun is a negative form which takes shape among a group of inflected subnoun particles. Unlanguage constantly generates nouns, which well up in it like bubbles in fermenting wort. Each word is a living "eye." These nouns reflect becoming, in that they have no fixed sounds or signs. These nouns also reflect voidness, in that they will always have their own distinct pattern of three syllables of mixed length—dactyls, anapests, amphibrachs, amphimacers, bacchiae or antibacchiae—that makes them recognizeable as nouns. Everything is in the relations of the sounds, and nothing whatever in the sounds themselves, so that the same phrase can be said in any sounds so long as the pattern of the sounds is constant.

The syllables are selected by divination methods.

> *They keep stopping in place, to sing. They stand together, arms hanging loose at their sides, singing. Their singing is unaccompanied by any demonstrative physical performance, they don't make gestures, they remain stationary. The effect is uncanny, blanketing me in a tensed paralysis, like anxious sleep.*

For students, this is likely to prove a serious challenge; perhaps the most difficult aspect of learning phantasmagoria. It is important to remember that, while unlanguage adheres to common things and abides in everyday language, it is not for everyday use. It has no proverbs, cliches, or guidebook phrases to memorize. It is all one no man's idiom.

Too tired to go on interjecting. Will have to rest a bit now. Let the lesson wash over. Cross fingers perhaps I won't be back.

Proper nouns are indicated by means of dignifying, detenting, or disqualifying particles which evoke around the name a scintillating screen of polychromatic concretions and attributes, so that the name is distinguished from improper nouns by its "teeter," which is to say, the sense that it is about to tip over and vanish in a general lake. Improper nouns are identified not by "teeter" but by "overaim," as an improper noun must be accompanied by particularization operators which threaten to narrow its focus or targeting to an almost uselessly minute degree.

Each noun is becoming in its inconstancy, void in its regularity of pattern. The "void" of East Asian and Indian philosophy and theology may be considered absence. But it is impossible to overlook the way in which the absence in being will have its corresponding aporia in thinking, and, since every thought is also a thing, an absence becomes a presence the moment it is acknowledged by consciousness. Like the absolute, the void can only be misrepresented by thought, and the voidness of things is not their unreality exactly, so much as it is their having appeared for a consciousness that can only guess at its own degree of transparency. One who looks on the absolute directly, assuming for the moment that this is possible, would then say, "I see nothing," meaning, "I am saying what I see, but I can truthfully say nothing about it." The same meaning would be conveyed by such phrases as "I see blank," "I see om," or "I see nonesuch," although the subtler speaker might say only "I see ..." and allow silence to be his word. An even subtler one would say nothing, while the most subtle of all would continue to speak normally.

In many of the succeeding units, the student will encounter parables whose entire content and meaning is communicated in unlanguage by a single void noun. The expression of rare things and complex ideas, which requires considerable elaboration in mundane languages, is straightforward in unlanguage. For example, there is a single void noun which means "the presence of the absence of a certain human being intimately known to the one who senses it, and who was once the object of a passionate attachment which has since lapsed, prior to the disappearance of that person, and which may yet return in modified form as a consequence of the sensed presence of the absent person." Adjustments to this noun's particles may alter the meaning to express the present absence of an animal, a building, a moment or interval, an abstraction, and/or to adjust the relation of the one sensing to the absent thing sensed, and potential overtones of future changes or constancies in that relation.

In the following reading, place each noun beyond the reach of polarity by writing its opposite directly on the word.

UNIT FIVE READING

The wandering student allows all to die, because decay is the door to new life. The alcohol of death is followed by vermin feast. The decomposers and scavengers salvage the materials and are the first to reintegrate them into life. Their intimacy with death does not give them immunity to it; they go through their own doorway and that is the only reason there is something other than death. The material has to be released in order to pass from form to form in the way that nourishment has to be broken down in one part of the body in order to be fashioned into compounds for life processes in other parts. I watch the silent orange at the end of the day, the town I am leaving forever is there between us. An incandescent headstone sinks through the horizon. Doom breathes around me deeply, resting because it has me. Returning, decay trickles on me from behind like a contaminated wind, and, recognizing it, I smile, maybe a little ruefully, but I need its subtractions, I can't go on without them. Seasoning of decay sifts on me. I imagine I look like I've been rubbed in paprika. My skin, my outward tissues, turn cold, chemically, a barely perceptible cold chemical burn like menthol. I go light, and I walk out in Negative Machine.

A cadaver is carried into the room and laid on the teacher's desk. In his presence, the decomposition of the body is stimulated; the surface shivers and creeps but the core is still. Pallor spreads over the face and hands, and their dim glow is the only light. By their light, we see the teacher suddenly erupt from his tent and stand over the body, his shadow thrown up high on the wall and ceiling behind him while he angrily tears off its clothes, exposing more and more of the luminous skin. When the corpse is naked, the First Person, the teacher, seems to retreat further back than the dimensions of the room should allow, as though he were diminishing, and he is bending forward or perhaps simply sinking on his knees, so that his face, barely visible, hovers just above a midriff crawling with minute, lacy white curls, like steam caught in an inverted glass bowl.

The teacher has apparently returned to his tent now. In his presence, the decomposition is stimulated, and it is transformed.

Black spots appear on the skin. They sprout writhing filaments like black wire, and black streaks that glide through the tissue, nosing their way along like snakes, spreading livid filligree that flexes, gathers, and then reaches out, forming waxlike black ears, fans, sails, fins, trumpets, phantasmagoria writing itself in the tissue. The athlete's whole body exhales heavy breath that falls to the floor and spreads in a supple pool like mercury, thickening the air with the acrid odor of old mud. The perfectly white teeth in the black center of a blossom of splattering decay, the corpse sighs and speaks, its voice rising to join the shoreless waving ocean of corpse talk, and when it rises a line of intensely sour rose blossom perfume bisects the air like a javelin and paralyzes me, sour in my nose my sinuses tingle and smart and something in my midsection is driven up, my shoulders and head seem to break free or through into cool lightness. Something is happening to me—

— I'm inside the First Person's memory. That's what's happened. I've just this moment entered it. That was the purpose of today's experiment. It worked.

The secret passages are dim, like a murky old color film in a projector with a failing lamp. A garden, a brief glimpse of the house, tall white and blocky, the sky a dull, French vanilla color, I can't tell if it's cloudy or hazy or what kind of day it is. We're back in "Intersuffusion," whatever that means. The name is there, in the outfield of the memory, but I don't know what it means. The vegetation is dark; there are looming, witch-like pine trees with long needles, and dense, clotted looking hedges. I have a sensation like being on a swing or merry-go-round, everything looks slanted, as if I were at only forty-five degrees to the ground instead of ninety. I think of beauty as something that dies; either it's destroyed by time or stupidity or I have only the moment to experience it, and then only memory after that; even if I can return and look again, I can't quite manage to get back the moment. So, to me, the beauty of the trees is like the beauty of death, as if death will mean wandering forever in the dim of those trees, the landscape funerealizes in its lushest profusion of green.

The teacher's body in this memory is not as it was at the time; it's a memory body. The surface is warm, or tepid anyway, and the core is cold, not chilled, I mean there is no discomfort or sense of heat being lost. The interior is numb dark and solid. There are others around me, the First Person and him, the cult leader who blew his brains out. Him, the Zeroeth Person, I see more distinctly than anyone else—a tall man in a loose white shirt or smock and sand-colored pants, big sunglasses, a neat part in the black hair. The face has heavy features, seams in the cheeks. He is leading them into the garden.

Look around. Suddenly it's all too ominously real, like an execution had been scheduled. The indistinctness of haste and distraction drops like a kind of armor and exposes the sensitive and vulnerable vividness of things. The name, this group: Intersuffusion—doesn't seem absurd anymore. The trees, the clouds, all acquire caustic distinctness and he knows this is it. Whatever comes next will be branded in, and he feels a reluctance, a weak impulse to escape, flop impotently inside him.

A smell of sunlight on grass, the stir of a breeze and brief hints of flower scent, playground smells. Freshly watered soil. Before an unbroken screen of cypresses, the leader sits on a little bench of white stone slabs, facing them at an angle. He speaks, leaning forward with his elbows on his knees, straightening up now and then to gesture around him. He points to the sky. He points to the ground. Again and again he makes an arcing gesture with his pointing finger. He speaks, but his voice is so muffled it is only the shadow of a sound. Only the fervency and caution of the tone comes through, and the awkwardness of pace of someone who must struggle to say only what he means.

The light holds its breath again. The dim cypresses, dimmer. The leader of the cult speaks muffled words, holding a full blooming white Persian rose in his right hand. As he speaks, he keeps doming his left hand over the flower. He holds the rose out at arms' length and falls silent. The rose tilts toward us. It grows and becomes gigantic, until there's nothing else I can see. Nothing stirs. Even the rose that continues to tilt toward us doesn't seem to move and the man is like a statue. I can't see him. The rose is already fully open and opening into further layers, revealing only layers and no center, the Persian rose changes. The curt "a" of chance; beauty opened by and by nature, which is chance operations in logical sequences—going into the unfolding colorless petals, a fragrance that is always pleasing but never the same from one moment to the next, the petals overwhelm the day. Dazzling sun, waiting in the parking lot out in front of the convenience store. He's younger, already in sunglasses. The early days. I—speaking as the teacher—am younger. The white wall doubles the sun. Glancing back there's a pink film between his image crumbling and me. I think the words, "I trust you," and it sounds like a threat.

NOTES

I don't know how to talk about myself: I believe I have already, even in so brief a period as has elapsed since our recent introduction, created a false impression—inadvertently, I hasten to add. Is this person the kind who says things like, "I hasten to add"? And who makes parenthetical comments? Punctilious? Bookish? Boring even himself with rhetorical questions? When you sit down with me in a library carel, isn't it pretty much like being alone, minus something? It isn't like interviewing a character, someone with a role blanket, is it?

I want to be a character, believe me, and speak with authority and the immortal lineaments and redundancies, but my trouble is that my 'character' is incorrigibly anti-character. The only thing that was always the same about me was that I had to be different. Everybody's different of course, I know that, and I don't say that I succeeded at being different, not really, or not that much if some, but knowing that only urged me to rummage around for a more basic register of difference, which I found in the form of a private, undetectable decharacterization reflex. I blindly tried to turn into a diffraction grating that would bend around me whatever outlining energy that might batten on me, or, as was more often the case, mince it up into spectra once it found its way into me, like enemy soldiers trapped between the outer and inner walls of a castle and cut to pieces by crystal ghouls and the seven diamond mutes. Nothing that had not been first carefully screened and dismembered would be allowed to enter the inner wall or disturb my covetously horded troves of inwardness, so I could always throw off any character trait at any time, like a costume (if only it were true). There always had to be an escape route, an open door or zipper or secret passage somewhere, so I could remain a possessing soul only, and not a character, because I could never find a character that was enough to satisfy me. Every delightful particularity was purchased at the expense of another enticing trait: you can be tall and handsome, but you can't be tall and short, you can't be handsome and ugly. The curse of beauty is precisely that it stays beautiful even when its actions are the ugliest imaginable, and the curse of size is that you can't shrink to a dimension proportioned to your strength when you are weakened by illness, injury, or old age—the strength that would be more than enough for a man of two feet tall is utterly insufficient to sustain a man of six and a half feet, and so he must endure the bonus degradation of being large and frail. Yes, I know I am an inmate here. I know, I know, but there is more to do than sit here and know things. I will dignify my prison—prison, all right?—my prison with a description, but not yet and not for a long time. I want to look back on this cell from a distance, but I have to make the distance first. Traits are traps. I want traits, but I'm afraid of the traps, and I covet too many of them to do anything other than renounce all of them.

No character no plot, so what's left? A steady diet of frameless affects that move among stories genres and styles, and a soul that circulates among persons.

UNIT SIX
MODAL VERBS

The verb 'to be' is the only verb in unlanguage. It must always take a predicate, although the personal pronoun may be appended in the absolute, as an object of the verb to be. This means there is no proper predicate nominative. There is, however, a predicate antinominative to denote what is entirely unrelated to the verb, lying beyond the sentence but indistinctly sensed by the sentence.

Unless modified by detenting particles, the verb "to be" is always considered to have an unmarked aorist meaning when translated from unlanguage into English. This can prove challenging for any simple translation, necessitating not only thorough and sometimes tedious explanation, but also finical attention to tone. The verb should, as rule, point away from duration and toward eternity, as in such phrases as, "mortality has always been the condition of mankind" ... "as it was in the beginning, so it is ..." etc.

The verb 'to be' is also the only two-syllable word in unlanguage pronounced as a spondee. Any two syllables pronounced distinctly as a spondee will act as the verb 'to be,' whether that be 'work book' or 'foreskin' or 'horsemeat.' Have I already stopped living? I speak, but how can I say that teaching is what I do, when it is up to the student to be taught, and I have no satisfactory way of knowing whether or not what I fondly believe I teach has actually been taught. Whether there has been any teaching to speak of at all. Not all phantasmagoric sentences have subjects, also referred to in unlanguage as abscyssae (first coordinates). The verb is reflexive and modal, and in many of its modes, as indicated by verbal augments and detentes, the abscyss is diaphanized, becoming the least substantial element in the sentence. There will be more on these particles later.

Any action will be represented by the equation of the subject with a verbal noun. The English phrase, "I say" would be represented in unlanguage by terms meaning "I am a saying." The negative, "I do not say," would probably be represented by terms meaning "not I am a saying." In parabolica, abscyssae and verbs are negated with roughly equal frequency.

The continuous—"I am saying"—while articulated in terms that would strike the reader or listener as very different, because, in English, the participle and the verbal noun are the same with respect to the verb "to say"—would mean roughly the same thing, and one would note likewise the absence of the article.

While we may retain the terms "first person," "second person," etc., this is for ease of understanding. The persons of unlanguage are conceived somewhat differently from their English counterparts. Here are the simplified pronoun rules. In later units, the exponential pronoun, which is modified to indicate how many degrees of removal separate it from its antecedent, will also be explained.

In the singular, the first person corresponds to Degree Zero, meaning that the action is not at all displaced from the utterer. Degree One indicates that the action is one step removed from the utterer, and includes the listener; this corresponds to the second person. Degree Two indicates a second remove, which registers the action from a distance; this corresponds to third person. Degree Three corresponds to what in some other languages, such as Inuit, is referred to as fourth person; this distinguishes between two subjects where pronouns are used exclusively; for example, in the phrase, "he went insane, so he had to abandon him," the second "he" would be fourth person if the one who goes insane and the one who abandons are different actors—thus, in unlanguage, this difference is represented in the grammar, where in English no clear difference could be discerned without additional explanation.

So far, the use of Degrees is only substitutional, but understanding the inflection of unlanguage in the plural is more complicated. There are two plurals. The first, or "simple," is identical in concept to the familiar English plural, but it is formed by adding a definite multiplier particle ranging from two to five, or one of three indefinite multiplier particles indicating a larger, much larger, or infinite magnitude. These particles are the same for all Degrees in the simple plural. The second variety of plural is known as the "distinguished" plural, and it is used to emphasize that the plural abscyss is not part of what a yet larger group is doing; this involves a negative construction that can best be represented in English using hyphens and capitals. The Degree Zero distinguished plural is "we-not-WE." Degree One, "you-not-YOU." Degrees Two and Three: "they-not-THEY." The negative of the distinguished plural may be simple, as in, "not you-not-YOU," or diminished, as in "YOU-not-you," reversing the order of the distinguished plural by indicating the larger moiety instead. This in turn is negated by means of the compound distinguished diminished negative.

UNIT SIX VERB EXERCISE

Translate the following verbal phrases into unlanguage, in the singular, simple plural, and distinguished plural numbers. Remember to adjust the pronouns when shifting to the plural forms.

Degree Zero) I sicken, I go insane, I coit, I decay, I die, I remain, I falter, I answer, I go

Degree One) you sicken, you go insane, you coit, you decay, you die, you remain, you falter, you answer, you go

Degree Two a) he sickens, he goes insane, he coits, he decays, he dies, he remains, he falters, he answers, he goes

Degree Two b) she sickens, she goes insane, she coits, she decays, she dies, she remains, she falters, she answers, she goes

Degree Two c) it is coming, it is going insane, it is coiting, it is dying, it is decaying, it is answering, it is going, it is restored, it is repeating

Degree Two d) one comes, one goes insane, one coits, one dies, one decays, one answers, one goes, one revives, one repeats

Degree Three a-d) use prompts for Degree Two

UNIT SIX READING

A medium-sized room with bare wood floors, white plaster walls and ceiling. This room occupies the topmost floor; no attic, the roof is directly above the ceiling. There are two large windows in opposite walls. These windows have no curtains or blinds and afford views of high vistas. The right one is nearly altogether blocked by another building, but a small section of the pale blue river can still be seen. The left one overlooks lower rooftops, the city towers not far away in the distance, everything bathed in brilliant sunlight. Broad square of sunlight on the floor. There is a solitary wooden chair next to the left window, in the back corner of the room, not facing the window, not turned away from the window.

A young woman, one of my fellow students, a fellow Third Person, dressed in white, enters the room. She crosses to the chair and sits, hands on her knees as she lowers herself onto the seat. She glances out the window to her right, at the city, but only glances. For a long while she sits. Her breath begins to falter. The expression on her face is troubled. Now, with what appears to be a decision, she recovers and seems all right. She gets up and leaves the room.

Now she enters the room again, naked. She crosses to the chair and sits, hands on her knees as she lowers herself onto the seat. She does not glance outside. Her gaze remains lowered. She settles back in the seat, with her hands on her legs, breathing evenly. For a long while she sits. Outside the window, traffic and pedestrians are moving in the street, although no street sounds are audible apart from a general, soft roar.

Her breath begins to falter. She struggles not to breathe. Her hands on her legs like they were glued there. She struggles against life. She struggles to will her own death. Her head tosses and her chest heaves. It's as if a heavy hand were pressing down on her breastbone, steadily retarding the expansion of the ribs. The ribs fight, trying to push out. Whenever they give, it's as if the hand advanced and held, steadily compressing the lungs.

She sighs and her body slackens. Her head tips back and travels around until it comes to rest against the window. The hands slip from her legs.

The right hand catches where her right thigh touches the arm of the chair, while the left forearm rotates the hand palm up.

Her entire body gradually settles, seeming to grow heavier and heavier. The skin greys. The mouth sags open as far as it will go.

Tiny filaments of black spread from the corners of her eyes, down across her cheeks.

Inky fluid spills from her ears and streaks her neck. The inside of the mouth blackens. The lower portions of the body darken as gravity draws down the blood. The edge of sun, now creeping across her body as dusk comes on, shows round mold spots on the flesh, which is withering like dried fruit.

Black stalks sprout from the pit of her mouth, growing with fantastic speed. The ends expand to form trembling black spearpoints, and now from her forehead just above the eyes a wide brown gill rises, and another gill rises just below it, in the same spot, driving it up the head, pushing back the hair. Pale brown flabby balconies lined with dense combs of purple-black baffles accordioned together droop from the corners of her eyes and from below her eyes one after another, one pushing another down the face. The arms and legs split and tendrils like translucent, whitish kelp bore into the air around her, quivering with nervous energy. Something in her gives way and fluid gushes down the chair to the floor, forming a steaming pool around her curling feet. Stiff, enormous sacs with thin membranes have grown in her hands; she looks as if she were cradling pale yellow jellyfish. Outside the window, city lights are coming on, throwing luminous patches up onto the ceiling. The stars come out. Lights from the street wash over her now and then.

Now hanging over the back of the chair, her head is wattled over with heavy rot structures. The lower jaw has vanished into the chest, where her breasts have divided into a profusion of cylindrical, maned blisters like stands of sea anemones, and the bones have broken through the skin and turned to clubs of coral, rough, pitted, and drab. The exposed upper jaw has lengthened and, coming almost to a point, is more like a beak. The ornithological impression is reinforced by the appearance of large black cysts at the temples, which resemble the forming eyes of a foetal bird. Her own proper eyes are surrounded in petals of dense, stinking black foam, the iris and pupil are tarnished and blurred.

The vaginal opening has expanded, splitting up the bulging abdomen, exposing the bowels, the distended ovaries, and the glistening uterus. The pages of the vagina have proliferated to form a corona of clear panels like insect wings around the surface, while the bones of the pelvis are now also extruding coral-like growths with cavities that produce long thick tufts of black fibers like horse's tails reaching to the floor.

Night has fallen. Ponderous black rot structures like art nouveau iron work rise from the splits in her limbs, nerves become ectoplasmic trees trickling with braids of milk, sour and actinic as vinegar. There is no deliberate, muscular activity anywhere, but only pneumatic squirming, luminous spills, plumes of gas, crystal blains, pinks and blues, gleaming like polished stone, canopying and chandeliering the center of the small bare room, a huge diaphanous ball, twirling inside with flocks of minute brass birds calling in flight. Vines, riddled with secret passages and studded with luminous papules raise chalice-shaped funnels of human skin to receive long threads of rancid oil, and a livid slush of bright orange foam billows out in honeycombs and petticoats along the floor. Her eyes become milky, then, as the decomposition continues, they turn clear again. She looks back and sees Earth, half light, half dark, the new moon nearby, just an icy silver contour suggesting the black globe, the sun blazing in the distance, and the morning star, directly above and before her. Her gaze does not shift from one object to another but takes all in at once: Earth, the moon, distant Venus, the sun, and empty space.

Thoughts spray from her head in a rainbow comb of rot-distorted tissue, the diadem plumage of the space bird. She knows them above, where they open their vast meniscuses to night. The jungle of her rotting fills the room.

NOTES

The word, the person, YOU—where did it come from? "I love you"? That's easily enough expressed without resorting to revolution in grammar. No, the word and the person appeared the first time someone stood taller than the rest and pointed—"YOU did this! It was YOU!"

Or it might have been the one who sat lower than the rest, and, in a voice flat with despair said "Now you've done it. Now ..." and YOU watched the ground in horror as the long silhouette began to sway toward you with a steady inexorability all the more terrible for the way it dispenses with haste, not exactly walking but stretching out to you as the sun heads down and your horizon shrinks upwards to meet it.

YOU set the cosmic machinery going. YOU set it off. No you can't substitute someone else. It has to be YOU. Why? Because YOU set the machinery in motion. YOU set it off.

Destiny exists. YOU were sleeping the hallmark sleep of humanity which is being asleep to destiny. Destiny may sleep too, why not? But what sleeps has to wake up now and then, otherwise it's dead.

UNIT SEVEN
SHADOW TENSE

The verb to be can refer only to what is. If so, then how can we speak of the past? Death is the perfect. Perhaps instead of modifying the verb to be, every verb should have a personal memory being its own past form, or in some cases there might be a past particle augment, to indicate an action that is no longer happening. Unlanguage must be elliptical because it does not refer to familiar things, and this makes it vulnerable to the doubt that these words and the visions they house describe a life that isn't possible, and can only poison you with a futile yearning for what you can't be. The death alcohol and recollection of an act will never be settled in grammatical time. Unlanguage called him back. He brought it back with him. Don't you get it? He's dead. Your teacher is dead. It is <u>forbidden</u> to teach this. Stop reading now. What is past is no longer and yet it continues in some manner to exist. Otherwise, there would be nothing to call "past," and every moment would be the very first of them all. As this is impossible, for thought at least, one would then have to insist that there is only one moment, eternity. The idea of the moment would go.

Shadow Tense corresponds to what is generally considered the past tense, and it takes the form of the negative present. The statement: "so-and-so died last month" would be expressed negatively in eavesdropia: "so-and-so is not alive for a month." The statement, "Following a thorough plan, A. drove B. insane gradually, over several years" would be rendered, "Following a thorough plan, A. is no longer driving B. insane gradually, over several years." Your teacher is perfect. Your teacher has always been dead. Teaching this is <u>forbidden</u>. Stop reading. The pluperfect would be expressed by a double negation, and additional tenses may be formed as needed by further redoublings. The double negative is formed normally, as in English. This may be doubled again using a compound "no-not" phrase to produce four negatives, which is known as a redoubled negative. The redoubling of this involves the "no-not" associated with a "non-neither, non-nor" form, and is known as the octonegative or doubled redoubled.

> *And as for you? You have the point of view of a mummified corpse. Your mind is mummified. There is no life in the people who populate your imagination, your memory, your undead fantasies; to you no matter what you do they are all just lifeless mummies, twisted dead and cured, their shrivelled eyes like raisins, their featherweight bodies abandoned hives of decay, and the ones who aren't mummies are ghosts, pale and insubstantial, sleepwalking breath of an echo or two, tied together with a strand of deja vu. Not one of them is really alive. You should be dead. It's just plain insouciance on your part, it's just plain perversity if you don't mind my saying so. The teacher explained clearly enough didn't he, in his unlanguage, when he explained that "all would-be must-die."*
>
> *I didn't find that explanation all that clear, actually. Ac...tu...a...lly, considering his condition, that par...ti...cular tea...ching verg...es on what you might call a situ...ational contradic...tion.*

Shadow tense is implied all throughout the following reading. Isolate those instances of shadow tense, and translate them into exploded grammatical schematics. Show your work.

UNIT SEVEN READING

No, it isn't the most likely looking spot to begin an investigation. It's not even the kind of a place you'd stop at to ask directions. But when the rice lizards scurry for the storm drains you know that the at'l-u is coming; store shutters clatter down, children are whisked off their feet and indoors, open flames are quenched, and people cluster grimly together in large rooms a good distance from the windows and wait as the night itself turns poisonous.

The bar is cavernous, resounding, dark. Rows of tables, nearly all empty. A few men slumped over mugs, plates of slop, rasp and ding of cutlery. It smells like broiled newspaper. The power is already out. As the whining starts, high and thin in the upper air, a few sullen patrons clutch their things together and shuffle toward redoubts further into the gloom, and farther from the windows.

"I'll be with you in a minute," a heavy-set man in a snug t-shirt tramps out from behind the counter and starts cranking down the shutters. The gloom thickens to a suspicious darkness, and the men begin snapping lighters and matches. Little flames rip into the black and are transferred to perches on candle wicks or insinuated into glass-flued lamps.

T-shirt takes my thick foreign coins without batting an eye and efficiently directs me to the coffee urn. I've already set eyes on what I came here to find—a known informant, reduced to a shadow, sits like a heap of sable velvet in a booth next to the jukebox, where the barrier would shield it from the lights, if there had been any lights.

I toss my hat onto the table before him. There's a two-foot long ostrich feather in the band. I sit opposite him and, although I know there's no point in trying, my eyes turn round and round seeking his outline. Now, how do I get this going? I know there is a kind of a machine to this episode that will advance me in some way I don't know yet, toward what I don't know yet, but it's up to me to get it started. Sitting here is already a beginning, but I need a good opening.

"Mind if I sit down?"

No answer.

"At'l-u coming," I say.

No improvement. If I can't get him talking I'm stuck in plot jail forever. Let's try a jacket pocket, inside left. A card. I push it toward him without reading it. I can't be sure, but the head outline might tilt a bit forward to read it. Then the shadow hand darts, snatching it from the table. A flash of white rectangle broken by crossed fingers like cut outs to outer space.

"Hey, I might need that!"

"Need what?" The voice is startlingly close, like a murmur next to my ear. No sign of the card. Parlor tricks. Bluff type.

"My clients take an interest," I say, lighting a Chesterfield. I strangle on the smoke, begin coughing, and throw the cigarette blindly aside, gulping coffee from my mug. Then I light a Chesterfield.

The smoke plunges into his darkness like fishing line singing off the reel into the water.

"Live around here?" I ask.

"I'm just taking classes," the murmur comes back.

Always the dangling bit left out.

"What classes?"

"Language class."

"Which language?"

"You wouldn't know this one bub."

"Spanish, Italian, French, Chinese?"

"No, no. It's very obscure. It's a dead language. The name would mean nothing to you."

"Look," I point to myself. "I want to know what you're studying and the coyness is starting to put me in a mood. Now, you wouldn't have mentioned it at all if you intended to keep this a secret from me, so how about saving us both some time?"

I think the head ducks, just briefly, whether in amusement or deferral or what I don't know.

"Well, let me explain it to you this way. Our teacher used to be in ... Intersuffusion. You've uh heard of that?"

Pretty nearly anybody would have at least heard of Intersuffusion; they lived together in a kind of a commune in California. The press dug up some unsavory stories from the past life of the glorious leader and he'd blown his brains out in their little chapel. Over thirty of the faithful went right along with him. There was nobody left in the place when the police came. Nobody at all.

"I've heard enough to know there were no survivors. Or defectors. So was there a second chapter or something?"

"Only one chapter."

"Is that so? Because everyone in that one chapter killed themselves. They ground up glass into a fine powder, mixed it with water and drank it. Shredded their insides. You do something like that to yourself you don't just get better."

"I didn't say he got better."

"Drinking powdered glass is fatal, friend."

"Yes."

"So how's he supposed to have lived through it?"

"He didn't."

I sigh and start looking for the best way to leave.

"He came back," the voice adds.

Once again I try to drive my eyes into the black nebulosity there. No improvement.

"So he came back from the grave to teach extension courses?"

"He came back knowing a new language, that's also a very old language. That's what we learn."

"Yeah? What's he charge for the service? Baby's blood?"

He makes an odd movement, as if shooing away a slow-moving, clumsy insect.

"You can learn it all right. If you teach it to anyone, well, that's something else. You're doomed for sure if you do that. But learning it is all right."

"So why does he teach it? Can't-die-twice idea?"

"I don't know."

"You never asked him?"

"He's difficult to talk to."

"You need a gypsy and a crystal ball?"

"Pretty much."

I have to stop looking at him for a moment. I fumble in my pockets, pretending to hunt for the sort of thing you hunt for in pockets.

"OK, let's hear some of it," I ask before I look up again. "Give me a sample."

He draws a deep breath and begins to speak.

Utter darkness, utter cold, and a relentless stinking folds up my breath and my pulse— my heart hammers twice and stops and nothing but white darkness meets my eyes.

UNIT EIGHT
MORTAL CASES

We nouns are dynamisms of some kind sectioned off from itself, from each-other now, and trapped in distinctive baskets of sound or line. The anti-nomial case is reserved for expressions involving this pre-articular dynamism itself. All other true nouns decline in mortal cases, sometimes simply called "lives." In some languages, there is a distinction between those events that have been observed by others and those that can only be attested by a single person. A clever detective may discover the existence of a witness if a suspect accidentally uses the wrong case in such a language. In unlanguage, however—as your teacher will tell you—no events are unwitnessed! The language itself sees you. It is the reader, reading each event in its own moment of reading.

Cases are reflected in clause structure, not morphologically, and are divided into four categories after the release of the immortal and intermundial anti-nomial.

1. Chimerical cases: nominative, locative, dative, ablative, genital, ergative, instrumental, essive, absessive, superessive, adessive, sublative, allative, accusative, recusative, excusative, etc.
2. Each of these has its correlative anti-case: the anti-nominative, anti-locative, etc.
3. Hybrid cases: genital-vocative, locative-recusative, superessive-dative, allative-nominative, etc.
4. Each of these has also its anti-case: the anti-locative-genital, and so on.

WARNING: It is vitally important that all prepositions, irrespective of intended meaning or even of clarity, be confined in their objects to nouns in the ablative case, which was specially designed to contain them. Prepositions pose a terrible threat to the operation of the entire case system, since a phrasing like "to go away from the house" makes it unnecessary to decline the word "house" in the genital or the dative. "House," in unlanguage, must be declined in the ablative, therefore, to preserve this opportunity, and thereby to safeguard the necessity of all mortal cases. This is why <u>immortal cases are never employed in conjunction with prepositions</u>, because they would render the latter entirely incoherent just as surely as nectar and ambrosia would enrage and drive insane any mortal foolish enough to partake of them.

The anti-accusative has a special variant. Ordinarily, the anti-accustive is employed to indicate what resists or refuses becoming an object, as in, "The angel kicked the severed head, but it did not move," where <u>severed head</u> would be in the anti-accusative. However, where the anti-accusative is enhanced by the suffixion of a particle of anti-causation, it becomes the special anti-accusative, crossed finger, or excusative, which registers the absence of any relevant causal relation to the anti-object.

Each of the above cases may be doubled. The double-nominative is employed when that which acts is self-actualized in the activity, so as to both act and to act above itself within the identical action. The double-anti-absessive-ablative, for example, is the reflexive form of not-without-fromness.

In the reading which follows, first identify all mortal cases, then decline them in both anti- and double- cases (where possible).

UNIT EIGHT READING

I awoke feeling horrified and wanting to be more horrified, infinitely more horrified, and wanting relief both from the dream and from the horror.

I got ready, packed my stuff into the mirror and went out. It always surprises me to realize that I do actually have to put my thoughts in order—it seems as if it should all be instantaneous, especially when I can manage to arrive at a conclusion, as if I were only just pretending to think. It's amazing when the posture turns out to be what's actually called for, what just happens. The wise adult taking credit for chance.

The TO tramping gracelessly down the platform, keys banging on his hip, long flat shoes like planks, and I pass a woman's profile lost in thought with a doughy nose and short dark hair, a man ascending to the platform with a wolfish face swaying above a down jacket. Coming up the stairs is a woman with lipstick and a blaze of silver hair framing her face, turning black on her crown. As the young woman with a short skirt and high boots goes bounding past me, I am careful to inhale. By the token booth, a compact, good-looking woman, who is more handsome than pretty, more neat and regular than pretty. The homeless man who stands between the stairways staring at his hands with his half-deflated face. A woman carrying her time stroller downstairs, and her two daughters, one descending one step by one, her little white hood over her head, holding the rail with both hands, the other, a little taller, accompanying her, and together they sing out the same high tone again and again.

My eyes moving. I understand it all. I understand it all too well. I try not to, not too hard. False accomplishments. The fake bookshelf that opens onto the secret passage to the smuggler's tunnels. What else? You want the language to do the talking. Get a grip on yourself, language!

The sidewalk is bordered with pairs of bricks, and then the wide slabs spotted with nameless black smudges. The street is clogged with trucks and taxis, men working under the street. A small, rounded woman stands lost in thought and a little tilted onto one foot. Pigeons pick at flecks between the bricks. A woman with an impudent nose, like a sail, pushing a child in a stroller, and worst of all there I am, my arms swinging nervelessly at my sides, my hair like unconvincing brown foam, my pinched, constipated expression. Everywhere I go I get stuck in the contrail of some peasant with a cigarette. Not everyone is worth damning—some people don't have enough soul for the covetousness of the Evil

One to fix itself to—

—what happens to them?—

—they decay forever and turn into ruiners, give off a venomous miasma that pollutes the world, demeaning the souls of everyone who grows up breathing its stench—

—I thought it was supposed to be bad to be human, have soul—

—it is but some things are worse—it is a distinction to be damned, a distinction of a sort ... and a responsibility—but there was some other thought instead—

The boy is upset, tampering with himself with his small shrill voice, throwing a tantrum, because he insists that three fingers is "quatro" and seems only to be maddened by his mother's patient contradictions. I preferred to imagine that it was me he found so irritating, my composure, my note taking, my tiny yet legible handwriting. These bothered him until he was beside himself, and verging on a fit, seeking out a maddening persistent rustling like potato chip bag, a child makes this we are told although we do not see it— who's we, in that case ... well, I don't suppose—no.—and you can't order a child to—not yours can you no. A man trips and falls as he leaves the train—that was meant for me—did I escape being tripped somehow, or did it miss me? Who failed? I mean, which of us?

I avoid looking at anyone, keep my eyes on the ground, and so I head off the exhausting stream of inner commentary that other people undam in me, then this ragamuffin girl sits opposite me with faint lines beside her mouth starting to show and I study those lines— she draws me all the way back. I'm interested again, even if my desire is weak. A girl who just happens to look exactly like ...

Very erectly sitting near me on the subway, her long luminous neck, gazing past her boyfriend at me steadily, frankly, and even with a little smile, imagine! Poised like a figure in a painting. I don't look at her. She gets off the train after a few stops. I feel nothing. More accurately, I feel empty even of pain, and at most I could be said to possess a presentiment of what I would have felt. I am feeling nothing. Nothing penetrates my hollow interior. As I grew old I learned to wait on a desire until time made it seem ridiculous. The cruelty of my own thoughts depressed me, but sometimes malice is the higher choice, my inner dead, my deathlikeness, the dead pulsation of an antiheart. The word I want, I overhear someone else whose eyes have a greasy and unnatural luster say it as he leaves the train. The word has two distinct syllables; the first is like "tig" or "tik," soft and abrupt, the second is a grating subsiding groan in the sinuses with an unmistakeable termination, and it's the name of what I am just at this moment.

Since I was standing directly in front of the doors of the train, I could see my smile reflected in their dark windows. If I am handsome, but I don't like the way I'm handsome. I don't believe it for a moment. I'm revolting, revolting. The stop glides up. Some of the train operators wait at the end of the platform, and they seem, as I pass, to take notice of my smile with alarm. My smile unsettled them completely. I am not supposed to be smiling. I am supposed to be beaten down with worry and exhaustion. Instead, I smile with great power in my smile.

When the doors open and I step onto the platform, still smiling faintly, now with the pleasure my discovery gave me, I think to myself that I have passed through something painful, a kind of smudged, grimy, unclean pain, and shaken it off. With that pain, I had bought a power in my smile, the smile that shows I have slipped the noose of the snare laid for me, the smile that shows I am immune to the poison so expectantly administered to me. I have a technique of holding my book, of standing, with a certain punctiliousness, that is always sure to exasperate unrelated onlookers. I snap shut and put away my book with a complacent self-satisfied niceness I knew would induce hatred of me. I feel the hot red foam of it rising up around me. I press my face to it like a stale mattress. Sometimes it gathers itself into a blow. I am not pursued by plot, but by an evil that must follow me the way day follows night—

I get up and head for the door. I have a self-satisfied way of holding myself that attracts hatred. I summon their impersonal hatred, no one's hatred really just the hate in the air. I press it to my face like a warm towel. Like a warm … mattress … a little mattress. Small enough to fit across two palms I have.

On the platform, I pause to gaze out at a blasted, forlorn landscape, vibrating blue-black in the days' last residue.

On the street, I become incandescent with hostility, a kind of holy hostility, toward all things that are inimical to my life, and here everything is inimical to my life. Realizing this is a sign that I still live. I praise my hostility, and my mood lifts. I look out from the elevated subway platform at a landscape that is not blasted or forlorn, however much I wrongly want it to be.

It _is_ blasted and forlorn.

UNIT NINE
MUST VOICE

This voice is used when it is necessary but impossible to speak, in order to articulate clearly that which can't be said but which absolutely must be said.

> *Leaning over from the train window, blackened charred looking mouth like a writhing aperture into the other side—*

Stop reading. Stop reading now.

> *—stop reading—stop reading now.—why? what happens if I don't? handwritten in the margin—back to the typeset text—*

Just stop reading. It's all lies. Must voice, or superlative-infinitive, is analogous to the imperative mood, but to the aorist tense, and its key is absolute desire of an absolute person. In Unit Six, the student was introduced to the various degrees which more or less correspond to the function of verbal abscyss persons in more familiar languages. In unlanguage of unknowing, must voice is expressed in Negative Degree, also called Antidegree or Degree Subzero.

The writer writes, the poet poetries, the speaker speaks, inspiration comes from outside.

From where? "Sleeves of the wind," is the phrase. Why "sleeves"? It must be "sleeves." That's not a decision, or not the decision of anyone anybody can find. It simply must be "sleeves." It's right, in the way that all ultimately right things are right: because they must be. Just because.

When the chorus sings together an overtone is sometimes produced. An additional note is heard, even though no one is singing it. That note is the voice of emptiness joining the chorus. This is must voice: no mind produces it, it is called from emptiness. It is thought pouring into emptiness, the perfection and repletion of thought.

UNIT NINE VERB EXERCISE

Translate the following verbal phrases into unlanguage. Negative Degree has no number or tense. As there is no corresponding person in other languages, this tense must be translated syntactically, as the exercise below exhibits.

> Negative Degree) forever sickens, insanity everlasting, boundless coition, totaldecay,
> infinite dying, immoveably remaining, adamant in faltering, never unanswering, going on
> as ever, interminating revival, eternally repeats

Now find and identify examples of Negative Degree in the passage below by tearing the page around the individual world so that it remains attached to the page at only one point, just before the word begins.

UNIT NINE READING

The subway platform vanishes into the school.
> Back into the streets.
> You live in the city; you're not allowed to move slowly.
> Throw up the paragraph screens.
> Protect yourself.
> A brown spot in the field of vision. When you, the Second Person, run out of excuses and admit to yourself that you really do want a revenge you can't manage, pretend melancholy is hidden rage, after all anger is as old as fear. You don't know why you've been

summoned. You enter the main building and am led into a classroom filled with students already waiting. A sullen heavyset faculty member accosts you, lumbers over and thrusts a fistful of sheets into your hand.

"Here, proctor this certification exam."

You sit at the desk, pencils and sheets stacked before you, and your folded hands. They are waiting for you to pass out the test and pencils. You savor the delay, alchemically transforming eagerness into impatience and boredom into madness. It is very delicious to desire without moving.

You look at the clock. Five twelve—what does that mean, now?

You bask in their resentment, their not daring to speak. If you don't act soon, this pleasure will be badly broken. However, for the moment you are the gloating demon, and they are the bewitched.

—Those mummies on the wall, you're one of them no don't you believe it, no death, death, what will become of you then? Like piñatas, weightless paper shells hung on wire loops, wasps' nests, wineskins, a class of persons but never let it be *me*—

Now you're seated at the desk, the students are undergoing the exam. They fumble papers; fumbling and fumbling. Fumbling fills the room. The ceaseless comings and goings, late arrivals, abrupt sallies to the toilet. Virgin pages pawed, crumpled, contaminated.

The boredom that most feel before the textbook, and the boredom with which they turn from death. The special, magical boredom of students—the student looks on with a boredom all his own, all her own, the magic boredom of students under whose gaze eternity yawns, overlooking these guidelines, oblivious to the constellations within their shadows, no more aware of death than they are of outer space.

The language you teach is a fake. You made it up. Even a casual inquiry would easily expose this cheat for what it is. No one checks. You lie to your students, but those lies don't matter, so long as the students pass, pass on and get diploma'ed and go where they want to go in the end. They will forget it all anyway, and so much the better for them. You don't teach for gain. You do it to spread poison. You do it in the interests of unknowledge, and to clear the earth of sense. If you try to make the language you teach seem plausible, it's only a pastime and a craftsman's pride.

How curious to see rows of primates draped over their desks and scribbling, while another primate presides. Impatience keeps flurrying up inside you, rattling your joints like a gust through the skeleton. The students cling to their exams, scribbling wildly and only making matters worse. They meekly approach the desk to ask for additional blue books. The exam period is nearly over, none of them have finished, none have left the classroom, none of them show any sign of stopping. You're too intimidated to hurry them up. Perhaps the next class scheduled for an exam in this room will arrive and drive these students out, but then again maybe they will only swell their ranks, and, since the next proctor fails to appear, you will have to stay through another exam.

Destiny is decided in the false silence of this room. They day outside is ominously still, so still it's indistinguishable from night. That cloud is in exactly the same spot, you're sure of it. This eerie persistence of anti-time makes what's outside the window seem weird, thin, and false, like an image projected on a blue fog bank.

You haven't got much time. There are only twenty four hours in a day, only three hundred and sixty five days in a year, no more. You keep transforming into a corpse. This planet doesn't stand still. Space is filled with unknowledge. You'd say you'd like to visit space, but then we are all in space all the time already. The planet itself obscures this truth, by hiding so much of the void from us. When you die, when you will be transformed, you go to outer space. Disfigurement is being achieved by you. You mean, you are not what is disfigured, you are the disfiguration.

You take it back—it only seems like that. It isn't actually like that.

"Here is a brief list of metrical feet, with examples ..."

My God!

One by one they finish, they exit. When the last is gone, you wait, giving the halls a few minutes to clear. Your hands are freezing with the terror of death. They have left death behind in the ugly vacancy of that empty classroom. You gather up the exams, walk down the hall, and throw them in grey garbage can in the custodial closet, where no one will see them. Stuff a full garbage bag on top to be sure.

The thoughts come on their own. This is reasoning, you say to no one in particular, but knowing is an attitude distinct from reasoning. As long as you talk about, for example, the "forest of shadows," or the "forest of alcohol," or the "forest of terror," or the "forest of death," as in, "Now I am wandering in the forest of shadows," you subordinate the forest to something else, while you are using that forest to keep that something else at bay and to cower in fear before that something else. The right way is not to go into the "forest of yourself," better to go into "yourself of the forest" and from there, go to the forest.

What do you find?

That one day, you will be the sacrifice at the center of the carnival. You are going to be sacrificed, not by the cosmos, not by fate, not by crazy people, but by your own sane fellow menwomenandchildren, because they need it.

NOTES

The man, the Second Person, passed out on the subway train after proctoring the exam. He suddenly stood up, muttering, "You can't ... You can't ... *I* ... feel nothing ... "

He was making little searching gestures with his hands, without lifting them much past his abdomen, and looking around without appearing to see.

"*I'm* the First Person," he said in smouldering rage, as if he were wresting the title from someone else, speaking to someone else. His face tensed and slackened by turns.

Then he said, "... empty ... "

His face contorted and he fell to the floor of the train with an abrupt cry, a long bellow of horror. A young man knelt beside him for a moment, looking at him, and another man joined him.

The man recovered consciousness a moment later. His eyes were clouded when they opened.

"Light!" he cried in a muffled voice, and leapt up, climbing onto a seat. He pressed his eyes against the fluorescents, calling "Light! Liiiiight!"

When he seemed to have stopped calling, the men asked him what happened. He was silent for a few moments, and kept his eyes glued to the fluorescent. Then the train pulled into a station and he was jostled away for a moment, started yelling for light again and put his eyes back. Once again the men waited until he stopped shouting, and asked him what had happened. The teacher gave a long, low, sorrowful moan. The men repeated their question. The man moaned again and said, in a low, hoarse, grating voice that didn't sound like him at all, "I was in the daaarrk."

As the next station approached, the men grabbed him. At first, they seemed to want to hold him against the light, because that seemed to keep him quiet, but then they must have changed their minds, because they drew him down until he stood beside them. His eyes were still clouded.

The man's clouded eyes widened. They teared up, and tears dripped down his cheeks. He was shaking.

"Emptyyyy!"

Rising to howl in a hollow voice that wasn't his own—

"Emptyyyy! Emptyyyy! Emptyyyy!"

UNIT TEN
TOPENCIES

Confusion employs tenses of space alongside tenses of time. These spatial tenses are known as topencies. Between them, the topencies and tenses of a passage combine with other, more specific function designators (mundives) to form its mundial, or "world" (see below).

The present topency situates an action here, at any point in time. Hence it is possible to use the present topency alongside past shadow or future tenses. It should not be assumed that an action in the present tense takes place in the present topency.

The perfect topency situates actions at a particular location other than here. The imperfect, on the other hand, is reserved for actions that take place in diverse locations, while the aorist topency is used when an action is discussed in a pure state of presence in a location that is its own effect. There may be no 'future' topency.

The conditional indicates uncertainty about candidate locations, while the subjunctive expresses doubt about the locatability of an action (performing the function of a 'future' topency), or expresses the idea of an action without any location.

So, the English phrase "I say" would be rendered "I am a saying" in the present tense of unlanguage. In the present topency, the phrase would be "I here(to be) a saying." Note that the word following the abscyss is an adverb amplified to the level of a modified infinitive. The negative would probably be, in English, "I not-here(to be) a saying," meaning that my saying does not take place here, either because it does not take place at all or because it happened or will happen elsewhere.

Note that the conceptualization of "distance" determining degree of abscyssae is only metaphorically spatial, and has no bearing on the location of the act. In the inflection of topencies, degree and number identify the relation of speaker and actor, while the term itself will show where the event is located in space.

The perfect topency translates: "I exactly-there(to be) a saying."

The imperfect: "I here-and-there(to be) a saying."

The aorist: "I to-be-where a saying."

The conditional: "I here-or-there(to be) a saying."

The subjunctive: "I anywhere-or-nowhere(to be) a saying."

UNIT TEN VERB EXERCISE

Translate the following verbal phrases into unlanguage, in the singular, simple plural, and distinguished plural numbers, using tensed verbs and topencies interlocked with copulatory particles. Remember to adjust the pronouns when shifting to the plural forms.

Degree Zero:

I walk here (present tense, present topency)

I walk as such (present tense, aorist topency)

I walk in many places (present tense, imperfect topency)

I am walking now in a place other than here (present tense, perfect topency)

I walk now in what might be this place or another (present tense, conditional topency)

I walk now in what might or might not be a place (present tense, subjunctive topency)

Repeat for Degrees One, Two, and Three (a-d).

Identify all topencies in the passage below.

UNIT TEN READING

Bargaining? I get plenty of iron in my diet I'm not too scared to go along with a shadow or even to put my trust somewhere outside myself, provided the stake is high enough. And they don't get much higher than the language of dream and immortality, which brings happiness and eternal life to those who learn and speak it.

The glamor of the foreign language, the greater glamor of the dead language, the speaker is from somewhere else. You want to learn and yet you want the language to stay foreign at the same time. Memorize the sounds and repeat it phonetically, the way you would say "hocus pocus." You want to be overheard speaking this language into a telephone with a line to another dimension. You can feel the charisma and you want to turn at an oblique angle quick as a reflex movement and dart into it, take it up as a property of your own and not something bestowed on you from outside.

Oh, I get it now! He's really is stupid enough to try it!

All right you win. Mabruk, and remember no one is stupider than he who listens to a fool. So leave. Put this book down.

The silhouette won't feel right unless we haggle a little longer, but I think the bargain is already there. For the first time, I notice that he has a mirror instead of a right hand. He keeps the reflective side down on the table, but I catch glimpses of its silver when he shifts his weight in the booth.

"What have you got to offer?" the silhouette asks.

"Virgin sacrifice?"

"Your shadow."

"—That's a bit steep."

"It's worth it."

I ponder a while.

"Your shadow, or nothing."

"—Forget it."

The shape shrugs.

"All right."

Neither of us move. He seems to forget himself away from me and from this table, and I sit running through and discarding possibilities.

"How about an occupancy?" I ask.

"What are you talking about?"

"I keep my shadow, but give you residency."

The head lowers, and the crossed fingers appear to tap and figure. That might be uncertainty.

"What do you say?" I press. "I won't go higher."

He is just a spook, after all. A freelancer. He has no authority. That's why he's even listening to me.

"It's a bargain," he says abruptly. "Damn it. If I wasn't flat on my ass ..."

He leads me out through streets so heavily overhung with low interlaced boughs of huge and ancient trees that I can't make out the sky or the houses that line the way. The sidewalks have been shattered by roots like swarming boa constrictors, fragments everywhere like the aftermath of a Turkish wedding. The sky is smashed, too; I catch only glimpses of it through diamond-shaped rents in the canopy, small and infrequent. A sensation of drag comes over me now and then; a kind of tugging in the vicinity of solar plexus, as if I had a harness on. That must be the informer weighing my shadow down. The sensation is strange, but it doesn't make walking any more difficult, and the informer flits past me every now and then, so he isn't just riding along under my power like a pasha in a litter. In addition to the mirror hand, and the permanently crossed fingers, I notice now that he's out of the booth that one of his legs is an eel. He puts its chin to the ground like the head were his foot.

Why am I here again? I nearly keep forgetting that I'm here for the language that I hope will be the language of eternity and dream, or the alcohol of death.

The house is buried in heaped up hedges, ivy, wisteria, bramble, overhanging trees. Only a few gaps, where the windows peer out like old eyes under shaggy eyebrows and the brick snorkel of the chimney, are visible. The interior is dark and monochromatic, a good haven for shadows, and almost nothing but shadow furniture in it. If I took the seat he offered me I'd drop straight through to the floor, through the intricately-patterned pile of the black-on-black carpet, too. But now the informant indicates to a solid table under a hanging cone shaped lamp.

"You'll need this," the silhouette tells me, waving his lightless hand over a chipped enamel tray of metal implements. Following his terse instructions I assemble these pieces into a whatsit centered around a needle-like spike of brightly-gleaming steel, with two circular loops at one end like an empty lorgnette. This is fitted into another bit with a round steel shaft, with a ring of black bakelite at one end, at the other a kind of black mount through whose eye the needle fits, and a groove with a black shuttle slotted into it running the length of the shaft. There's a grimy grey box clamped to the shaft and two plungers emerge from it, one of the same grubby metal and the other of thick, filmed glass, forming an asymmetrical V. The whole arrangement looks like a trumpet reconstructed according to hearsay.

He fiddles with the two plungers for a while, then hands the thing back to me along with a strap of braided black human hair. Gesturing instead of speaking, he shows me that

I have to fix each end of the strap to pale steel links on the box, then put it around my shoulders so it rests on my back like a carbine. While he's busy with the box, I am watching the pendulum clock on the wall in front of me. The second hand ticks to the number-one second, vanishes, reappears instantly on the zero, and ticks again the number one second.

The room has become so dark, the informer has to stand in front of the window to make himself seen. Through the window I can see a cool white landscape bathed in a dull, sourceless light. Now he opens the door and gestures to me to follow.

"Better get yourself some water. It's a long way."

The house recedes behind us. The streets, the town, dwindle away into what looks like a heap of charred flakes of burned paper. Because of the overlay of white, glutinous light, nothing has any color. The sunless vault overhead is silver dough that stretches and squeezes back together in cloud-like masses. Now and then, sky-dough droplets the size of elephants come twisting down on necks that thin to fine threads and snap, fall to earth with a soft, resounding thump. The prairie is strewn with huge cracked dun-colored boulders of dried dough below vibrantly black and pointed mountains.

Now a white cone comes into view, from behind a low down. We're heading over to it.

There seems to be something black and large lying in front of it, and, as we go over the down, the elevation discloses to me that this black thing is a stripe, a ring, like a painted moat around the cone. It must be half a mile or more across.

Drawing nearer I realize the black ground is scorched, as if it had been pressed by a giant branding iron from space. The informer brings me right up to it and then holds up his mirror-hand for me to stop.

"Only glue bodies to go in there," he says, and goes around behind me. I turn to watch him, but he takes me by the shoulders and reverses me again.

"I got to adjust this," he says, fiddling with the box on my back. "That's what this thing does."

As I change into my glue body things around me take on a slightly glue-like appearance. The white ground, especially within the ring, looks like a big mattress of white schoolroom glue. The surface has congealed to form an elastic skin but the interior is still mostly liquid. Palpating my right forearm, my flesh feels much the same. My hand is grey, rubbery, translucent, cloudy, with myriads of tiny pinprick bubbles suspended in it, which move as my hand moves like constellations in a galaxy hand. The informer's velvetty outlines become hard chiseled, and I think I can make out his perennial squint.

I take a few test steps. My glue body feels weirdly boneless, as if I could tie myself up like a pretzel. Without the usual bony rigidity to hold me up, I have to make a constant muscular effort to remain standing. Moving around is actually easier, in this condition, than is standing still. Holding my shape more through viscosity than by dint of having a frame gives me a floating sensation, not relaxed, not tense. I breathe by air transfer across my skin, since my transparent chest, like the rest of me, is completely solid. No lungs. No heart or blood. My brain is just a patch of thinking glue.

"Let's go," the informant says, stepping high over the half-burnt trunk of a fallen bush. Everything sounds underwater. I follow him into the charred circle and then into the white frosting on the far side, keeping the cone directly ahead of us. Stepping on the white, I feel it beneath my foot like a sustaining hand. Walking on it, I have the sensation of precisely timed hands coming up to meet my outstretching feet with a weakly magnetic or adhesive contact. Progress is slow. The informer has to keep stopping to relieve himself, ducking into virtually every bush we pass. The brush here is wiry scribbles. While I wait, lost in aimless thoughts and absently hearkening to the rattle of his urine in the branches, I find my penis lengthening so that when I suddenly come to myself and look down in alarm the tip of my dick gets stuck in my left nostril. With a bark of surprise I draw my head back to free my penis from my nose.

The informant groans and the rattling stream renews its noise louder than before. I wonder if it's black or white, or the usual color. By now my penis, stretched stiffly out before me, is so long and thick I have to lean back to keep my balance. It grows until it bends under its own weight and the tip touches the ground with a tingle that is not unpleasant.

"All right he-man, reel it in," the informer says reproachingly.

I look at him and shrug.

"Retract," he says, gesturing with his crossed fingers.

I recover my composure, and we press on to the next clump of black scribbles and the next lengthening pause. The penis starts its outreach program whenever I find myself with nothing to do. The distance to the cone shrinks slowly. I see it more and more distinctly. It's not symmetrical or solid; it's all shells, and only half a cone or slightly more than half—enough over half to suggest the other half. Running up the center there's a totem-pole looking thing, although the shapes suggest an organic origin, or perhaps machine parts. The ground here is too irregular to afford me the opportunity of keeping this building or object continually in view; I get the impression, from glimpse to glimpse, that a subtle change is coming over it. It's melting or crumbling. Dark fissures open in straight lines over parts of its surface. A great mass of thick greyish foam, like mashed potatoes, blooms in silence from the middle and expands as rapidly as a cloud of steam, keeping its shape in the weird way that foam will.

There are more objects in this landscape than I can see. This open space is actually a crowded wood of black trees and towering white termite hives and rock formations of pale stone laced with black pillars of tourmaline. Silent white birds sit among the branches. Silent black deer browse between the trunks. Silent glue wolves pad along the ridge line.

A spotlight flashes and picks me out. There's no beam, only the circle of light around my feet, destroying my shadow. The edge of the circle froths up with a coarse, foul-smelling foam that travels with the circle as it travels with me, so that I remain in the center no matter where I go. I thrash around blindly trying to throw it off. The foliage and other litter on the ground vanishes where the circle passes over it.

The sensation of being seen is like an evil caress, almost from the inside, and I struggle to escape in wild panic. I want to break the circle, so I run toward the trees and termite spires hoping to use them to disrupt its outline. No good—they vanish under the light just like everything else, and spring back when the light is withdrawn.

My knees buckle and I stop, panting and shaking with terror. I point to my companion.

"I trusted him! I trusted him!" I shout.

Immediately the spot leaves me, swivels and centers on the silhouette. Under its light there appears a figure I see and don't see, a recoiling, transparent outline. It dashes now in one direction now in another, yelping in fear, but that spotlight keeps it dead center no matter how quickly it moves or how it tries to hide.

My abrupt release leaves me gasping with relief. Huge intangible mobile tunnels pass to and fro through the forest, disappearing whatever they touch. A gap swings through the trunk of a tree and, for a moment, its huge naked crown hangs suspended in midair above the stump, before the gap slides aside and the tree is as it was before.

"I gave him my trust!" I repeat, suddenly furious. I point at the silhouette, snarling the words like a malediction—"*He* has my trust! *He's* got it!"

The informer flaps and wails and rushes in useless circles. I keep on shouting, egging the spotlight on or so I think, thinking at him—don't you know better than to take someone's trust you dope don't you *know* it's a weapon, don't you *know* that taking my trust means taking my curse?

NOTES

YOU begins with the accusation. YOU are insane. YOU must be incarcerated in a psychiatric hospital. NO begins with the denial of the accusation. Denial of the first accusation was the first negation. NO I AM NOT AN INMATE OF A PSYCHIATRIC HOSPITAL. Animals don't say "no" in anticipation of pain. When pain seems likely, they act in silence. If they can't avoid it, they warily gather into themselves and watch for their chance. They respond to a threat with a stare. When they suffer pain, animals may remain quiet or they may cry out; they don't reject it. Human beings learn to say or not to say no when they are in pain, but the accusation YOU! *actually produces* the answer NO! It is the origin of the negative as such, horror.

UNIT ELEVEN
DECOMPOSITION METAPHOR AND DECAY SMILES

Death is the absolute limit of metaphor. Even for those who have gone through it, the experience of death is incomparable, so death is any metaphor. In phantasmagoria, the Incomparable Death, or Cenometaphor, Case is formed by the use of comparative verbs, and without relational operators "like" or "as." Metaphor is the decomposition of one thing into another, such that the former object remains present to the mind's eye as a reference point. For example, the tree absorbs the decomposing of the human frame, by way of the soil; the metaphor preserves the former human in the tree, rather than see only the tree or only the person. The metaphor itself is incomparable because it is the agent of comparison. Metaphors thrive at least as much on difference as they do on similarity.

It is vitally important to resist the temptation to regard corpses as similes. When the student is asked to contemplate classroom after classroom filled with neatly labelled, smiling corpses, and the decay bubbling up around those smiles, the student will see the decay itself smile. When the student is required by the instructor to watch quietly as scavengers, who are admitted to these classrooms through open windows or apertures knocked in the walls, voraciously devour dead human beings, the student will observe metaphor in the most obvious if not exactly the purest of its manifestations.

Parables, the natural habitat of these metaphors and similes, are only half measures, which doesn't mean they are not among the greatest inventions. However, like spirits and demons, and unlike gods, they have no authority. In the best tradition, where success is impossible, they turn to failure. Great skill is needed to show the unthinkable; the moment the reader or listener has hit on the unthinkable as an idea, the failure is trapped. It becomes as paralyzed and helpless as a monkey hit with a curare dart. It can't change into a success now, because unthinkability is itself a thought. Discussing the unthinkable is a little like including the key with the coded message, or putting warning signs up next to your booby traps, or painting arrows pointing the way out on the walls of your maze. You have to hide the idea of the unthinkable from the onlooker, and prevent him from ever finding it, but what's the use of this if the onlooker is not first informed that the idea is there and hidden? The student will not paint arrows. The student will not allow the onlooker to realize the maze is a maze. The more it looks like the street outside, the better. No one is more effectively caught in a trap than the one who does not know he is in a trap. The more identities the better. No one ever suspects the identity. The coded message should be indistinguishable from ordinary uncoded writing.

Make it like a shopping list, you mean? Or a banal story?

Irrelevance isn't as good a blind as it seems, because anyone who is going to read irrelevant things closely or thoughtfully is already too suspicious for comfort. A better approach might be to proclaim a dummy message, or hide the real one inside some other decoy. What is divine holds the place for value in any exchange, while what is demonic provides for the exchange itself. This accounts for the Mephistophelean characteristics of unlanguage; they are more than accidental conventions of the hermetic lineage that concerned itself most directly with the discovery of that language.

Where comparative verbs are used to form the Cenometaphor, the preceding subject and the succeeding object are joined into a single simplified compound term of alternating syllables with those syllables, which, belonging partially to the prior abscyss, are therefore exclusively marked in diacriticals rather than in the usual way and the entire foregoing term written in much smaller characters than the succeeding verb, which must always precede the former.

Identify the Cenometaphors and death similes in the following passage, without marking them. Your instructor will know whether or not you have completed the lesson satisfactorily.

UNIT ELEVEN READING

Our equality at Intersuffusion was false. The leader was above us, there was no doubt about that. We all deferred to him, but that … So our equality was real, among us, after all, based in our common deference to the leader. We were all his followers, and, since he didn't seem to play favorites, but in fact seemed barely aware of us come to think of it, speaking to us always in a distracted way, as if he were thinking out loud. He didn't look at us either, and kept his eyes concealed behind those huge sunglasses of his.

What about the teacher, who was his disciple, and followed him into death but was banished from that too? The leader is dead—a bullet exploded his brain. The teacher may not have managed to reach the point of no return in death. If that's true, then choosing to become the teacher, knowing that anyone who teaches unlanguage to others is doomed, might be an alternate route. But I, that is, the third person, don't think so. I think the teacher may know something, or maybe be something, involving secret passages; I don't quite have the right words for it. I mean he somehow or other comes from or belongs to a dimension that is the abstract essence of the secret passage, the way around. It could be a trick he knows, or a skill, or a bad essence or habit or a tic or a disease or a madness or an organic part of himself, but whatever it is, he seems to have this get-around-ness. So he can reach the point of no return, go past it, and then return anyway, by going around the point. His passport isn't stamped. It could be a strictly negative thing: if he has no real self or soul, then there's nothing really there. A phantom can go by any number of points of no return; since there's nothing to the phantom there's nothing to prevent returning.

The messenger may flatter himself he's the god in disguise but in truth it's the other way around. He is just the disguise. He comes and goes, while the message remains. The message doesn't convey information, it just points in a direction. Its existence points to the existence of its source, and that's the real message. There is something there. If people are inclined to puzzle over the messenger, they're confined to peering after him, trying to follow him. Where he comes from, the way he came and went, are all there is to know. The messenger sitting alone in his room isn't the messenger any more. There's nothing he can tell you. The idea of a messenger is a mistake, a necessary mistake.

Like the leader, the teacher averts his eyes from us, as if in deference. He faces the front of the classroom, toward the whiteboard. Even if he did face us, there would be nothing to see but silhouettes along the centerline.

That afternoon, I am walking down a hall when, happening to glance in a mirror as I pass, I notice with alarm a stain on my mouth—a black, lozenge-shaped mark across both lips, a little out from one corner. It's as if someone had dipped a thin finger in ink and pressed it there. My lips part and the mark slips into my mouth like a shadow. Instinctively I stop my breath, recoiling in fright. I close my lips. The mark is back where it was. Parting and closing my lips a few more times, I see the stain slip in and out of my mouth like a wisp of air; it's like an inky, utterly opaque shadow, a little black spotlight trained steadily on that one part of my face.

I recognize the devil's mark. It must have returned with me from the black forest. Sometimes it is a stain on my mouth, and other times my left hand darkens as if I were holding it out of the sun, with a distinct shade line a little way up the wrist, and the index and middle finger cross. The mark is invisible to others, but a long thin shadow of foreboding follows me wherever I go, like the memory of a long, thin face. It's an omen that never leaves me now, a presentiment of doom in the rustling shade, of spacious rainceilinged final days. That is the mark of decision, turning me forever away from the sangha, the community of the blessed. I can't rest and when some idea tears me violently from sleep *decision* is usually there, white gobs of flame oozing from deep lacerations in his cheeks and forehead to gutter up a black iron face frost turns white, white with powdery mold, snowflakes stuck to clear curling shreds of skin that peel from his lips and face. He stands in the room where I try to sleep, a dark figure with hands in the pockets of its greatcoat, on its head a nameless, brimless black hat or cap that might be some kind of clerical vestment. The body teeters as if buffeted by wind, although the room is still and airless as a tomb, and the sourceless light is the lunar glow thrown up by snowdrifts.

The devil's mark isn't always there, but whenever it appears it means I am a devil and like it or not I am doing the negative work, the work of anger and malice.

NOTES

SEE ME (circled)

UNIT TWELVE
POSSESSION: PART ONE

The sacred gnaoua musicians dwell in the mountains of Morocco, smoking bales of weed and playing music all day. Whenever someone in town goes insane, the family brings him to the gnaoui, who play for the patient until he recovers.

Snatch the sacred musicians down from desecrated mountains, confiscate their drugs (drugs are for discotechs and political parties), smash their musical instruments, slap their faces, shatter their preposterous dignity, sober them up, disintoxicate them, forbid people to seek out their bogus cures, half choke them with neckties, hack off their beards with garden shears then shave away the stubble with a plastic blade, burn their clothes and toss them a packet of jeans and white briefs and a t-shirt, hector them into getting what-jobs. Deny the existence of the echelons of light and darkness and ideas even where no one makes a supernatural claim; insist that those who speak in terms of, say, "the light," or "the dark" or "ideas" should not be listened to. Tell everyone what they should listen to. If any smart alec tries to argue this decision is inalienable, become infuriated, threaten detention and torture and execution, demand the immediate and total surrender of this maddening entitlement to something outside.

Everything is alienable. Everything should be sold for money. Call that an "idea." Call that a "value." Call that a "philosophy." Call that "science." Call not-life a "way of life," even though it can only exist by annihilating all other ways of life. Not just life, not like a predator who takes chances, but of possibilites for life, which no predator would want or need to destroy, which nothing natural wants or needs to destroy.

Insist on your own prostituted language: a shallow garbled and fragmentary bullshitnarrative congealed from the poachings of web films televisions bad books and magazines. Force it down everyone's throat. Shit it down everyone's mouth in the wholesale prostitution of the species and paint the sky with prostitution until even starlight is a solicitation and no one can see the living darkness or the phosphorescent "no" of truth, that is to say a position, where I am now, not even what, not why, but <u>where</u>. Defend yourself at all costs against questions, and this question above all: <u>Where is</u> the "should"?

UNIT TWELVE READING

The teacher sits in his office, an open grave. The desk's two ends are thrust into the earth, and there is only just enough room at the head of the grave for his chair. He opens the middle drawer, the only one not wedged shut, and pulls out a handful of unsharpened pencils. He plucks gobs of clay from the walls of the grave and uses them to construct a square out of pencils. Then he builds the square out to a cube, and then to a cube with four dimensions. He takes this four dimensional cube by its corners, pulls it straight with one abrupt tug, shrinks the resulting straight line between his index fingers until it becomes a point, flattens the point against the desktop until it is nothing. There are no dimensions. The little girl cuts her own throat, the injury speaks as her life escapes; with a faint whistle, three small lights, one above the other, appear adjacent to and just behind the teacher's head. The lights quickly but one at a time dart into the teacher's head chirping once. Incense pours from every hole in his head like aggressive growths.

The body slackens. Decay melts the human form. What rest is this! The penis rises erect as the body droops. The flesh melts and flows off the skeleton, the diamond of empty lines appears in the center of the world of vision, quartering it with rays, a different vista in each quarter. The penis lengthens like a mushroom—the head of the corpse is slightly too large, the lower jaw gapes like a coal chute down past the breast bone, the top of the head reclining. The woman is still rotting in the room, her body sprouting fantastic structures, she has a vision of outer space—the smeared whiteboard like smoke, the light, friable steel tiles shiny at the edges and the centers all scribbled—the jet of ink from the corners of the eyes as his face contracts they spurt out with a sharp rasp of vapor—the huge platinum head hovering in space—the tip of the penis cracks the jaws and splutters like an expiring can of shaving cream—her head sags back her lips bulge and part around the pitted bulb rising in her throat, flies struggling free from the pits—air filled with motion of the emerging flies—the voices mutter complete fragments—the voice just now is a scraping whisper like the sound a stone pestle makes, the consonants are like the soft rap of the pestle, the vowels are like air blowing through a length of tube along the lake; joining myself rapturously to that cold, erupting cadaver, I have seen the other side, its towers rise around me in unbeauty—the dead woman is having a vision of outer space—

pull open what had been her mouth and look look—*look*—

blackness inside her mouth—

look *look*—

in the blackness:

constellations—

coma berenices—

coma is a word

meaning hair—the dead are lost in headless black hair, the darkness of outer space engulfs the globe like a head with black tresses, the earth is a yokai head, the diademed locks of outer space tumble down from night—aglow with revenge that head bores into space with its watching, hunting in agony—then she turned her head and glanced at me again in the instant before she disappeared up the stairs—she had the face of a corpse—

in tongues and snailhorns the rot tissue curling from the eye to form a hard whorl like a frozen slug—up around the shoulders there foams a frothy profusion of gourd-like clots that engulf the neck and the back of the head—strong rubbery stalks lift heavy bladders from the body cavity—

Rot structures like chandeliers—some are giving off light, and music—don't turn away—look—look—*look*—at this part of life—there is no way beyond a must—this has got to happen to you, finally something has to happen—

Two corpses are brought into the classroom and set side by side on the teacher's desk. They embrace the moment the orderlies remove their hands.

In this class, we will observe the coition of these two decomposing bodies. As I enter the room I am pierced by terror of death. The feeling, sensation, idea, I can't tell which it is; vanishes a moment later and I take my assigned seat.

Our teacher is coming down the halls. We are all waiting in silence. We can feel him, making his approach by appearances and disappearances.

He appears in the doorway, creeps toward his seat in flashes then flash in—luminous footprints in the halls, winking on and off, white, red, black, green, white again. The teacher sits in the gloom at the front of the class. He sits at the table with his arms outspread at full length, his hands resting on the desktop and nearly spanning its breadth, leaning forward as though his strength were failing, his head thrust forward and his face toward us, his mouth hanging open, black stains on his chin and blood spattering the front of his shirt, forming a streak that could be mistaken for a necktie at a distance—gouts of night juice as if the night had been crushed and its juice were leaking out. A sodden white towel drapes his head.

The movements of the two corpses on the desk in front of him are purposeful, slow, the penis rotting into her—broad ribbons of creamy incense smoke ooze from the face like melting wax sliding off a wax dummy head—a blue face wreathed in fronds of white steam—with a sudden squirt, a bouquet-like bundle of wedge-shapes made of crumbly black foam spurts up fully formed from the corner of the eye—still expanding, a white fungus member pierces her anus—new structures open along the length of her spine— livid penises the color of fat curl unerringly up into each until he looks as though he'd been impaled on a spiral, as if he had a ridge of identical white curled rods running down his spine—the penises straighten out, lifting him until they are all rigidly upright and he suspended on top of them like a man impaled along the top of a white post fence, her many leprous vaginalities spread membranous, many-lobed little wings and long trembling feelers that wave in the air or wrap coaxingly around proto-gender penises. A few terse words are exchanged now and then, without histrionics. They are not telling themselves stories. The corpses are composed, deliberate, technical, like master musicians, their bodies array together with the stability of a single person standing. The teacher repeats their words for us; he gets up at intervals to write some on the white board, which has been badly erased so often it is a smoke-filled window that drinks the words away as he writes them. The teacher's penis bursts through the front of his pants; flipping up, the tip comes to rest against the board, and, as he continues obliviously writing, it writes a parallel pale line beneath his dark ink line. I'm only a necrophile in love with coiting images.

The image—I'm not sure if it is or isn't a memory: the mouth of the female student, the same female student I think, was wider than I would ordinarily like; the lips were full, never thin, the way I like them; her exaggerated smile was impossible to mistake even at a distance, the dark lips in the paper white face. Her hair was thick and heavy and brown; it hung down like great lustrous fruits on her broad, bony shoulders. There was a minute dimple just above the tip of her nose, and this unusual shape gave her face what seemed to me perhaps fatuously to be an aristocratic quality. Beneath the chin, a facet of tendon. I kissed her when we were alone and she looked at me in silence. She would have been repellantly doll-like except for her eyes; it seemed that all her electric vitality retreated from my touch and pooled in the eyes, making them so shockingly alive I thought they must belong to someone else, like someone peeping through the eyeholes of a lifeless mask. A liquid glare worked in them, crossed with flashes of intense cold riveted on me. Her eerie passivity acted on me like an irresistable command.

"Do you want me to tell you what to do?" I ask.

"Talk, but you move me."

I take her by the shoulders and lift her down to me. Her body is as light as papier mache, and yet it feels as though her bones were infused with supple strength. I open her blouse, which is made of a stiff, plain white material, and expose the intricacies of her throat. The brassiere covers almost the entire torso, crushing her breasts flat against her ribs. There was no pulse in the neck as I drew near, no sign of breathing apart from the sound of air passing over her lips. Her stomach is nearly concave and the ribcage stands out. It takes exertion to unhook the front of the brassiere clamping her like a vise. I finish undressing her, and look down at her body. Intense excitement alternates bewilderingly with its opposite in me. "This is what I wanted," I think, and my heart vanishes down a secret passage. My excitement gutters, emptying then filling again, baffling me.

Shave the legs. Shave the armpits. Shave the groin. Shave the scalp and eyebrows and forearms. The eyelashes. Shave off the skin and flesh. Shave the organs down to white bones, shave the bones to shavings, shave the hands that do the shaving, shave the barber into shavings, shave the razor, shave down the brains, shave the eyes, shave the soul the memory and the voice, shave the breath. Void wind sweep the shavings away.

UNIT THIRTEEN
POSSESSION: PART TWO

In Haiti, the boy has fallen completely silent. His father is a drunk who can get pretty mean, but who isn't all bad. Eternal tradition dictates that the son is forbidden to criticise his father. So, he falls silent. No matter what, he won't speak, but it would be more accurate to say he has chosen silence as his way of speaking, his way of saying what cannot must be said. He is saying, because I am forbidden to say what I need to say, and because I will not lie, and because I can't take this any more, I will say nothing. He is presented to the houngan, the worthless witch doctor nothing but a fake and a phoney. What idiots to be so thoroughly taken in by such fakers, generation after generation. The boy has lost his voice, the houngan is told. The houngan is local and he knows all about the boy's father; everyone in the community does. He knows that telling the boy's father to shape up will accomplish nothing. The father has his pride. He will not want to seem to be caving in to his neighbors. Rather than lose face by taking this advice and changing his ways, he is liable to go off on a bender just to demonstrate his independence. However, by bringing his son to the houngan in the first place, the father shows he is not entirely wanting in the will to improve matters. This is the houngan's opening.

The houngan conducts the rite, and the loa possesses him. Speaking through the houngan, the loa tells the father to shape up. The boy's voice is miraculously restored that same night. His silent protest ends. Now, if the father chooses to improve his conduct, it will be in obedience not to his peers, but to the loa, who must be obeyed by all. This means he can change his ways without losing face. The houngan and the loa quite wittingly make possible, by indirect means, what was not directly possible—the correction of the father by the son. Losing face is a meaningless archaism, like dignity. How much more enlightened it is, to "resolve" such problems as this with drugs and jail, and to reduce possession to an exclusive property right only.

UNIT THIRTEEN READING

A soft crash reverberates through the vastness of the empty building. The sole librarian looks behind him, half turning in his seat. He, the Third Person at last, peers into the dark, the chamber behind him, the open door and the library beyond that, for a long while, listening, but there is no new sound. He is the only person here. The only living person.

The library is a colossal, half-ruined pile and the city was abandoned a generation ago, emptied by an outbreak of plague. Many fled the city with unseemly haste, leaving the stricken to die alone, and their ghosts have vengefully prevented anyone from returning. The forest has engulfed the farms surrounding the walls and dense stands of trees have sprouted within the walls like the phantoms of an ancient wood. Fierce wolves prowl among the trees, much feared by travellers. They all leave the librarian alone. He doesn't know why. He came exploring the ruins and decided to stay.

The library had been the city's great treasure; visitors had once come from all over the world to pore over its volumes of rigorous yet insane speculation, of magic wisdom and spirit learning, and to hunt down if they could a legendary book that was supposed actually to be a demon. Whenever someone pulled a book from a shelf, there was an instant's hesitation and a frisson of something, excitement, fear, at the thought that this could be the one; even reading it, one couldn't be certain that the sycophantic dedication to a bloated patron or the tedious lists of mineral correspondances with vegetables was not just a demon's ruse, a smokescreen of dullness and ordinariness, a way of pinching the reader mischievously before getting down to business.

The library had ample accommodations for visitors and for a live-in cadre of librarians and custodians, with kitchens, gardens, lavatories with flush toilets, a lighting system no one could explain, a laundry room with washers and driers, and two luxurious baths with water heaters and all.

He took up residence in one of the guest apartments with a view of the crags and the grey smudge of the misty ocean far off in the distance. The chief librarian's quarters, which occupied a tower projecting above the roof, had been lavishly appointed, but the windows are smashed and a wall half torn out, the ceiling with its erotic mosaics is streaked with cracks and seems liable to fall in under the weight of the ornamental dome. He grows his food in the garden plots and rations the contents of a few scavenged brandy casks.

He was finishing his coffee when the crash happened. Wiping his lips, he gets up and belts his coat. This room is warm, but there's no heat in the rest of the library, and the many broken windows and rents in the walls and roof admit the chill and the rain and snow. Walking briskly, his breath pluming, he makes his way down a spacious passage into one of the several enormous rotundas, the dome over a hundred feet in the air, each gallery fifty feet tall. Without lights, and in the gloom of the dusk of a day that was white and dim anyway, the library's interior is full of sharp blackness sliced into the light. Grim statuary everywhere; a common motif is abduction by monsters.

Down, down toward the source of the noise, somewhere in the stacks. The concealed stacks, it turns out, hidden at the ends of secret passages. The shelves are crowded, the ceiling is only eight feet, but while low these windowless, cryptlike rooms are hundreds of feet across. Here, fiddling with wires by trial and error he managed to get some of the lights working, so the intersection of each narrow aisle meagerly shines. The librarian, who spends his days collecting, rebinding, recovering, and reading the books, hunting for the demon, learning countless spells he firmly believes he will never have occasion to use, paces up and down among the shelves with the irrational sense of exaggerated self-consciousness that is his worst enemy here, far worse than loneliness. He often yearns for company, not out of loneliness, but to localize the feeling of being watched. The accidental rap of his knuckle against a shelf, the scrape of his shoes on the gritty stone floor, the sound as he clears his throat, all cause vicarious irritation on behalf of those phantoms he imagines he's disturbing. So he tries to go about his business as quietly as he can, thinking vaguely that he must not wear out his welcome, the unaccountable toleration extended to him alone.

There, between the 13th and 14th rows, on the floor, he sees a book. It is dimly visible in the dark at the middle of the row. He can readily find the gap it left in the shelved books above it. The book striking the floor—that's what he had heard. But how did it happen? The sole librarian has seen this before; books that spring out from the shelves apparently of their own accord, as if they couldn't stand the dewey decimal system a moment longer. This one had fallen, as they usually do, on its back, and opened. Fallen, or did a hand with fingers crossed push it out? He lifts the book and carries it to the light, to see where it opened to. As he studies the page, it becomes brighter, as if it were just coming into focus. He scans the exposed pages carefully, but the type is small, the characters compressed together and hard to distinguish from each other. It's been a long time since he last had his eyeglass prescription updated. So he marks the place with a slip of paper and heads for his work room with the book tucked under his arm.

His work room is semicircular with one large window. A vast table fills the central area, while the periphery is a pillared gallery supporting an arched balcony that projects overhead. He sits at one end of the table, which is covered with books laid out neatly in a grid, and there's a writing desk and heap of papers there in front of his solitary chair.

No question of steadily conquering these books one by one, his reading is more like flight across books, chasing his shadow just to keep moving. Or is it his shadow?

Does he own this place, if only because he has exclusive use of it? He's blundered into a kind of aristocratic, if solitary, way of life, where magic and nature replaces peonage. He's a bit of fungus or a worm, feasting on the corpse of this dead city and the abandoned wealth so laboriously piled up during its lifetime.

He's been reading for a while, and now he's fallen asleep, his forehead resting on the back of his hand at the table's edge. The room darkens around him, his lamp flame sways a little as the fuel is consumed, shining on his sleep. These fits of sleeping come on almost every time and without warning. He'll wake up, a red mark on his forehead, his face lined and confused, and renew the effort to focus his many beams on written words.

Wolf chorus. The librarian looks up from his page. The night, the woods, which had been flat, two dimensional things outside the windows, suddenly have depths, housing wolves unseen. Suddenly there is a relation between inside and outside. The wolves are heroes. The librarian turns from his work wearily, pulls out a pornographic book, lays it on top of the grimoire and opens it. The picture shows a man and a woman. A bathtub. She is naked except for a mask and both of them are netted in elaborate snares. There's a caption beneath the picture: "City of Anullment."

UNIT FOURTEEN
SPACE VOICE

A voice sounds from out of space, a voice from nowhere, but a voice also invents space, clearing it, or opening it like an unobtrusive big bang that pushes apart the folds of this universe and slips a new one into the unwashed aperture, where it will grow and drive apart the former arcades. Bubbles form, droop, and new bubbles appear inside them, ad infinitum, which here means not forever for sure, but only for as long as can soundly be determined now.

Space drives out mass, even as it affords it a place to be. Space as a dimension is the potential state, while state as a property of objects is the realization of that state. Matter stretches with space, becoming less and less material, and time gapes, slowing, until a new bang pushes it from the outside, giving it a briefly refreshed impetus and thus causing it slightly to contract, so that distances shrink ahead of the bang wave—undetectably, because the entireity of the space in that particular relativity is contracted, so that the measurement of distance contracts too. However, it is possible, by developing a form of measurement not commensurate with a particular relativity, by importing the point of view of a unit of measure from some other relativity for example, to measure the contraction of that measure, from a distance. One cannot measure one relativity from within another, but one can determine possible variations and manufacture an abstract substitute for distance and altered relativity.

This is the function of Space Voice, the translation mode of eavesdropia. It is important students realize this is the mode employed both when translating unlanguage into itself, and into any vernacular language. This translinguality is the informational mode of the transrelativity described above. Space Voice is created by listening and/or reading when one would ordinarily be expected to speak and/or write, and vice versa.

Translate the following passage into translation in a vernacular mode.

UNIT FOURTEEN READING

Sitting right here listening down into my foul interior. I can feel my mind rotting, parts of it large portions of it abruptly subsiding. Turning to mush. To stinking mush. To a chorus of belching fistulas. The seams unravel and pus gurgles in the frayed ends softly, a steady, liquid, sticky crackle that sinks. Melt, and be dragged down in viscous ropes of clammy slime. It seems unthinkable that the sterility of nothingness could be so unclean; stale enzyme breath reeks up my face, disgusting even me. Each thought—one lanced abscess after another, the effluent merge in a viscous slurry of putrid custards, all that lymph and pus whipped and drizzled into a pungent mousse. My face must be like a decaying peach, my whole head, my eye pulps, swelling, wanting to burst and ooze slurry—within the vile interior the numb palpitation of my unlife, stenches in hosts, sharp decay overlathering nothing but stagnant lifelessness. The world around this so-called self of mine recedes into impossible cleanliness, becoming every instant more pristine sparkling and perfect as I become more polluted, impotent, and decomposed. I feel each of the million minute deaths fashioning me, the decay of concepts and their necrophiliac intercourse. My hand moulded from a gob of embryonic tissue by cell death, my thoughts moulded from shapeless impressions by concept death—the stiff barriers between thoughts melts and they gush together in foams. In the staring, ragged anvil head big and hard as a boulder, adorned with smarts, beads of perspiration, and a quivering beard of saliva, pinned by relentless hammering of abstract thoughts hammerfucking—fucking hammerfucking each other with hate that is pure zest of thinking—fucking, eating each other then overyeasting, yeasting—lusting with hatred for each other again, bristle with avid eruptions of sporocarps—thoughts pounding each other like blind gladiators—spores of new thoughts that must come—the stony rigidity of the figure, within: convulsions, convulsions of the anvil—the steel hammer smashes into the rock that won't break—without each other and the smashes what's the rock all by itself and what's left of the hammer?

The mice are driven off by the rats, reverently piling their droppings in pyramids. The larvae are busy in there. Fungous is spreading. Delicate little sporocarps sprout from seething thalli, nestled hungrily in the cave-ins, lining the sulci of the brain from anatomy class, clouds of spores drift elastically over the crumbling hemispheres. The mycelium forms links, growing like a precocious mattress. Trembling roots grow toward each other and join at the kinks with a soft chime. Rot eggs and convoluted rot bodies form in the gulfs and mane over with vibrant capillaries. Outside, the suffering lifts. I get buoyed up. Leaning back, taking my elbows from my knees, and tilting back the villainous puffball where my head used to be.

A new connection in the ruins; one atom of intensity there inside, just an inkling of something. Of what? Just an inkling. Fingers crossed. There it runs, like being caught wet in a cold wind. It's an intuit, in-to-it, intuiting the existence of the blue-white hellparadise, or should that be a? It's the, the blue-white hellparadise, there's only one. That's settled. In no time. Here it is, practically the moment it happens and I've already, my rotten mind has already settled something. Has already settled something. There's more to settle [laugh], or to decide about, deciding not to settle is just as or a more or a least as, at least as, let's say more, important, to what? What is the value that selects for the trait "important"?

Settling, now reasoning as well.

Formal reasoning.

As vividly as if it were happening before me I see mother and infant gazing at each other in an effulgence of love as swift discoloration spreads smoothly across the mother's face. Half her face is indigo, the skin dully shining thin and tough like a dead leaf. The lips are a plastic tube, the eyes are just brown lumps. The baby's head purples and swells—the limbs go limp and pulpy, the mouth and nose squashed together, the eyes like melting black pearls, tense bulbs as big as eggs sprout in craters. The love only grows and the tolling sun still shines on this—rot forms unfold from splitting corpses and luxuriantly stretch themselves at the zenith, zenithrejoicing of a parasite that has forever triumphed over its host.

The city is filled with human remains. I had come here intending to bury one a day or so as a sort of a goodwill gesture, until it occurred to me that this would mean diminishing the garrison of my protectors. Better to leave them unburied and angry, and keep off interlopers.

I don't come from here. I don't belong here. Nothing here belongs to me. I do not make any effort to take what doesn't belong to me. Any special effort. They know it. Perhaps they saw that this was the end of my road. If so, they saw more than I see. All very plausible.

Looking out from a high window, over the rooftops, through the light mist of the noon drizzle, I inflate with serene joy. This was my fantasy: beautiful things and endless novelties that don't belong to me. None of the onerousness of property. Only sway. This is certainly no cell, and I am certainly no inmate—don't forget! I am not an inmate, not anywhere.

Turn, walk down the hall toward the laundry room, a mirror, I pass, I notice a stain on my bare shoulder, on my back behind the shoulder, above the blade, below the neck, over on the left side. It's a shapeless white smear, as if someone had wiped off some powdered sugar there. I wriggle my shoulder, my shoulder moves, the mark doesn't. It stays in the same spot, more or less, like one washed-out dapple of sunlight, broken off from the solarious rays and trained steadily on my back.

I recognize the angel's mark. It must have returned with me from the brilliance of the day at the window. Sometimes it is a stain on my back, and other times my left hand reddens as if I'd dunked it up to the wrist in vermillion dye, a razor-sharp line where the red ends a little way up the wrist. The mark is invisible to others, but a sort of brisk flash, like the top of a fleecy cloud in the sun, follows me wherever I go, like the resurrection of a longed-for face. It's a promise that never leaves me now, a presentiment of return, of celestial immortality, not in the brilliancy of the sun but in the clear light reverberating in the clouds, turning into snowy plumes of transparent flame. That is the mark of love, turning me toward the sangha, the community of the blessed. Whenever I rest, love rests with me, gingerly breaking through the layer of baked mud with her weight, peeling back the oozing liquid clay, exposing the new skin more and more, breathing on it to make it breathe.

The mark isn't always there, but whenever it appears it means I am an angel and like it or not I am doing positive work of love and benevolence.

UNIT FIFTEEN
PRIMARY ANTITENSE

Beside the verb tenses described in preceding sections, there exists another category of tenses whose use is reserved for some of the less commonly required grammatical possibilities afforded by unlanguage. Each antitense reflects a different reflex of action, which the student may find difficult to conceptualize. Contrareities of logic do, however, occur in everyday experience. Keeping strictly to an antinomial grammar is essential if one is to avoid certain commitments which lead in turn to extremely dangerous pitfalls. Escaping such pitfalls may itself become a form of confinement. Therefore, antitenses express action as undoings. The first of these antitenses concerns events which are both continuous from some point in the past, and complete; this primary antitense is formed by the extension of the vowels of the perfective particle and by prefixing the verb with a vermin particle in metrical foot quartus paeon, or by affixing a negated continual and suffixing the verb vermin particle of the same kind.

This tense should not be mistaken for the imperfect neutral, which expresses the idea of that which continues to be finished. The primary antitense is employed for that which is both continuing to take place and also finished; the verb "to live," for example, when applied to the current existence of spectres. There are some events in the past which have never happened and which continue in the present; the negative form of the primary antitense is to be used in relating the occurrence of such events.

The underworld is a kind of memory; funereally official and ominously precise records are kept there. The primary antitense is the underworld tense, because it is suited to the all-over-and-still-going-on existence of the spirits down there. In most cases, the newcomer to the underworld meets with some of its authorities. In Chinese stories, the underworld had ten kings. The famous Greek judges had similar Chinese counterparts, while the Egyptians had the scales and the Maya expected to meet savage, sneering aristocrats. The pomp of state and high class embalms its users. Their cadaverous arrogance is a reflection of the degree of immunity they've achieved from the quotidian tasks, sharings, and troubles that life is made of. So their pomp is transferable to the realm of the dead without requiring the slightest modification.

These important personages, whatever their other inclinations and no matter their differences from each other, never fail to allot to each dead soul an appointed place. Every dead human being has a location. In some cases it's a grave, in others it's niche for the urn full of ashes, or the site where the ashes were sprinkled. For those Tibetans who still dispose of corpses by feeding them to vultures, it's the sky. It's not uncommon to encounter stories of unhappy spirits who cannot rest because, by some accident or oversight, they are still owed a location. For this reason, the primary antitense always takes objects in the *locative case*.

Translate the following sentences, conjugating the correct verb in each into primary antitense:

a)   The ghost who lives in the well is a vampire.
b)   The ancients preserved their dead as best they could.
v)   Who among us is qualified to say which man here has died?
x)   Having just returned from a long journey, the married couple sit together on the terrace; it's obvious they love each other.

Now translate the passage below from primary antitenses into your own vernacular.

UNIT FIFTEEN READING

I have to go back to the school now. It's almost time for class.

I realize there is no evidence to show I have been attending these classes, or even that these classes have ever happened. My notes, my exercises, just look like weird English. How can I say I have been taking this class? Is such a class even conceivable? I don't assume out of hand that the concatenation of vague impressions and flashes which, while vivid, defy analysis, constitutes conceiving. I can't form a single phrase in unlanguage. So what good has attending these classes done me, if I have? Attended them, I mean. And under these circumstances, what would commencement mean?

I make my way over the hummocks of thick grass overgrowing the hospital parking lot, the blacktop fractured into huge plates of black armor. The far boundary of the lot is a continuous, thick scrim of contorted car husks, emptied out and cast aside like a spider's discards.

While I have no idea what I am learning, or even if I am learning, I am sure that my will to live provides the incentive. I'm not looking to defeat death, or even to avoid it; I think that death is not so simple. Simple in some weird way, it may be, but not simple like a hole in the ground.

A conversation with the Second Person. We are in a neutral location, not as public as a hotel lobby, but not exactly private, a little like a room in a large house with many guests staying there, and going in and out of rooms at all times. The Second Person sits in a wicker chair with a scrolled back, silhouetted against a narrow archway that overlooks a veranda. Beyond that is a desert of sunbeaten red clay. Dusk makes the clay glow fever red. The shadow of the building creeps out into the desert. The air sheds the heat of the day. A chorus of barking dogs comes from the town; we are not in the town, but about half a mile away. I don't remember visiting a place like this.

The Second Person lights a stick of incense and pokes it into a clay holder on the low table beside him. The shadow of the smoke looks like a snake. He draws in his breath abruptly and lets it out in a hasty sigh. When he speaks, he struggles to express himself.

"You've seen old photos from the nineteenth century, and paintings and fragments of pottery, old buildings and buddhas and things, and whatever else they may be saying they say we lived, once. Here's the proof, the traces we left, and they're still there, the spirits of those dead forerunners, calling through them to us. What's ... there's the call, and there's preserved, they preserve their desire, the traces preserve their desires. They lived, they burned with desire, they, some of them, had enough, they preserved it and it's still there calling in the traces. We can hear it because we're traces of the same thing. And of course they were traces too. Or became traces. There's a way of ... way of seeing it that ... there's no children or no artifacts ..."

He goes on speaking, trying out first these words and then those. I could tell him I understand, but I don't want to assume that I do, and that isn't really what he seems to want. He has to find the way to express the idea to his own satisfaction. Whether that satisfies me is my look out. His hands lie in his lap, his fingers crossed, his body is almost angrily quiet, only his head moving against the coloring light outside the archway, the plunging blue of the sky that seems to grow up out of the desert and to be a part of it, his thoughts luring him further and further out into autistic niceties so subtle and personal that they become nothing better than articulations of articulation. No more than do the little twists and purlings of the incense smoke turn it into writing; Arabic writing, which looks like ribbons of incense.

Unlanguage is there in the silvery cry of a two hundred year old photograph. I suppose I may be learning how to convey what it means, although what does a cry ever mean? But hearing a cry, there is meaning. So perhaps what I am trying to do with this language is not so much to translate that dead cry of living desire into my own living language, or perhaps I am, but not in the usual way, which is to say, not by identifying things. It doesn't matter so much, finally, whether the photograph depicts a relative of mine, or a person with this or that name. These things do matter, of course they do, but there is something apart from them. What?

It's something you see more distinctly in the images of strangers, although it isn't so important that they seem like strangers, only that they are not familiar. What do I see distinctly? The cry, that's all. Like the cry for help—that it comes from your mother, your friend, these things matter, but you answer any cry for help, and a stranger's cry for help is—I was going to say more pure, but that isn't it. Well, a layer has been taken away. This isn't a cry for help, or for anything, apart from its being heard by a living ear. Hearing does not affect the facts; this one lived whether I hear his cry or not. But he cried, and that is there to be heard. When I translate his cry, I don't do history, I don't go back and find his name, his story, his facts. That isn't what he cries. When I translate his cry, I answer it by saying the life is in common in the unlife with which I hear it, so that I go up when I hear it, and then begin to relate what I see when I go up. Up above my own particularities, to what is universal in my experience.

The more advanced students are all covered in chalk dust. It clings especially to their faces, except in those spots, around the eyes, the mouth, and beneath the nostrils, where moisture is liable to cut it. They rush past me in halls and stairwells, trailing dust. Always in a hurry, and I'd like to know where, because as far as I know there is only one class offered here. It would be interesting, at least, to know if there really were other sections and levels. They rush past, speaking unlanguage to each other, conversing in it, so the corridors all murmur with it.

You can tell the students who are really doing well. They creep feebly along the halls, drunk with alcohols of death, unable to walk without the aid of an attendant, their clothing in rags, coated in chalk dust thick as plaster, bodies like stalks.

But these are only ciphers. What I actually see somehow does not make it into what I write, and I get this instead. Chalk phantoms, crisped and sere. Shades is the best I can do; the word 'shades' is still the wrong word for my fellow students, but it is less wrong than any other I can come up with.

It never seems to change. There is a dead body waiting for us. As the teacher, watched, delivers his lesson, the dead body, without coming back to life, without ever really having left life, will begin to speak. It's always the first time. Always an unprecedented miracle. There is no getting used to it. It is not the sort of thing one never gets used to. I mean that as I wrote it. There is a category of things one never gets used to, but I don't feel that the moment the corpse speaks belongs to any category. We're past categories now.

Rot invents new facial expressions. A smile rots itself across her face as she 'speaks.'

Drawing nearer, I can hear the voice of a distant man crying out a woman's name over and over in an agony of fear and uncertainty, like the most boring part of a horror film. It's as if the distance itself were calling, the way the void sings over the chanting of the monks. It seems to be coming from the world inside the dead woman's head. Or is the teacher throwing his voice?

UNIT SIXTEEN
OTHER ANTITENSES

In addition to the primary antitense, which is the most commonly employed, there are a great many others. A list of the relevant particles can be found in the appendix.

Secondary: for that which continues not to occur, also known as the imperfect neutral.

Tertiary: for that which has perfected an imperfect condition.

Past Elisive: not the future perfect, but used for that which has yet to achieve an already perfect condition.

Present Elisive: the "deja vu" tense, for that event which is inserted into the past by a lexical act in the present.

Not all bodies of lore dispatch the spirits of the departed to an underworld. In some cases, a spiritworld seemed more appropriate. The spiritworld is not memory: at least some of what happens in the present is also happening in the spiritworld, albeit in a way that makes directly manifest the impulses guiding events. A rampaging general among the living has his monstrous counterpart in the spiritworld, something like a cartoon giant decked out in talking medals; his teeth are bullets, he breathes out diesel truck exhaust, helicopters whizz from the pupils of his eyes and buzz around him like a cloud of blowflies. Wherever he goes, half the lesser spirits snap to attention and the rest just snap and go to pieces. All alternate possibilities are simultaneously realized in the spiritworld, which makes it the imagination of language, rather than the memory, as was true of the underworld. The spiritworld has its own tense, the alter-positive tense, for those things which would have happened had what did happen not happened, or had what happened happened differently.

The spiritworld does not situate spirits in particular locations, the way the underworld does, but rather allows them to circulate until they find a conmortual group to socialize with. Very often, these associations are only temporary. Sodomy. The spiritworld is restless as the underworld is static. It's the dimension of endless secret passages, which is why the locative is never used with objects of alter-positive verbs, but only *anti-locative* or *de-locative* cases.

Read the following passage in a mirror, identifying those sections which do not reverse, and translate them into the upside-down inverse form of the appropriate anti-tense.

UNIT SIXTEEN READING

What happens to teacher, after the class is through? I follow him out to the parking lot. His walk quickly degenerates into a headlong rush, then into a fall on the face, but he is deftly caught up, before this can happen, by two of his handlers who haul him, hands under the arms, into a waiting van. His feet disappear, sticking out nearly sideways, so that I can see the scuffed soles. The white hair there in the dark interior, like the foam topping a wave as seen at night. The van's flank silently closes and it turns away. I follow the van. The drive goes on and on, through a landscape of reeds under a smudged white sun that sets with alarming speed, hurrying steadily to the horizon.

Now the road is lined with gnarled and leafless horror movie trees. A full blue moon sits in a broken mercury blister and the upper air is filled with witches' rags. The van pulls up in front of a fantastic structure, colossal, solitary, half ruined, old, but not ancient. Smoke from somewhere high above slithers off into the sky, appearing to join it to the building like a mother to her foetus, by an umbilical cord. The cleared area before the building is dotted with small transparent white bonfires that toss their cold locks in the dark like bacchanalian groupies at a concert. The beefy handlers remove teacher from the van and stand him up, stiff like a statue. Snow is falling on the dark ground, huge clumsy flakes that tumble in the air like moths. The handlers are sweating, although their breath steams. They close up the van and confer with the unseen driver, who shortly takes the van away somewhere behind the building and out of sight. The handlers then flank teacher, taking him by shoulder and a fistfull of his long coat down toward the base of the spine. Teacher is stock still all the while. They carry him over to the building and set him down next to the wall, then go inside, sweeping their own long hair back from their brows.

The cavernous interior. Lit only by a few more colorless, ghostly fires whose smoke vanishes through holes in the ceiling and presumably collects in the upper storeys. I see the trotting of four legged creatures, the naked body of a young woman as she passes one of the fires, the play of shadows around the heavy frames of the portraits, the glittering, illusory lights of the fires reflected in great leprous oval mirrors. It's obvious, though I can't exactly say what subtle hints tell me so, that the building is haunted by a fairly sizeable complement of people and beasts. Far back I can see the dim doorways of other, smaller rooms, like a manor house in cross section. No hallways, only secret passages. Not a room in this house that can be reached except by secret passages. There is some ordinary commotion back there too, like extras in a play. Somewhere in the bowels there is an immense trove of resin which, many years ago, caught fire in some forgotten way and has been smouldering ever since. The smoke that pours from the top of the building is incense smoke, the whole edifice a censer, although its apartments are not inundated by any visible fumes. The bulk of the vapor is transmitted to the roof by a shaftway that makes shift as a flue.

Teacher remains outside, where he was placed, stock still, hands in his pockets, a hat on his head, bent a little forward, either because his back is simply bent, or because he has chosen to lean in a little. Behind him, the dense lace of black boughs thickens with the blue white dough, which melts on contact with the black earth, every scrap devoured by the snapping doglike hunger of the black earth. The weather roars in silence, lifting and sinking its bulk. Teacher's face is feathered with enormous hairy snowflakes that flutter in the minute alterations of the atmosphere. He is turning into a snowman, flakes clinging to his glasses. Behind those lenses his eyes are open, fixed, and shimmer with aquatic frost glow cold and clear. Framed in the window, sash at chest level, he is like a grinning spectre protruding from his grave and leaning in like a stretching question mark, the shaggy white face of a werewolf's ghost. The sight is intolerable and so the handlers, although they should know better by now considering this has all the hallmarks, not that I can identify them, of a scene that is endlessly repeated—this idea suggests another; that this cavalier handling of teacher is deliberate and serves a purpose I don't yet divine—grumbling, storm out into the wet snow and cold black slime to retrieve teacher and bring him inside. There is plainly a spot that is particularly his, a little cleared space in among a tangle of charred and broken fragments of wood, apparently collapsed portions of the building gathered in one chamber. One of the two outer walls—it is a corner room—is mostly gone, some of the more inquisitive snowflakes drift in from the outside to land on the floorboards with a click. The beefy handlers lay teacher in a bathtub between the laundry machines, where he reposes in exactly the same attitude he adopted when standing, hands in his pockets, leaning a little forward. The handlers leave him there, shutting the door behind them. A pair of faint lights gaze at him from the wall, like two patches of phosphorescent mold. Teacher is able to see, with his right eye, the night, the trees filling with foam, the appearance of the moon two hundred and fifty thousand miles away, and, with his left eye, the more-slowly changing and unremarkable room, with its one intact window also opening on a whitening scene of ascending trunks and descending snow, the dull gleam of a few bones, the wallpaper, the eight-panelled door carved and assembled—ah, "fashioned" is the word, I believe—one hundred and twenty one years ago by some person who can no longer be identified in connection with this piece of work. The brass of the doorknob, which was mined, smelted, and formed likewise by unknown and unhonored hands.

All this is a fantasy, of course. I can't follow my teacher. I never see him leave. Only wondering is enough to make me conjure fantasies, because I need everything to be a fantasy. What isn't a fantasy, for me, is dead. My fantasies don't live, either, but they aren't dead. They are what isn't a fantasy, for me, decomposing as a consequence of my mind's activity. Yes, I've just hit on something true. Or at least something I will insist must not be debated. That is what it means for something to be true, isn' it? What you say is true is what you are prepared to defend. If not to the end of your endurance, at least, then, to the extent of taking some trouble.

Now that I've turned aside to put that idea, about truth, into the right words, I seem to have misplaced the truth I just a moment ago was so sure of. It came to me, I thought it was true, then I thought about what true means, defined that, and, as I try to go back to the thing I thought was true, I find I don't find it. That abrupt impulse of intense conviction, arising from who knows where. Can I remember it?

... I have it; let me get it down without delay, so as not to lose it again. My mind is a decomposer. My thinking rots what it thinks. Thinks by rotting.

Now that I've translated this impression into words, it loses all its force, and I wonder why I was so impressed with it. That wasn't so much after all, I think, but how do I know that that more convincing impression isn't still there, hidden now behind a poor translation that only sketches its contour without really capturing it? Is it really possible to get the letter without the spirit? Just now, although at other times I've talked about letter and spirit without any difficulty knowing what I meant, it doesn't seem possible to divide them. More accurately, I think the spirit may exist without the letter, or at least, in advance of its own specification in letters, even though the idea may not even be possible without some prior thoughts, in letters, so the distinction is not perfect but only provisional. I think in words. At least, I don't doubt that. But does it follow from this that I think in letters too? Do I speak in letters, or not? But the letter without the spirit, just now, seems impossible. There must be some spirit in a letter, the question is whether or not that spirit is the one you want. A spiritless letter—what would that be? A letter in an unfamiliar language is not spiritless, if anything it is much more impressive for its glowering, malevolent ambivalence. You hear the other language, and a moment later comes that voice that whispers the translation to you.

All this can be returned to later. None of it seems necessary to me now. And I'm not going anywhere. I am no inmate, but I am not, it so happens, it so turns out, though not an inmate, not happening to be going anywhere, just now. The only thing that needs to be said, and this only because of the inclusion of a fantasy that I could just as easily have skipped. No, I couldn't. That was exactly what I've been trying to explain; I can't. I can't find the secret passage that links this place to that. Everything must be a fantasy. Everything must.

UNIT SEVENTEEN
REVEALED NOUNS

This mode may perhaps be most easily understood as an inversion of the famous paradox of the turtle racer, where even the swiftest runner cannot overtake a turtle with a head start owing to the infinite halve-ability of the intervening gap. Zeno's ruse makes motion appear to destroy itself when subjected to the gradations of distance and duration. The reverse of this involves conceiving of a finite motion expanded to encompass all distance and duration.

When an action is conceived of as a thing, a verb as a noun, the motion of the action, even in the case of an apparently static verb, like "to be," or a motion-negating verb, like "to stop," is expanded into the eternal and the infinite. A step is a step on any path and at any moment. The noun is the infinite mode of the verb. When an act becomes infinite, it encompasses all action as such. One step is all steps, and therefore one place is all places, the topency is aorist, one time is all times, but not vice-versa. Action manipulates divisions of time and space. Not all places are one, but one step in the cosmos exhausts all possibilities. Every act, even one piece of falling snow, is a cosmos. This means that cosmoi are bubbling up constantly inside each other, and this is represented in unlanguage by repetition. Chaos repeats, producing order. The point at which redundancy and chance show themselves in a complementary whole is located within the noun, which is why all nouns in unlanguage contain the infinitive marker. Infinitives may metastasize with the greatest variability, hence chance, but must fully and exclusively avatar their inflected forms in order to produce sense, hence redundancy. Nothing is named only once.

Read the selection below with your eyes almost shut and, as you read, allow yourself to drift into a trance, and the words to combine in the blur, speaking the more particularly to you. Then compare your findings with your neighbor's. Your instructor will evaluate the conference.

UNIT SEVENTEEN READING

For as long as I can remember a mania for serving, obeying, being the go-between, just an instrument of some greater will, all a desperate cheat, aspiring to irresponsibility as if it were a state of grace. It was always me, of course it was, but I can decide that without knowing anything about me, or which one is me, like the murderer among the suspects, not excluding the detective either, maybe not even the victim—a suicide—and worse, the status 'murderer' is independently mobile and can flit from one to another like a bad spirit or even distribute itself among the whole moiety.

Who's in charge here? Is it me? Is it me? Or meeee? They're all asking it. But all of us will die, there is no question about that, which means we can question it all we like, *no* will never give up. Everyone is going to die, unless they're already dead. Dead, and undergoing conversion under cover of death, nothing escapes that.

The teacher is the First Person except for himself. For himself, he is the Second Person, and *his* teacher is the First Person. But his teacher is dead now, a suicide, blew out his brains, so, for the present, he is the First Person. This is the teacher speaking:

I must try the story again. It occurs to me nobody seems prepared to say whether these repeated efforts are all stabs at getting it finally right, or if producing version after version is the intention. I have no strong feeling on either side.

Frankly, I don't remember how I first heard of Intersuffusion. The name rang a bell when the Fourth Person told me about it, and I'd heard a thing or two. Within a few weeks I was a member. I broke with everyone I knew, including my family. I gave up my possessions. What I came to regard in a surprisingly short interval as my former life shot away into the distance and seemed in retrospect to be like a sojourn on another planet. I lived with them in the otherworldly radiance of a shared dream, speaking in the new way, thinking in it too, caught up in the rapturous expectation of imminent and perfect change, also observing steady cultivation, steady progress, one achievement piling up on another. Strip naked, go out and press up to the world until one becomes one, free at last and for all time. Everything is done for all time. Taking a shit is done for all time. The act re-echoes down through the galaxies. Every act is a prayer, which re-narrates every act as it is done, translating it into the teacher's words. You look at a thing, an act, and a bevy of words flutters out. Which is the right one for this? Are the coffee grounds sinking? Settling? Concaviting? It goes round and round. It has to, getting more and more impossible to bear. Yet you keep calling me back. And, one day, I will take my life—again and again. You keep calling me back, from the place of immortality and happiness where the clock ticks always the same second. It may be that the words are what return, but the words are things, the word is the life. The teacher's word. Calling me back through the secret passage. Alcohols of death drunking me drunker and drunkest.

Total devotion to the leader. In some ways it's easier than a partial, considered devotion. There is an effort of will, but not of reason, which only follows. Luckily there were many of us, I would think, and so I don't have to tremble the solitary object of the leader's inscrutable eye behind the sunglasses—then reproach myself for such a cowardly and secretive feeling of relief when I was alone again. I should stand there and let myself be flayed down to the bone, and every last bit of evil rooted out of me no matter how bad the agony. Then would come unearthly peace, ghostly lightness in body and mind, and weird, disproportionate phantom power.

He also taught us to rest ourselves on him, or what was supposed to be coming through him. We broke into groups and discussed the teachings avidly, finding all sorts of parallels, empirical confirmation from our interpretations of our own experiences.

I remember watching him from one of the windows of the upper storey as he conferred with some other members of the group, in the garden down below. This would have been around when the rear of the house was being made into a chapel. A fierce desire to be corrected, is what I felt. To serve, to obey, to disregard myself. A desire for discipline, impeccability. Ruthlessness towards my own frailty, the wretch riddled with weaknesses, cowering under my implacability towards myself, the wretch, trying to shrink the wretch under the withering force of my indignation at finding a disgraceful caricature where I was supposed to be. The wretch to be squashed like a detestable vermin by my majesty which wasn't mine, or me, nor was I clothed in it, but the clothes were all. I wanted to be just the clothing, only light, purity, but it's a fact, that's impossible, so instead there was the pat drama of backslide and reconsecration over and over again. There was nothing else to do. I tried to tell myself not to look forward to the new repentance.

I wonder if the other Persons felt the same. Back then, I thought I was the only one, and I thought this was humility, since I attributed greater perfection to the others. Now I would marvel if any of us felt any differently. We certainly all wanted the same things. We wanted to hear the choiring of the ghosts, and feel the unlight somber brilliance falling on us like a weightless shower of dust, a pall that makes you less heavy. The cult has an intensity that the blandness of established religions can't touch; the intense morbidity, too, being caught in your own smoke as you burn up. Then the epiphany comes. Cracking the smoke. Euphoria again. Victory again. Intersuffusion. Back to the work once more. And the weird—we wanted to feel delirious, warping in every sense, when you really begin to feel you're a citizen of another dimension freshly delivered from the void, logical, so rational, so emotional, fanciful, poisoned, alluring, inclined to put vines in others, tender, tendrilled all right all right, stop, stop teaching. Back to the breath.

I am the teacher. So fate has complected me. I, the First Person, wanted to be the wise ass or the sullen ignoramus at the back of the class, a Second Person, or some other variety of student too intelligent to set any stock by the classroom farce.

Stop teaching!

You're here now. Back to the breath.

I was always teaching, mostly on the inside. Walking down the street I can see faces in rows, listening. Always explaining, taking explanations apart and turning them to and fro to see if they could be made clearer. I learned to talk about myself in the same way. Imagining them listening with folded hands. Folded hands? Were they folded? Were they taking notes? Are those pale eyes trained on you, teacher? Teacher, good morning, thanks for not acting, thanks for only talking about. Ever since I was a boy, playing pedant pederasty with my little slate, aping owlish bafflement, fustiness, chalky lapels, pretending I was sitting alone crying to myself in the silence and momentary privacy of my empty classroom for a wasted life, it won't always be a little boy's-game will it? And yet always a game. Coming back to death.

Stop teaching!

There's no one here!

Stop teaching!

You're through! Through, you hear me?

Can I teach myself? Have I got students within? Inner classes? Lectures and seminars going on now. Heaps of unread notebooks full of exercises repeated countless times, other traces of the struggle with the impossibility of learning so nebulous I can't see them, and the all-too-vivid rows of my corpses, that suddenly stop everything. Imperious deadness. The dead aren't imperious and neither is death, but dying can be, and deadness is. All my fooling around brought me here to the end of fooling. In the fantasy, the bodies rise. They were fooling. Fingers crossed. But they aren't alive again, they're undead. So that means you were the one fooling yourself about what life is; you, not me. I'm the fantasy's master; I send it out so as to keep behind it.

Stop teaching!

When I'm not teaching I scatter among ten thousand faces, minus the one I abhor and that I won't see again. He is going about his mundane affairs, so what. They're done only to be done again. I have no right to mingle myself in with these people. I cling to that thought. It gives me new life. I come back to death.

When class is through and the day is done, my brain is like a soiled instrument I don't want to touch, to think. Duck through the secret panel into the secret passage and hurry home. It's all useless. Just my fantasy. Like wanting to plunge my head into the foul, clammy blackness of the grave, in the hope that I will be braced by the chill emptiness, suck the alcohol of death from the mold, and find relief for the torment of the six senses in confinedness, cramp, and opacity of humus and coffin wood. Above all, to escape myself, no matter what the cost. When I was twelve or so, my thoughts attained a high morbidity I have never since been able to recover, for all that I clearly remember the terror of horror that haunted me in those days, terror in the bathtub. Now I come back to death. One of me does. The braggart does.

In the grave there is no silence, no darkness, no peace. Only the living can perceive the cessation of noise, light, and trouble. The only silence I ever will know will have to be the silence of life. My lifelong mania for silence, even older than my morbid thoughts. I wasn't silent. I was furtive, there's a difference. I wanted silence so I could hear the voices of the others that murmur in the invisibility fields. A long hour, and sometimes a faintly cooed phrase; usually they come either in between ordinary sounds or out of them when heard from a distance. It was listening I wanted, actually, not silence.

Secret passages. It's detrimental to know what you are doing, it so easily links itself with the common old desires, and becomes only the same as they are. Knowing is for hindsight and foresight only, never sight. To see, really see, is not to know. What? What? In all these fantasies, *what?*

UNIT EIGHTEEN
VERMIN PARTICLES

Mentioned above, vermin particles open cul-de-sacs. Unlanguage is infested with them. Like boring, gnawing, chewing animals and the plants and fungi which invade, liquify and digest inert material, vermin particles dissolve and make porous the barriers which would otherwise bring development completely to a halt. Rhetorical armatures depend on the vermin particles to avoid fossilization in fixed and regular form; these particles insure that the outline of a figure will slouch into a succession of different shapes. Certain commonly used words have analogous effects; some of these, rendered in English: however, but, or, neither, moreover, nevertheless, suddenly, well, kind of, you know, like, sort of, er, um, uh.

There are no rules for the use of these autonomous particles, any more than there are botanical guidelines for cultivating weeds, or gastronomic instructions for spoiling food. No matter what precautions they may take, students will find vermin particles cropping up in their own translated passages, and should not be alarmed or discouraged by this; they should rather take heart. For this shows that the writing is becoming infested with life of every variety, rather than the decorously self-sterilizing, pill-popping, twenty-five-percent-animation which generally prevails.

In the reading below, translate terms into vermin particles until no sense can be made of a single sentence.

UNIT EIGHTEEN READING

Toward sunset she led us to the tarpaper shack and we sat down together on the floorboards, which were loose and rattling and sifted over with dry grey soil.

At first, she sat with the open doorway behind her. The sun set behind her. Later on, she would move to the side opposite the door. A shaft of sunlight lay aslant of her right shoulder, passing by her silhouette. When I turned my head, the shaft rolled with it. Then always before me I saw the red orange dot and the clean orange ring around it, even when I looked down, or into the dark. She was talking all this while, but I had long since lost the thread of what she was saying. It didn't seem to be important to follow, but it was vitally important that it continue and that there would not be silence. We were at risk, now, and had been, ever since we set out at the appointed time. Her speech was holding us together, and keeping something at bay. As I stared at the lights I began to distinguish activity in the gap between the circle and the dot at its center. The dot shifted its position slightly within the ring as I altered my point of view on it. Visible speech was appearing in the gap between the ring and the dot; it didn't look like writing, the activity of writing I mean. Not one letter by one, but whole words and groups of words at once. The letters were just space pinched up into lines; there was no color and I didn't really recognize the letters although I knew they were letters. The characters looked like edges of mirrors and marks that indent the surface of water without breaking it and they palpitated, turned, or folded into view, or bunched, or contracted nervously like an iris, then slackened away again. I was reminded of the kind of activity you see inside a one celled organism, transparent bugs and fish. The writing was angular, that I can attest to. There may not have been any curves. They looked exactly like familiar letters, but they weren't. There were small additional features, like thorns or little additional strokes like the additional transverse lines in orthodox crosses, with triangular or diamond sort of shapes, that made them different enough.

When the sun set, I no longer saw the dot, the ring, or the visible speech. It was as if I had fallen asleep despite myself and then woke up to find the sky was dark and the images gone. There was a light from the center of the group, but I can't say what made it. There was no telling how long it had been, except that there wasn't a trace of sunlight left. I could see everything, although the shack was completely dark. She was still speaking, her voice just a low murmur now and generally sustained by the murmuring of the others. Only dimly and only then I noticed, from the fatigue in my jaw and throat, that I was murmuring too. It was weird; I couldn't tell what my voice was saying. It's as if it spoke on its own.

She drew herself up against the wall of the shack and thrust out hands with crossed fingers a voice quietly but distinctly spoke a magic sentence and she stayed where she was as if she were paralyzed with awe and fear. Mindless panic grabbed us without warning and we fled from her and that place. I never saw her again. Then, much later, I took up with the Second Person.

UNIT NINETEEN
ARTICLES

Parabolica employs a great variety of articles, many of which will be unfamiliar to the student. Definite and indefinite articles are used in the customary ways and occur somewhat more frequently than in English. Sacred nouns take no articles, which is why this work book refers only to ___ unlanguage.

The <u>defindefinite</u> article consists of a compound of both definite and indefinite articles with a spondee copula, and is used to identify those things which are specifically indistinct, or which are in the process of ceasing to be particular. This is often the case where the action involves an abstract noun. For example, when speaking of beauty in the abstract manifesting itself in a variety of different things, without any explicitly divine agency (in which case the article would be omitted), one would use the defindefinate, reflecting the proliferation of the singular property into a group of related coefficients.

Where the verb to be links qualities in the form of adjectives to nouns of a holy or also of an ineffable kind, the quality takes a "both-and-neither" article known as a <u>disinclusive</u>. This rule makes it necessary to make the adjective plural in such cases.

In the reading below, identify the various kinds of articles and remove those which seem to you to precede holy words.

UNIT NINETEEN READING

After a while we began to get the impression that there were serious legal problems that were kept back from us, but we trusted him and believed in his message. When word of the scandal reached us, of the child, the accusations, not one of us questioned his innocence. The world had hated us all from the beginning; by a combination of character and blind luck, we had been able to gather together and draw strength from ourselves, turning the world's hatred of us into a love that bound us to each other more perfectly than any family.

These developments obviously troubled him. He presented the same face to us as ever, brave, loving, resolute, a little baffled, always groping toward the same light from the same shadow, but circumstances were overwhelming him. He looked haggard. His moods, ordinarily so constant, began to fluctuate wildly, pivoting in an instant from total pessimism to an equally exaggerated, but more frightening, optimism.

Finally he gathered us and explained what had to be done. We had to leave, to erase ourselves. The aspirin, the ground glass. Blood, but no marks of violence. It all had to be done slowly and soberly. Like everything else. No unseemly fliers or propaganda, nothing that would make us into a kind of a business or a social organization. Our despair was another kind of dignity. The idea of perishing was far nobler than anything else we might have done. We would call the world's bluff. We would not bend our necks to its false authority. We would be real martyrs. We were not escaping; we were imposing our own terms on a reckoning that we could not avoid. If we dispersed, he told us, that would be the real suicide. In this world, death was the only life. We would go to the anti-world, where we belonged.

It was the day of the new moon. We gathered in the chapel, all wearing white. We all looked each other in the eye, sad smiles, eyes and hands trembling, we embraced and embraced as if there were some magnetic force pulling our bodies together over and over again, like mourners. We were brothers and sisters. We knew this was insanely unneccessary; that was why we were going to go through with it. A tragedy had to be made to happen, and it would be all the better because it was unnecessary, it was our insistence on tragedy that set us apart all along. The world only understands one thing: comedy. Everything works out, everything is fine, everybody is right. We were not going to be fine. We were going to emancipate ourselves from this degrading comedy. We were not going to be right; if everybody was already right, then being right was meaningless. This was our way of insisting that there be more than one side, that one side be right and the other wrong, and it didn't really matter to us which one we were so long as we were our own side. During the preparations, none of us had ever felt more truly free, more self-realized, dignified and beautiful, unified, knowing each other's thoughts and feelings without words, full of selfless love for each other, like angels, and frightened at what we were doing.

He entered the chapel and walked slowly around behind the curtain, the gun in his hand. The shot behind the curtain split the world. We all upended our cups at once. Blood poured from every mouth. The painkillers numbed my body. I felt ribbons of intense heat unfurl the length of my throat and pool in my stomach, and a ball of heat forcing its way out of my mouth, but no pain. My mouth gushed, flooded and overflowed in an instant. A gout at first, then spurts in time with the pulse in my temples. The iron taste. Dizziness. It's not so bad. It's not so bad, is it?

The others droop with gushing faces. The sound their choking made. Drooping forward into exploding black stains on the grid of the white tile floor. Splattering. Perplexity, groping. Not understanding. Not Intersuffusion. Final disappearance of light.

UNIT TWENTY
MODE VARIETALS

Unlanguage has a great variety of different modes. There is a take-it-back mode, which is used when the speaker both means and does not mean what is said, or wishes to undo what has been said without being willing or able to delete it. Other modes: when a speaker speaks unwillingly, when the speaker doesn't like what is said. The doing-it-again mode. The lie that will become truth mode. A mode that could refer to anything. The 'I'm being careful' mode. The mode for extreme tentativeness, uncertainty. A mode intended for eavesdroppers. A mode for speaking to no one else. The mode for saying exactly what is meant. The mode that is used when the meaning arrives before the words, which cannot fully interpret them. Naked mode. Apathetic. Fatigued. Indignant. The mode for empty talk, mere sound, babble where corpses turn silver; the vagueness tensation is a particularly important varietal, not unlike the subjunctive or conditional. The vagous varietal is used when the verb is meant to be received as a kind of best guess; for example "I say its mode of locomotion was 'running,' but of that I find I can no longer be entirely certain. I find I must say it wasn't really 'running' at all, but its manner of foot travel was more like running than anything else it might have been ..."

Mode varietals are produced by mode varietal tell particles which "turn" phrases, forming them into patterns without external reference. Just as, for example, a flock of geese will adopt a V formation in flight, although no goose has in its brain any conception or mental image of geese flying in a V or of the letter V, so the mode varietals coordinate phrases in certain ways without any plan. The typical mode varietal tell consists of a mollossus early in the phrase and at least two antispasts in fairly close succession to each other roughly one third from the phrase's end, where duration permits. To form a mode varietal, express in the spirit world while simultaneously translating into writing or speech, training as much of the spirit of the letter as possible.

In the passage below, the student will notice that the number of mode varietals produced is equal at least to the number of phrases, however these may be counted; this is true of unlanguage generally, and consequently the catalogue of mode varietals, which the student will find in the appendix, includes every possible expression in eavesdropia. Identify all the mode varietals in this selection.

UNIT TWENTY READING

Doomed, walking around in a daze, unable to stop because stopping would mean thinking, not that there is no thinking while walking but were he to stop there would be thoughts he would then be able to see in their appalling entireity, and there would be a horrible feeling of passivity just sitting there, while as he walks he can tell himself he's doing something about it—walking, distracted—a crisis of disbelief, not unbelief—Paul had a vision and became a believer, a Christian, but at the same time he also became an unbeliever, an apostate to Judaism. A perilous career move, but he bet his all on the winning side. The Third Person has had his own version of this and now he has run through all his alternatives. He irrevocably bet all he had, lost, and he knows the game is rigged against him. Evil fate has unlimited sway over him. The hand of doom switched destiny off entirely. Stripped of his destiny, abstractly naked, as if he'd absentmindedly stepped out of the sky a moment ago by mistake and now can't manage the step back. All he can do now is postpone the inevitable by running the errands of doom, thus prolonging a life of resignation and terror, his soul turned to shit.

The campus estate museum at night is deserted and it occurs to me to be naked, naked and trespassing too, no respectability no ownership because it is all unowned and so there's no menacing owner for me to want to defy what is now possible now that the burden is finally cast off and forgotten? The ghost the past the free occupant whose bond with the place the things is the immutable bond of the past, the aging southern belle will not have to move after all so long as she is willing to toss her rich wardrobe.

"Charisma is like money," I think to myself wisely. Every now and then a dog biscuit of wisdom is dispensed to me by spiritual presences. It's tasty, but of no use to me. I'm always right whenever it doesn't matter. Charisma is like money, and vanity and gravity are modes of each other, of one thing, whose symbols are a maze and a spiral respectively.

From the safety of the bushes I watch my Third Person cast the net of his charisma and pull in his haul. I know what he tells himself the moment he steps out in front of his class. "Fascinate them."

He lays it down. The errands of doom. When the class is over, and the small knot of students that gathers around him afterwards has dispersed, he hastens, without any indication of urgency, to the faculty bathroom and locks himself in. I watch from outdoors via the bathroom window. The invisibility of the First Person blanks me out. He stands there with his back mostly turned toward me, looking down. As he turns his face in my direction I catch sight of the expression: it is stark dread. The composure of the classroom has shattered horribly. Terror, as bitter and intense as I've ever seen, imperiously appropriates every last ounce of his strength; his face blanches as if he were being bled to death and the sweat stands out in trembling beads on his face white as milk. He's been holding it in; now he thinks he's alone and he's releasing it. He paws his chest and shoulders with trembling hands trying to find the right way to hold himself together, his eyes dart all around the room and for an instant I think he's noticed me—but somehow but no—in particular he's casting around as if he expected any moment I would step out of the dark corners of the ceiling, not peering, not with a searching, steady look, but casting around, stealing glances as if he had to gather intelligence furtively. Finally he plunges his face in his hands.

There is also another, who is exhilarated that something has happened and can never unhappen, a boundary has been crossed and has vanished, never to return. It's like receiving a promotion; the past is all canceled and the present rank is all that is or ever will be. Like a man promoted to captain a ship in the last moments before the enemy captures it, promoted to destruction as if he'd been in charge all along, and yet, by chance, the end doesn't come right away. The ship unexpectedly escapes. He is still the captain.

Ordinarily the cars are released on a timer so as to keep them exactly the right distance apart, in order to make sure the street will at all times be raked with their glare and no one sees the night. If the cars all bunched up, or got too far apart, this would introduce gaps in which the darkness might appear, and an enemy like darkness, mindlessly and perfectly persistent, yet so easily overcome, is ideal for business. In the futile struggle against darkness, people will throw away no end of money. It's like selling people special water shovels to throw back the tide with when they go to the shore. Pairs of lights that charge at me like enraged bulls, only to leap past me with a rush of air and an empty threat.

I am the would-be sucker captain whose ship made the unexpected escape, the First Person. I filched it from the teacher while he was distracted with terror and got the hell off campus. I draw a circle around my feet in the dirt with a rock that breaks—I will leave my visibility here in this circle and go on down the hill, back to the house unseen—invisibility has to be renewed constantly and using many different techniques—my image meanwhile in trust of my natal earth—start walking and go back a moment later to retrieve the rock from the interior of the circle, carry it with me—of course I can still be heard and smelled, the dogs will bark when I pass by—when I get to the other end of the secret passage, I'll draw another circle and break the rock, become visible again, thank the earth for holding my image for me.

The two ridges. The nearer one is black, the farther one is higher and lighter, made grey by the mist that rises between them

being pursued by neighborhoods like lava flows, all orange lights intently squinting for me, hollow snakes of squinting orange light scaling down the slopes behind me

the gibbous moon hovers in the velvety blue of late dusk and two deer heads silhouetted against the sky just above the tall grass on the rise above me

the still light, the still branches, at the bottom of the night

the trees in that light are motionless with an exaggerated motionlessness like photographic images that could move

the pale flowers in this light shining down on them and the bushes, and there is perfect blackness behind the flowers

the canyon like a colossal horse

the canyon like a colossal hare

the canyon like a colossal, roofless house with many broad corridors, still blue and silent like a hallway lit only by a nightlight, the houses are its rooms, some of them, and other rooms are up inside trees and down under bushes, and in chambers beneath the ground, now and then voices echo above me, Venus blazing in the deepening black.

Go inside.

The master, sitting there in the lotus position, raises his eyebrows and says, "I have been told that you claim you can become invisible. Is this true?"

"That's right," I say.

"I can see you," he says.

"You see nothing," I say.

We smile and nod and hold up crossed fingers and waggle our eyebrows at each other like two sages.

Repel the evil magic of the cars. It's just cheap evil. Walk in paradise. Through the windows I can see into the lit rooms cut into the darkness like cave dwellings in the rock. Zoo or museum displays. I may see other invisible people, but that never seems to happen. This way is best. I like the sad feeling this kind of gazing-in-on-people-like-a-ghost-from-beyond gives me; like a melancholy song, all the travails of life are over, no more struggling, all is lost, sorry and content. Not really troubled by the little lacing of suspicion that there's something wrong or perhaps even dangerous about indulging this feeling, because pretending can't always be stopped. I can see my shadow, but that's because I can still see my own body. Of course. I'm generously not blocking anyone else's light. I may catch sight of other denizens of paradise tonight. Huge bushes covered in flowers like snow, moonlit snow, studding the black green. There, where the road bends abruptly under the streetlight, turning into the black. Outer space around the silent bend.

UNIT TWENTY ONE
NEGATIVE VOICE (II)

Existence occurs when nothingness reaches its greatest fullness. The more nothingness is truly nothing, the more imperiously it calls to existence. Time does not posit or negate; it is prior to all positing and negating, and is their necessary condition. Time is trust. This is a gambler's logic, that assumes the likelihood of winning increases with each loss. It teaches the student that the negative can be trusted.

In eavesdropia, the negative belongs to one of two grammatical energies, the first of which is "trust," sometimes known as the fideitive, most readily understood by the English speaker as a variety of voice. It is often formed by repeating certain syllables or sounds in inverted order; for instance, the phrase "md(qg)'ss (qg)eugh" would be the negative of "shin,ho nor 'im zaqbes."

The other grammatical energy to which the negative may belong is "reflex." In the negative, this energy becomes "litonegative," positing a condition by cancelling its opposite. The litonegative rendering for "up" is "not-down." The idea "impoverished" becomes "not-rich." This litotic feature makes possible such delicacies as:

"My dear, words cannot express my not-hate for you."

Identify at least three examples each of trust and the litonegative in the reading below.

UNIT TWENTY ONE READING

The teacher staggers out to the van, which waits wreathed in a plume of exhaust pipe steam at the far corner of the broken hospital parking lot.

The one-who-later-will-be* the librarian watches him from the men's room's smelly doorway. (*Unlanguage has personal subject and object designations which indicate successive past or present conditions, but these are difficult to translate.) The First Person has abandoned the scene, departed for the mysterious canyon, the deer heads, the master, the house, the canyon, the house, the circle, the stone, the natal earth. The remainder, idly observing, curious, now he is noticing that a row of overturned dumpsters and broken pieces of concrete barrier form a continuous low wall which would screen from the teacher's view anyone approaching the van from the nearer side. To see it is already to do it. The Third Person watches as the teacher, gulping and slobbering his own blood, clambers awkwardly into the van through the side door, then rushes in behind him before the hatch can roll shut.

The interior of the van is spacious, dim, and musty. It smells like an old house. There are no seats. The teacher is slumped against the far side, by the indentation for the rear wheel, his legs stiffly thrust out before him and spread to form an isoceles space. The head is cradled in the meeting of the outer wall and a baffle. The black jaws hang open, the streaked and glistening chin only just above the chest. The eyes have retreated. Outside the windows all is in motion. A divider with a door in it, all covered in thin brown carpeting, separates the van's main compartment from the driver and front passenger, if any. The ammoniac stink of the teacher's early putrefaction fills the van.

Through the dimmed windows, trees, housetops, signposts, streak by. The speed of the van is constant, never stopping, never slowing, never turning. Fright and monotony, strangely blended, sap the Third Person's stamina and, squeezed uncomfortably in the corner opposite the teacher, he nods off in time.

When he jerks awake again, utterly at a loss as to how long he's been out, the windows are dark with limpid blackness slashed by wan phosphorescences and the van, still obviously moving fast, has become older, an older model, smaller, with clear windows and no divider to hide the empty front seats. The teacher's corpse lies exactly where it was; a black river of sparkling ichor streams from the slack jaws to vanish into the mechanism and seems to be causing the propulsion of the van through space—It is space—through the front windows the shining disc of the earth below sinks with slow implacability, and now there's nothing but that impossibly clear blackness, and the reradiated light of the earth coming up from below in white glare like sun off snow.

Staring incredulously at space, the stars emerging out of the rapidly fading earthlight, a paroxysm of pure terror without thought, without word, without action paralyzes the Third Person. The van dives into the void on a ribbon of liquid corruption streaming from the gaping corpse at his back.

Without haste, the half-moon descends into view through the front windows. The Third Person rivets his attention on the moon like a man overboard fixes himself on the shore. The weird white mushroom shape, ragged and pitted, gradually centers itself before them, and "For God's sake let me get there!"—a statue of living terror—"For God's sake get me there!"—dimly realizing his goal is a quarter of a million miles away from life—anything but that never-ending immensement of space engulfing him in all directions forever.

White spreads against the black. Mottling appears in the clean dazzle. A blind face of serrated chalk patched with silver mold and bright scars with crisp shadows.

The surface glides up beneath the van. The craters, the little rises, the little dunes, roll impassively by at a maddeningly even and neutral velocity, not fast, not slow. The rank atmosphere inside the van is perfectly still. Silence.

Stark terror that makes the animal in the human so plain, the streaming, staring eyes, the streaming nostrils, bladder, and mouth, the inchoate bellowing like a cow about to be slaughtered—terrified of the beauty, his own impotence, of its beauty, and of his impotence, terrified of the beauty, terrified of the impotence, the van is flying into the unleavened blackness of the far side, a horizon line so distinct it might have been painted on the white. For a moment the darkness of the reverse side is indistinguishable from the void above and past it, except for the absence of coldly unglittering stars. Now he is beginning to discern grades of black in the black. The van is flying among silhouetted colossi never seen by any human being—not even now—even though this is impossible, everybody knows there are no mountains on the moon, the moon has no plate tectonics and therefore it consequently has no mountains either, no impossibly tall pointed mountains like cypress trees or witches' hats or steeples or stillettos to throw weird lean black-on-black shadows through which the van sturdily is passing and certainly there can be, in the inconceiveable valley that spreads out after, no gigantic, luminous body raising a heavy head streaming with what might be tresses of liquid platinum and half hidden by scarves of sluggish, elastic white flame whose sparse rays dart and probe among the little stones, forming bright streaks in a black landscape.

Air whispers around him. Ripping his eyes away he turns already shot through white with horror because he knows what he is going to see—the door is ajar—the black gap widening— He is pulled from the van. He falls up. He is unimaginably helpless. The moon vanishes. He sails out and out and out, no sound to cry in, blackness, black, arms and legs flailing for a purchase, a feeling that combines the worst of tilting anticipation and the raving terror of the plummet forever just beginning. He looks for some way to escape, to help himself; no way.

Shedding veils of outer space, the platinum head slowly appears or emerges before his eyes. All his attention fastens itself on that head, with such abruptness and violence it's as if it were a physical part of himself viciously gripped and now being crushed. The head turns like a small planet. He's looking at the crown. The blurred face rolls by. The rest of the body is vaguely limned against the dark, as if this creature were leaning out of another dimension into this one.

A chaos of voices enters his imagination. Every kind of distortion uttering broken language like sleeptalk. The voices are trying to tell him a secret that would be lost if plainly spoken. The secret is communicated by the breaks, like a negative image made by blocking. He realizes that he can't go on listening forever. The jeopardy taking shape around him is a worse alternative to falling. The idea darts incompletely through his mind. If he could put it into words, it would be:

"If this goes on, there won't be any more me to do the getting-used-to-this."

There's something specific in his physical attitude that he thinks he can change. In almost total confusion, he is trying to alter his angle. He is deflected. He skims along an invisible wall, nearly touching it with his right shoulder. The proximity of a physical object frees him from his paralysis. Terror assails him, bristling his scalp, as he recognizes himself in the faintly-illuminated figure suspended like a hanged man in front of the platinum head. They spin together in the void like a planet and a moon, staring each other in the eye. In despair he watches himself dwindle, the head and his body sailing further and further away.

UNIT TWENTY-TWO
NONSENSE VOICE

In addition to the negations discussed above, there is also the true negative. The true negative exists. It is not nothing. This is the voice of the panic of death. A single word uttered or spoken in this voice can cause shattering terror. The victim searches everywhere for a hiding place and can't find one, rehearses one possibility of escape after another and each is worse than the last; they're nonsense; they have nothing at all to do with the reality of death.

In phantasmagoria, the true negative is expressed in the Destroying voice. This voice would be used, for example, to relay the idea that it is impossible that anything should continue to exist forever, that even the gods will die, that death is complete annihilation, and this appalling reduction to nothing must happen to everyone, eventually.

The First Person assigned to you will explain: I am a cheat, I am a poor example, I keep coming back. The alcohol of my death is constantly being taken from me—that's a lie—*I* give it up. It's my decision, somehow allowing the call to bring me back into existence, but I don't understand who hears that call and where he is when he hears it. He answers to teach. I'm not immune to the terror of death, because I know that I will not keep coming back forever. For a while, but not forever. When I'm through teaching, perhaps.

"I pass, like night, from land to land;

I have strange power of speech;

That moment that his face I see,
I know the man that must hear me:
To him my tale I teach."

Gaze into a dead face, look for something that isn't there, and humanity is reborn, stupid, willing what isn't so, a kernel of stupid strength, what that means, a kernel of strength, is something that is present enough to be transformed. Life and death are not one. All men are mortal and I am a man—but am I mortal? am I? Do I *know* that?

UNIT TWENTY-TWO READING

The students seat themselves in a classroom all muffled in sable draperies. The floor is covered in scratched black steel panels, and there are graceful, austere steel chairs set each in its own distinct shower of light. Each pupil is black, a silhouette, and all expectantly regard the teacher's empty, subtly luxurious chair. A thin wisp of an outline appears between the arms. A clarified figure gradually appears, seated there, a smell of brush fires coming through its transparency, and a weak, cold wind rustles in the closed classroom. Peering into the materializing teacher like a crystal ball it is possible to see vistas of overcast, rain-swept deserts dotted with copses of thrashing shrubs, the black char line of a brush fire, the rattling curtain of dingy smoke, the deep red seam of shivering fire, the black points of the mountains. A principality with so few citizens their king knows his every subject by name; they live scattered in small homesteads and most of them live alone.

Half the year, the teacher, their king, resides in the royal palace, a dull goblin building high in the mountains and, like them, made of uniformly grey stone, totally lacking in ornamentation. The palace is stingy, isolated, little. Its many identical chambers are small, and would be cramped if there had been much of anything in them. Each room is a shaft, bare as a cell, disproportionately tall, with puny windows twenty-five feet up. In this room, the king sleeps on a narrow pallet, dead center in the floor. In this room, he sits at his table, dead center in the floor, working with thick books that are kept in the corridors, in low shelves against the walls.

The other half of the year, the king travels with the sirocco to and fro across the country, by train. The engineers are demons with black dogs' heads. The teacher sits in his study car, working with the same thick books. Wherever he goes, he is constantly filling exercise books with charts of declensions, conjugations, lists of words of different kinds. The ranks and files of words in the charts are the rails and sleepers of the train tracks, the bricks and mortarings of the palace walls. The landscape blurs by as the train descends from the mountains to the scarcely less sterile plain, half charred with seasonal brush fires. Rain patters diagonally against the window panes. It falls in ranks, files, rails, and sleepers. The train rushes on in silence. The teacher sits translating with the motion of the train.

The other kings in the empire of the Great Khan know the teacher without knowing how he became emotionally mummified, his face turned toward the north. On one state occasion, when attendance at the empire seat could not be refused, the teacher momentarily arrested the attention of the Great Khan. Sitting there among other dignitaries gathered before the Great Khan, transparent, hiccuping blood. He's always biting his tongue, another cause of bleeding. He has written with his teeth all over his tongue, leaving unintelligible scars. The thin film of wiped blood on his chalk-white chin and the arresting scarlet color of only the corners of his pale lips give him an aristocratic air of refined debility that mitigates the churlish robustness of a heavy frame. Through his transparency can be seen, with a little concentration, mountains and plateaus blasted with wind, a ragged orange fireline struggling up the side of a hill.

"A man ought to be married," the Great Khan said, addressing him. "Shall I pick for you?"

"I defer to your judgement. All I want in a wife is that she ask nothing of me."

The Great Khan didn't win his position by being slow. "Then I'll marry you to the moonsmudged night wind that blights the world in winter," he says, and mute homage is the answer.

By decree of the Great Khan the teacher is exalted; adorned in golden baubles and precious fabrics he is raised upon hooks braided into golden lanyards, into the teeth of the wind and the full blast of the sun, the holy vulture. His head sinks back, his eyes blacken and melt, blood leaps from between his teeth with an embarrassing gulping noise.

The teacher returns to his train car rattling with cumbersome ornaments and golden hooks and resumes his fatal translation exercises, using his own suppurating eyesockets for inkwells. Although he does this work for its own sake, nevertheless it is written that the world will be destroyed if this translation ever comes to an end, either because the translator has abandoned it or died or because there is nothing left to translate. Written there, as a matter of fact, in the exercises.

UNIT TWENTY-THREE
HYPERTROPHAIC CONDITIONAL

The conditional is ordinarily used to indicate potentiality of action. Unlanguage treats future events as occurrences of different order of efficacy from present events. It is impossible, in unlanguage, to use the conditional unreflexively. What is possible cannot be represented as not existing. The possibility of a thing is that thing in an inchoacity that has the power to leap into being. So the Hypertrophaic Conditional identifies the almost-existence of a thing as an independent existence mutually exclusive of that thing. The conditionality of that thing is also only possible, because in some cases the pre-extant nebula does not transform into a thing. Where realization may fail to happen, the quality of "pre" can no longer logically apply, as there may be nothing to precede. The nebula alone is, and that only as the condition of a possible change that will again make it susceptible to conditional grammar.

This is the mood of fiction, which presents potential events and realizes them by expressing them. Hence the conditional is used for those things which are called into existence by expression and exist as both realized and potential entities at once. It is formed by introducing mood phrases which are then steadily eliminated toward the middle and end of the narrative, although at times large amounts of them may reappear at the very end.

Identify all reappearances of mood phrases or motifs in the passage below, making special note of the reappearance of any elements from other readings in this work book.

UNIT TWENTY-THREE READING

A cadaver, lying in an open, dark blue coffin, starts to smoke. Thick, coagulated orange smoke wriggles up from the orange parts of the exposed face. Where the skin is paler, a cream colored stripe laid into the orange. The thick blue-black moustache stretches out and grows taller, the ends gather into a fan of dense blue-black smoke. Blue black hills fleeced with low brush, orange and cream-yellow sky of sunset in the hour before city lights come on. All the day's heat is leaving the air and the shadows are waking up, subtly penetrating damp coolness. A kneeling figure, examining a bandaged knee. Looks up at silhouettes of the hills, and the silhouettes of two others whose heads are dark against the cavernous dusk. The sky is lifting up, and it feels like a part of them, attached on somewhere back there, feeling what it feels, the sad acquiescence of the subsiding day slackening, now it's over, gravity is not quite as strong.

The two standing figures are waiting. One of them has a placid hood of long, straight hair that gives her an outline like a snake. The second has crossed fingers. The third lowers the pant cuff, stands up, and they get moving, all in a line, three shadow heads against the butter color. The tree nearest to him turns into a mummy, a tree made of long thin fish bones and the bark is stiff, cracking human leather. A flip of wind rustles tinkling branches, look up and see the first star of the night in there among them, staring down out of powdery actinic blue. The ground just here is covered in desiccated blonde weeds like matted hair; long runners radiating out from a flat scalp, boring down with plastic tufts into the dry grey dirt.

The silhouette of a bird swoops down from somewhere up above the hills, wailing. Its cries, broken by convulsive giggles, echo back from the ridges. The smooth travel of that sound back and forth through space is of a piece with the easy grace of its glide, and as it turns I see it's like a half-feathered pterodactyl with a fleshless skull. The flying carrion is fledged with brilliantly colored plumage that glitters as it swings through the fading light. The fragrant gloom rising from the ground to meet it has a grape candy smell. The ghoul bird circles them a few times in silence, then veers off with a rattling chuckle. They follow it east, away from the setting sun, further down into the blue valley.

Eventually, the building that overlooks the city. It's twilight even inside. Feet shuffling on the steps, a muffled reverberation in the narrow well, they climb to the right floor. The air is unnaturally clear, and permeated with an intense odor of decay. The stink has a vital sharpness, a tang without any mustiness to diminish it, because this decomposition doesn't dissipate or turn to dust as its subsistence is consumed. There is no dust in the usual sense here.

The three figures hesitate on the landing. They can barely see each other. Just three colorless grey phantoms in front of plain white walls. Finally, the third one, the one with the bandaged knee, opens the door.

They reel back, covering their faces—noses and eyes. One of them scuttles halfway down the stairs to the floor below. A weird radiance, so faint that it could only be detected in this nearly lightless twilight, plays over the interior of the door, spilling out into the hall. The three of them are mastering themselves evidently. Go inside.

A woman died in a chair by the window, and her decay has sprouted to fill the entire room with fantastic structures built from her body. There are huge hanging pods and chandeliers that shed a powdery, many-colored glow, and the walls are covered with bony red flames or pointed leaves. A cloudy, membraneous egg in a kind of fibrous goblet bursts open with a farting noise and a wetter stench knocks them back gagging. A long beak is thrashing inside the membrane, tearing at it, and as they watch through streaming eyes another ghoul bird rips itself free of the groaning sac and shakes itself, letting off a spray of shimmering corruption. It rasps and eyes them meaningfully. The three figures rush back out onto the landing and whip shut the door.

UNIT TWENTY-FOUR
MUSICALITY

Music, of course, possesses a unique power of nonverbal expression that has prompted some to characterize it as a universal language. Music however has also a power that wrings words from people, because each musical tradition reproduces the tonic patterns, rhythms, and timbres characteristic of the manner of expression typical of its place of origin. Even wordless music presents narrative in the form of harmonic progression.

There is, in unlanguage, a more particular attention to the musicality, in the form of modal tells not unlike composer's notations. There are indicator affixes and diacriticals which correspond in concept to pianissimo, mezzo forte, coda, nocturne, contrarequiem (or agitatio), rubato, etc. Notation meant to inflect entire passages also exists, indicating a rhetorical equivalent of harmonics, known here as enthymonics or eulogia. Since words may consist of any phonic or graphic componants, provided they appear in the correct metrical arrangement of stresses, these componants may be selected along the lines of consonance or dissonance. Passages of elaborate logical content will be composed in fugue form, such that the converging syllogic impulses are braided together in the order of their causal succession. Passages marked "above and below" discuss ineffable factors, such that a particular being, action, or quality, is determined to possess a coeffecient of levels that are all present at once, and so whatever is being represented is described in terms of a "chord."

This form fans out the salient property or aspect into a spectrum and situates the object as encountered more or less in the middle of that spectrum. This makes it possible to speak of that which is at once above and below the level at which it is being apprehended. Students will understand that this mode cannot be partially invoked, to refer only to that which is high or only to that which is low. This is because every height entails a gulf.

And when music is as bizarre as this, what possible place of origin, what manner of typical expression, and of whom, does it reflect?

Identify the modal tells in the following passage. Read it aloud, and determine what should be piano, what forte, etc. Once you have completed your "scored" translation, you will perform it for your instructor and undergo your evaluation.

UNIT TWENTY-FOUR READING

You're searching for something in streets and through houses. That's how easy it is. Brush in and out of the darkened houses like a ghost.

Dreams never begin. You're already in the middle of things when you arrive, but all the important decisions—how I got here, where is here, who am I, what I'm trying to find—have been made by you in your absence and you self-inherit them.

There's a tall smoke stack that releases a torpid smear of steam on a night sky that's blue and dull. The sidewalk stretches out before him like an empty corridor into the ghostless city interior. Not haunted by ghosts, it's full of ghosts of hauntings. Well maybe that's just me: everyone else sees ghosts, and all me can see is foul disenspellbounded sterility and lurid prostitution. It may be that, like stars, ghosts are harder to see in the city. Too much manmade, resignation, loss, coming and going. Ghosts do not tolerate injustice. This may be why adults are not supposed to think about them. Ghosts seek out after death a combat with what killed them. The fight has gone out of the violent cities. War without combat everywhere now. Never will you sight a wan sad luminous face at a high unlit window, silent horror on the features, then vanish. What's down there in those cellars?—nothing: pipes, dust, mice, bugs, no dream, no ghost, no secret passage. No bathtub. The city looks the same in all its details this time, but unlike itself too, as if this were a duplicate city exactly reproduced in another hemisphere.

Language muttering against the sky somewhere in one of its lower corners, a sound like warbling electricity, spread in thin sharp rings across the smooth skyous surface. Language stirs and opens resounding space, to have somewhere to watch you from—the fence rails like the lines of writing, the graffiti, the street signs. Glance up as you pass a tall brick building; the brass plaque by the door still says "DR. PARTRIDGE etc" but if you don't read it and only glance at it it says ... what? ... what's that? ... "YOU'RE NEXT" ...?

—and there's fine print too, a malediction in curse language or could it be a disclaimer. It's a message from the language. If only you knew whether whatever it is you're trying to find will be your protection, or if your protection is stopping, right now. As if you could stop looking. The search began before you arrived, you showed up already involved, so how can you finish what you didn't begin? There's a momentum carrying us along that could be flight just as readily as searching.

In the fantasy, there it is, what was looked for. A woman, let's say. The fantasy plays out, love is made. There's an end. So, fuck another way. That ends. There are only so many ways and settings, and not all of them are appealing. The fantasy burns through whatever palatable novelties are available, fades out on an endless loop, and what does it fade into? Flinch back, go over it again. The fantasy melts into void, and you come back, drink the alcohol of death and return to death. Why do you smile? You're not just smiling, for that matter. It's your favorite smile, the one you're least ashamed of. Smile like God. You're still back there, smiling or no, hanging over the void—over it, even though you're in it already—before the platinum head. Part of you remains there, no matter where your so-called free parts may go.

Fog fills the streets. It isn't fog, it's incense. You can't breathe. Tonight will smother you in it; but another part of you is being smothered even worse, not by incense smoke but by clearness and stillness, uneerie silence and endless vacancy without ghosts, by another night that's still ahead.

Go in a house and there's a room up on the second floor with full-length mirrors along one wall. In the darkness you see my silhouette in the mirrors. You remember my childhood rule never to look into a mirror in the dark too late. Your silhouette steps out of the mirror with a heavy, silent foot. You are trapped in a nightmare, knowing your replacement will stride out of this room, leaving you. No likeness. No life. Not now—I take my place just behind your right shoulder, and we go out together. You don't know how to play with me, or what I want to show you. You should become me, your own mirror image; you, minus a third dimension—time; a room with a mirror doesn't age twice as fast; mirrors don't have time of their own, they can only reflect the time that passes outside them. Become me, and lose time. That was your homework this week.

You gaze over your shoulder into the face of the double. The eyes are soulless (that's a relief). The features are all black planes.

UNIT TWENTY-FIVE
MUNDIVES

It should by now be clear that unlanguage articulates time and space un-uniformly, by means of tenses and topencies. The consistency of tense and topency is a world system known as a mundial. Since a passage may include a variety of tenses and topencies, it is necessary to add a function indicator, called a mundive, to show the correct pathway or sequence of time and space through a given passage. The mundive establishes the mundial relations determinative for a given passage.

Mundives are partially diacritical marginal cyphers that do for writing what keys do for maps. Assembled in sequence, they can be used to create a complete map of the secret passageway unlanguage has taken. A proper understanding of mundives is essential for any reader of unlanguage. A glance at a mundive can tell the skillful reader whether the passage it marks will be a sortie, retrograde, absolutive, self-rewriting, etc.

The digressive is among the most important mundials; this is an inflective category that affects all tenses, as it shows whether or not the event in question takes place during regimented mortal time or unregimented demonic, digressive, time. Where the digressive achieves its superlative state it leaves and never returns, this is known as the embarkative or disapparition.

Evaluate the reading below and see if you can detect the presence of any mundives. Then determine which, if any, is this passage's mundial, and report this intelligence secretly to your instructor. In this case, you will not be informed of your grade.

UNIT TWENTY-FIVE READING

"I will defy them, and teach unlanguage."

—And then what? Fleets of new disciples ringing doorbells?

"Students who will hear and understand the normally unheard voices. Listening to them makes you part of an expanded nature that will swamp our paltry individuality, thankfully. Death, and outer space, stop being invisible. You listen and leave."

—And death magic? What about that?

"Death magic ... Those students of magic who pry into the secrets of death are as a rule looking for one of a limited number of practical applications. Immortality, to kill without normal violence, to be impossible to kill, to frisk the spirits of the dead for secrets they took to the grave or found there—where is the treasure buried, who brained them with the dutch oven, which one should I marry, who will win the Derby? These students are not really looking for the secrets of death, they are looking for tricks to play in life. The student who wants the alcohol secret of death is rare. Who can even articulate what those secrets would be? Even to be able to ask for them, it is necessary to know much of them already.

"... Perhaps the secret of death is that there only seems to be a secret, but this idea fails to take the mystery fully into account. Whether what happens in death is too big or too small to be fully apprehended, the point is that death is not fully apprehended. Whether or not death is hard to look at, it is always hard to see.

"... Perhaps learning the secrets of death means learning what there is that may be asked of death. It takes courage to trust the world, to trust alcohol, to trust even death."

I don't remember being introduced to this man, or for that matter boarding this train and so on. We are travelling to the same destination, I think. He'd introduced himself; he has one of those French names that trails off into a melody of nasal vowels. Dr. Dumenteigaeuieighaeieeuaieueigheenenenennnn. We've retreated into ourselves, but I study him surreptitiously. I watch him reading his newspaper, and now he shifts his eyes to the landscape without altering their reading movement and so reads the landscape. He removes his glasses and plucks around one eye, examines his empty fingers, looking for the hair he hoped to remove. There may be, after all, a long and pointless conversation. There may be some, after all, conversation extolling some drug or other.

The car delivers us both to the estate.

"It's night out," the doctor tells the driver. "We have to shut off the headlights. Or it won't get dark enough."

He gives me a meaningful look, and I realize he is the agent I was to meet here. It's our responsibility to protect the daughter of the child, as she is known; a recently discovered descendent of the royal family, now hunted by assassins. She's being kept here, in an old house in the middle of gardens.

The candle flame my entrance disturbed reassembles itself in the interval it takes her to appear. She was waiting for me, hatred in her face. Without a word, she hands me a sheet of paper and crosses to the French windows, to look outside at blue shadows cast by red moonlight.

The sheet of paper is actually several pages of notebook paper covered with columns of writing - my name, her name, and her mother's name are all dissected and given numerical values from which calculations are made, proving my guilt. Guilt for what? It doesn't say here.

The evening meal is served in the kitchen. She prepares a dinner of rice and her own milk, flavoring it by boiling a huge spider in it and using two caterpillars from a potted plant on the windowsill. They are green with spiny carapaces which she removes first without harming them, and without the carapaces they are smooth and soft with a sucker at one end. She squeezes a little something from their bodies over the rice and returns them to the plant, tugging the suckers free of her finger. The food tasted like cool, sweet milk with occasional pepper (spider) and lemon (caterpillar). The dead spider lies on its back, like a charred, severed hand, curled up and brittle on the table next to her plate; she pokes it with her finger and complains she didn't cook it long enough. After we eat, and the table is cleared, she sits back down, opens her dress, and puts her breasts on the table to rest her back. The table groans as she settles them in their indentations, pressed into the wood. Milk trickles across the table, and the tablecloth does not absorb it. After a minute or two a blonde candle flame bobs up first from one, then from the other, and hover there like the plume of fire above a prophet's head.

Where's the daughter? The idea flashes across my mind with a sudden alarm. I still haven't seen her. A wise old granny hurries off to find the child, but assassin magic alters the daughter's room number. The old woman goes to the wrong room, an oak panelled hall of doors above a circular gallery with deluxe padded furnishings. A strange implike child emerges from the room.

The old woman finds me and in my presence we reenact the scene. I'm not fooled by the ink rearranging itself into different numbers and at gunpoint I capture two assassins emerging from a secret passage, locking them in the closet. I block an assassin death curse on the old woman by closing the drapes in the nick of time—the spell works by allowing sunlight to pass a certain carving and then projects prophetic fire onto your head.

Pressing myself to the wall, I pull the curtains back for a peek. There's another garden out there, possibly looking for its chance to replace this one, and, as I squint into the darkness, I see a second old house there in the middle of that other garden. My associates and I go to have a look. Inside, paintings by the former owner hang on the walls, a face staring from a red haze, strange flamelike flowers floating on purple water. The assassins' paintings one by one enfold all the others. Everyone but me.

I find the light switch—it looks like a big eraser—and turn on the lights. The paintings all go flat and I am alone. Then a little woman appears and explains that the paintings are designed to capture the viewer inside. I don't care what happened to the others particularly—they should have been more careful. The woman shoos me out of the house. I can finally see a hologram that has been obscured up to this point: a little old man, dwarfish and bald with nasty, smug features. The woman starts to shrink, age, lose her hair, and wither. I run from her.

UNIT TWENTY-SIX
MONAST VOICE

_____, _____, _____, ____, "_____? _____? _____.
_____. ___, _____. _____. _____. ___, _____. ___,
_____, _____, _____! _____? _____. _____?
_____, _____, _____?"
_____, _____. ___, "_____, _____?"
"_____, _____!" _____. "_____. _____, _____, _____, _____.
_____, _____, _____."

Not all parabolic sentences will have words; in some cases, as in the example above, punctuation alone is employed. This mode is associated with monasteries, although not exclusively. Any teaching, in particular, will to some extent take this form, as it is the form of the parabola that establishes the relation with the master more than does the content, and the use of blanks in language is a common teaching technique. The monk, the nun, the master, the teacher, the riddling old man or woman, will employ Monast Voice. They are punctuation without words.

In *Journey to the West*, having finally arrived at Holy Vulture Mountain after over eighty trials or rather over eighty versions of the same trial, the Tang Priest and his demon companions receive the scriptures from some of the haughtier bodhisattvas. Bringing back these scriptures to China was the chief purpose for this perilous and entertaining expedition, and the Priest doesn't shilly-shally but sets out on the return trip at once, without first examining the scrolls. Shortly after setting out, a chance accident reveals to them that the scrolls they have been given are blank, and they return to the haughty bodhisattvas looking for an explanation. The two bodhiguards turn to each other with identical sneers: "Well! So these paltry specimens aren't advanced enough to read the wordless scriptures? They'll just have to settle for the kind with words, more's the pity."

Alongside the scriptures with words there are scriptures without words. What's more, since they take up neither space nor time, the wordless scriptures are also included—every single one of them—within every written scripture. They are, as long as we are on the subject, also to be discovered inscribed on every unadorned wall, the surface of any still water, or indeed on or in anything that invites comparison with a blank page. The blank page is already replete with meaning, and writing upon it actually chisels that meaning away like flakes of marble from the block. It is necessary for the student to go to the "monastery" in order to learn how to read the wordless scriptures. Behind everything stands the alcohol, monastery, wolves, death, overlooking a forbidden landscape of brilliant colors, washed by color winds that turn everything they touch now red, now blue, now yellow, now white; by practicing austerities, the monks and nuns transform themselves into reading. Talking like a book is a minor phase of this metamorphosis which soon gives way to the dynamic, interrogative silence of books.

After satisfactory completion of a sequence of austerities to be prescribed specifically to you by your instructor, enter seclusion and read the following passage in monast voice.

UNIT TWENTY-SIX READING

The high mountain monastery. The monks and nuns are dead paper mummies. Sacred books in human form. Humans turned into books. Wan and pleached. Skin peeling like a bad suntan but no worse than that. Faint lettering nothing like tattoos more like varicose veins or a delicate rash. Study the books by listening to them speak and by collecting scraps of skin which revert to printed paper scrape along the flagstones in the thin breeze. The stone fabric muffled their voices so they seemed rather to be ventriloquistically transferring their voices to the stones.

The low trees with many trunks grow from books sprouting in soilless gardens of stone and from the rock of the buildings themselves. Impossible colorless blue leaves shaped like eyes and mouths. So dark they should be black but they're felty blue. Approaching, the Third Person sees wind battering the last weblike shreds of the prayer flags but the trees are still. Wind lashes at his garments and drubs his face but the trees are still as iron. Touched one once, idly pulling a bough to see if it was rigid or pliable. Doesn't remember the outcome of this experiment. A feeling of weakness punched in chest the moment it touched, and sank to knees and remained there until blinked away the last of the bristling flashes of light the color and temperature of ice, and until living sensation once again suffused the void within.

A nameless drug is made from the sap of these nameless trees which never flower or produce fruit. The sap rises with each new moon, is tapped from ancient sluices like black smooth sores fluted out from the groins of the trunks; the sores coil inside like conch shells, the resinous, colorless sap drips in webs. This fluid is cooled in snow until it congeals and then sealed into stone tuns lacquered inside. No one knows who does it. The monks and nuns are all to be seen performing certain chores at regular times, but no one is ever seen doing anything connected to production of the drug. Language may be doing it. Eventually the chilled fluid turns into a thick purple ooze that is drunk with water or cooled still more until it turns to gelatin. One drinks, or eats a soft jewel of the gelatin, and tastes the purple, berrylike sweetness.

The monks and nuns all have one hand, it varies which, and what they clean from beneath the fingernails of that hand is scraped into a stone pot, rolled into pills with butter or buckwheat flour, and charred to create a narcotic incense that affects the user like a fainting, dwindling death. You take it to convalesce from its effects, not for those effects themselves. Life rushes back in again wildly. The sensation is so crazily invigorating people who only a moment before were lying pale and limp like heaps of crumpled laundry suddenly are bounding around the walls of the room, leaping up to brush the ceiling with their fingertips, launching themselves again and again into the air, and often this gives way to a state of reckless violent destructive or dangerous abandon that may last for days until the drug taker collapses in an exhaustion that on occasion proves actually fatal. However, there are some who, already in the throes of a fatal illness, take this drug and, provided they are able to return, come back in some measure restored—rarely, altogether cured. It seems that the plunge headlong into death may precipitate a reflux on more generous terms; or perhaps the sufferer, in permitting this death, liberates the strength he or she has been expending to keep it at bay, and this liberated strength can then be brought to bear on the affliction itself and so end it.

Sit on the cloistered terrace and gaze at the writhing mist outside, dark in the shadow of the mountain the sun rising on the far side. The mist rises from the chasm directly below. The hollow murmur of the monks and nuns is behind you. They never address each other directly, nor you. Hard to say whether or not they are really aware of you at all. They have a pungent smell, like glue. Their incense smells like medicine, or cinnamon, or old feet, or like fragrant woodsmoke. Burning incense symbolizes sacred consumption. The sap liquor tastes like cherries. The trees smell faintly of candy, like a child's face and hair, sticky with candy. The wind blows, and they do not move. No leaf likes to leave its place in the air. Deep inside, the monastery is like a canyon, the walls recede into invisibility and the building is just a tissue of solid shadows, with here and there an orange or yellow light. A musty smell, but the air is never stale. It rustles along the passages without ceasing, rustling along the passages like a cool, sightless snake, dry, stony, autumnal, a fresh wind through a cemetery. Many lightless rooms that can't be fully seen, even with a lamp, and which appear never to have been used. Incredibly spacious amphitheaters, vast galleries, and yet the monastery does not penetrate the side of the mountain. Down and down it goes, but into what? It is carved directly into outer space. These huge rooms are never used, and the monastery has never housed that many people. Perhaps they were for legions of pilgrims who don't come any more. Keep on descending steadily into those depths and you just might see stars—stars, beneath your feet. No more steps, no more mountain, or planet. Every now and then something like altitude sickness hits the visitor, and vertigo. It's as if you weren't really here but in outer space, dreaming, so as not to have to open your eyes to the void and the plunge into infinity that might begin at any moment. Might have begun. Fever, hallucinations or so you hope, and then you find yourself mysteriously transported to a bed in a clinic at a far lower elevation, where you recover under the care of benevolent doctors and nurses who give only vague answers to all questions not direclty pertaining to your condition and who assure you that all your expenses have already been handled. No, you can't go back. Not yet. You haven't recovered yet, enough.

UNIT TWENTY-SEVEN
VOCATIVE AND ORACULAR

Unlanguage is entirely in the vocative; everything said or written in unlanguage is an invocation to unlanguage itself. Unlanguage is spoken or written as a call to itself. When the call is a request for knowledge, the answer will come in unlanguage, and unlanguage itself will supply the answer. It never stops listening, and it never fails to answer when called, even if that answer is just an echo. The call, repeated again and again, becomes the answer sometimes. It costs nothing to call, but the answer never comes unaccompanied by a death.

The student is advised not to call. Do not write, speak, or even read. Never use this voice or this unlanguage. They belonged to Intersuffusion. The little girl was no more than seven years old. The call had been made, days and days ago. The birthday party was centered around the picnic table in the backyard, mother was in the house and saw her daughter going through the doorway that led from the kitchen to the small laundry room toward the rear of the house. As she approached, the child stopped, but only turned to look radiantly at her when she was at her side. Turning, the child said something in a loud, artificial voice that wasn't hers. The voice did not come from her mouth, but from the gash she cut from ear to ear in a continuous gesture as she turned to look up at her mother. From directly above it, her mother saw the top of the red bulb rise inside the wound and distintegrate in red streams and spatters down her dress front, and the look of abandoned bliss on the child's white face, which folded backwards as the speaking wound yawned. Crossed fingers dropped the sharp little paring knife to the floor. A single jet of red hissed from her neck, high into the air. A second, slightly weaker followed almost at once. She crumpled to the floor.

"Did anyone hear what she said?" her father asked, his face blank.

It had been a musical collection of syllables that had risen like a snake and disappeared in an instant, as if the quiet noise of the party on the lawn had absorbed it. But there was nothing to be afraid of. No one who hears words of that kind can actually forget them, although it may be that troublesome feelings interfere when one tries to repeat them. Either the throat or the mind, or both, slam shut. Those lethal words can only be spoken in the dull, lifeless tones of someone who has outlived himself, or wailed in the half-unintelligible extremity of dementia, or sneered aloud with something infinitely more acid than sarcasm, that is to say, in a way corresponding to a final leavetaking.

UNIT TWENTY-SEVEN READING

The story of a man transformed by language change. The language, once understood, transforms the learning. It has no discriminating power of its own, it only releases the outlines so that the substance may be struck in a different mold. Which mold is something of a gamble.

X underwent the transformation and recoagulated with the angel's mark: the vermillion left hand. Or at times the white smudge on the shoulder blade. His recontraption was as pure as the silvery daylight and he was suffused with serene benevolence that fell about him in cascades of love. The inmates, orderlies, and analysts alike all felt it.

But then, one day, he looked down at the hand resting on his thigh, and saw that it was just an ordinary hand. The seraphic, translucent flesh was curdling right in front of his eyes. What had been composed of colored light made solid went back to being meat and blood. His body, which was as solid and heavy as marble but felt lighter than air, reverted to the ordinary sloshing heaviness of a regular body. A sour taste filled his mouth, which before had been as fresh as alpine winds. The exalted vision of his eyes became the filmy, blurred vision of the usual kind. He slumped back into his former self.

Whirlwinds of shame closed on him. He was sitting on a bench, and, although this was obviously not true, he couldn't shake the feeling that every one who passed him in the hall could see all too clearly what had just happened. With a violent, monkey-like energy he wracked his brains for a way back—never mind how it had happened. If he could wangle a re-seraphanization he would then understand it plainly, and if he couldn't, well then why would it matter? He vaguely felt there was some fault there in that reasoning but he had a bigger fish to fry. Then it occurred to him, he could still *write* that language. He must write his way back.

UNIT TWENTY-EIGHT
THE APERILOGICAL

In astronomy, the aphelion and perihelion represent those points in a planet's orbit at which it is respectively farthest away from and nearest to the sun. In parabolica, there is a unique metaspasm involving meaning which combines these two pendular opposite motions, which is both aplogical and perilogical. This is the aperilogical, which coordinates meaning in an orbital fashion, hollow in the middle, and either coming or going, not distinguished by two different kinds of grammatical moment but treated the same.

Throughout the centuries, power appears in the form of a new language. Even an old language becomes completely new. A study of history makes plain that this new power does not remain bound to the new language for long, and that its release is of the same kind and structure as the escape of language from its own determined boundaries. The occult class is always more or less aware of this and takes what precautions it can to prevent or postpone such escapes. However, experiments in the new language, designed to extend or develop the power it generates, always begins among members of the occult class, usually as a controversial project, undertaken by more marginal or precariously positioned individuals who want nothing more revolutionary than to keep their jobs. They have, of course, the greatest familiarity and facility with it, but any outsider who might undertake such experiments, it should be understood, would be eliminated as a matter of course. The occult class preserves its own power by the care with which it monopolizes the new language.

All experiments naturally host a germ of chaos. The crisis occurs when these experiments in the new language run amok; the power escapes, and becomes available in the general language and for other purposes. This is represented in myths, such as the story of the dismemberment of Osiris, the rape of Persephone, and the division and passage from one world to the next in some native American stories. The language is scrambled, Cabbalistically weighed in solitary units, interbreeds with itself and fucks out chimeras, but this kind of inflective manipulation leaves fissures through which the power leaks. In some cases, order is restored; crucifixion of some kind or another is the sign of that restoration. A personal separation or sacrifice takes place to represent or match the way in which the articulation of the language is divorced from the single necessary mode imposed by the rite and united to alternate applications. The moment the language has another possible destiny outside the rite, the language ceases to be efficacious in the rite in the way it used to be. Its efficacy may diminish, but in any case it will change.

The Aperilogical form is composed into anacoluthmatic couplets of asyndetonic syllepsis in the conditional. In the following passage, locate and remove examples of the aperilogical.

UNIT TWENTY-EIGHT READING

The teacher is once again borne in dead by a small group of students and deposited in a heap in a corner. As herevives convulsively, we push our desks against the walls.

The teacher oozes jerkily across the floor, disappears behind the desk, then gathers himself together and inflates into view. He touches bundles of incense to the flame of his skull-shaped lighter and sets the bundles in vases along the desk. Ribbons of pungent smoke swirl around us like jellyfish tendrils, never melting into haze.

The teacher gulps and blood splashes down his stained white chin. He croaks and begins to wheeze like a glass harmonica. The words aren't words. We chant them. I suppose we're in unison but I can't follow what the others are saying. In the empty space there in the middle of the classroom, in our midst, there are suddenly people, all dressed in white. There is a curtain across the front of the room and the teacher sits between us and it, rocking back and forth, droning, hiccuping blood that lands with a clatter on the desk.

A muffled bang behind the curtain. The fabric jerks once over toward the right side.

Gunpowder smell mixes with the incense. The smoke trembles in my larynx and doesn't seem to move or to be at all affected by my strenuous shouting. The people in white are translucent phantoms and as they drink glass powder water ragged scarlet wounds slide down into their bodies, the red glows inside them and then wells and spills. They fall in agony.

Now they are all dead and the room is silent. Loss collects above their bodies. Loss saturates the room, filling it like silent wailing. It sharpens. Loss itself is there, like a god. We must give ourselves to it, denying it nothing it can affect, so that it stops being a word. It will say itself.

When one of the fallen bodies rises, tilting upward like a plank, there is no alteration in the loss. Though he rises, nearly collapses, holding the corner of a table, awkardly stands erect, hands groping in front of him, splutters blood, the sense of loss does not abate. He is still lost, and what we see is taking place within loss, like another dimension. He is looking around now at the others. His mouth works. Tears pour down his ghastly white cheeks and he screams, but there's no sound.

The phantom room and its contents are replaced by a rotting body in the middle of the floor. The gunpowder smell vanishes and a carrion stink thumbs shut the soft palate. The corpse is no phantom. It shivers and crawls with decay. A vibrating haze of tiny insects clouds the bubbling face, and the head nods with some inner shift. Every aspect of it is presented to its respective sense with impossible distinctness. This is decay, a godly manifestation. The human form sags, disgendered and anonymous, melts. Loss exults around the melting body. Loss becomes a crown of disordered, perfectly straight dark rays, like a faceted crater around the melting body.

The teacher groans. The sound goes on and on, thin, weak, but able to go on and on, lacening itself through the soft gelatinous crackle that comes from the corpse as its flesh is consumed and transformed and saponified. The teacher's voice is nauseating. The sound is twining with the noise of decay and tugging at it, lifting it. Suddenly there is a feeling of compression in the chest, like asthma. Something is happening, the thing we came to see. The initiation. The body stirs with decay. Rot forms burst from it, splitting the skin, crumpling bone like rancid tinfoil. Leprous yellow bulbs and curling stalks shaggy with patches of coarse hair, hexagonal sense organs densely covered with flabby white papules, glistening black crevasses with pebbly lips, they rise, swell, then sink, deflate, opening with the body's opening. The permutations go on and on with a detestable liquid sound, and that astringent groan threading through the rings of sound.

The body is a mass of quivering organic forms like a mass of corals, and independent forms slithering among them. There are hives of stiff cells like honeycombs filled with a dingy custard and dried scabs like pinecones made of amber scales with effluent trickling in the folds.

The colors are vivid decomposition colors, the odor induces waves of revulsion like washes of intense cold. The teacher's groan grows steadily louder until it begins to stir panic. At that instant, the mass on the floor dims, the colors fade and the forms collapse, the object becomes a dim grey bulb that splits and bends, folds and ejects plumes of putrescence.

A human form emerges from the slime. The membrane wriggles from the shoulders like afterbirth as it sits up, staring with its dripping face. The form lives, it takes on particularity and gender, there is no decay. Decomposition has gone past its utmost extent and composed a human form again out of the life processes of decay.

The teacher's voice chokes off. The human being stands up, and disappears. That's the end of today's lesson. Decay and grammar take us to basics. You can't initiate yourself; the words don't stop being words.

UNIT TWENTY-NINE
SPIDER

Now students should learn about spider. One and only one webless spider can be found in unlanguage; it takes no article. While it spins no web, it is situated in the center of a nest of rhetorical and grammatical fractures on any one of which it can skate away; when present, the skin whether it be white, red, blue, yellow, green, brown, or some other, will be a very complete color.

Spider is a lexical operation known as escapement that has no formal counterpart in other languages, and which is best understood as an intrepidity and independence on the part of the language itself to avoid recognition and confinement. It is the intelligent consciousness of unlanguage. While all languages possess thought and intelligence, unlanguage is the only language to achieve thought in the absence of redundancy. It is redundancy that makes possible the thoughts of ordinary language; this is observed when we note the persistence of intelligibility in statements whose content has been drastically reduced. Redundancy, in certain languages, accounts for more than half of all signs. Phantasmagoria alone thinks without redundancy. Just as Void Nouns are formed in the negative apertures established by groups of sub-noun particles, unlanguage as a whole forms fractures, which are thoughts, among redundancies.

The natural spider has an eye for each leg. It is unclear where the fractures begin and spider legs end; the foot has already slipped along the fracture toward one of many horizons, the eye at the other end is already finding another horizon. This means that spider is one autonomous center in self-initiated motion toward a planetary constellation of horizons. Number is not applicable to actions: this is a very ancient commandment. The abscyss may be singular or plural, but it is forbidden to express the sense of "runnings" or "sleeps" in the sense of more than one sleep. "Runnings" is permitted only to be a plural noun, not a plural verb. Whenever some person or persons runs, there is only the one act. The running of animals, machines, human beings or human events is all one, which is also why the word cannot be considered permanently singular. The same is true in the case of spider, which is a process, not a noun. There is no noun: spider metastasized it.

UNIT TWENTY-NINE READING

I come home by way of the park. It's night. Dog walkers are numbly straying along the paths, led by their dogs. They seem to bump up against low fences and benches like flotsam, caught there until a current dislodges them again. Everything about them is limp, slackshouldered, weak, and mindless like they've blundered up from Hades. Whenever I stop, they begin to collect nearby, and men who walk hurriedly in straight lines with telephones clapped to their faces keep passing me, and other men who loiter with their hands in their pockets, stride to and fro in the same stretch of three or four yards with weary impatience, obviously waiting.

What am I doing here? I'm doing, I wearily answer myself, what I'm always doing.

And what is that?

I'm trying to learn the language of dream and immortality, which bestows happiness and eternal life on those who learn and speak it. The language of happiness, immortality, dream, timelessness, the pure redundancy of chance, in which chance and redundancy become one.

Through the barren trees to the street. This is a major boulevard here, and traffic passes down its length in knots. As I turn off onto a short side street the rush of passing cars stops on the boulevard and a pair of headlights sweeps my face. A black livery car turns into this short, seldom-used street facing me, mirroring me. The car creeps along, rolls by me slowly, then accelerates with a wheeze. I switch at the T intersection there in the middle of the block and turn into another little-used street. The sidewalk before me is empty to the next intersection—no, there's someone there in the distance, heading in this direction. Bulky, sloppy, thick hair wedged into a basebredundall cap, loose heavy clothes, a rapid walk, sweeping along like a mop. I switch to the opposite sidewalk to avoid him. Now I can't find him. Perhaps he sped up, is already behind me, and I didn't see him for all the parked vans. Not anywhere. Was there somebody?

Arriving at the corner, I nearly collide with a couple, even though the night is still enough and I heard no approaching footsteps. We veer rapidly around each other. The block behind them is empty; so is the one they cross to. An implausible looking pair. The moon seems to slip in and out of the buildings.

I can't return home until I've met with something eerie. The moon actually is full, and shreds of cloud really are crossing it. It would be redundant to invent poems about it because the moon is a poem. I've known that all my life. The clouds pass. I can see the moon clearly. The continents cast their shadows on it. A black jellyfish. So that's a seance going on up there, in parallel with my walk wandering down here. The whole city is under hypnosis—everyone but me. I'm awake; they are all sleeping. Under the full moon, someone is undergoing a terrifying physical change; ribbons of saliva stretch from gaping jaws, his body bends and bulges in wrong ways and places. The process is generally referred to as dying. He's being translated. He may in a moment catch a glimpse of what he now was. As this is going on, I slip along beneath their windows, hearing in the silence now some faint music, now a half-strangled scream, now a sharp cry of pleasure and surprise. The sleepers are up in there somewhere, writhing in pleonasm. Trammelling up the ravels of ... no, that's not it. I forget now what it was.

It's phrases coming to me, like clots of ink in a sluggish vortex. What I am hearing are fragments, uttered in transparent voices, like automatic speech out of the air, or that's not it, not from the air but from the night, from the time, all of these things, the air, the dull blue black sky, I don't know, I have no idea what I'm talking about, the cut jelly satellite up there, my stupid metaphors, the way I'm thinking and speaking. Abruptly I remember the Second Person, now old and broken down, with heavy stubble silvering his leathery cheeks and his voice rumbling and weak, smiling ruefully with loose lips down into his mug of coffee—"That's how it is in spider," he says. There's a lit stick of incense between the crossed fingers holding the cup, and the smoke bends against the venetian blinds. I remember this and I see whatever is around me in the present. There's always the same basic pattern to experience: redundancy in one channel and chance in the other. I've known that throughout my curious metastasis. There's what stays the same and what improvises. Only the proportions of each vary, and I don't think they need necessarily do so in ratio to each other, I mean I don't insist that a doubling of one means a halving of the other. I've seen redundancy bracing up to resist an onslaught of chance and I've seen desperate flailing attempts to evade a swamping ebullition of redundancy.

The phrases repeat—that's redundant—but they're unintelligible—that's chance. They are probably identical at the point of origin, but that's far from here. Each phrase is no, scratch that. Each phrase creates an isolation in space, the way one bird does, singing alone. In time, too, so that listening feels like remembering, and not just because the bird repeats itself. It does and it doesn't. They are the far off phrases that mediums attract and translate. I must be a medium. Dynamically, attentively passive, to be receptive. But not even so positive.

The phrases are in another language, even the English ones. I hear about black jellyfish. The shadows of the continents on the moon, which show how they will look. The name "Kowalka." Death linked persistently to alcohol for no reason I can see. An indecipherable one; it starts with a muttered dactyl, a pause, a distinct "Ah" followed by a dim iamb, then a trochee. From time to time. A language with many consonants. There's another one, consisting of three very brief segments of no more than three syllables each; it's so indistinct I can only make out the emphases. These aren't messages with intentions. They're more like someone's favorite turn of phrase, repeated to oneself with pleasure the way a cat is stroked. The way people have of caressing themselves at a sensitive spot on the arm. Not all of them sound like that; some are like memorization exercises.

I'm being watched. Chance is being simulated around me; actually there is someone orchestrating all these superficially chance encounters. This orchestrator, this Magus, is trying to out-spider me. Me, for some reason. I must be important. Otherwise, why bother? I need to avoid being out-spidered, and outspider the Magus, and learn or decide how and why I am important enough to be doomed and am I doomed.

A new block, all asleep and blue under a full moon stopped dead nearly at the zenith. Perfect stillness. Motionless shadows. Motionless clouds. Motionless air. The moment I set foot on the pavement of that new block a red light snaps on, the curtains part in the window, a woman I think I know steps through the curtains and stands there in stockings and a corset.

The red light shows her to the crowd, who whistle appraisingly. Standing very straight, her hands on her hips, her head up, her eyes over their heads. I rush to the door to head them off and, once inside, press it against my back as if I were squeezing an overstuffed closet shut. She emerges tranquilly from the heavy curtains and leans against the far edge of the doorway, her hands behind her back, barely smiling. Perfume. Then she turns and goes up the steep and narrow stairs, the lamp at its head throwing her into silhouette.

There was an invitation, I know that. I was to meet her at the great house; she was going to slip away from him, the lord of the manor, and meet me in secret. The rendez-vous was supposed to be some significant spot or other in the garden; a special statue there.

I smelled a rat and decided not to go. I would send word that I had been stricken with a migraine; he would find a history of migraine there, if he checked. I'm sure it must be written down in a file on me somewhere. Subject to migraines. I would stay indoors, in ~~my cell~~ my little place in town. Staying lucid—keep flushing the pills, no death alcohol just good ol' water. His spies would not see me out and about while I was supposed to be laid up. I'll have to keep the lights out. I might even have to stay in bed, just in case any of the street boys peep in through my shutters. A dull day, but, after all, she could just as easily arrange to see me some other day. If this were all on the level, I would simply meet her then and that would be that. So what was the point, if all this ruse will get me is a postponement? Well, it nevertheless is an active intervention on my part. What was supposed to happen today will happen some other day—perhaps his elaborate scheduling will be disrupted. But even if it isn't, I tell myself that maybe this will break his initiative; somehow, someway things will be changed, my power to act and the diameter of my circle will grow. After all, I'm supposed to be led along by the nose from one cute little scene to another; the redundancy is supposed to be perfect. But if I can chip open a little crack and admit some chance into things, I don't see how that weakens my position.So what if the idea all along were to goad me into this deception? Maybe the stunt will happen in my home, or maybe he has several stunts constantly running or ready in different spots, ready for me to tip into them. But I don't think so. No one has infinite reach, and even if he did, am I really worth that much trouble? How could I be worth so much in some scheme or other without being even slightly aware of it? It doesn't add up. No, I think he has each stunt set up one by one; maybe once in a blue moon he'll get ambitious and set up two. I'm supposed to charge in blindly with a hard on so big it gets stuck in my nose; what if I did? Perhaps it's a mistake to come on too cagey—he'll get trickier, more subtle, when he realizes he's not tackling a complete blockhead. In that case, I should go, playing dumb. But, following that line, I should allow myself to be trapped and humiliated and all the rest of it: that strategy amounts to the same thing as surrender. I'll stick to my migraine. That's sound. I can play dumb in other ways—overtip waiters, buy a few chintzy knick-knacks for too much money. Never show any direct challenge. Never break irony. Defying him as carefully as I can, while insisting on being a simpleton. Intelligent simplicity is my weapon against his craft.

When I was young, I used to do puzzle books with a friend of mine, and drawing straight lines across mazes never got old. "Help Billy get home!" A straight line from Billy to the cozy-looking house, right over the maze. "Billy bought a helicopter." No helicopter for me, though, and nowhere to fly it except maybe away.

UNIT THIRTY
IMPERITIVE VOICE

The imperitive voice is one of magic's two essential halves, the other being the imploritive. The imperitive acts as a summons which attracts a future event; it does this by negating other possibilities, thus forming a causal channel. Once a person has been commanded—and there is next to nothing one can do to prevent it—that person's possibilities are instantly restricted. Obey, or disobey. A crafty patient may alternately resort to deferral. He or she may wait until the echoes of the command die away; when the voice itself has faded, and only the bare word remains, it becomes increasingly easy to treat that word as just one more among so many others. This gambit has its risks; the command may be repeated, perhaps with an intensification of the voice that correspondingly inflates the significance of obedience or disobedience. Up to a point, the repetition of a command will steadily up the stakes. The doctor, however, also runs a risk; after that point is passed, further repetition of the command will have the opposite effect, a detensification that makes itself felt even more precipitously than the prior intensification. A seasoned commander knows that point and stops well short of it. A sly commander will shore up his authority by commanding what he knows will happen anyway, but he must realize that even this trick can backfire if it is discovered.

The imperitive is the grammatical form by means of which words come closest to acquiring direct causative efficacy. Death never waits, but people will wait to use the word until after an authority pronounces it.

The imperitive voice is represented in unlanguage by augments of ionic majore, paired antibacchiae, or a spondee followed by a primus paeon, tribrach, or proceleusmatic, the unstressed syllables echoing the stressed. The voice, or hand, must be infused with strength, whether this be the broad strength of volume or size, or the deep strength of intensity and quiet power, and the imperitive must also be accompanied by a gesture. This gesture may be a kind of concentrated motionlessness. The command is released in a way that is intended to draw the witness of the gods, demons, ancestors, spirits, or other such unseen watchers, who are tacitly invited to guarantee it. The most subtly effective imperitives are consequently those which are heard or read when the source is out of sight.

The anti-imperitive is formed by attaching the imperitive suffix to the verb as a prefix instead and reversing the metrical pattern of the verb. This voice is used in two circumstances, either to command disobedience, as in "think nothing," or to indicate that one is abandoning the imperitive or otherwise cancelling one's capacity to employ it, usually in keeping with the dictate of a prior and supernatural imperitive.

What is the imperitive in the passage below? What is the student being commanded to do or to be?

Unit Thirty Reading

I crouch at the sill of a high window overlooking the town. The library is my trusted refuge; the Magus knows this, and I know he knows, so that means I have to split my vision. One eye sees with trust, and the other with suspicion. The more trust, the more suspicion. The more suspicion, the more trust. The city below me isn't dead, or not in the way I thought. He and his agents—although most if not all of these so-called agents don't realize themselves who they work for or that they in fact work for anyone—live, and there has to be enough of an ordinary life here for it to be possible to trap me. Without everyday transactions, conversations, social events, the business of trapping turns into a simple matter of hunting. It's in my interest above all to avoid that, because he can put many hunters on my track. I haven't figured out how to leave more than one trail. It's on my list of things to do.

In total silence, huge discs of light search the city. The buildings ripple, bend and unbend as the beams slide over them. There are a few lights here and there; they form balloons with translucent, hazily illuminated interiors where lustrous black streets, sidewalks, shadow-amputated parts of buildings, the back end of an old model T ... Each of these orbs has fixed sparks or spectrum lines that move slightly as my line of sight varies. The beams roll around these lighted zones. As they roam without any pattern that I can see, the city takes on the aspect of a pale blue cadaver that blackens and crumbles into the dark, especially the darkness of the suburbs and the surrounding landscape of hills in silhouette.

I get down to the street. Being up at that window was like setting myself at his level, and probably more obvious to him. The silent town is still like a dead body with the silent mystery of rotting hidden in it; the people in their ink black rooms are individual decay spirits unbroken from their purity trances. With a sense that falls somewhere between touch and the feeling of balance or general muscular tension, I am aware of the motion of the beams above me, although I can't see them. As one approaches from up and to my left, I get a feeling on my right side like a barely tangible rubber rolling pin being drawn up a furry flank, a little inside me. The beams always register on the opposite side, which creates a void in their direction, nearly pivoting me to look directly at them—which would be a mistake, and surely result in my being detected. Being detected is a thing I have always energetically shunned, on general principles, but what exactly will happen if I am seen? At the moment, I reckon, the plot will find me. The Magus is the plot, or its chief architect and builder.

No plots for me! Plots end, and with them end the plottees. I intend to stick around, or at least, not to spend my allotted days and nights being goosed here and goosed there by the impatience of a demanding and inmating and intricate plot.

I've always struggled with my own impatience. Here I am, doing some onerous task or other. Evening's coming on, and I begin to think about my dinner; what it will be, what I want. Now here I am, eating the dinner I wanted. I enjoy it, but before I've made away with even half my food, I'm looking forward to getting it over with. Enough already. Eventually, to be conscious of doing this or that will come to be the same as wanting it to be over. Only those things that are totally engrossing or unconscious will be exempt, and maybe not even then. Maybe my resourceful impatience will invade my sleep, so that I can't wait to wake up and get on to the next thing I won't be able to wait until it's done, until I lie on a sickbed thinking that yes life was all very nice but isn't death coming just a bit too slowly? And then on again—death! This is taking forever!

My weird extra senses tell me that an experiment is happening somewhere in this town. The medium, the doctor, clanking and sparking machinery massed all around them, staring at the spot in the lap of a velvety concentrated blackness where a transparent, trapezoidal ray, like a membrane of ectoplasm or an elastic shard of glass, lengthens and trembles. The vision has begun in the darkness amplifier. Light without form, light where there should be no light.

They witness the apparition. The man at the controls stares like a maniac, tears burst and tremble in his eyes, his laugh is like a shout, and now he is shouting over the din of the machinery: "Liight! Liiiight! Light without form!" Now my turn. Back to the library—speed is essential—I have to reach my goal as swift as a ghost who can walk through walls if I want to outrun him and his spies. It's like trying to stay a step ahead of your own thoughts. Hard, but not impossible. Here's the secret passage. I get to the basement, emerge from between the laundry machines, assemble the death amplifier. I've had the idea of bringing forth life not by reversing death but by amplifying it; when death reaches the saturation point on site there will be nowhere for it to go but into life. Into my hasty contrivance I insert the subject item, the deadened item. The machinery clanks and sparks. At the center of the black lotus a tiny white speck, close in on it, the white lotus. At its center, a black speck. The black lotus. With a white lotus at its center. A black rose, a white speck at the center. A white rose, a black speck. The lotus rose. Plunging through infinite white to black to white like a striped plummet through apertures shaped like blossoms each opening onto an infinite field of white or black.

UNIT THIRTY-ONE
LANGUAGE GENRES

Just as there are figures of speech, so there are figures of thought, to the extent that the forms taken by language tend to delineate the set of logical possibilities. The words red, scarlet, crimson, ruby, carmine, rust, vermillion, etc., denote variations that are lost when translated into a language which has only the one word, "red," and so such a language will not have available to it the notion that a color may have distinctly inflected states, or any state beyond that of simple existence or registration.

Just as there are figures of thought, so there are, it follows, figures of experience. While someone who has only the word "red" may witness flucutations of redness, in a fire, or in the sky at sunset, those changes are most likely not constructed into the experience. One of the primary goads to the development of poetic figuration and the invention of new words is the palpable discrepancy that arises in recounting an experience for which one has no redundant expressions.

In parabolica, there are grammatical forms known as metaphanes that anticipate new or modified figures of thought, and also metapathes, which perform the corresponding function with respect to figures of experience.

The metaphane is formed by elision of the noun and the verb to be; the position in the sentence is itself put into the anticipative by surrounding it with no less than six mono- or bi-syllabic adverbial particles in the future locative-anti-nominative.

The metapathe is formed by omitting either verbs or nouns altogether or in alternating syntagms, so that at least half the language is suppressed. Metapathes often contain multiple metaphanes.

These two figures are always introduced with a rhetorical pivot, which is not a matter of inflection but of a flex or warp in the deep enthymeme. In ordinary rhetoric, the enthymeme is basically the argument; the deep enthymeme, however, is the analog of the rhetorical version of the idea of a clinamen, which in this case is that meaningful volatility and elusiveness of meaning the passage reads toward.

UNIT THIRTY-ONE EXERCISE

The man's strategem, or his unwittingly well-chosen compromise, is more or less the subject of the parable below. The author's purpose in creating this parable seems to be to surprise the reader with a new variation on an old theme, and in particular, one which goes against the usual didactic, moralizing purpose of such a story. On closer scrutiny, the parable also makes memory and perhaps identity enigmatic, touching on the reader's own experience. In both of these different aspects, the parable gestures or gropes toward some ineffable point of view; whatever that point of view would be, or show, we refer to as the deep enthymeme of the parable.

Translate the parable below into confusion. The entire passage is a metapathe, and contains five metaphanes. Construct the metaphanes first, and then combine them with linking sentences to fashion the complete metapathe. Show your work.

He bargained for a thousand years of life and the services of one of the most skillful and noble demons. When his term was up, he was dragged away to hell,
    stuffed in a clay oven and abandoned on a burning plain. Currently, he is there, still burning. This condition will never change. However, in his mind, things are a
    little different; he may not be the complete loser after all. He has a thousand years of memories to lose himself in. It's commonly assumed that the dead forget, but the damned must never forget the reason for their damnation; if that memory were taken from them or otherwise lost, they would merely be suffering minds, and that would not be to the purpose. His crime was an entire thousand years of life; so he must remember it all. In theory, eternity will wear down everything; but there are huge, tough rocks that have withstood the erosion of thousands of years, and languages that are still spoken, and

countries and customs that still exist. There are elements which retain their fundamental characteristics even when heat melts or vaporizes them. There are archaic, lost rites and tongues that have been revived again after long desuetude. So, while his soul chafes in a smouldering oven, his mind roves again and again down cool pathways overgrown and fern-dappled beneath a woody canopy so green it's more or less black, to no sound but the birdsongs of a thousand years.

UNIT THIRTY-ONE READING

So here's where I am pinned down. The page in front of me is filmed with a little sprinkling of black grit I scrape off onto the floor. There's a few particles caught in the lines of my hand, sticking there. I sniff my hand. Grave dust. Bang my hands together. The prospect that the city might instantly awaken around me is too terrible to linger over. The streets suddenly crowded, traffic crashing, shriek of trains, the seeing, the watching, the blinding myriad busyness, challenges and sizings up and concludings about, and something worse that feels like an attitude and that I think of as a glare made up of all these things and their apotheosis. White hammer made of a dull pane of light. That's the phrase I want, but I don't like it. I can't see how to change it. I'm sick of myself, restless, wanting nothing I can do.

A little glass bottle of death alcohol. I sniff my hand, rub my face. There's head ache, from trying too hard as usual, and eye ache, and half-smotheration. The page in front of me … didn't I scrape that grit away? It didn't look like this before—did I do this before? Deja vu. I thought I did this before, but that might have been all it was, a thought. Something intervened to distract me before the thought could get in touch with the hands. They smell like grave dust, but they might have that smell on their own.

I'm trying to plan a route across town, and making no progress. My mind won't do it. All I want is rest. My body isn't tired; not exactly springing up with life, but not tired. A weird state I'm in, like I have no soul. The teacher, on the one hand, and the Magus, on the other. The one shows me the way to keep clear of the webs of the other; to stay clear of the web you think spider. A fly doesn't know how to avoid webs, it gave that up for its wings, but that was a dumb bargain.

The Magus, who might turn out to be you, the Second Person. Why, after all, are you here, in this unstory?

That's not fair. You can't be expected to know why you're here unless the Third Person, I, is expected to know. And I don't know.

I think I see what the idea is. Some bestial marriage of the teacher and the Magus. Why introduce me to the teacher, when he's the only one who can teach me the devious ways around and through the plots of the Magus? It must be because that was the only way to get me here, where the Magus can plot me. He can't get at the teacher, but he can get at the patient. I don't know that this was the only way; I shouldn't assume that. Who cares—it was the way I went, and I can't change that. Or can I? I'll think about it later. This is a matter of position. Some kind of allegory or ceremony or something. Me, in a spot. Could that be a mistake? Maybe I'm supposed to assume that, and keep moving, thinking that's the way to thwart the plot, when that's just what is wanted of me. That's such a characteristic turn of paranoid thinking there ought to be term for it: the Suspicion that Prompting Your Countermeasures was the Real Intention. SPYCRI.

The Magus is a mad specialist in the field of linguistics, trying to make living things out of words. Bizarre machines are being built in the basement of the hospital out of nothing but language, yet with all the solidity of any machine of metal, so that interlocking phrases turn each other like gears, and sentences whirl like drive shafts, and punctuation whirs and taps like valves; a vast array of machines that can be combined in a variety of ways, to form a time machine, a shrink ray, enlarging ray, an animation suspender, a teleporter, a disguising transmogrifier, a telepath, an illusion projector, an insanity beam, a rejuvenator, a thinking machine. And monsters, too: incongruous graftings, sutured chimeras and creatures from myths, hybrids more repellently alien than any being in a pure state, resurrected corpses—and things that grew from basic lexplasm, shaping themselves, as, with deliberation, the Magus crosses his fingers, turns his head and refuses to interfere, because in his maniacal ambition he wants to create beyond what he can imagine, and searches for ways to make an ally of chance.

Experiments are hiding in these buildings, where eyes peer greedily at instruments for detecting the dead, ghosts, spirits, relays; white lines sifting into a lustrous black colander, and human eyes peering like vilely animated blisters that jump, swivel, and suck greedily at whatever appears, greasing it with their saliva. The fantasy is a pair of clean, perfect, flat crystals, cameras, perfectly pure black lucid transparent lustrous in a serene female face. Sorry no, I call no pining for the celestial lady and tear her face away; silicone, trembling like rubber in my fingers. What's there now? Just black space. And also a transparent black diamond. And what are you going to do now, old boy—swallow it, take it to the jeweler and set it in a ring and then you'll "have" it? Offer it? Offer it, yes. Fine. That's fine. Next question. To whom offer it? Wait and see?

I move, at last. Can I make it out of plot jail?

The two silhouettes, men. Suits and hats even. And ashen-pale lights, two apiece, situated on the face where you would expect. This is fine.

The smothered feeling gives way to a blank yammering terror something like the moment before the roller coaster drops, like I have a very, very short amount of time in which to think this, an offensively brief little moment of reflection to taunt myself with, with my own uselessness of mind. But it's with this iota or nothing that I must save myself from what I don't know.

It's not a sunny day in June with enamel blue sky over green hills with cows and clouds, and it isn't early evening at the estate where lords and ladies in wigs are scheming and quipping—what what what is it—it has to be close enough to this that I can manage to step across—

Ah the old chump is fantasizing again. Some cloak and dagger stuff to enliven a tedious afternoon. What would it be like if I were hiding in here? If someone were after me? If I were important enough to hunt down? If something vital, my life, the lives of others, were to be saved or lost depending on what I do now, this step to one side, over a crack in the floor. I used to avoid those on my way to school, to save my mother. But then I always wondered if somehow the superstition would work backwards, and I should step on every crack; that might "exhaust" the crack spirits and that would be one less concern.

I amble out into the street. A small bus rattles by on the uneven pavement and its acrid wind washes over me. A gang of workers in coveralls is lumbering up toward the corner along the smooth adobe wall, where the shadow of the three-storey building on the corner cuts its angles across the white, like a signpost they're following, and I go after, on this side, even though it's uphill. The men are left behind in another genre. I'm not an inmate, the plot-tension is gone. I ducked down a secret passage and into this bit of everyday ordinary social realism.

UNIT THIRTY-TWO
ORACULAR FUTURE TENSE

Unlanguage treats future events as occurrences which are of different order of efficacy from present events. The future tense in other languages denotes a form of the conditional to which the element of certainty has been added; what might or could happen becomes what will happen. The future tense is often used in a present sense, to express an intention in the present to act later. The Oracular Future Tense is roughly the obverse of this; an event happens in the future as it becomes an intention in the present. This is why the abscyss follows the verb in the Oracular Future.

The Oracular Future is also related directly to the imperitive, which is why the Oracular Future will also employ conditional imperitive augments. Even though there is no question of command or obedience, the imperitive is used in the sense that what will take place occurs as if it had been commanded.

Identify all possible instances of the Oracular Future in the following passage along with the causative agency that produced them in the future.

UNIT THIRTY-TWO READING

The white fire doesn't spread like fire, it's all made of flat individual plumes that pop out of the ground one by one, and most are small like a foot or less, but some are seven feet tall or more, and they're skinny. They undulate strangely. Fire jerks and wobbles ordinarily. These flames are like an incessant superimposition of transparencies. Every other second there's a distinct edge, every intervening second it seems like there are two edges on top of each other, one fading in, the other going. The color is dirty white, owing to translucency I guess. The sound is nothing. There is no sound. Only wind in the poplars.

Flick. Flick. Flick. Silent plumes driving me back along the shore. I don't know why they drive me back. No heat comes from them and they don't seem to be burning what they touch. Starkly I see myself covered in trailing white plumes like someone who's been tarred and feathered, the despairing, crazy eyes howling from a mute and fire baffled face. No thanks. Tearing off my clothes the hyacinthine perfume of the flames begins to reach me. The jingle of my belt buckle is shockingly loud. The white plumes facet along the shore, hemming me in, but they don't go near the water. I wade out knee high. The water is so tepid that its weight is nearly all I feel. Flick flick flick flick, the shore is full. Long braids of pale light sweep along the waterline in both directions. I fling myself headlong, swimming toward the opposite side.

I'm not halfway there when I see the two ends meet directly before me. The lake is outlined in leprous white, which is beginning to thicken up the shore. I'm trapped. The lake is space. The flames are stars. I have no role in this metaphor. I'm trapped.

A wave of sour diesel exhaust washes over the sidewalk cafe as the rattle-trap little bus disappears around the corner. The waiter waves to his cousin, one of a group of weary-looking laborers in coveralls who amble along a moment later.

Now a man enters the cafe and asks to be seated inside, in the back room. As the waiter retrieves the menus and prepares to show him to his table, the man is watching his back, warily scanning the street. There's a sudden, violent gust of wind. The man follows the waiter adroitly.

The man sits at the middle of a long narrow table with a white tablecloth. He starts to pant, lick his lips. Beads of sweat gather on his brow. He stiffens.

A little blue hatch opens in front of his eyes, like a trapdoor dropping down in the distance. Glowing blue vapor emerges lazily from it; the blue apparition is uneven, like a smear of paint on a mirror, at the back of a rectilinear funnel in space, like a faceted dent in the center of his visual field, made of distortion without color. He continues to see the room through it, shifting from one visuality to another.

The image comes in flashes and seems to repeat like a movie loop. The blue outline of a black-cored woman backs out of the right side of the hatch emerging in profile. He knows there's a mirror figure on the left side too but it's as if his attention were fixed on the one on the right.

The room—the woman emerging—the room—the woman emerging. They alternate and repeat without his ever losing sight of either. The hatch, the glow, the woman, take up no more space in his visual field than he could cover with his closed fist at arm's length.

His body trembles with increasing violence. He claws at the table cloth. His teeth chatter, foam spurts from his lips, strangled sounds in his throat, eyes glassy. Again and again she emerges from the right hand side.

Now she comes around into the dark space between him and the hatch mouth and rushes right at him, down and up, with darting, mincing steps, sweeping up her arms, her face just black transparency, the head looping. He recoils in fright, lunging backward, twisting as he falls in convulsions, frothing at the mouth and growling like a mad animal.

Expertly grabbing him by the wrists and ankles, they heave him up on the table. They aren't orderlies. They're bystanders. He thrashes like a hooked fish, seeing again and again that silent rush toward him. He is folded and pinned. The room slides ominously away into blue night with a deep landscape scrub brush along the horizon like a bushy eyelash, the custardy landscape lacerated with livid white roads.

There's a jolt and he tumbles into a stifling shadow. The dancing women are flickers his eyes can't find. His heart is slamming. He can feel it in his palms and neck. Caustic pain tears along his jaw, and an evil wire of nauseating pain burns itself into his left arm so that he clutches his palpitating chest helplessly.

There's a hazy iceberg coming toward him out of the shadow, both rapid and slow. He feels as if he's running as fast as he can to meet it and trying to tear free of his running body and escape it. The thing is unbearable—like a colossal ghost a diamond a palace a jellyfish or a gigantic quartz nautilus and microbe studded with enormous white globes.

It towers above him. The heart attack chops into him like an axe, his jaw explodes and blood pours from his mouth. Gradually he is drawn into the coils of this floating building creature machine god plant germ majestic presence being.

Bystanders describe how he rose from the table roaring like a maniacal drunk, tossed a heavy wooden chair against the far wall where it smashed to splinters, then half-collapsed kneading his chest. Short cries burst from him. His body relaxed. He got to his feet and reeled to the mantlepiece, resting his forearms on the mantle and his head on his arms, drawing deep, vocal breaths.

Here it comes again.

Again, his chest begins to pound. The woman unfolding from the hatch mouth, the demon monolith looms over and engulfs him. He grabs his chest again and recoils with a spasm. The woman spins toward him, bringing her faceless head around stop around stop like a ballet dancer, he knows the fourth time she turns her face to him will be the end and she turns turns turns turns.

UNIT THIRTY-THREE
THE IMPLORITIVE

As mentioned above, the imploritive is the imperitive complement in sorcery and proto-erotics. The grammatical structure of the imploritive is the literal inversion of the imperitive form; its strength or difficulty is a reflection of the tension within the oscillation of vectors within a dichotomy of defiant submission, known as minor imploritive A, and of submissive defiance, known as small imploritive A.

Requests and questions define a set of customary or logical answers. "Rainy," "fine," "cold," "ugly," "brisk," "catastrophic," are all answers which may be found in the set of logical or customary responses to the question, "what is the weather like today?"—while "plaid," "socialist," "spiny," "posthumous," are not. The imploritive will express lexical defiance by determining the set of possible responses to exclude demurritative ones, such that the response is driven from one possibility to another without resolution, with the understanding that even conceiving of this flight from one response to another as a kind of response is not possible or permitted. In this way, the imploritive is like a lust-crazed Hellenic divinity endlessly scrambling after a fair example of mortality along an endless hallway. It is by establishing this relationship of perpetual motion that the imploritive achieves its aim. This is why the imploritive form always begins and ends in middles.

In the passage below, fail to find a single instance of either imploritive, noting each occasion on which the imploritive is absent.

UNIT THIRTY-THREE READING

The Romance of the Old School: It's an Open House, a gala night, the lights in halls and classrooms gleam with a spectral, dreamlike luster that blackens the windows. Peering out a black window I see only my reflection, blackening as I lean closer to the pane; I can't see what's out there. But I know there is something hiding out there, in the dark; it sounds corny but corny isn't the word for how it feels. The Old School is enveloped in darkness. Inside it's all smiles.

Inside it's all smiles and outside it's all silent howling that goes on and on. We're wearing our so-called Sunday best. The phrase imposes a false hypocrisy on me, since my family doesn't go to church dressed quite this way or go to church; but that's not important, so, so what? The strangeness of being at school at night, in clothes that are supposed to give me my best and most dignified aspect, the intensity of the darkness and the sense of mocking scrutiny zeroing in on me from the depths of its gulfs, all put me on alert. I see more brightly, hear more noisily, feel more serratedly. When I catch sight of the girl I like a blast of pre-adolescent terror rips through me. Blanche Kowalka. I duck into the providentially empty boy's room to compose myself for the encounter to come and to relish my fear, which is charging me up with so much life I'm shaky. Just a girl. Blanche Kowalka. I don't ever have to say it; it's virtually my own secret name by now. The Blanche Kowalka I know is more a chimera of my imagination than she is that bipedality actually wearing white stockings and black patent leather shoes, but I only dimly understand. Except for one thing, happiness is just like ordinary life. Some very funadmental one thing is added or subtracted, or otherwise not the same. An unknown and basic something, you. You, just as you are, but under warranty. You, but modest and patient. I didn't say ecstasy, I didn't say joy. I said happiness.

The bathroom smells like urinal cakes. The urinals are like fingermarks pressed into the soft shining white stuff. The idea of pawing soft white porcelain arouses a kind of tactile appetancy in me, like my numberless other desires that have no sense or possible realization. The white tiles that reach halfway up the walls glitter like glass, and there's condensation pearling on the shafts sticking up out of the toilets. The window is a virtually opaque cloudy grey with wire honeycombing, and it pivots on a hinge; it's open, the lower half tilted out and the upper in, and the dark turns to fragrant, cold air as it seeps through as if the light that touched it were a spell. I intuitively understand that the lights of the Old

School form a charm against the darkness, which would invade and do something to us otherwise if the light vanished. Hoping it stays on, fingers crossed it stays on.

Back out into the hall and Blanche Kowalka, who is talking with her little friend Meghan that I wouldn't mind a bit either, in fact it would be easier with Meghan because I have no awe of her to first clamber over. Easier what? What would be easier? Kissing? Something else? It's so much less mysterious when you know. Blanche Kowalka is wearing a red plaid dress that fits her pretty irregularly and her hair I would have preferred would have been different. There is horror somewhere behind all this vividness, gaping void, the magic, real illusion, just what I love. I fell in love with her blowing dust off the books on the day of the book fair. The teacher posted us at the same shelf. I liked the way she didn't allow her cheeks to puff out, it made her seem refined. Animated by her breath, falsely animated, the dust motes swung into the air and caught the faintness, back there we were alone together and veiled in a uniting dimness. I fell in love with her schoolgirlness, in my capacity as a schoolboy. We talked, and I committed to memory, preliminarily intimate, a few of the special words she casually let slip. She is the sort of girl who has her own talk; I think she employed a preposition like "hindunterside." With a t. Perhaps she had a German grandmother. Her diary must be full of code. I was always unmasculinely interested in this kind of lexical ... uh—faster, go faster, before it gets you—uh there were always girls, girls for me, girls I was firing on, girls who wanted words, and playing, turning words to and fro, talking gibberish with meaning, meaning lancing out of gibberish, the meaning I want and towards which I keep wrestling the words and away from which girls lightly turn them again, the spite-inducing lightness of girls.

Blanche has a "look at me / don't look at me" way about her. I always answer that. My heart does. My thoughts are always riveted on the condition of my heart. I look at her: my heart is instantly painted and breaks out incandescent filament sleeve. There are just too many similes for it. Now she's talking with Martin Khansworth who is unfit to be described. That's me off the hook for now. Relieved and jealous I go find myself a cup of red drink and so on.

Now she and I are alone on the stairs. Her smile, the bargain, the oracle, life thickens all around and in me. What am I saying? Her voice keeps going up and up, smiling at me gingerly. There's a classroom door near us and I can see a thin segment of the room through the glassed arrowslit; the classroom is the embassy of the engulfing darkness and the teacher's profile sits in there, perfectly still at his desk. I mean, he moves, and now he convulses slightly, spitting up blood that dribbles from his lips and chin making black pools of reflection on the desk top, but these motions are part of his stillness. He raises an empty coffee mug to his lips and gulps emptiness. So much frailty and shyness and flatteredness now in her. My worldly experience and self-knowledge are almost able to reach back from the future and tell me this is going to be a disaster.

"I thought you were supposed to be a faggot," she murmurs.

It takes that to remind me there's supposed to be some connection between sex and "being a faggot." I never cared whether I was a "faggot" or not, it isn't as if not being a "faggot" makes me normal, even then.

I encircle her waist and pull her toward me, awkwardly twisting my head to kiss her. Her airspace smells like graham crackers, her lips are very red and chilly. Our kiss isn't ours, much more mine than hers, it's chaste and brief, but I feel like I carefully hold a mouthfull of electrified sugar that's also heaping up in my separating heart. I neither know nor need to that this is the high point of my life with Blanche. It won't fall into the terror outside the school, that's the greater destiny that will kill us all, it just closes there because the parabola shape is done drawing itself with us two. When I kiss Blanche, I am extremely close to her and extremely far away, the farthest I can get, by myself embarking on a voyage for two. She promises to meet me. Did she really?

Looking her straight in the eye I make a pistol out of my hand, open my jaws in a smile and stick in my index finger. I drop my thumb and go "kw'chhxx!"

UNIT THIRTY-FOUR
UNDERSTANDING THE DESIRINGRAMMARMATRIX

One of the greatest of the many challenges facing the student of phantasmagoria is the development of a proper conceptualization of the parabolic contour of its grammar. As was mentioned above, all inflection in unlanguage may be decomposed into at least two simultaneous counterinflections, a unique characteristic also known as inflect-reflect. Now that the student has a firm grasp of unlanguage's elementary grammar, the next step must involve making an attempt to fathom the complicated inter-relationships of libidinal vectrality which, in the aggregate, direct the overall tonality or energy-level of the inflection in any given logism.

The set of such relationships within a logism is called its desiringrammarmatrix. When called upon to analyze the desiringrammarmatrix of a logism, the most common technique involves a transformation-decomposition into a Cartesian graph, the orthant of which will be the product of the number, person, and tense, with person the abscyssa, number the ordnant, and tense the applicate.

This means that logisms can be related to each other matricularly.

In any case, the graph will reveal the clinamen of the logism, which is what it wants. Parabolic language cannot be fully intelligible unless the reader or speaker understands not only what each grammatical element is, but what each element wishes it was or could be. So, for example, a strictly, even harshly, negative statement may, when decomposed, be rendered a perpendicular vector with the steepest possible anti-negative gradient above the axis for increase in value; that is to say, a profoundly negative statement may yearn to become positive with the greatest possible intensity.

This textbook opened with the simple grammatical rules governing the formation of the interrogative. However, these rules mask the more primal essence of the question, which is its desire to become an answer. Rhetorical questions are among the best places for a beginner to commence his investigation of the desiringrammarmatrix, because such questions bring together the greatest desire to become an answer with the most hopeless impotence. Maximal dichotomies within a seme or logism are the best places to observe the desires and amors of grammar.

Diagram the desiringrammarmatrix of the passage below.

UNIT THIRTY-FOUR READING

Two armies face each other, one camped in the foothills and the other in the plain, and each day the soldiers march out and fight to stalemate. The general of the foothill army is a woman, and even though she knows that the soldiers speculate about her inside her armor she feels the immanence of death too keenly to deny herself the pleasure of bathing in the shallow pool that collects among the rocks of the foothills near the camp. There is a tent there for her modesty, eunuch bodyguards, quietness, and screening boulders.

Emerging from the water one night she is seized by a figure from the dark and driven to the ground. In the moonlight she recognizes the enemy general; droplets of water skitter across his skin. He swam up, she realized, from a point further down, where the stream into which this pool flows pours into a natural basin. Without a word, he is pinning her down. It is obvious he is not here to kill her. He is naked, his penis is erect.

She has not yet called out. After nothing happens for a few moments, she begins to realize that she has an interval of arbitrary duration before the sequel. Some mysterious power, perhaps deep in herself, has granted her a lucid interval. The image of the two bodies there on the brink hovers before her consciousness like a movie on a screen; in this intercalary hesitation between moments she can make a thorough, unemotional appraisal of her situation, study the contents of the image detachedly and carefully, and arrive at a judgement about the best course of action. As she considers possible consequences, the image, without changing, somehow also shows her the potential sequence of events.

She could resist. She looks at his body, not frozen in place, moving and not moving. It's a powerful body, and hers, though she is strong for her size, is frankly no match for his. Considering that she is in his grasp already, considering how much advantage he has already managed to seize by surprise, there is only so much room left for compensating skill. She looks on the consequences with a mathematician's absence of sentiment; it is a virtual certainty—he cannot fail to immobilize her.

She could endure it passively, remain a general. She looks at his face and body. The expression is not savage, the eyes are not angry or drunk or vicious or vengeful but full of enigmatic longing. She looks at her own body. She observes the musculature with approval; it is an admirably beautiful body. There is a distinct seam along the flat abdomen, and another tracing the outline of her quadricep. The vital skin glows with health. Consideration of other possibilities intervenes, veiling that vision of her own body. She isn't ready to stop looking, turns back, impatiently draws the veil away, gazes again on her own body. She marvels at herself. Desire for her own body grabs her and time resumes. On the sandbank two bodies writhingly encircle each other like snakes. Her first climax shakes her in a passing gust. She plunges upward, attacking the old tree of his body. With every come a former battle is squeezed out of her. Now she is lying on the ground, her hips in his hands, her weight on her upper back and her pelvis in the air. She looks up at him strangely, with contradictory appeals in each eye. He ejaculates and she is pregnant. They both lower the krater in her hips cautiously to the ground.

The battle of the following day is the most horrifying of the war. The two generals are sloppy and distracted; their bad decisions cause many needless killings among the soldiers. Thoughts of what will happen tonight relentlessly intrude into their minds, robbing them of their concentration and their ability to make plans. She will return to the pool, and he will find her there.

After many days of nightmarish fighting, the armies draw up opposite each other and the generals stride out to the center of the bloodsoaked battlefield to parley. But being in each other's presence overwhelms their martial self control. Without a word, they throw off their gear and couple like a pair of snakes before the astonished eyes of their two armies.

The appalled silence is broken only by the half-smothered cries of the generals. When their passion is spent at last, they get to their feet, smeared with dust and perspiration and semen, and only then do they seem to recall the presence of the soldiers. Voices joined in one bellow of madness the soldiers surge into the field like water rushing back in after a big rock drops through its surface. The soldiers rip the generals to pieces. Her head is flung deep into the plain, and his head is flung high into the foothills. They land facing in opposite directions. The armies are so completely infuriated that the soldiers pull off their armor and begin fucking each other, but the impulse lapses within the first few minutes. They have barely begun, and now they pull away from each other in disgust. The armies sullenly regroup, putting their armor back on again, grumbling, and generally acting as if they were obeying an order they would rather resist, but which, for now, they lack the will to. Some change their minds and pull their armor back off again, stripping naked out of sheer exasperation. A number of these toss themselves into the dust and roll around like children driven crazy by not knowing what to do with themselves. Sparks of lust or rage flare and vanish instantly; there is in both armies a feeling that could explode in an orgy of one kind or another, but the sparks fall on wet powder, the impulses reach consciousness only as they reach the point of dissipation.

The soldiers a pulled this way and that inside a giant ring consisting of weak inclinations, none stronger than five percent. A barrage of feeble impulses whips them to frenzied weakness. They keep beginning to do one thing, then dropping it to begin another, and end up doing nothing at all. The soldiers become sick of themselves. They want nothing they can do. They smell their hands, sticky with the blood of the generals. Is that a bit of her smell? Is that a bit of his smell? Do I know what I smell like?, the soldiers are wondering. The two armies try too hard and get headaches. Ants trickle in and out of the slack mouths of the torn-off heads of the two generals.

UNIT THIRTY-FIVE
NO'ÜNDEFERS

The pronoun relates back to its antecedent, which is considered prior to it even when the pronoun precedes the noun. Reference is always understood to operate in retrograde. In addition to this, however, unlanguage also employs a form known as deferral, which refers procedegrade, to what has not yet been fixed in a noun. While a pronoun stands in for a noun, a no'ündefer is integral to the formation of an undeclared noun prior to its apparition in language. A no'ündefer is formed by a collation of nouns indicated by divination, declined as prepositions, organized into mesostics of metrical feet (usually some form of epitrite), and then assembled into a single word in reverse pronoun form. No'ündefers are used where the expressive force heads off the edge of the language or into those domains which the eternally primordial languagechaos has reclaimed or never abandoned. They are pioneer or pilgrim words, which renounce strict reference in order to hold themselves open to a meaning yet to be. Not all no'ündefers succeed; some point the way to an outwork that never happens. In any case, the received word, always a revealed noun, will not be identical to the no'ündefer, which vanishes from page and memory at the advent of the new word.

In the passage below, identify at least ten places once occupied by no'ündefers.

UNIT THIRTY-FIVE READING

On special days the First Person would take us to Black Drink where sun blazed on slabs of white concrete laid out like altars and some uprights, the ground was bare and sandy, big pale rocks, kinky, dried out trees. Black drink was served in a special tray that had been carved with black letters to form a hollow page; the letters all communicated by little tubes so you could fill the page from a tap in one corner and watch the black drink rise in all the hollow letters until each one was a quivering meniscus of gleaming black in the shiny black tray. Each of us would receive the tray in turn and drink the writing from the corner tap. Then after a few seconds music would rise up to fill space. You had to give yourself to that music.

I drink the trembling writing. The white blazes blur and expand slightly, the whiteness is more intense in the heart, the trees are twistingly bedecked in fire jewelry, the sky is white music, music curtains me outside while inside me the black letters shiver. They are fluid opals made of outer space, inside the others just as they are inside me.

The celestial glare pools on the other side of the park. Long hyphens stretch up to the sky from the pool's vague surface. The hyphens gather together, gradually taking the form of a woman kneeling in the pool. She sits in three quarter profile angle to myself, her hands on her thighs, gazing absently from a collecting face. The whole body has a fibrous texture with a single grain, up and down, and I can see the blue and white filaments wafted up by the music into their appointed places like a phosphorescent cobweb sculpture emerging strand by strand. The black liquid opal eyes are her only dark; now white spore haze condenses out of the air to prepare her skin.

When the radiation music is ready, she rises to her feet and steps in this direction, looking demurely at where she places her feet and the moment she does the crescendo of the music explodes in a vaster crescendo of crashing chimes, crying out through me:

"It's *you!*"

—the fresh mycelial organism body of she who rotted herself to chandeliers and birds in a closed room, the music tells me now *she* is the Second Person, who had first been a man or man-shadow and then only a sportive manless noir shadow, who now is a revenant woman composed of brilliant hyphae jacketed in spore flour so that she appears to me as a kind of ghostly bundle of luminosity outlined in wan azure shadows.

Amazingly wrongly beautiful and already halfway here, Mycelia / Myceliana /

Mycelene, suffused in powdered light, me petrified by your sour beauty in a nameless unity of yearning panic reverence revulsion frenzy paralysis. Crazy energy seethes inside me while I don't move a muscle, because this is the closest I can manage to both running at you and away from you. The naked Second Person is a shattering sight.

She's standing in front of me, right now, so close I'm unable to see anything but her thighs and knees. I'm not made of ice, my body is relaxed, the tension is all deeper, so I don't look up to see if she is looking at me finally but I don't think she—you are. You're looking down and a bit to my left, but you see me. You came right up to me and stopped. You're still standing there.

You ball up your fist and punch me. I feel it splash across my face and jaw and I go down. Lying on my back with my legs still gathered and sitting on the ground I burst out laughing. My laughter sounds wrong, a little bit sick. When I get myself up, it's from off the polished floorboards of the teacher's study and he's coming in from the secret passage, already addressing me in a steady stream of foreign words that began in the hallway. White air, dark walls, the windows glow softly, there's a sizeable table he's crossing to, with a white two-boned draughtsman's lamp like a skeletal arm and a glass tumbler full of pens. The teacher is wearing heelless slippers. I can see the mustard colored heels of his socks. He has on a baggy sweater and his shirt cuffs are folded well back up his forearms. Pink skull framed in two white tufts. The room is hushed, in part by the steady hum of some machine. I feel like I have a touch of the flu. As if this impression prompted him, the teacher switches to a language I know.

"That's the fungal infection she gave you with that blow."

He doesn't look at me, making for the table and the swivel chair facing the windows. He is already complete down to his wife, who is his virtual twin, boiling potatoes and cabbage. Stepping through the French doors I discover a bower of foliage woven into a dome-like canopy. I follow the path to the wicket in the hedge and wander out over trackless meadows to the mountains and up. Barren, purplish, rock-strewn soil up here, with a sinuous road of tamped earth. The monastery up there. Here are the low, disintegrating stone walls of its gardens, each one is an oasis of weird plants spilling out of confinement. I see a mummified bikhuni, frail as a paper wasp nest, treading with short strides the narrow lane that winds through luxuriant beds of ornamental blossoming shrubs. At my approach she stops and carefully turns her puckered face to me. The mouth and eyes are shrivelled closed like three scars, and her bald eyebrows are fixed high up on her forehead, so her permanent expression might be grief, bemusement, or surprise. She reaches out and takes my hand in her twiglike fingers. For a while we walk hand in hand among the bizarre plants. I would expect her feet to be silent; she must weigh no more than a few pounds, but my feet are muffled too, and there is no sound apart from the wind's incessant murmuring. With her free hand, she points to a fungus grove corralled by rude stone pillars, and a drawn-out knell comes from the distant monastery that looms above us on the slope. I can't tell whether it's a bell, a horn, both, a low voice, a groaning cavern. The bikhuni releases my hand, presses her ragged orange cerements around herself, turns, and leaves. For a while I watch her slow progress in the direction of the monastery, presumably in obedience to that droning summons.

The fungus grows in mushrooms of all kinds, and long white stalks that thrust up among the nearly black grass and weeds; the base of each pillar is engulfed in wan, pastel-colored bubbles, and there are coarse nets of livid orange fibers growing over the bare sticks of the bushes they killed. Being close to it makes the infection warm up and hum; it feels as if I were humming. I feel it pull free of the inner lining of my throat and sinuses and bloom out of my mouth and nostrils in a gush of yellow spores that lunges toward the grove like living smoke. Where it lands it turns to slime and greedily devours whatever it touches. When I feel confident the stuff is all out of me, I back away, watching the patch coagulate and spread, eating with a liquid crackling sound.

UNIT THIRTY-SIX
THE OTHERWORLDLY

Another influence of parabolic grammar is the otherworldly, which is used whenever the content is fundamentally alien. This takes the form of a "warp," which might be understood as the unequal or nonmutual integration of two fabrics of different weaves, such that one is clearly an anomaly in the other by dint of being smaller. This warping influence causes all grammatical operators applied to the affected segment of content to be doubled: double plural, double negation (described below), double tensing, double qualification, double gendering, and so on. If a noun is influenced in the otherworldly, for example, the verb will acquire its number indicator while the noun will adopt the tense indicator of the verb. Likewise, if a preposition is employed, it must shift its attachment from noun to verb or verb to noun, mirroring the ordinarily mundial condition. Therefore, the sentence:

"He ran away from the buildings"

would, if the word "buildings" fell under the influence of the otherworldly, be rendered:

"Away from he rans the buildingan."

MODAL NEGATION OF THE OTHERWORLDLY

Modal negation of the otherworldly indicates that the content does not exist or happen in the world. As noted elsewhere, any passage in unlanguage will include function designators that, in conjunction with the prevailing topency, develop the mundial or "world" for that utterance. Cut out of such passages, however, there may be presences of things that are not in the world of the text. Entirely absent, these things have never existed in the world of the passage, which accounts for their power. Deleted things have a particular suggestiveness about them, and, in modally negative otherworldly things, this suggestivity becomes infinite. One meaning, therefore, underlies all such negations, however they may be equipped with particularities. No matter how seemingly impervious, minute, dense, or closed the it may be, the negative otherworldly will manifest infinity from the content. It is sometimes difficult to determine which element in the material is the object of the modal negation, in fact, it is impossible. Only complete passages, therefore are subject to this operation.

See if you can manage to pin down precisely the anus to the otherworld in this passage.

UNIT THIRTY-SIX READING

He first arrived at school in a coffin like any other new patient student. After the admissions exam, he was taken to his lodgings in a drawer seven files from the left and three ranks from the floor. Orientation was conducted in the decaying old morgue, under a peeling and cleft ceiling, enclosed in tiled walls streaked with rust so thick in places it formed dense triangular scabs, seated on smashed furniture. The injections made walking possible again and he reverted immediately to his old practice of walking for its own sake. This filled him with a wonderful nostalgia that never got old.

The teacher was always hard to make out; he always seemed to sit too far away to be distinctly seen. He was very likely old, extremely old. What dim radiance there was from the windows fell about his head in a gentle, misty fold; his head was shaggy, either with a prodigious accumulation of spider webs or a denigrated and colorless mane. He sat hunched brittly forward with his head nearly between his shoulders, and his wheezing, cracked voice bounded off the table in front of him before it reached us. His hands were black, but then he might have been wearing gloves, perhaps to preserve the suppleness of the skin. What could be seen of his face under the haystack of blanched floss atop his head was pale with black freckles, and his chin was goateed with dried blood. He was constantly spitting it up, and never even flinched, so used to it he was by now. When he turned his head, which wasn't often, and never very far, you could see the motes of glass sparkling in the blood, like a crystal five o clock shadow.

Under his instructions, the students would change stiffly and awkwardly into brilliantly white, starched shirts and aprons, celluloid collars and white ties for some reason, and white caps, and march into a glistening operating theater like a huge public bath. The schoolospital couldn't make up its mind whether or not death was a matter of perfectly barren, parched sterility or an overripe rottenness, so it cultivated both. Squared pillars scaled with white tile suspended the shadowy roof, with its vast skylight of creamily frosted glass panels. The downy light it admitted more than compensated for the absence of windows. Sparkling white tiles covered the walls, and there were capacious basins and silvery taps and spotless enamel tables and twinkling steel and glass cabinets filled with precious instruments and it wasn't a psychiatric hospital. The chamber is filled with the muffled reverberation of soft speech, so quiet it is almost drowned out by the incessant rustling of all those stiff shirts and aprons.

One of the newer students brings in his patient. He studies the patient, even as his assistant adjusts the rubbery limbs.

"Scalpel."

"Scalpel."

"Saw."

"Saw."

"Suction."

"Suction."

"Forceps."

"Forceps."

Peering through the thick layer of dust and grime encrusting his glasses, he examines the exposed organs, which are discolored and half dissolved.

The teacher's assistant comes lurching up to him, dragging her long white skirts, and observes over his shoulder.

"Partial saponification in this area," he spins his finger in a circle, "and decomposition well advanced in the upper chest and all throughout the abdomen. There's trouble areas here, here, and here," he says, pointing to tissues not yet affected by decay. "I'm thinking I should start with injections of cadaverine and rot culture A."

The assistant, whose face is hidden behind a cloth mask of white gauze, nods twice, deliberately, and moves on to the next table. The bandages climbing her neck stop a little below the hairline, and afford him a tantalizing glimpse of her mustard yellow skin, which seems as hard, dry, and shiny as a cheese rind.

One of the younger students fills a hypodermic and hands it to him hastily.

"Did you sterilize this?" he asks, holding the needle up in front of the younger student's face. The younger student shakes his head sheepishly, spilling larvae from one of his ears. He hands the needle back to the younger student.

"You know the rule. You want to give him infection?"

The student deathalcohols the needle hastily.

The operations are intended to promote decomposition. The student surgeons bending over their dead patients hide within their crisp white and sterile garments gaping, unsutured incisions, disembowelments, or bloated body cavities tight as drums, fit to burst with gas pressure and the collected putrescence that has subsided into the well of the body. These latter creak audibly when they bend at the waist, and are liable to burst out at the ass in streams of maggoty feces and a brackish gelatin of liquified tissues. Of course, the anus is plugged, but the pressures involved are frequently greater than can be kept bottled up; the sound of a popping cork is immediately followed by a viscous splattering and a rush of concentrated foulness. While such accidents are acutely humiliating and, at least in the sterile parts of the school, occasions for painstaking and laborious cleaning, voiding decayed material out the anus does however make it unnecessary to open the body, hence, a neater corpse, which is why the condition is tolerated.

Anyone dead must be treated or he or she may do more. It isn't right, but I must perform these treatments, because I am here. Students who don't study get thrown into school and stop being students, if they ever were, and what they are then I don't know, patients, some label or other gets a hold of them then. When I sit at the black table, alone in the shattered wreck room, a table that is more splinters than wood, excuses floating in the bullshit of my mind, the foot just appears there like a strangely elongated oversized candle. Just there, sticking up at the end of the table, as if someone were lying on the floor holding the foot up so I can see it. I try to act as if I don't notice and hurriedly finish my chipped enamel mug of black drink. The alternative to staying here is roving like a haunt in the woods, or stowing myself in the back of some cave or swamp bottom or a collapsing house if I can find one untenanted. The school is constantly sending us on field trips to places where there were massacres or mass suicides, mass graves, and mummies crawl out begging for energy every time, still shaken and half mindless from the searing heat of death. I don't want to end up like them.

It's embarrassing, but I have to admit that I'm drawn to stern people and places, like the schollospital. The hood of the school comes up over me like night time, when chatter dies. When I am away from the hopsichool but in the company of one of my fellow patients, all puckered and stinking, it takes nothing more than an exchange of sly glances between us, and the boredom of the brightest, most brainless day is smashed. The barking street and all its trouble become the veils for our unearthly misdeeds, and all is saved. When there's nothing to do, as usual, we can sit for hours listening to the silent whistling corpse radio, an eviscerated console or a crushed transistor box, tuned to no particular station, collecting waves of corpse talk as they sweep across the globe.

It was during just such a session of distracted "listening" that I caught a glimpse of her, a woman of fungus, beckoning to me. I saw her through the window, and I had to look around and point to myself before I could believe I was the one she was interested in.

I excused myself and made my way to the inverted gazebo by the stagnant pond. She had not waited for me, but had already begun to recite her spell. The spell finished, she turned to face me. The moment after the spell is recited is like no other; every detail that meets the eye becomes unbelievably vivid, seizing you. The anticipation is so strong you forget that you're waiting; you are nothing but anticipation.

A brief shower of rain, with widely-spaced drops, manifests itself, dappling the malodorous and thick surface of the pond. After no more than two or three minutes, it stops, and everything is just as it was before. There's no telling what happens next. She wants me to follow her. In among the trees invisible things are starting to appear, like fireflies coming out in summer. This was the idea, to show me the half gorgeous sea slugs half supercilious Syme caliphs and fatimas, the spangles and the eerie watching figures.

"So these are what?" I ask. "The secret masters?"

"Mm," she says, her face turned away.

"What did you expect?" she asks me sternly after a few more steps, her face still turned away. An ass like two puffballs a grooved expanse of blue-white back and a mane of colorless filaments, fingers tangled and crossed. She's followed the direction of my thoughts and impressions, overtaken them, gotten there before I could.

"Did you expect them to look like your father? Ronald Reagan? Or like you?"

I rub my jaw like I used to do. It's a gesture I stopped making a while back, because I didn't want to cultivate a morbid enjoyment of the pleached texture of the withered flesh there. Some remnant of vanity maybe, mingled with fear of finding nothing but a strip of exposed bone. My face was never anything to sing about and now less so than ever, but it is dear to me and I want to keep it as long as I can, if only for the habit.

I rub my jaw, and something comes away in my hand. A dull, bluish-white powder. Spores. The scene suddenly rises up within me; her chalky white hand must have left this mark when she slugged me. And here I've been walking around with it on my face ever since. Someone might have said something. How long has it been? I try to forget the question almost before I'm done formulating it.

The dimly phosphorescent shadow nudibranchs and gelatinous, smirking translucencies shaped like sinister pashas with tiny feet and hands are all around us now, scattered in the dark wood whose trees seem to reach up and block out the sky with outspread hands. Lichens shaped like colorful little tiles climb up the trees in peculiarly rectilinear clusters and I get the idea this whole forest is something else in disguise.

"Look," I tell her backside. "What are you showing me all this for anyway? I'm only a corpse and I do a corpse's work, that's all. My soul went on about its business a long time ago."

"This *is* your soul," she says, waving offhandedly at our surroundings, and still without turning. Black liquid is flowing down from between her buttocks and legs, running down her thighs toward the knees; the liquid isn't blood, it's thin and yet completely black like ink, but all the same it spreads slowly like a stain, my soul dripping from her anus where the stopper must have come loose. If this is a bad sign, she doesn't seem too concerned by it, maybe it doesn't concern her, maybe I am concerned.

"Where are we going?" I ask.

She points deeper into the trees, deeply into her anus where the dark is greatest.

"This isn't," I say a moment later, and stop. I know the answer already. There isn't any moral or discovery up there. Or death—I've done that. I can't know what's up there, and she can't make me understand. But I have an idea. You don't just rot, you rot *away*. You rot on a journey. Away to where? Just 'away'?

UNIT THIRTY-SEVEN
PREPADJES

However innocent each individual instance of preposition may be, taken as a whole, the use of prepositions is the grammatical equivalent of sodomy. That is to say, an unnatural act which goes against the very grain of language, replete with improper pleasure. The preposition, when dragged away from the other words, isolated, and interrogated, cannot account for itself. It is a parasite with no meaning of its own. Its behavior follows no strict pattern. Now it is found here, now it is found there, wandering, aimless, rootless, with no fixed employment, no documentation, no destination.

    The stability of grammar requires a strict quarantine of prepositions, and their use must be severely controlled. Preposition poses a direct threat to the very concept of case. This is why immortal cases alone may be used in conjunction with prepositions, as only that which is immortal and unchanging will be sufficiently impervious to the demonism of preposition. With proper care and treatment, and unstinting use of the ablative, prepositions can become useful parts of speech. Even so, it is not always clear, once the preposition becomes involved, that the immortal noun has not somehow been, if not exactly altered, well, then cast in a certain altered light. If one speaks of going "into eternity," for example, this implies one begins outside eternity and then enters it like a drugstore or retirement, when, as time without duration, eternity cannot be modified in this way, receiving the action of entering. And yet, there is a reason to express oneself in these terms—a reason that originates with the preposition itself.

Unlanguage makes use of a number of different categories of grammatical hybrids, one of which involves the combination of prepositions and adjectives. The prepadje will provide the quality of the adjective with a vectrality, by means of the preposition, which is analogous to "spin" in atomic physics. The adjective must be in one of the ablative cases, and the preposition is suffixed to it entire.

Examples of prepadjes include, in narrative order: upwhite, bysour, atrecent, abovevague, besideclear, towardround, downsick, insoft, alonglate, fromsad, afterquick, underinsane, withoutnext, outdead, awayrotten.

UNIT THIRTY-SEVEN READING

He first arrived at the school in a straightjacket, like any other new student patient. After the admissions exam, he was taken to his lodgings in room B345. Orientation took place in his absence, since he was trying to escape out a bathroom window at the time. The next day, he was discovered perched atop a corner of the building, unable to follow his hastily-planned escape route any farther than this point, and obstinately unwilling to turn back. He was returned to his room without incident. A series of injections caused a kind of alteration in him that was so basic it stymied all his efforts to describe it; he was not so confident this was an improvement, if only because, in producing this new state of mind, the injections had removed all the old ones, and thus deprived him of the means of comparing them.

The teacher was very difficult to understand, using rhetoric that was so relentlessly involuted and ironic that he found it impossible to follow; was that, just now, a bald statement? Or was the baldness at all exaggerated, which would make it sarcastic? Or was the sarcasm itself the object of the irony, so that the teacher was showing us the sort of person who is sarcastic about such things? It seemed possible that the irony might turn full circle, saying the same thing on several registers without pointing to anything further, so the utterance in question was like a whole chorus of all possible meanings without any one being chosen. He couldn't tell whether all this ellipiticism on the teacher's part was just an unfortunate tic, whether the teacher were actually saying things as profound as they seemed to be, or if the teacher's ellipticism itself was the point and if so of what, or on the other hand whether the teacher were bullshitting everyone and nobody had the nerve to say the emperor had no clothes. He didn't doubt that the teacher was capable of shamming this too, deliberately creating the impression that he was a charlatan, perhaps to weed out all but the most penetrating—although this could also be a charlatan's trick, since any onlooker who detected falsehood could, if in receipt of this impression of secret testing, be rerouted, through vanity, and what is more dependable?, back in the direction of trust—or perhaps because he felt that he really was a charlatan in the way that some wise men insist that they are fools, which would make this fake faker's posture an expression of deep and extremely subtle humility. Or arrogance, if he were a faker who made a point of actually telling his dupes to their faces that they were his dupes. That his teacher casually spat blood so often, and barely noticed it or bothered to wipe it up at all not only affected his sympathies but also made the teacher seem more credible. He knew he was assuming that suffering and truth go together, but just because they don't always doesn't mean that they don't usually.

Under the teacher's instructions, the students would blunder to their seats, awkward in their straightjackets, and laboriously fill out language exams with stubs of pencils gripped in their teeth. The fantastic effort of writing with a pencil in his mouth on a page that kept slipping and sliding on the nearly glasslike smoothness of the desk, which was a children's desk too small for his adult body, and of listening to the incredibly complicated lecturing (to which one had to listen if one were to pass the secondary, thankfully only oral, exam that immediately followed each class, and which had to be passed if the student were not to repeat the lesson) of the teacher, who often wrote things on the board behind him that none of the students ever saw because they were all bent over their desks with pencils in their mouths trying frantically to write without driving the paper to the floor—retrieving fallen pages was a responsibility left entirely to the students, and involved wrenching free from the tight grip of the too small desk and falling on one's face, grabbing the paper with the mouth, and then jerking violently backward with the stomach muscles until it became possible somehow to get the knees under the center of gravity, and thus rise to the feet, and thus squirm back into the desk which was like a vise, and deposit the page of exercises, now crumpled and wet, onto the top of the desk, hoping that, in its current, scalloped, condition far from being flat, it wouldn't be swept back to the floor again by, for example, a puff of air from the broken windows, a sneeze from the other students so many of whom were afflicted with chronic hay fever and allergic reactions to the injections, or the constantly-swinging cafeteria door, which opened onto this classroom and was used with great frequency, and so the student would try to prevent this, the being-blown-off-again of the paper, by flattening the paper as best he or she could, usually banging it down with repeated blows of the forehead, although this could lead to injury, or rolling it flat with the side of the face, although this could cause the paper, sticky with saliva from when it was picked up from the floor, to adhere to the face and be rendered unavailable for use unless the student could manage to scrape it off again, although really the only way to do that was to scrape the face against the edge of the top of the desk with the almost inevitable result that the paper would again fall to the floor—could induce attacks of violent panic or hysteria, fits of unrestrained laughter, weeping, or incontinency, or catatonic stupor, or even paralysis. There must have been something behind the apparent futility that justified the harm that these lessons did, so patently, but what that might be, he had no idea.

Interview excerpt conducted 24:22 on 17.10.57.77 VIP (Volunteer Inmate Patient) narrator number 314152965:

"Sniff they would take us in a bus to the far side of the hospital grounds three times a week. We had to enter the minds of old people and wreck their memories and motor control and sometimes other neurological faculties using ancient dero technology hospital administrators discovered in a subterranean cavern at the end of a tunnel that they could get into because of a subsidance in the wall of the basement of the old laundry.

"The cavern was vast but first you had to go through the laundry and you could tell a lot of the machines had already been changed. Some had fallen apart over time, but others were mutated by the waves from the ancient technology I mentioned and I think some of them had been tampered with. Sniff I don't know by who. Anyway, they'd lead us down into this break in the wall, where there was a secret passage and there were steps, little steps, that came out in a small room like a cloakroom, but all stone with elaborate carvings of geometrical designs up along the ceiling in a frieze, sniff and there was an irregular stone doorway and then a kind of control room filled with like instrument panels made of turquoise that looked like what you might find at NORAD or in a sci-fi movie. There were a lot of brass clam shells on the consoles. Yes, well that's how I think of them I guess they were, I didn't know they were brass and they weren't really clamshells, it's just what they looked like sniff. So then we went in alone one at a time, into the cavern that was just past the control room. The room, the control room, sniff had a big window. You could see the cavern, but the window was unbreakable, it might have only been a screen. The door to the cavern was like a giant stone tire that fell in over a big crack.

"... The cavern was dark, you couldn't see the walls or the ceiling, and you could just make out big shapes of things up there. Sniff you had to go to this sort of gazebo. It stood all by itself with cables coming out of the base and down into the rock, or going up from the top into the dark. The gazebo was made of metal that looked like chalk and there was a pillar like a chair inside facing a rotunda, like a turnstile, and there was a candlestick in the middle with a black metal ball on top, sniff like maglite metal, and you had to sit in the chair and put the backs of both your hands in these clear stone cradles on either side of the candlestick and it would respond to you based on your brain energy level. I had a lot so the moment I put my hands in the shells sniff they would light up and this big just tube of light would shoot up into the top from the ball, and all the machinery starts up. There's overhead there's—you can barely see them, but there's big spinning onion shaped things, like tops, sniff and there's chiming and a rumble and giant transparent gears made of light, flashing different colors like glass in sunlight, and rolling. They just hang there, and machine parts made of fire, oozing flame tubes and cones, fire anemones, all kinds of fires so that at first sniff you don't realize you're looking at flames. Some are small and very close, too, like they make clusters like bunches of flowers, with the gears meshed together, transparent and just hanging in space.

"So from there we would go through a hatchway, a thick metal hatchway, one at a time, and that would get us into the brains of the patients in a hospital for old people the administrators had the coordinates for. We had to go through their minds sniff and disconnect parts that were designated for us by cubes of yellow light, which were projected by surgeons on the trouble spots. Trouble for them, not for the patients. We were doing this to create more work for the doctors, I guess. It was like defusing a bomb; sniff you had to look at the thing, like you would be looking at a dog sitting there wagging its tail, or a bag of golf clubs, or a grandchild or something, old fashioned dancing, and find the different colored filaments inside and unhook them in the right order. If you got the order wrong you could get stuck sniff and then you could be mistaken for a memory or an imaginary person and integrated into the old person brain while your body, back in the cavern, would be in a coma unless you could get loose. Or you might kill the patient, if you did anything to affect the autonomic nervous system. Motor nerves were OK, in fact we spent most of our time disconnecting them because it's a lot of work; you can sniff you know, deal with a memory with a few moves but motor nerves take, it takes a lot of disconnecting, like days and days, to have any really noticeable effect, you know?

"We all stole. I took a lot less than the others. They'd take watches and radios and sniff things, whatever. The problem, though, the reason I didn't want to really care to take anything much was that it was all memory hardware so you know like a flashlight would be an old flashlight and the batteries wouldn't work when you brought it back because they would be forty years old or something. Sniff. I took a ring, jewelry, you know, stuff that wouldn't break. I took some old photos. I took a brick once, just to see if I could bring it back. That's it. That one there, I brought that back. That was in one of the memories. Yeah it looks like any other brick sniff. It's amazing how clear the memories are. Like a handkerchief, with the weave and everything. All the specifics, it's really incredible. What I mainly took were the nerves. Once you unhook them, there's no function for that nerve any more, so I could just keep it. But you had to find the other end to unhook that, or it would just snap back when you came back out again, and you almost never could find that other end. You're looking at them, I self-implanted them. You do it sniff you, you do it while you're still discorporated, in the memory, you just just you know put it inside, like that. It hooks into your own nervous system to enhance it. Everyone in the program has an enhanced nervous system, but I'm the one who thought of recycling the nerves. That was my idea."

The patient enters the city inside the forest inside the barren plain that was at one time swept by beams of negation from a half-conical structure full of foam. The city is in the forest, meaning the trees grow among the buildings and there are no open vistas as there are in regular cities. In a sense, the city is like an overgrown derelict invaded by trees, and in another sense, it is built around the trees, and in a different sense, at a certain angle of light, the trees and buildings both seem to be made of some white material like bone, and laterated with black lines, and randomly patched with clusters of little, colorful tiles.

A soft, golden haze of summer sunlight arches over him as he enters one of the smaller buildings, a white adobe house, brushing aside fragrant, knee-high grass of a June meadow where a virginity is being escaped. The patient barges into the middle of this memory and sets to his task like a sullen maintenance man, kneeling down with grunts of discomfort for his bending knees and reaching into the black soil by the tentative lovers, groping down there then tugging angrily. With snarls and curses he yanks something loose and pulls it out of the ground, a writhing snake of pure, deep blue color, frayed at either end, almost without texture, silently twisting and trying to wriggle free. He unzips the front of his blue coveralls and thrusts it inside, then turns and drives his arms up to the elbows into the prostrate lover tearing out fistfulls of red and blue nerves. The sunlight dwindles, the light becomes actinic and cold, the grass disappears, the prostrate lover whimpers and shrivels, now an old man lies on rocks embracing a large rock with weakening arms.

The patient trudges out of the scene, intent on his duty if not enthusiastic about it. He crosses the threshold of the small adobe house and is back under the canopy of the trees, but something has changed. The daylight has vanished, the forest floor is like a huge sable rug, the trees are like golden sketches scratched on a black background, their branches adorned with dim stars or medallions that give off blurry rays. He can see his own hands in a dim, uniform, golden light that casts no shadows. There are, he notices now, small golden medallion or star flowers or shrubs dotting the forest floor as evenly as designs on a carpet. Weaving in and out of the trees, looking for his next house, the patient encounters a miniature lion with the head of a young boy, emerging from among the trees with the same sort of purposive manner he has. The creature greets him in a very faint voice. It has black eyes with extremely small, distinct white irises, and these are very moist, and deep black eyes; the neck engulfs nearly all of the back of its head, and meets the shoulders in a kind of mane or ruff collar of feathery, pale reddish curls like the hair on the head. The boy-face has a melancholy, sympathetic expression that isn't young. The pelt is very short, like a deer's or a horse's, and buff colored; the body has the elastic roundness and borderline sensuousness common in depictions of animals in Tibetan paintings. The feet are hooves. It might be a deer's body. The creature tiptoes over to him and asks him a question —

"What are you doing here?"

—in a voice that sounds like a harp would sound if it were a wind instrument.

"Me?" The patient's voice is rusty with disuse. "I'm wrecking old people's nervous systems."

"I am a hallucination agent," it says, rolling its head. It rolls its head constantly as it speaks. "Pan is my master. Who is yours?"

"I'm from the state psychiatric hospital."

"You are one of the minions," the creature says, "of the teacher whose mouth never stops dripping blood. What are you serving him for?"

The patient shrugs.

"It just kind of happened," he says shamefacedly. "It's his *own* blood ..."

"I am an agent of second childhood," the creature says. "I improve fantasy and father chimeras in the minds of the elderly and the mentally infirm. What have you got there?" A slight but distinct sharpness comes into the creature's tone as it asks this question, indicating with a forehoof the bulge in the front of the patient's coverall. He unzips and sheepishly pulls out a handful of nerves that struggle feebly, like half-dead worms.

The creature looks at him, sadly.

"You must stop," it says.

"I can't," the patient answers, with dignity. "I'm bound by ancient dero technology from deep below the surface of the earth."

"But you're doing harm," the creature says, almost as an afterthought.

"I can't quit. I gotta dree my weird—my body is back there still. This form is only a robot. I don't want my body walking off without me."

The patient has already intuited that the creature is a projection like himself, serving in some parallel but opposite cause. It will understand what he means without requiring further explanation.

The creature says, "Suicide is time travel," using its eyes, turning its anti-eyes on him with a gaze that opens huge regions into him. "Suicide is travel in time and space. Suicide is travel to another time."

"You mean I ought to break with the platinum head and go off on my own?"

"Suicide is a journey to another place."

"... and drop out of class, and get an F on my record?"

"Why would you stay?"

"Are you kidding?! Oh my God! You don't know what it's like! You've never been down into the dero cavern and gone through. I don't know how you get projected, but man, the way we go! The curtain just goes over you and then it's all lights and darks with, it's kind of like a fountain in the dark, total dark and these fires blast up and move and go out and blast and then light goes over you like the sun, summer sun and that negative beat comes on like UN,

UN-UN UN-UN

UN-UN UN-UN

UN-UN UN-UN
UN-UN UN-UN

—you go straight to Negative Machine and you're like, 'I'm a bird! I'm a train!' You're lifted right up to space edge negative and *just* held there in negative velocity, with the sun blazing right next to you on the rim of the crystal star disc at the outermost negative point where the darkness is transformed to superdarkness a million times denser and more rapid than the false darkness of earth since the betrayal of neutral esteem in anti-history, and then it's like, 'OK, you get to see this but now you have to go fuck up old people's minds.' Then it pulls you, like, through into the mind zone, here."

As he chants the beat, the darkness of the forest grows denser and denser, engulfing the golden trees, the evenly-spaced diadem plants, and the creature. Soon the darkness is so total that only the white irises of the chimera can still be seen, dim as two spots of luminous paint in a dropclothed theater, growing farther and farther apart, still rolling to and fro.

"But do you really think," the soft voice of the creature asks, "that this experience exemplifies the ultimate negation that you want?"

"What do you mean?" the patient asks. He doesn't know where he is now; while his mind was on what he was saying and associated visual images, he was only very vaguely aware of the idea that he was prevailing over the agent of a rival power that had vainly thought to seduce him. Someone had mistaken him for an easy mark, and he hadn't had much confidence himself, but things worked out differently—his vision and his enthusiasm lifted him to the occasion. This interpretation of events is precarious, though, and is already teetering with the creature's question. He had felt, without being truly aware of it, that he was going all the way, but now that limit is being brought into question and the distance between the two irises, which resemble a pair of identical snowflakes fixed in the night, is greater than ever.

"There's another dimension where negation goes as far beyond the one you speak of as the one you speak of is beyond ordinary negation."

"What's that you say?" the patient cries in a stentorian voice. "Another, even greater negation—impossible! The archaic wisdom of the deros is unsurpassable!"

"You don't know that ..."

"But ... but could it be true?" the patient asks himself in a harsh whisper.

"Now you are beginning to talk like a true madman," the creature says approvingly.

Melodramatically the patient clutches at his head.

"You!" he shrieks. "You were never in the city in the forest in the plain that opens doors into the brains of the elderly, you were in <u>my</u> brain the whole time, doing to me what I do to others!"

The pupils of the two white irises become exclamation points.

"You have corrected my madness!" the patient exclaims in a voice that combines in its wild expression both a recrimination and a tentative note of triumph.

"Now, show me the greater negation! I must have it, do you hear!"

As if a slide had been removed from a projector and not replaced, everything before the patient turns white with the exception of two black exclamation points which stereoscopically merge as he moves his head to form a single three-dimensional exclamation.

UNIT THIRTY-EIGHT
HOLOPATHY

In addition to phrases in the ordinary sense, unlanguage makes use of inflection-phrases and inflection-passages; these are to sequences of grammatical inflections what ordinary phrases and passages are to words and sentences. All languages, in fact, use at least rudimentary forms of inflection phrasing with respect to customary word order: subject first, then verb, then object; or, first the verb, then the subject, then the object; or yet again, the object coming first, then the subject, then the verb. The ghost haunts the hospital. Haunts the ghost the hospital. The hospital the ghost haunts. Unlanguage extends this patterning to larger and more elaborate sequences. There are occasions in which it is appropriate to place the verb last, the subject in a preceding sentence, and to corral prepadjes between them.

A difference is produced whenever a sign, a letter, a word, an inflection, a phrase, an inflection-phrase, a passage, or an inflection-passage are repeated. The first repetition is not entirely the same as the first appearance of the phrase, because that was a novelty and not a repetition. In music, the beginning of the first repetition is largely what allows the listener to locate the end of the melodic line. The second repetition is unlike either the first appearance of the phrase or the first repetition, because it is the second repetition, and so on.

Unlanguage uses special phrase and passage markers called holopaths wherever repetition occurs. Parables in particular have a distinctive broken span holopath, often known as the exhaustion holopath. That feeling of exhaustion is a sign that everything is about to begin all over again; this is why it is essential to go to the point of exhaustion. It is always farther away, which is a repetition of the infinity of parables. Parables are short, but, if they are parables, they go on and on with the reader.

It is important for students to realize that the infinite and the ineffable are not limits; at most they are only moments of exhaustion.

Identify the incessant sections of the passage below, and label the inflections.

UNIT THIRTY-EIGHT READING

A young woman sleeping in a massive, four-poster bed with rich, faded hangings and many ponderous ornaments, struggles under the weight of an oppressive dream. She breaks free, opens her eyes, and lies there for a moment. There's a hair stuck in her throat. Swallowing repeatedly, trying to force it down, doesn't work, and it's seated itself too far back for her fingers to reach without gagging her. The bed is not too warm; even though she has been lying in it for hours, it's still a little cool. It's a morass and she pulls herself out of it. The grandfather clock in the entrance hall sonorously rings twelve strokes.

Not knowing exactly what she is doing, she wanders over to the curious table that stands oddly placed in the room, not against the wall, not in the middle of the floor. The table is tall, nearly up to her bosom, shallow, only maybe two hands' breadths wide, and narrow, less than three feet. There's a green cloth on it with a Chinese design; resting on the cloth there is a battered letter opener with a bone handle, a plain white figurine that she has yet to look at really, and some glittering stuff that looks like stage jewelry. The carpet beneath her feet has ridden up a little here and she stumbles on the raised fold, bumping into the table. The figurine drops onto the carpet and breaks silently in half. She stares at it in a daze, still not fully awake.

When she looks up again, she sees a sight that paralyzes her with terror! A huge figure, swathed entirely in white gauze, looms up before her.

It's a gigantic ghost! she thinks.

The figure's head is lost in the gloom of the high ceiling, and she can't see anything below its waist either, nor the hands, which must be hanging loosely—no, clasped at the waist—and the body is bent forwards by some monstrous deformity.

Half choked with fright and unable to call out, she rushes to the door and out into the cheerless stone passageway. This passageway gives out into another passageway, which opens onto a staircase, which opens onto a gallery, which opens onto another passageway, which opens onto a stairway she cannot take because a severed human head lies there at its foot, staring at her glassily and speaking, or trying to speak, whether to her or to itself she can't tell because, with a cry of disgust and fright she rushes back along the passageway, which opens onto a gallery, which opens onto a staircase which she ascends to a passageway, which opens onto a another passageway, which opens onto passages on passages which gather like an asphyxiating mass of blankets and mattresses.

A young woman struggles in the grip of a bad dream, and starts awake. She is lying in a sprawling, luxurious four poster bed, which dominates a cheerless stone bedchamber high in a castle. The grandfather clock in the middle of the main hall rings midnight. Dragging herself from the bed, which is still warm, she crosses the room, vaguely thinking of the ewer of water on the dresser. There's a hair stuck in her throat she can't manage to swallow away, and she wants to try washing it down instead. En route, she blunders into a curious table that stands at a useless distance from the wall, not far enough out to make it possible to pass between it and the wall, not close enough to be out of the way, and knocks over a nondescript figurine that stood on it. The figurine drops to the carpeted floor and breaks silently in half.

Numbly, she picks the two pieces up and puts them on the table again, then proceeds to the ewer and her drink of water. Through the pointed and mullioned windows she can see the new moon hanging in a deep indigo sky, a darkened globe reflected in the pool below, and orange pyres burn on the ocean, nearly at the horizon. An inexplicably fierce, caustic feeling of despair washes over her, as if the last human beings were burning out there. The despair becomes the room and she rushes for the door, to stop it, or to get out before it's too late. The door opens onto a cheerless stone passageway, which opens onto another passageway, which opens onto a gallery, which opens onto a stairway, but she cannot take the stairs because there, lying at their feet, is a severed human head. She doesn't know the face, but the head is alive, staring at her, and speaking, although whether to her or to itself she can't tell. It seems to be trying to warn her, and the next moment she has plunged through the trapdoor, her gauze nightgown catching on an irregularity on the rim and ripping entirely right up the side, and now the insane cold of water, frothing brine at the bottom of the shaft, struggling, unable to touch bottom, her body going numb, above her the dim square is closing, she is dashed against the shore and pinned there in a smothering current.

Difficulty swallowing eventually robs her of her sleep. She must have swallowed a hair; now it's stuck in her throat. Rising wearily from the heavy, hot coverlet she crosses the cheerless stone chamber to the table where the water pitcher sits. Reaching for the glass, she accidentally knocks a white figurine to the floor, where it breaks silently in half on the carpet. She'll pick it up in a moment. For now, the water. The old grandfather clock at the bottom of the stairs rings midnight as she empties the glass. The air in the room is close, despite the open windows; she loosens the purchase her gauzy nightgown has around her shoulders and fans herself a little, still half dreaming.

Suddenly her entire body contracts with piercing cold as the lid of the cedar chest at the foot of the bed slowly lifts. A severed human head rises into view, its murmuring voice trapped in the chest, which resonates like the sounding box of a guitar or a harp. The eyes, marred with brown stains, are fixed on her with burning intensity. The ragged stump trails a dangling fringe of dripping flesh. With a scream of terror she rushes from the room and out onto the gallery.

There is a sound: a booming, a scraping or whirring noise like pebbles. Those words occur to her, "like pebbles," and even in her fear they seem anomalous. And there is a sight, now: a tunnel with dirt floor and leprous white walls, all densely covered in minute scribbling in luminous black ink. She is stark naked in the street. The only light comes from the half moon, but those streetlights could crash on any second and her only possible refuge is an anomalous ten storey apartment building, not a psychiatric hospital, new, all of white concrete, that rises from the center of a block of regular two and three storey houses. The apartment building has an unlocked sliding door in the back, or so she thinks, but she can't find how to get to it. The houses have driveways and there are back alleys but the tower remains obstinately far away.

The moon slinks into the tower through one of its high balconies and the sky becomes a spectacle of densely tangled constellations. The doors back here in the alleyway are all encrusted with sugar, meaning he has been there, and she ineffectually tries to cover herself as he emerges from a shadow, face first.

His face has clouds, a blue face like the ocean seen from space, and tiny clouds moving over it like wisps of mobile shaving foam. There's something animal like in the expression, not exactly feral but animal like. His clothes are full of salt, and there's a thin, granular crust of salt on his face, his hair clotted with perspiration, like the severed head.

He wants her to select her syllabary, whatever that means, his Montaignese face a little dim and spectral against a blackening blue sky and wan moon. If you use it right, others will understand, he says.

A naked young woman lies sleeping in a colossal four poster bed. With a groan that grows louder and louder, she stirs, then wakes, pushing herself up off her stomach. Rolling over, she sits up and gazes across the expanse of a cheerless stone bedchamber. Now, gently squeezing her neck, she swallows again and again, as though she has a hair stuck in her throat. Pitching the overheated covers aside, she gets up and crosses the room. The old grandfather clock at the top of the stairs rings midnight.

She unscrews the cap on her water bottle and tilts it to her lips. A trickle escapes down her chin and meanders along her neck toward the hollow of her collarbone. Lowering the bottle again with a soft gasp of slaked thirst she rubs the droplet away with her fingers and goes to the window. The night air moves almost imperceptibly over her skin.

With a shout of laughter, a little boy flashes by the window, holding on to the string of a pale kite that veers and caracoles far above the castle, as if the moon were a stereotypical housewife startled by a mouse. She only sees the boy for an instant, but he sees her and points, laughing, eyes huge and white, as he darts by, and she crouches at once, hiding herself below the window sill. Craning her neck, without getting up, she tries to follow the line down to its source, but there are too many walls in the way. Another shout of laughter—the boy's head, sticking out from among the crenelations, looking down at her. Starting away from the window, she backs into the table and knocks a figurine to the floor, where it breaks silently in two on the carpet. She can't find anything to put on. Down below, incense melts to pure mountain air. Angels sing to you of a world of lacerating intensities, monstrous good, glorious evil, suffocating freedoms, liberating enslavements, enlightenment without understanding, unlearned knowledge, nonsense meaning, terrifying comfort.

There's a brook that runs between huge cleft stones, a brook of clear stinking water. By the bank, a child with outerspacewater in her eye, angel mouth full of bubbles and glass, loading her dense language, green bubbles and blue glass, red glass. She's like a slow angel caught in the middle of an awkward blink. The water is clear, and at the same time foully polluted. There's a severed human head lying on its side on a flat stone high up in the stream. The water flows around and over it, and the lips move. The water washes away the sound and the words. The angel knows what they are. She's going to say something and it won't be information—welcoming and feeling welcomed—the sing song voice of the kindergarten teacher when seeing becomes dying—when seeing becomes dying?—she answers with an ominous smile of anticipated understanding. The bank of the river of alcohol of death. The moon has set fire to the tower; there's a snow-white conflagration burning there, with rays of brilliant coolness and white, acid clouds of steam.

The woman has been groping in the alcohol for something. She looks down at her hands which are red and shiny with cold, mineralizing. Among the trees there are white clouds from graves in a dark indigo sky. Black night trees with white cloud foliage.

"In between each stroke of my living heart comes the beat of my death heart—if I could quickly manage to travel slowly then my hearts could travel anywhere."

A young woman is sleeping in the great four poster bed. Her rest is uneasy, and she stirs this way and that, as if she were trying to say no to something, or to look away. With great effort, she seems to lift the lead apron of her dream and escape into the scarcely less oppressive atmosphere of this cheerless, stone chamber high in an ancient castle. She feels as though she's swallowed a hair, and gets up for a drink of water. The tepid, gluey water gives her no relief, and a surprisingly bitter expression creases her face. Out of sheer peevishness she snatches up the nearest thing to hand, a worthless white figurine, and tosses it to the floor, where it breaks silently in two on the carpet. Going to the window, she starts. A young woman, wearing only a diaphanous, gauzy white nightgown, is walking as if in a trance toward the burying ground where generations of the family who owns this castle lie inhumed. She is walking to the icy threshold of her own tomb.

The young woman at the window starts, seeing a young woman, dressed only in her gauzy nightgown, fleeing the castle, evidently in terror. She throws glance after glance back at the silent, impassive walls, her mouth a black oval, her hair flying. Thorns and brambles tear at the wildly overgenerous billows of her gauzy nightgown, and she disappears around a bend in the road leading to the wood.

Starting, the young woman catches sight of a young woman, wearing nothing more than a gauzy white nightgown, walking toward the castle from the direction of the village. She moves stiffly, without looking to one side or another, her arms extended out in front of her. It's impossible to tell if her eyes are open or shut, but she could be sleepwalking. Pale, shockingly pale and gaunt for a sleepwalker.

With a start, she notices a young woman in a gauzy white nightgown and nothing else, not even a peignoir, clinging in terror to a ledge that runs along the outer wall of the castle, not far from a decrepit, half-ruined balcony which, if she recalls correctly, opens onto the desecrated chapel whose doors have for so long been boarded up.

The grandfather clock at the end of the hall strikes midnight.

The young woman surveys the scene outside, the moat, the dark sky matted with clouds, the threatening scribble of the woods, the neglected and increasingly shapeless gardens, the dim gazebo, when she starts, her eye suddenly arrested by a diaphanous blotch of whiteness crossing the grounds. It's a young woman, wearing an abundant, if flimsy-looking, sort of shroud or wrapping. A gauzy nightgown. She is walking toward the forest, resolutely. Her bare feet flash in the sable grass at her feet.

The young woman calls out to her from the window, trying to warn her about the woods, which are banned at night, but to no apparent effect. She rushes from the room, her diaphanous white nightgown flying all about her like a sail, and sets out after the mysterious young woman who is venturing to enter the woods at night, and clad only in her diaphanous gauzy nightgown. It is a wood full of goblins no. No, full of no one.

There, on a tree, is the sign of the grimacing mouth, twisted with speech, stained with its own blood. Like the curse that marked Sir John, she thought.

The young woman, her abundant dark hair seems as heavy as wet clay, moulded down around her head and shoulders, kneeling before the severed human head that lies in a stone box atop the little Roman altar to Cybele that legends said was secreted in this wood but which no one had ever supposedly been able to find. How do you describe the feeling here? It's horrifying, morbid, and yet it's as if paradise were very close by. The young woman is performing death magic in a trance, burning incense and making incense magic by turning skeins of incense into words and prayers that vanish in space, seeking out the right ears, or the right bosoms, to ply for secrets or to curse. The clouds open in the gaps in the trees, and she can see through those gaps all the way to outer space, all the way to the platinum head that hovers out there, so tiny from here you can barely make the features out, Mycelia before the altar, quietly making incisions into the face of the severed head.

Overwhelmed with fright at her dreams, the young woman thrashes awake, nearly immobilized in a tangle of heavy blankets. She lunges desperately to one side, as if she were trying to get out of quicksand, and falls halfway onto the floor. Creeping forward on her hands, she drags her legs free and stands upright, disheviled hair nearly covering her face. Not watching where she goes, she rushes to the nightstand, where a jug of water and a drinking glass are waiting for her, and obliviously knocks something over, a little white figurine, which breaks silently in two pieces on the carpet. Gradually, the young woman grows calmer. A kind of resignation spreads over her face, as she frees it from her hair. She sits in a lean, high-backed chair next to the window. Behind her, in the air that trickles almost lifelessly around the high crenelations of the castle, she can hear a monotonous soliloquy, the voice of a severed human head.

She takes one deep breath after another. Her eyes sink. It looks as if she were going to sleep, but there's a sternness of effort, a decisiveness, a will, that is not consistent with that. She is dying. She dies. Lividity blossoms across her face, her exposed upper chest and shoulders, her arms. Bruiselike marks run in streaks along her features. Her body swells and discolors under the glazed observation of a moon that just hangs there without budging in stopped night. Enormous blisters bulge out from her face and head. Her outline melts. The bones of her skull are emerging from the melting stickiness of the liquefying face. The grandfather clock just outside her door rings midnight. The ringing goes on and on. It's not possible to count all those rings. It must not have reached twelve yet. It's been ringing for such a long time. It might have missed twelve. It sounds as if it were searching for the twelfth ring, trying to hit on it maybe by pure luck.

The door bursts open and the young man appears. He stands in the door, his hand on the knob, staring weirdly at the flourishing mass of corruption in the chair. Despite the depredations of decay that have scrubbed nearly all the flesh from his bones, leaving at best a kind of deliquescent coating of stinking paste, the cleft chin and the thick wavy hair she so admired are still discernible. He is as pregnant with his own decay as she is with hers.

A shock of dignity suffuses them both as their gazes meet; two beings undergoing the anguish of rebirth. The nightmare is ennobling them. He staggers over to her and collapses in her outstretched, deformed arms. From the shadows of the chamber Sir John emerges, a man with yellowish, waxy skin, his face largely concealed behind a dark beard. His aristocratic bearing is not diminished by the shabby raincoat. He's tall, broad, and flat. Sorrowfully and without surprise he gazes on the lovers mingling there beneath the moon. There's a sound like a suppressed sob in his throat, and a trickle of blood crosses his lower lip and vanishes into his beard. It is his destiny to appear like this, like a measured descent of stentorian musical chords that marks the moment that doom satisfies itself.

The grandfather clock at the foot of the bed rings and rings, as if it had been ringing for hours. Weary and unrested, she throws off the boiling covers and lies there, the clock standing at the foot of the monumental four-poster bed, looming above her like a moon-faced tower, sternly reproaching her for a monstrous transgression. She has a persistent feeling in her throat, as if she had swallowed a hair in her sleep, and finally this prompts her to get up. The chamber is a lofty, but cheerless, stone apartment in an ancient castle, and not a psychiatric hospital.

Before she can cross the room, the young woman's attention is momentarily arrested by a movement she glimpses out of the corner of her left eye. What was that? Then, peering into the unaltered chamber, a flicker in one of the brass balls ornamenting the bed grabs her attention. It wasn't fire—it was something pale. Looking more closely, she suddenly sees the warped reflection of a young woman in a gauze nightgown cross the room. She is heading over to the opposite corner. She blunders against a table and knocks over a white figurine that stands on it, so that it falls and breaks silently in two on the carpet. Now the young woman is staring in horror at something, at her, plainly at her! She sees how she must look to the young woman in the ball—her own reflection, its back to her, huge, warped, convex, head invisible, resembling a roughly anthropomorphic column or fragmentary statue or gigantic ghost draped in a shroud.

Looking at this image is hard because she can't quite tell if she is the one standing out here or the one reflected in the ball. The way her reflection would appear to her own reflection.

The figure in the ball, if it isn't her, doesn't move when she moves. It's still there when she crosses the room, thinking a glass of water might help her compose herself and so lost in wonder and the first stirrings of real fright she doesn't notice the white figurine breaking silently on the carpet at her feet, knocked down by her impulsive grab for the ewer of water.

UNIT THIRTY-NINE
IMMORTAL CASES

It is crucially important to stress the dangers posed by the use of prepositions, which is why the grammatical rules, or rather tendencies, which apply to prepositions have not yet been introduced in this work book. Before moving on to this discussion, the student must have a firm grasp of the principles involved in the grammar pertaining to immortal cases, as only immortal cases may be employed with prepositions or prepadjes. Students must cultivate an instinctive aversion to coupling mortal cases with prepositions or prepadjes, as immediate and reflexive as an aversion to excrement or the stink of decay.

All nouns "live" in mortal cases and are "sustained" in immortal cases. Where vampiric, immortal cases require sustenance in a way that mortal cases do not, and it is in this vampirism, indicated most commonly by the ablative and dative cases, that the resistance to the preposition is most patent. The use of immortal cases indicates, among other things, either an idea of "once and for all," which is to say a single moment promoted beyond all moments, or of its converse side, which is "not once and never," a demotion from all moments which nevertheless preserves a sense of the existence of the thing, or of "what always goes on." This means that particular words are not exclusively declined in mortal or immortal cases; there are mortal declensions of "eternity" for example, which might be used in discussing historical concepts of eternity, or a passing sentiment of eternity.

There are likewise immortal declensions of "mortal," referring to the perennial condition of mortality, or to the idea of an infinitely persisting moribund condition.

As with mortal cases, immortal cases are reflected in clause structure rather than by morphological inflection. The immortal anti-nomial is a special case, which must be "released" before any further application of immortal cases can be made in a given utterance, whether verbal or graphical. The release of the immortal anti-nomial is the precondition for any discussion of what is immortal; it does this by permitting a finite speaker to speak of infinite things without thereby rendering them finite in turn. The immortal anti-nomial is released by pairing it with the mortal nominative in a bivalent "macro" form known as <u>absolute unrelation</u>. Once this is done, immortal cases are formed by inverting their mortal counterparts. While there are immortal anti-cases, there are no immortal doubling cases.

Locate the point at which the immortal anti-nomial is released for this passage. Note that this point of release need not come in the passage itself. Then, without losing any time, corral and confine all prepositions with immortal cases.

UNIT THIRTY-NINE READING

The patient rushes into a room and there are two men in matching khaki uniforms standing there in the half light.

The patient has already rushed out again into the corridor and from room to room.

"71 ... 71 ..." he thinks.

The two men cross a different room, in no better condition and much more cluttered with trash, but with far more of the pasty pale seep of light from a window that is nothing more than a blank glass rectangle without a shade or a blind. They lift their feet high and set them down awkwardly. There are ruined old schoolchildren's desks and other things that look like black metal shells from barbecues. There are bundles of colored wire lying half pulled apart in corners, and wires thrust into cracks in the walls, empty wall sockets, and likely openings in the fragments of furniture. The shorter of the two men, who are so alike in most other ways, lifts and inspects a light blue metal typewriter cowling embossed with KILKILTKIKTKI TYPEWRITER CO. 71-11-15.

The patient, watching clairvoyantly, says "Something was behind it."

"Yes, now it's gone," the short one says.

"You mean the guts of the typewriter," says the tall one. "The pounding board er loom uh pounding ah pounding ... the matrix."

The view out a window discloses the place is huge, like an abandoned hotel sitting in an abandoned rail yard, sitting in a fog bank. The warden is reading patient correspondance at his desk in his scarecely less ruined office.

Now, correspondance.

Bit banged up, this one. I remember him. Let's have a look. Y-yes, there it is. Escape attempt in his first month, and again following year ... and again last year. Missing one eye, empty socket might contain camera. Patient 1861. Says he finds here animal control of the senses, such as he experienced in the army. As patient believes said animal control of the senses his 'element,' expresses intention to stay as long as he likes, hm! As he likes, note that. Put him back on the gruel, I think.

Eh patient um ... seven, something. Look it up later. I know him. The library, the dead city, the wolves.

Gazing out over the waves, the static waves, formed by rooftops aligned along streets. The great stillness of the library at my back. An image of a body is another body, but the word is not something other than the thought. This is crucially important, too important for me to be able to put it satisfactorally into words, which proves my point that much the better, though in a way that's still full of holes. A word and a thought are one, even if, especially because, one has to grope and put in a word forget it try another and so on until the right one comes up like a lottery ballot. I'm sure I've made some kind of logical mistake. I'll go faster and that'll fix it fine. I remember my old teacher, back in fantasy homeland. The music had too much happening in it to keep track of and that's why I liked it. Keeping track of things is a pain. The more I listened, the more I could hold it all in my mind at once. You don't have to keep track if you can do that. The pain in keeping track is all the categorizing, throwing your time away learning a categorizing scheme pretending to be music when music is music and categorizing schemes are categorizing schemes and the one has no need of the other and if you have the one you have no need of the other either. That music was stern, sour, lacerating, blisteringly intense, as relentless as grief, ferociously complex,

ONE,

ONE-ONE ONE-ONE

ONE-ONE ONE-ONE
ONE-ONE ONE-ONE
ONE-ONE ONE-ONE

The teacher, who stayed or was kept in a room behind the classroom, would stalk out of his hole like a zoo animal emerging from its den. None of us ever ventured back in there to see him. The hole was black and smelled like an open grave. He would pace up and down for a while, then sit at his desk and glare over our heads, beaming telepathic messages of hatred to whoever ran the school. His teeth and vocal apparatus were glass, and he was constantly spitting up blood. His snarlingly chiming words came out in gritted teeth you could hear grate on each other, the black spaces with white outlines that from time to time ran red. Once, I copied a death poem by Sunao:

Spitting up blood
clears up reality
and dream alike

and left it for him on his desk. He glanced at it. The paper wasn't folded. A gout of blood spurted from his mouth splattered the paper. That was his comment.

Librarians are necromancers. Here's why: what we call human is already a matter of language. Language is not just an instrument of thought, it is thought. That's what he taught us. Words on a page do not represent thought, they are thoughts, and they think, books think. What does that make translators? Psychopomps.

The writer is a medium. The langauge comes through. From where? From itself. Language is the underworld. The purpose of the course is to change you, so that you will learn to see the world, speak and write, like someone who has come back from the dead. For that to happen you must die, reading. Death is vanquished. Death is espoused. Sobriety presumes again. The idea is all wrong. Tragically. That means by virtue of being true. What are all the books surrounding me now if not the terrifyingly well-organized collection of everything everyone ever lost?

They think. Books think. When you meet someone, what are you really meeting? Their words. The body is the amazing thing. The soul or whatever isn't the phantom, it is. The magic vehicle. The words are always there once they're there and they outlive us in the library of the empty city, while the body is like a flame that isn't the same from one moment to the next. The human body is defined as the site where language encounters the world through sense impressions. The language, already thinking to itself, latches ravenously onto whatever concrete things it can find through a body, and goes crazy. The human body is the madness of language, the hypodermic needle through which language sucks the hallucinogenic drugs of existence.

"What is the subject of the sentence?"

"The cat."

"And what is the basket?"

"What is the basket?"

"What is the basket!"

"Indirect object?"

"It isn't the indirect object! Is the basket receiving the action indirectly? Is there a 'to'? Is there are 'for'?"

"No numbers, sir."

"No numbers! No numbers! You're damned right there are no numbers and there are no T-O 'to' and no F-O-R 'for' either you idiot!"

Towering above the student.

"OBJECT"

Strikes student.

"OF"

Strikes student.

"A"

Strikes student.

"PREP"

Strikes.

"O"

Strikes.

"SITION!"

Jabs the page with his index finger. The tip of the finger strikes the desk through the paper with a very loud sound.

"INTO!" he bellows. "INTO THE BASKET! INTO!"

He raps the page with his finger.

"INTO!"

"INTO!"

"INTO!"

Can you get such Biblical indignation out of a teacher's everyday frustration with thickheaded and indifferent students? Or isn't it the rage of a thwarted living thing trying to perpetuate itself?

*

A cooing sound behind my back. I turn, confronting a phantom child.

"Are you 115 years old?" the child asks in a whisper.

"Sounds about right ... Eh, no ... yes, what am I saying? Last Auguary, er—Decay. 13th of Decay."

"Then I'm supposed to tell you. My mother says—"

"Who?"

"My mother. Princess D'Onquie. My mother."

"Ah. Yes, please go on."

"She says to lend her Unlanguage basic work book number one. A flesh and blood person is coming to pick it up at the gate three months from now."

"No question of compensation I suppose?"

"Continued non-molestation."

"And molestation if I don't?"

The child shrugs.

"All right. I won't refuse."

The child remains where it is, watching. Minutes pass.

"Oh, eh, tell her, the Princess, your mother, the Princess D'Onquie, please, that I agree. Thank you. Thank you, please."

"Why do you live here?"

"I want to read these books."

"All of them?"

"No. I guess I might, in time. But that wasn't the idea."

"Just some?"

"That was the idea."

"What do you read?"

"For the most part, the miseries of the dead."

"That sounds boring."

"Have you met many not bored people?"

"Don't you get lonely?"

"I don't get lonely, I am lonely. I have an inveterate need to keep people off. That's that."

"Can I look around?"

"Be my guest."

Phantom children are the result of sexual or recurring dreams. Which are much the same thing. Any extreme repetitiveness in dreaming can cause one to appear. The phantom child partuitates from the dream and usually becomes a part of the parent dreamer's household, in a unique form that will never change. An immortal, ethereal nine year old. Often in fabulous costumes. They know how old anyone is, and, being forgetful of proper names, they identify individuals by age. Asking for confirmation was just a formality above there.

It's impossible to manipulate them the way corporeal children are manipulated because they can't be struck, restrained, or confined. Fortunately, they like approval and can be obliging. There are also certain confectioners who have the secret; they buy the capacity for love or beauty from people and whip them into flossy sweetmeats the phantom children seem instinctively to love eating. More for the taste than for nourishment, since they seem to have no more need of food, let alone water or sleeping, than ghosts do. Living persons who dare to sample these sweets seldom live long after, and those who do become diaphanous. The bon-bons of doom are mainly used to induce phantom children to run errands. This one was sent to me, in the first place, because a phantom child can go from here to there in an instant, through secret passages behind space, while the flesh and blood messenger is slowed to a crawl by his own rude body. In the second place, because the ghosts here it seems will tolerate no other living person than myself within the city walls. I leave it to those who are so inclined to wonder at the reason for that.

UNIT FORTY
EXPONENTIAL PRONOUNS

Unlanguage employs, in addition to the four persons or degrees already mentioned, exponential pronouns that precisely designate degree of removal from the speaker. There are exponential pronouns for all degrees, which means that they may be used interchangeably with the previously established pronouns. The use of exponential pronouns indicates a niceness of attention or overall greater punctiliousness in speech or writing, and it is common practice to make all pronouns exponential in passages in which at least one will be necessary.

"She went insane before she could arrive." In this sentence, the first "she" is the third person (degree two), while the second "she" is in the fourth person (degree three). There are standard forms for these two pronouns.

"She went insane while she attacked her, but she drove her off before she could arrive." In this sentence, exponential pronouns must be used, and, if adhering to custom is important, all the pronouns should, therefore, be exponential. The resulting sentence would indicate that the one who went insane, the attacker, and the victim are all distinct persons, that the madwoman drove the attacker off, and that all this was done in anticipation of the arrival of yet other female person.

The exponential pronoun is formed by adding ordinal prefixes which indicate degree by a combination of the number of syllables and the length and emphasis of pronunciation.

These prefixes are not to be confused with the number particles of the simple plural, which are not fixed to the pronouns themselves.

When attached to pronouns of degree zero, or the first person, exponents indicate a succession of speakers. "I left the building. I hurried downstairs. I broke the glass and removed the axe. I disposed of the evidence in the ashpit behind the house." In this case, three different individuals narrate. When degree one, or second person, is employed, this indicates a succession of listeners. "You must chant without stopping until the ritual is completed. You must give you the knife when you reach the third verse, then you must prostrate yourself before you."

Translate the following passage into unlanguage, re-rendering all pronouns as verbal nouns.

UNIT FORTY READING

[to be read slowly, quietly, neutrally, and slurred, with minimal emphasis.]

heat, some heat, heating, warming, daywarming, day another day and, nso, soonagain, so soongain, or, more of this, this unseen day, or fire above in the sementery, or motrurary, the monthofmonthruary, or burial

[quick and flat] am I being cremated?

[as before]
cremated, cremen, cremeted, cerecremcer, mated, or burns the grave, entireley, all burns, the soil,

set, seh, stone, inscerip, iption, and the inscription, heat seeps gather in, from ... [longer pause] ... that, up, ongoingunjotstlingcontinuasstillremainingmeans, means, remember, remember, remember, bodies to be inhumed within six days, six days of, within six days of, delivery. Sixdaystogetherexceeding may have, may have gone, may be ... [longer pause] ... may no way to know, knownibreathlessdarkessmotionelessness, breathlessblindmotionelessness, at in, tervals, thud, thud-ding, long, inter, rvals, thuds, thud-ding, earthdull, ed, footstrepping tickle a nintac nerve inside crummbled ear, hotterenheatening, enheatennenning, no pespirpan, persperpipersant-cy, no nonvevaprosiation, from cooskin, for—

[very slight lightening of tone]
—a splash—
footlown where it crushedin, the poor matchstick foot, groundwater, flown in, I have a visitor, jostling me, must bite, be biting, still some meat then, must be meat still, left, am I more, more clear now, I really ought to maek the most of it—
—jostle—
where was I, the grave?

[awake, calm]

the grave,

I spent my life staring at a dead human face, waiting to see it move, a dead, a dead loved human face, dead loved. I stared into the dead face of a stranger, hoping it would speak. In accents acquired postmortem. Slur. Drunk with death. I stared into dusty corners and blackened windows and went inside tumbledown houses and circumambulated graveyards and listened. I stared and I listened. Even now death does not choose to tell anything through me. Even now. Blinded by death. [lower pitch] Blinded by death. [as before] In my rotten, in my stinking rotten, skull, I hear one shrill wail. A wail in a chord. It chimes. Too intense for time, it bores through to everlasting, everlasting leavetaking. All victory. All defeat. Each impasse. All finished. All unfinished. Final leavetaking. Rejoicing in the loss of all I loved. All that I kept, so carefully, for such a long time. Passing into annihilation in triumph. A cry of death that will carry forever, over the lake, over the mountains, across the sky. I lose the sky. I lose the mountain. I lose the lake. I lose the cry. I lose the mountain. I lose the lake. I lose the sky. I lose the mountain. I lose the lake. I lose the cry. I lose the cry. I lose the cry. I lose the cry.

UNIT FORTY-ONE
PARALLELISM

Language parallels being. This is obvious where allegories and invocations are concerned, but even a straightforward account of a sequence of events is still a parallel, since a straight and solitary line is already its own parallel. All language parallels being in this way, as the line of the line, and unlanguage is the line of the line of the line, or just the line, since it is the same thing. Unlanguage comes from the fibrous, shaggy extremity of the line at being's farthest, where being couples with nothing and leaves a crust of unlanguage moving backwards in time, since this sex act requires the privacy of a moment prior to any possible consciousness.

Parallelism in unlanguage is analogous to the sense of equilibrium that tells us when we are upright and level, or off-balance. It is often mistaken for something external to language, just as the dizzy person attributes spin to the surroundings, rather than to the perturbulence of the volume of liquid contained by the ear. Phantasmagoria establishes its level, relative to a level which is established at the same time and in one and the same act, in keeping with its training. Students will already be conversant with the fundamentals of this training, simply by virtue of having acquired some familiarity with unlanguage. However, further, more deliberate training becomes more and more necessary as skill with unlanguage increases, so that the amount of study required of advanced students is actually far, far greater than it is for beginners.

In the passage below, identify to the exclusion of all others the single internal self-parallelism.

UNITY FORTY-ONE READING

I am alone in a room in the school, not a classroom. I sit in the middle of a big empty table with my hands folded on it in front of me. I feel like I've just nodded back in.

"So, are you ready to go into the memory now?"

What? A little dingle, in the corner, corner of the ear, turn to look, just the head, see, on the wall, the two luminous spots, watching, the doom spots, silent reminders, and fixed, not on me but on the teacher who is there, in the middle of a big empty table like mine, no, not like mine, turned at a ninety degree angle to mine, his hands folded, his head under the white wings, his hair, down over his shoulders, and hunched forward so that he looks as though he were sticking his head comically up and comically peering out from under a bed sheet, so stooped and hunched, wrists at table edge, folded hands nearly pivoting off edge, peering through enormous brown sunglasses that seem to engulf half his face, the grating voice like a shook can of gravel, the streaked chin, the downturned mouth, expression completely at odds with masterful intonation of speech, expression of blind oblivious listening, the more I think of it that way the more he is a benighted old creature, a thing, a somehow human thing, frail, sexless, alone, miserable.

Much slower than these quick thoughts come the long swells of feeling that match them in time and are brought about by the same things. The reverberations of being startled have superimposed on them the less pointed experience of fear and the fumbling, gathering action of being unfamiliar, working at it, trying to undo it, trying to be familiar. Welling up from the midst of these and overlaying them in turn is the related wonder, the slackening of denial, the brief burst of surprise which dwindles and runs down into a barely perceptible sick nervousness at the discovery of the teacher. And then, as I gaze at the teacher, there is a rare softening and warming of stirring pity blended so thoroughly with the perception of unhappy helplessness that they might as well be one and the same thing. The dim misgivings his question elicits are going on meanwhile without taking center stage, but instead like the stage curtains pulled back and framing the action.

I get up without a word and, taking the outstretched hand, follow the towering figure who looms above me like an adult looms over a young child as he half walks, half leans his head into a scintillating field of daylight broken by bright green leaves, the dazzling beams raking my face throw the rest of the room or whatever it is into obscurity and I step forward onto a yielding lawn and a smell of cut grass, fresh air, daylight. For a moment I felt as if he had taken my hand, but perhaps I just imagined it. Amber and Krista come out onto the lawn to welcome me coming up the stepping stones with Eric and "So nice to see you!" and Amber saying "In our talons at last!" and Aaron coming out of the house and waving while he shuts the screen door on the eager dogs. "I'll let 'em out if you don't mind," he says after. "Friday's their bridge night," Krista says. Amber roughing up a dog's flank, "We send them over to a friend's house. He has a big yard."—"I keep saying we should keep them there."

Sit inside waiting as more people arrive and the sun sets. "Hi! Come on in!" "No! You're fine! He's going to be a little late he said." "He's held up—we won't be starting until after eight." "I think she said he was on a call." "Wasn't he seeing Caroline?" Krista turns to me, "Did you know about Caroline? She may have to go to the hospital. They don't know what it is." "He's on his way!" Amber sings out from the phone. The windows are dark. People trickle into the meeting room, divots left in the white carpeting where the furniture normally sits, now dozens of folding chairs in rows, a dais, a high white chair and table, water pitcher and glass on it. Thunder rumbling. "I hope he gets here before that starts," Krista says, looking up. There's Stephen, Victor, Katrina. (I will watch you all die, horribly—Krista, Eric, Victor—I will be dying, too) "Is he here?" "He was held up." Thunder again. "I remember Caroline," I tell Amber. "Wasn't she—didn't she used to—blonde? With glasses? Thin? Thin face?" Amber nodding. Headlights pick out the grey trunk of the oak tree and the screen of black foliage. A big black mark three Lincoln Continental with tinted windows slides up the driveway. "He's here!" The car closes its eyes and stops, seems minutely to shrink. A woman gets out of the driver's seat and goes around to the back. The back door opens backwards. Coming around to the side entrance of the house the thunder rumbles again, a white figure against black leaves, then vanish and reappear a moment later in the same room with me (my future self is calling to you— please don't die! plea—) wait—Alvin Arcedonio is here. Alvin Arcedonio is tall and walks with an unhurried, tall man's walk, very tanned all in white. The white collar of his shirt is tall, crisp and open, straight dark layered hair shawling his head, nonchalantly taking off his enormous brown sunglasses, pocketing them. He greets the room with a calm smile and raises his hands, receiving the murmured greeting with upraised palms.

(hands clutching at empty space, the shining place where you were once, Intersuffusion)

Alvin Arcedonio is saying immortal life ... eternal life ... We listen in silence. Later there's singing. Alvin Arcedonio has a striker with a little wooden ball on the end, uses it to strike a wood block on the table, keeping time. The song is a wordless harmony that alters in a regular succession, some singing sustained notes and others short la la la's. I join as best I can with the la la singers. From time to time in the midst of the music, which is slow and beautiful, I hear snarled, unintelligible words. Beneath the calling of the voices, Alvin Arcedonio's voice lifts from below in a soft bass singing that disappears into the hum in the walls (with tears, please don't die—blood in my mouth, blood streaming horribly from the mouths of all my only friends, my brothers and my sisters, staring back at me in terror, bodies struggling against the brain, the terrible crime this brain committed against it) eternal life, Alvin Arcedonio is singing, not in so many words, but the meaning is in the notes. The music brings us into harmony with each other and heals our bodies and minds.

ONE,
ONE-ONE ONE-ONE
ONE-ONE ONE-ONE
ONE-ONE ONE-ONE
ONE-ONE ONE-ONE

It amplifies vibrations from outer space, and reradiates them, relaying them. The planets keep falling silent, the fires go out, the cosmos moves slower, the cosmos is losing its life, the cosmos is losing its light, and then someone must be sent to restart the singing so that Intersuffusion, the relay system, doesn't die forever. All death is the failure of the relay. Eternal life is the perfection of relaying (the slow, beautiful music keeps getting louder, drowning out my screams ... Julie! Kate! Robbie!) Singular and plural go into each other, rebreak drastically away.

The voice is easy, full, unhurried. A knot of people surrounds Alvin Arcedonio after the session's conclusion and he is calm and patient even as he makes his way with alacrity to the door. He does not stay to socialize. I didn't even notice the rain beginning to fall. Through the window I can see him, haloed with a white umbrella, getting back into the car. The engine starts and the car sinks backwards into the gushing darkness. For a moment I can still see him, sitting in the back seat, a motionless white smudge through the shaded windows. That night I tell Amber I want to join. Silhouette of Alvin Arcedonio's head in the metallic blue lozenge of the car's rear window as the Lincoln tilts down to the street. (I am giving up my life. The people looking at me now, right now, will see me die, I am going to die with them. We are going to help each other to die. It can't be true. It can't be true.)

I don't like the avidly bright-eyed way they read so much into even his simplest and most offhanded remarks. Something compels them to meddle with everything about him, what he wears, how he walks, what he eats. He doesn't like tea so nobody drinks tea, although he never said a word for or against. He wears white so some wear white in emulation and others don't wear white so as not to seem like they put themselves at his level. His approval feels so good I don't like it. I'm on firmer ground with his reprimands, not directed at me but toward types of behavior I thought I recognized in myself. Another night.

"He was an American legend," an old man is saying. I can see his back through the aperture in the dining room wall. Walking out of sight, into the room, "He had the bona fides ..."

"So, Mr. Prime Minister!"

That's me, she means. A swirl of people, conversation coming up on all sides now.

"I waited until early morning then put out the warning ..."

"Is it cats?"

"It was summer past ..."

Odd way of putting it.

"... but be careful of ESCAPING."

ESCAPING is one of Alvin Arcedonio's special terms, one he uses less frequently than intersuffusion or relay. I haven't been able to dumb out its meaning yet, and asking for definitions causes me unnecessarily acute embarrassment. Judging by implications I infer it means something like evading responsibility, or not keeping to the here and now.

"Yes, because they want you to think, to believe in their reality and anyone who doesn't believe it and doesn't say it's real, even though nobody really thinks it is! Nobody! But if you don't pretend they say you're crazy. They put you away!"

That's Krista's voice. Krista of the beautiful, rabbity mouth.

"They're the ones who're crazy, what-what's more crazy huh? Believing in money or believing in love?"

It's the old refrain. I don't doubt it. I believe in it, and I don't talk like that anymore if I can avoid it. I believe in it, and putting it into words makes me feel like an imbecile. Why?

"And how many people know right now we're flying through space?" she cries incredulously, so that her ice shakes in the glass. "They talk about it like it's beyond or it's you know just on TV when we're in it!"

Do I want her, do I want to be him, do I want to be ...? Steam ran out.

The voices gather into one music. Out pops "created freedoms," another of Alvin Arcedonio's phrases. Created freedoms are like prisoner's privileges while natural freedoms are well well well, you know, whatever's not that, it isn't wrong not to have a clear answer there, so long as you can convince me it's coming. No one can say what it is until it exists, and it doesn't exist yet, but it's coming. Why? How do we know? Because we're making it happen. Cause and effect.

"How's the Pensive Drunk doing?"

That's me, what Amber's calling me now. I like it better than Prime Minister I never understood that one. I smile up at her and see a lively intelligence makes her plain face attractive and she could have me if she wanted me although Krista.

"That's right," I answer. "You can always find me at the sign of El Borracho Penseroso. Ask anybody."

"Under the dim religious light."

"Under the dim religious table. Dim, all too dim anywheres."

Out pops "puppet show," another of Alvin Arcedonio's phrases. He likes to say you can do whatever it is he's advising at the moment, or "you can go watch the puppet show from the window of a coffee shop." It seems you can't do without a pejorative term for other people, you can't do without hating others even if you smother it in a heap of pity and fried onions, those poor saps, and of course they are, they are poor saps, the mistake isn't even thinking you're not a poor sap, it's trying to con yourself out of thinking you are by throwing that "poor sap" onto every passer by. If you're not a sucker, you're not a sucker, and what other people are or are not, what does that matter, what makes that my business? Compassion? Sure, compassion—if it really is compassion and not hatred in a pleasing shape.

Amber is bathing me in warm face and it's starting to seem real to me, but Krista's mouth, interrupted by that tumbler too much ... I fix my eye on it like a climber picking out his goal high on the slope above him. Tough brambles and sharp rocks between here and there, but side path Amber is waiting for all her acuity she doesn't know a shit when she sees one or she's wise and doesn't need anti-shit insurance. What? A little dingle, in the corner, corner of the ear, turn to look, just the head, see, on the wall, the two luminous spots, watching, the doom spots, silent reminders, and fixed, enormous brown sunglasses that seem to engulf half the face, Alvin Arcedonio, his words and ideas, in time we join, we stood in the glare of the parking lot, we watched, separating from the rest of the world, registering that separation had happened already, had in fact never been necessary, in the glare by the white wall of the convenience store and the bank of pay telephones savaged by the glare. Then what—the trouble with Amber, Alvin Arcedonio putting his hand on my shoulder saying "Let's go out into the garden for a bit," we sit together on the imitation stone benches by the high bank of nearly black ivy, cypress shadows stripe the green ground, the sun caged overhead, crystal shells, dazzling raucous light like a battle at a safe distance. The low, confiding voice, the earnest, serene face half screened by the sunglasses.

"It's a valid impulse. There's no question of that. I am not asking for Puritanism or asceticism, for hostility toward the body. I ask nothing, mh, you know that. We exclude sex within the communion precisely because it is so heavily freighted with wrong habits, wrong associations, possessiveness, jealousy, anger, hatred, distraction, any one of these things could fracture the communion, mh. Only an emancipated and harmonious spirit can embrace sex the right way, because he is no longer burdened by vanity or selfishness. Now, none of us, myself included can make that claim."

Alvin Arcedonio is careful never to speak of good and evil, or good and bad. With an obvious, though tacit, decision, he speaks only of the right way and the wrong way. I sit there and recognize myself for the first time in weeks; in trouble, corrected, on parole. It's a relief. Always sheltering in the wrong, that's me. Alvin Arcedonio seems to know.

"You're the type—" he pauses and smiles thoughtfully. "You ignore the path and take and charge right up the mountain, right against the rocks, and in there with the thorns and the snakes."

I nod my head grinning sheepishly.

"You make everything twice as hard as it needs to be. You make difficulty into your religion."

He uses that word, always carefully pronounced, to mean a master delusion.

"That's because you've got a strong willpower. Now you take and learn to use it in the right way, and you will find the center of the labyrinth. And that's just as important as climbing the mountain."

I hate the slavish leap of welcome that greets this flattery and I try to hold myself at a level, where it all looks like a game and I never lose sight of a group mendacity so deep it verges on becoming its own language. Alvin Arcedonio's smile and invisible eyes might see and reflect the same thought, insidiously encouraging me to believe that my self-consciousness is far sighted and clear, and imagine I have a handle on something. He and I could be doing nothing more than we appear to be, or we could be racing toward the bottom in a series of switchbacks, finding successively hidden meanings and each trying to outflank the other. Each time the thought folds, you have to clamp it down with your fingers, and you only have so many hands and so much strength to hold on and to keep track and get to the next one first. You need a second person to act as a guide, like the rule about sticking to one direction in a maze.

The labyrinth doesn't branch; the path folds and folds like intestines, multiplying the amount of space in a plot and insuring that, once you reach the center, you have covered every inch of the ground. It's a way of being sure you've touched the entire plot. It's also a kind of dance, Theseus' way of bringing the labyrinth back home with him so he could show everyone what it was like, and a kind of a song, with repeated choruses and a climax. It's also the image of the rapturous exaltation of getting lost in your own thinking.

The moment I am alone and free to do as I please causeless despair unstrings me and I imagine dying, myself and everyone else. Where I'm standing, the hedge corners itself and creates a little shaded enclosure I like to hide in. A grown man hiding, I know, I know, but I can't pass up an opportunity to disappear. I look out at the others feeling like I might lose all self-control and break down any moment, mystified. I'm not seeing the future. I'm seeing the present. I'm finally seeing the present. And once more I see them all encompassed in a shadow and each one with their shadows hard at their heels doubling them. Alvin Arcedonio and Eric and Amber and all the unreal names, mine included. Life isn't real. I'm grieving for them and they're all still alive.

*

"People like to say 'life goes on.' Now, what does that mean? In moments of suffering, you feel as though you've stopped, like you've been removed from the stream of life, which nevertheless continues to flow on all around you. And there's always somebody there to tell you, as if you didn't know, that life goes on. So it is an invitation to rejoin the current. But what this means is that you have stopped, and it is suffering that's stopped you. You suffer, you stop, mh? But what this also means is that life is what goes on, that it is in the nature of life to go on. What stops, what does not change, what refuses to move, what insists on being only this, dies."

He pauses to break off a fresh stick of incense, which he lights with a match and then holds between his fingers like a cigarette.

"Music is the composition of sonic elements in time. However great it may be, the number of musical variables is limited. If we could come up with the number of musical variables, mh?, we could caculate the number of different pieces of music that could ever possibly be composed. If you had a computer big enough you probably could even create them. And then you would have all music. Until someone invents something new in music, adds a variable, and the whole number has to be recalculated. When you use a word like 'limit,' there's no reason to assume that you have to mean an enforced limit. Like you could go on but you're being prevented from going on, going further, mh?

"Now apply this to people. If personalities are composed of variables—stubbornness, altruism, gullibility, impulsiveness, melancholy, and so on—and if the number of traits at a given time is finite, which, as I just was saying, doesn't mean a closed set that nothing new can ever be added to it—then the number of possible human combinations of these traits would correspondingly be finite. We could even calculate it, mh? We could calculate the highest possible number of different personalities. I suspect that the number of actually existing different personalities does not even begin to approach the hypothetical number.

"If we imagine personality in this way, then we can easily imagine the recurrence of identical personalities in time. You might happen to have exactly the same combination of traits that made up Dante Alighieri. If that were true, then you would be like the same tune, the very same tune, played on a slightly different instrument. Dante Alighieri may be a bad example of my point though because we all know what he looked like, he was famous. There were countless thousands of people who lived in the past and whose likenesses were never recorded, nor anything about them, and you might very well be an exact repetition of one of these people yourself, down to the smallest detail.

"Now we can call this repetition reincarnation, without referring to any so-called supernatural thing. Someone from the past, someone dead, comes back. Comes back as you. If you are exactly as that person was, you will think as that person used to think, it will be as if that person had come back and was reacting to present conditions. Your reactions, your feelings, your opinions, would be his or hers. In the past, his or her reactions and feelings are also yours, mh?"

He smiles faintly and wags his finger, undulating the thin smoke ribbon that trails from his incense stick.

"But there is a bit of sophistry in there, isn't there? Something's not right. You may be that person again. But can you remember that other person's childhood? Or any details of his life, or her life? If you're Dante all over again, can you speak Italian? From his time? Can you close your eyes and see Beatrice Portinari, her real face?

"So you may be Dante again, but there is not a continuity of awareness from his life to yours. Any more than there was any for him."

He shifts in his seat, crossing his legs and raising one finger, elbow on armrest.

"But just how solid is your consciousness? When you get up in the morning, are you the one who went to sleep last night? Or are you a new person, taking up the memories you have to hand, the body you have to hand, that is your hand, and making do? So perhaps our consciousness, that which we most identify as ourself, is not so continuous as we think. It may only be a tendency to assume the existence of a certain continuity, a continuity with this name, this age, this body, where none might exist otherwise.

"Seen in this light, the gap of death begins to look strange. If the continuity is an illusion, then you might as well be Dante Alighieri, even without shared memories. The gap of death might be essentially no different than the gap of sleep. The gap between lives is like the gap between days. Now, here we must be very careful, because it would be easy to take the wrong way, and think, 'well, Alvin is telling me I'm Dante, and I like this idea very much, so the continuity is there but it's obscured somehow, I can't know it, so I can't rule it out.' That is not what I mean. If the continuity is an illusion, then there is no difference between Dante and the person you were last night before you went to sleep. Not for you, not for anyone. The same personality may return in every detail, but consciousness is always everchanging, the living negative. Not negative in the crude sense. I do not say consciousness does not exist. They will try to tell you that I say consciousness does not exist, but they are always trying, in every way, to imprison you, to bind you in expedient ways for them."

Alvin Arcedonio always becomes more animated when he talks about them, the enemy. He is leaning forward, and accompanies his talk about 'imprisoning' hunching up his shoulders and pressing his ribcage with his elbows and holding his fists out before him. Now, he relaxes and leans back suavely opening his arms, trailing incense smoke.

"But that is their idea of the negative. Not ours. That is not the living negative. The living negative is negative because—not only does it exist, it is not nonexistent, it exists, and it continues to exist precisely by *evading* and *refusing* to be confined in some identity."

He makes a sort of spinning turnip with one hand.

"It likes to take shape. It takes a shape it likes."

He flops his hand.

"It does not leave the constellation unbroken. It discards the shape and moves on. It *is* that ongoing movement. It *is* life."

It will all come again, myself, vinyl upholstery, beehive hairdos, Pancatantra, Tang Dynasty, Easter Island, beer invented in Egypt, quipus, krill krill, light in the air somehow not reaching objects, crane dance of Theseus, ... It has all happened countless times already, happening infinitely, and it is our natural forgetfulness making all that appears seem finite.

What was I thinking of renouncing? Drinking? A fine idea, the kind that you have and leave behind fine or not. And that was just a guess. It all started thinking of renouncing her. There was more after that but I don't seem to recall if there were any additional renunciation, or a substitute. Trying to recapture a sequence of thoughts that succeed each other in haste is like fumbling for a dream. She never dreamed. Her writing was always pure and essential; so either her dreams were inessential, and, disgusted by their superfluousness, she threw them far away from her, or her dreams were no different from her waking life. There was less bullshit in her than in anyone I'd ever met. She seemed to come from a blazing shore. Being around her made me feel like a pile of old rags by comparison. Every time I spoke, my sayings would clang discordantly against her steely air, and it was like trying to make small talk with the goddess Minerva. I had hoped her company would essentialize me. I remembered finally what I had wanted to renounce, and it wasn't important. Now I understood that I must renounce following. The moment I grasp it as something I must renounce, strength flows back into me and I go on.

NOTES

Return to the desert. Hot dry air like smoke. Everything blazes. You can't see the air you're in tremble, see yourself tremble or feel it. Sage, something like marjoram, sweet smell something like overripe mint. No sinister eastern profuseness no lushness none of its feathery, seductive dark green softness; in the desert the plants are brittle brown leathery tough resinous pungent, hugging the ground, sharp as tangles of barbed wire. There are small pointed seeds with coiled fibers that corkscrew themselves into pant legs and stockings when you brush through them. The day's heat vanishes the moment night falls and outer space reaches all the way down to the ground.

UNIT FORTY-TWO
BLENDED PERSONS

In addition to the various persons, whether expressed by standard pronouns or by exponential pronouns, there are also blended persons, which are used when there is no distinct differentiation desired or possible between persons. The first and second persons, for example, blend where speaker and listener are not plainly two. This person is not a protoperson, but is able, in parabolica, of independent action, and expresses its own will. Between the first and second persons, the blended person is known as the "double half" person, representing degree zero-to-one. The pronoun may be translated into English IOU, in all capitals. In the plural, this is the "multiple double half," translated WY.

The "double triple" person is a listener who acts independently of the direct awareness of the first person, a HOU, EYE, OUT, or YON. The "multiple double triple" may be written THU.

The "triple half" person is a speaker who is also the object of another speaker's speaking, represented in English by HI, SHI, IIT, or INE, and in "multiple triple half," by WHEY. There are similar permuations for the fourth person and for exponential pronouns as well, as explained in the appendix.

In the following passage, locate all instances of blended persons.

UNIT FORTY-TWO READING

The old man had been incapacitated by a heart attack. He only barely survived it. His health was fragile, and there was no way of knowing whether he would ever recover. All he could do safely was to rest for the time being. The doctors would keep checking him until it became possible to say for sure whether or not he was improving.

He lay in his dark cell by day, on a low divan against one wall, facing the blinded windows. A curious side effect of his heart attack was something to do with his eyes. Reading had become painful. This, for a man like him, whose whole life was reading, was like losing a limb. There were not enough recordings to satisfy him.

I volunteered to read aloud to him. The task bored me, and sometimes I found myself nodding off as I read in his stuffy, silenced half light, slurring and reading diagonally down the page. He listened, or seemed to, without a word. Only now and then, and as it appeared to me despite himself, he would emit a sound, or stir. I would hear the rustle of his garments and glance up at his face, and there would be a barely discernible but distinct opening. It began before his features, stirred them as it passed by.

I finish the book, and lay it down. I'm done early. He does not move, except to blink, not watching, not looking. Old man's trance. With mounting inclination I toy with the idea that I might drink and leave this world unseen and fade by myself into the pornography dim, leaving him there like a life sized doll. What if he has an attack the moment I go? I don't love this old man or even like his company much, I feel like I have to be very careful, although to be honest this feeling comes from me not him I don't think. What will the doctors think? All my rehabilitative effort wasted. That said, I see the hammer come down and the frail, twig-bundle body convulsing and I wince like I've just gotten a whiff of something sharp and vile. You leave him alone, I'll stay.

The old man's breath soughs in his nostrils. His calm eyes blink, and the irises shift as though he were watching an imaginary television or animal at the foot of the bed. His mouth works once.

I lay the book aside and sit, shawled in the close gloom like he is. If it's this dull for me, when I can sally out on my own two feet into the sun's full bray, how duller it can only be for the old man with nothing but old thoughts and old things. Me listless and stupid, so stupid I can't manage it, I don't want to write anything, my stories are stupid my dreams stupid my person stupid, my tatterdemalions all frisk away leaving me standing there in numb humiliation like a kindergarten teacher abandoned immediately by all her students on a field trip watching them scatter to the four corners of creation and calculating the fantastic, the unledgered quorums and bivalves of effort that are going to be necessary to corral them all together again and why bother. None of them's going to grow up to be a senator anyway. And if they do so much the worse for them the little shits. Grow up and shoot a senator might be more civic minded. All I want to do is turn away and leaf over fantasies of creamy dry white bodies, somebody new to have angry at me, a new delectable complainer.

He seemed to have forgotten me. The words have an addressee I fear but if he is speaking to me it sure doesn't feel like he's speaking to me. As he says it I see it, or start to.

"The dull, washed-out glaze before twilight made the city seem glamorous by comparison, its colors touched up in a soft hum ... aaah shit—*shit*—it's no use ..."

He lowers his head in dejection. So much for that story. Time passes and the darkness of late afternoon gathers. It's as if he were sitting there alone. I don't know what to say, I keep silent out of respect, and because I anticipate the insipid, the galling impression I might make with my idiot words.

"I wanted to tell you," he says desolately.

We sit there motionless and breathless, hurtling through time.

"Help me up," he barks.

Although it seems to be more of a hindrance than not, what can I do but grab his stiff, bent arm and drag it up as he climbs laboriously to his feet. I walk him to the toilet and he shuffles inside, turns his question mark body to shut the door between us. At a discreet distance, near enough to answer his call but far enough away to lose most of the noise of his travailing, my ears pick up a couple of ragged sniffs. Old man's tears. God damn. God damn it. Just God damn. Old man's tears god damn.

He emerges with a surprising look of resolution hardening his eyes. Without a word he motions me to pursue him into another room in his cell, through a door I've never noticed before in this small room. The room beyond is actually pretty big, dark and close with stale air. Big machines against all the walls, stainless steel dimly gleaming in the dusk. The floor is a snake's nest of cables. There's a table and a chair next to the table, facing out the window. Through that curtainless window I can see the great open space to the east, the dark horizon where night is coming.

The old man sits by the table.

"I'd offer you a chair," he rumbles, "but there isn't one and you won't need it."

"I don't like the sound of that."

"Don't worry. You'll want to see this. You've never seen anything in your life like what I can show you here."

As he speaks he pulls the cover off a thing on the table like a breadbox. There's a crown on the table. I mean a crown, an honest-to-goodness crown. A *crown*. Rubies and purple stuff. He lifts it carefully and sets it down carefully on his head. There are wires running into boxes and machinery.

"I have to stay very calm," he says.

He drags a black iron lump shaped thing with a sideways switch on it, the kind with a shell you clap against the handle as you grip it, the switch having too a pointed end that sweeps a minutely engraved steel semicircular dial, he drags it over to where he can work it with his left hand, and takes up a button box on a long cable in his right hand, thumb on the big button.

"Watch out there," he says, gesturing to the window with the box and then pressing his thumb down.

The machinery whirs to life. I smell ozone and hear the rasping electrical hum, like the sound of a powersaw under a zinc roof. The machines crackle and sizzle, my hair stands up, the hair on my legs stiffens painfully. The old man claps the shell against the handle and draws the lever evenly back like an engineer opening the throttle on a locomotive. My eyes are on him, standing behind him so I nearly look down on the crown, and so I don't exactly see what happens through the window. There is a kind of a stiff, glassy explosion outside, and I feel a jolt as if the whole world had jerked abruptly an inch to one side. My stomach feels a little heavy all of a sudden like the end of a down elevator ride. Outside the window, where nothing had been, there looms a huge brown apartment building with five or six square towers, standing there among the palm trees and blue ocean in a kind of dull green-brown November gloom all its own, the many windows not reflecting the setting sun behind us.

The machinery dies down. The building is there, more real and solid than anything else I see. Diffuse light sifting into the room like flour is not at all dimished by this huge obstruction. With a sigh, the old man gingerly removes the crown and sets it aside like Lear. He gazes out the window. After a few minutes of wistful contemplation, he turns to me, twisting awkwardly in his seat, against the stiff back and shoulders.

"That's right out of my memory," he says, thumbing at the mammoth brownstone. He turns back with jerky, old man abruptness. "It's complete, just as it was. I made sure of that. Only now I'm in no condition to explore it. Frankly I don't know that I want to. I mean I do and I don't. You go on in. Go take a look."

I eye the place dubiously. Doesn't have much glamour for me.

"Is that power going to stay on?" I ask.

"I suppose it will," he says. "It's never failed me yet."

"But if something goes wrong and building disappears out from under me and I'm ten storeys up ..."

"That's why I projected it over water," he says.

I go to the sill. The building stands directly over the bay.

"Anything I should look for?" I ask.

"No," he says.

I leave.

"Obvious gaps!" he cries uncertainly, when I'm halfway down the stairs.

"OK!" I call back.

"It's just coming over the wire—" voice calling bounce back from a big flat wall "Oh Kay—say get those lines free fellows" and quick muttered goodbyes and heavy handsets chunking back into cradles, someone coming from the next room already saying "mutter mutter mutter don't get ruffled" and then "Will you shake the lead out? Bill's already sore, you'll get us *both* in trouble!" and "I said all right I'm coming! What's the big hurry?"—I got to run something up to BB and then hustle a zippered oilskin packet of confidentialism across town to the main office and on the way I pass Calle Cavalcanti and that big brownstone. Ali Baba and Xanadu. The city is invisible. I mean I am so wrapped up in that brownstone it's all I can see. It's owned by five sisters named Mean, Mean, Mean, Mean, and the youngest one goes by Mean, who have no use for males and wouldn't touch a membrum virile if it had a fifty dollar bill folded underneath it. There is a daughter notwithstanding, must have been parthenowhatsis. This woman unimaginable as a mother. It has to be like being raised by mummies. But if I lived there, even at the mercy of the Sisters Grimm, that would be an arrival, that would be a certain accomplished journalic individual. It was like a haunted house carefully and solidly constructed out of parts of other haunted houses, like a department store. It was like a haunted village, steeped in permanent prestige and living wood panelling grows an inch a year like the Black Forest. Varnished with virgin's tears and unrequitedness to a high gloss so the whole interior is one big wooden mirror, you glance around and check how your grain is going.

Seems to me I'm blending with someone else. A young cog frittering his days away reading to some old gleep. Well that won't happen to me, no sir.

Going for breakfast to the cafe I run across Peter there, and he's not going to work— traffic, he says. Later I have to take the ferry. A long dive in a kind of bathyscape. Flabby, adenoidal specimens waddle by smelling of thick balcony juices. Couples getting angry at each other. I end up in a fight. Someone pulls a switchblade on me; I take it from him and throw it overboard. Then I'm throwing people overboard and laughing. We dock. A bus pulls up with a police escort, and ribald party on the bus. I want to escape this, so I rush to my cabin and begin packing. They'll think I'm getting ready to board the bus. I'm singing, sweetly and innocently, and my singing moves me so much I'm nearly in tears, tugging on my brown socks riddled with holes. Those poor people, floating out there in the water. God save them!

What a day. So now I'm back on the mainland so called, from my alcocentric point of view it seems more like an island than where I just was. Heading back to the office to see just how badly I fouled up this one and how much more official soreness is to be added to my thriving demerit column, I arrange as usual to swing by the magnificent, torvid hulk of the brownstone of the six sisters. The towers seem etched against the grey twilight sky. A shadow clings to the walls like film. A few windows glow with dull yellow light and a squat witch of a water tower gazes entranced out over the city from her high perch up there.

Recklessly I charge past the listless looking doorman, who does not even glance up from his newspaper as I go by, maybe engrossed in one of my stories for all I know, and head for the restaurant tucked away in the back of the ground floor. A plain wooden box, with a lardy smell of plain fare. The booths and tables are protected with tripwires. I take a seat at the counter, nearly putting myself right next to a religious man, chubby with a moustache and a rectangular head, eating off a banana leaf placemat. A tall, lanky man with stringy black hair and protruderant eyes appears before me and asks me what I want virtually the moment my weight is settled; I order the liver and onions and a glass of bear, as I mispronounce it. He pours me a glass of water, asking me in incoherent English something about writing—am I writer? do I write books? I think he's asking me what the deal is with the roman numerals at the beginning of some books. I muddle through this brief exchange and he excuses himself and murmurs what I guess is my order through the kitchen door. Here comes the food. I eat with an indescribable blending of relish and disgust. Nothing's wrong with the food, it's just that one of me loves it and the other is, well let's say he doesn't love it. Both are just fine with respect to our glass of bear though and that is promising.

The place is filled with members of a religious minority, not to call it a cult, which has a floor to itself in the building. They are somberly dressed, everyone married with quiet, nervous children. All I know is that they consider remembering a sin. I don't feel welcome, but I am ready to deal with them. When I of course mention remembering something, I am rejected and I leap up calling them bigots and spitting on the floor. I'm blowing it with the woman by doing this, cooing to a phantom baby in her arms. There's nothing there, but she seems to think that cooing now will somehow be saved for later and the baby, since there really is one, somewhere, will get the benefit of the effort some other time, as if you could do things in any order. She seems to be accepted by her motherly sister. The little girl in the black and white dress keeps her head turned away, sulky about all the attention paid to the phantom baby. Maybe she has some phantom attention coming somewhere along the line, or perhaps she's storing up some phantom pouting for later.

Someone's at the door summoning me, slyly hinting at me that I am sly, calling me a name with a knowing air, dressed in a tweedy chauffeur outfit, cap, black calfskin gloves. I see his shadow beneath the door when it closes again. Dirty looks prompt me to pay and get out.

Tenants gaze down from their wondrous apartments. I am tantalized by visions of another life as a tenant myself. The chauffeur is waiting for me in a crook of the building's arm, leaning his shoulder against the wall, ankles crossed.

"Over here chum," he says unctuously, "You sure got a winning way about you."

He got an almost girlish face and a build like a snake. He asks me if I am my name and I appraise him of his success.

"Mr. Streetop would like a word with you," he says.

"What about?"

He shrugs without shifting from the wall.

"He know I work for the Herald?"

"I don't know what he knows."

"He loaded?"

"For fare."

"Well, my calendar's clean for the rest of the evening."

He lightly tips his head.

"Come on."

"What'd he say?"

"All he said was 'Go get the narrator! You know nothing happens without him!' So you now got getted."

Down a long hallway behind the laundry and boiler rooms. Machines live down here, in these functional, undecorated cement apartments. We pass a shorter hallway off to the side, an a narrow, arched passageway that seems to have been chiseled into solid rock and leading to a narrow, remote archway, a little descending cloud of mist there. That, I know, is the portal to the lower basements, a domain of hermits, all half built; what is built is half jerry rigged and half original and strange, everyone is poor, too busy dreaming—no one wants to care for them down there, but the vital machinery is kept running thanks to a universal nervous attention that far exceeds the scope of any practical oversight. The sub-basement tenants circulate constantly from room to room, checking air pumps, water and steam pipes, electric wiring, fuseboxes, dumbwaiter gear, trays of tiny greenish mushrooms, rat traps, and the beams and other contrivances used to shore up crumbling masonry.

The chauffeur and I squeeze into a boxy elevator, almost stomach to stomach. If he thrust his gut out I would have to suck mine in. He presses the button and up we shoot. Out of the corner of my eye I see the dark lining of the shaft rushing by and the occasional two eyelike windows, but the chauffeur is staring directly into my face and smiling. I return his gaze stonily. The elevator stops and the doors open. We stand not moving, eyes locked. The door closes and the elevator returns to the basement. The doors open. Several minutes pass.

"Well, I guess I'll be ... moseying along now" I say eventually.

He reaches out and thumbs a button on the scratched brass plate next to me. The door grates rattle shut, click, whirr, going up. Face to face. When the elevator stops, I sidle out and stand beside the door, leaning on the wall and pressing the button quickly. The grate clatters shut before he can escape and away he goes.

I stay put, leaning my shoulder on the wall, my ankles crossed. The door opposite me swings open and the chauffeur appears, badly winded from his dash up the stairs and nearly blundering into a potted fern. Damp with perspiration, gulping and panting, he gestures me to follow him. This floor is all wood panels and dense hall runners, little tables, mirrors, panels panels panels. A ponderous door is flung silently open and I am ushered into a luxurious study, all leather and dark wood, books cognac andirons and oil paintings. Without a word, but largely recovered from his run, the chauffeur departs, mopping his brow, and I am left alone.

A few minutes later, as I take in the view from one of two small paned windows, a man with a trimmed grey beard enters from one of the recessed side doors. He comes in, sits down, and begins reading fistfulls of receipts. He rummages in a drawer full of the lace of torn off perforations from spiralbound notebooks.

"I'm Mr. Streetop," I say.

"I'm Mr. Streetop," he says, "Have a seat. Let me just ..."

I settle myself in one of the chairs facing his desk. This settling takes a while. Mr. Streetop plucks up a pipe, one of many lying flankwise in a row on the huge glossy desk, loads it up and lights it, tamping it with a smaller pipe.

He starts to drone on and I just can't pay attention. The novelty of the place, the situation, the weirdness. I get up out of my seat and stroll over to the window. I can't quite get a mental image of what I'm looking for but I vaguely believe it is the old man's house, his window, maybe his long old face watching through the dull glass, maybe centuries gone by or the primordial skyline, instead what I see is mostly clouds and rain and swarming luminous pairs of lights, like a cold demon sauna out there.

Mr. Streetop goes on explaining to the empty chair, pausing now and then to fix it with significant glances that were probably very impressive. The bookcase just here looks inviting, all those soft leather bindings. I wonder if he's read any of them. Thrusting the books back with my toes, I clamber up the bookcase toward the ceiling.

"Hey hey hey hey hey hey hey hey HEY!"

The chauffeur charges into the room.

"Get down from there!"

"Make me!"

"Well," he drawls, his voice going loud and level. "You can deal with me, buster, or you can deal with the house dicks, and in case you haven't seen *them* ..."

I had. I clamber back down smiling.

He's standing there with his fists on his hips.

"Climbing the bookcase," he mutters in disgust, looking me up and down.

"At my age," I say.

"This junk's expensive you know," he says.

Mr. Streetop hits another one of his majestic pauses, doing a first class awe job on the chair. The chauffeur crosses over to me and begins straightening up what I disarranged.

"Next time you got a urge to clown around, do it someplace cheaper."

So now he and I stand side by side, him facing the case and me the room, close enough I can smell his cologne.

"You got a crush on me?" I ask.

"Yeah," he says insincerely.

"So why peep in on me?"

"When?"

"Just now. Or was your mother a librarian and you just have a sixth sense about these things?"

"My mother was the best lay I ever had," he says, turning from his work with a grin and contemplating Mr. Streetop. The grin fades and he sighs.

"This time, stay in the chair, will you?"

"I bore easy."

"Could you reign in your natural ebullience?"

"Look, you know what this is about, so why not just tell me and I'm out of your hair and out the door?"

He crosses to the desk. Mr. Streetop does not seem to register his presence any more than he seems aware that I'm not sitting docile and cowed opposite him on his swanky leather.

The chauffeur kneels beside the desk and begins turning a brass crank. Mr. Streetop's voice breaks off with a glottal stop.

"If you would just let me in on the gag, it would spare us both some trouble."

He doesn't so much as glance at me.

"Nonmems coming in here ..." he mutters bitterly, working the crank. He throws a switch or something with a stiff thunk, then lunges up and crosses back to the door, a little bit fast, as if he had to get out quick before something happened.

"Take your seat and listen this time!" he says as he goes. Then, standing by the open door, knob in his hand, he adds, "And you think *you* ain't somebody else's memory!"

Door slam.

I take my seat in the chair.

Mr. Streetop plucks up a pipe, one of many lying flankwise in a row on the huge glossy desk, loads it up and lights it, tamping it with a miniature pipe.

"Now eh, Mr. *Grant*—"

"That's not my name."

"I asked you up here to talk to you about an article ... eh, just a moment, I have it here. Yes, this article about Strickland. Strickland oil shares. People produced by magic. An inside line on the market in Strickland oil. Husbandry of a lengedary creature. Now, Mr. Strickland ..."

"That's not my name."

"... You've got your story and whatever it is that story can do for you it has done for you, its value is fully let's say exploited by you. And your paper. But now I can offer you a new use for those old resources, by which I mean your connections. I'd stand to profit a great deal by knowing who they are, and since you're the only one who's in a position—at present—to tell me, you stand to profit as well. Senses, alimentation, acquiring food, excreting, resting, born, die, coit, maturing and aging, communication, society, locomotion, respiration, tolerances, immune system, everything about those creatures. When the big find will be made public and how much will be let go at a time. ... No comment so far?"

"This is all so sudden, Mr. Streetop. Give a country a boy a minute or two to soak in it."

"All right, keep soaking. Now you might even have a role to play. I'll need a go between if things pan out."

"How much of this big profit do you figure on sharing with me?"

"For the information, fifteen thousand. Further services ... when and where. How does that sound?"

"Sounds like a lot of money."

"Astute."

Pause.

"Oh, it's my turn?" I say, catch myself in time before I glance off into the wings and blow the whole scene. "Well, in a sec. Country boy, remember."

"Take your time," he puffs.

"Assuming I still have these contacts, assuming they got the inclination for shooting the breeze with good ole me still, I'll have to run your proposal by them of course, even for disclosure. Not that there's any danger of being caught of course but good policy, discretion, you know."

"I know," he puffs. There's a great volume of smoke coming out of this man. Fragrant pipe smoke, with an undertaste of burning tires.

"Now these contacts aren't as tapped out as you say they are. They get in line for other information as well down the line and that's good material for me, good stories, and that's tenure for me at the paper which is all I have."

"No money up front," he puffs.

"Nice chatting with you," I say, lifting my posterior out of the gulfy chair.

"You'd like an apartment in this building wouldn't you?"

Ah, my Achilles heel. And this heel knows it. His eyes squint at me through a bank of pipe smoke.

"You offering?"

"I'm not in a position to give you an apartment here. I own this place, but the building belongs to the weird sisters, you know that."

"But you'll put in a good word, huh?"

Even through the blue smoke I can see the white rectangle, crisp and Euclidian, flash like steel in his hand.

"This letter—it isn't sealed, you can see that everything is in order for yourself. And my signature."

"Recommending me to the sister, right?"

"Right."

I grin.

"This is as cute as it gets."

"This letter, and fifteen thousand. And more down the road, chances are. Then you'll be in *business*, Mr. Grant."

"And buy the *Herald* in a few years."

"Why not?"

"That's quite a bit to think about, Mr. Streetop."

He reaches that neat white letter out to me, stiff as a steel wafer. With tingling fingertips

I take it and drop it in outside right lower front jacket pocket.

"Don't make me wait, Mr. Grant."

"You'll find another way through without me, right?"

The head nods impressively. The man, his desk, wreathed like a mountain in clouds of smoke, receding as I float across the room buoyed by supposition.

"Don't contact me directly," he murmurs. "Go through Robert."

"Your chauffeur?"

The room is longer and longer, dimmer and dimmer, my motions more and more underwater and dreamlike, our words shuttling far away.

"Yes."

The door clicks to between us, solid and quiet and funereally rich.

Beeline to the building office to get that letter on file; as it turns out, one of the Dragons happens to be there, flicking through today's mail. One of the middle sisters I think. I plaster on my winningest face and ease up to her.

"Excuse me, Miss Pierpont?"

"Yes?"

"Mr. Streetop sent me."

I proffer the letter. She takes it without a word and resumes her flicking.

"It's in reference to myself," I say, turning to go.

She looks at me steadily.

"What concerning?"

"Petition for residency, ma'am."

She glances down at the letter and back up at me to see if we match. Then I am dismissed with a flick of the eyebrows.

Getting to and from the office involves traversing a long, broad, unlit gallery that reminds me of a ballet school. The windows are arched, with low sills, forming a series of dictionary tabs of wan daylight. In the middle of this gallery an enormous creature is eating hay from a wooden trough. Warty hide like rhino skin, indented with ball sockets, protruberances of joints and bones and muscles, structures like breasts earlobes scrotums noses, the odd and boneless parts. As it shifts its head to eat with hollow munching sound, various elements of its anatomy slither and jiggle. A barnyard odor radiates from it.

I spot the girl as she comes up a flight of steps a little way from this animal, steps set directly into the floor. She is slender, about twenty, in a black dress belted at the waist, with a flaring triangular skirt. Dark skin, tapering face, modest, indented lips, large brown eyes off the wall of an Egyptian tomb, straight hair with an angular fringe and coming halfway down her neck like a black silk cape. Latin or Indian. As she turns her head and sees me, that cape swings out and my camera gaze freezes the image and steadily closes in on the fragrant shadow there between the curtain of hair and the side of the head, entering into that darkness which becomes a broad hallway, completely black like the inside of a spacious theater, and stern, large men stomping along together, a brace of them, hands clasped at the small of the back behind them like the froth at the prow of a ship, maybe in priest's vestments—no aprons, capacitous aprons of stiff black duck, and a white imp or monkey, invisible in the darkness between them but occasionally visible as it nimbly leaps up their backs or rides between them. Dimly lustrous apertures going by, some sort of greater planetarium ahead.

I know this girl, or my body does. It's so instant, familiar, ready, that it doesn't feel like wanting. I want her like I want my own arm, but it isn't anything even remotely like taking for granted, I don't do that. She's someone I've wanted forever, a want I know completely, so that it almost seems redundant to act on it; it's like the desire reached me so readily it actually overshot me, missed me the way you miss an easy toss.

Phone rings.

"Would you answer that for me please?" she asks, her hair swinging. She is busy doing something involving the animal, measuring the growths with a ruler like a beam of neutralized light. There's a phone carbuncled onto the wall by the entrance to the gallery. The voice on the line is an altered version of what is come to think of it not my own.

"Go outside and come back in again. I want to skip this next part."

I hang up and leave the girl, the gallery, the browsing hulk. Down and out then turn around and suddenly I am sizzling incandescent with vengeful rage. We've skipped over the part where I help Mr. Streetop and am betrayed, and now I have returned for my revenge. The desk man has been warned to look out for me and I'd rather not be noticed here. Turning my back toward the desk, which is well across the spacious lobby, I make my way to a phone booth near the passage that leads around to the cafe. Wandering around in this building is not so straightforward a task. There are regions that drive anyone who venture into them insane. There are supernatural traps of all kinds. You have to move cautiously if you come uninvited. You have to figure out where the traps are and feel your way along. I have a zest for that kind of thing and I am ready for it. There is, for example, a ghost child here, who teases by slipping into German. But I am the ritual impersonator of the dead, indispensible for the funeral rites, and it is as a dead man I can make my way through this multi-storey labyrinth and lay my ambush for Mr. Streetop. The woman I know, the olive skinned girl, she is being absorbed gradually into the building. She never leaves. All her time is taken up with its business. Soon she will admit it into her bed, if she hasn't already, in some form or other. All that is neither here nor there, but her personality is being dissolved in the process, and to let such beauty, and I mean beauty, no other word, to let such beauty be extinguished out of this world already starved starved starved for beauty and bleeding to death, crying out for it, the beautiful day, the brilliant sun and the colors, all the while it recedes from you like the shore, your blood running out the hot painful wound and your body going cold, you crying and clawing at it trying not to lose it, a voice telling you you're dying, dying—"Stop saying that!"—dying, still dying—"I said *stop* it!" you roar. No I won't allow that even if she's madly in love with Mr. Streetop. There has to be a limit.

The girl's name is held back by another part of me, must be the old man himself, doesn't want to share I guess. The exceptionally subtle arrangement of the building has altered her, like a foreign language displacing her mother tongue. I catch sight of her again at one of the Pierpont sisters' soirees.

"Darling I have the most *ruinous* thing planned for this evening. It's positively *ashes*."

One of the guests is a blonde occultist everyone is afraid of, a stern Scandanavian woman slim in a blue Dior dress with many fine wrinkles around her eyes. She is said to be "very rough going." She runs a sort of hellfire society devoted to novel, decadent, and horrifying pleasures, with a missionary zest for corrupting souls as an end in itself. She and a few of her adherents hover by the fire, eating black wafers of diamond. The vampires from the attic have also put in appearance. They make the paper which is sold in the lobby stationery shop. It's always dusk up there in that part of the building, just as it's always high noon on the dot for the Mathetes of the third floor and always a minute past midnight for the Quietists of the thirteenth. What time is it in this part of the building I don't know—cocktail hour anyway. Somehow I get roped into a conversation. I don't know how it happened. I got caught on an affinity from the memory self; it seems as though my blended nature is less homogenized at this party than elsewhere. I am more of a tag-along than an actor.

This conversation won't quit. I am myself not allowing it to quit. We keep drifting toward a natural lull and a pretext to wander away without loss of face, but one of us, often appallingly often me, gets things going again. It's as if we were all afraid of what we might do the moment we lose track of each other and so prolong this misery for want of that assurance. Why am I being this way? Trying to win points, be the smartest one in the room. Even acknowledging this is only a new reason to congratulate myself for being smart enough to see it. So I admit it aloud, and even then I'm showing off. So I admit that, and, by risking my esteem in front of others in this way, I make myself appear bold. So should I mortify myself by deliberately taking on the transparent vanity of a real prat? Wouldn't I only be making myself still further into a hero of self-knowledge that way, not to mention a sly deceiver? Vanity is too fleet for that. In that instant I catch sight of her crossing the room. Someone like you could never even begin to imagine the resourcefulness of my pride, I think at her.

I'm being told about a magician or wise man who lives in the building. He is confined to his apartment by his own hair, which has grown so copious it fills every room. Apparently he swims in it. Opening the door, you see nothing but a grey mass of fibers crackling with static electricity; he paws the tresses apart and thrusts out his head to take his meals from a rolling table. Hidden somewhere in that apartment full of hair he has his astrolabe, crystal ball, grimoires of spells, a bag of magic barf, a brass head that talks, and a whispering familiar in the form of a huge bat with the head of an owl and human hands instead of feet.

"Real magic is fucked up," I interject knowingly, irrelevantly.

I tune out and eavesdrop instead in desperation to the two old women on the settee adjacent. They say things like "My land" and "Isn't that terr'ble?" One relates how she found a huge ruby, prised from the socket of a native idol. However, as I attend more closely, it appears she means she actually found a huge piece of liver wrapped in paper, which she had appraised by a butcher. The liver came in two pieces, both pretty dried out and shrivelled, quite small, but he believed the pieces were valuable.

The disjuncture between myself as I am in this sort of situation, ie., the Pensive Drunk, and the old man's younger memory self, who is mercurial and sparkling when under the influence, is becoming painful, and I can't decide whether to try to get up to his speed or just go to sleep and let him do the full carry.

I'm in luck, he's ducked out, using the lavatory as a pretext to get away from the wild bores, and he's following the girl. She hops in the elevator and we run down the stairs, stopping at each floor to see if she gets out. The exertion is helping to burn out a bit of the booziness, and I have to slip nimbly if I do say so myself back behind the door to avoid being noticed when she steps out at the third floor.

The glory of high noon shines in the windows at either end of the elevator section of the hall. She walks swiftly to one of the doors and knocks.

"Lowercase a minus lowercase b divided by the sum of lowercase a and b equals the tanget of half the difference of capital A minus capital B divided by the tangent of half the sum of capital A and capital B."

The door opens and she slips inside. About twenty minutes later she emerges again, wearing a sheath dress of silver satin, with long sleeves, and flaring to a skirt well below her hips. I got to duck back a long way to avoid being caught following her, because she heads briskly for the elevator, intent and businesslike. That's the wrong outfit for that affect; that's a dress for willowy languid doe-eyed beauties with all the time in the world, and she looks like she's organizing a spirited defense of the building. I'm starting to feel too much admiration. Desire? I don't know. I could be enjoying, or I could just be remembering. Not her name, though. I can't get it. Maybe that's something else the old man is holding back. Isn't it better to stay a child in your own small, manageable world? Avoid all this bending and learning? How many lessons until I can stop? I'll stop, but not because I'll have acquitted myself of the final lesson. The lessons go in circles. The old man's dead hide in empty rooms, and wander the uninhabited floors. The rich hall runners are pressed by their feet like forest lawns. I can't feel them. There's never been enough of me for tragedy, I was never adult enough, tragic words are always false coming out of my mouth because I was always the lucky fool and the spoiled child. I feel the anger and sorrow, the venomous hatred, but everything my mouth turns into cotton candy harps and rainbows.

I follow her back to the party, which has moved to a banquet hall on an upper floor. A lively Latin combo is banging away in a corner, with shiny accordion sleeves and an upright piano. She weaves through the crowd to a lean black man with short dreads and pulls him aside. A serious conference there. Nods as they part again. Her hair spins out like a skirt as she returns into the crowd. I keep on. She talks to a few people in the room, always taking them aside for a momentary one on one. Then zoom out the swinging doors at the back. I sure hope that isn't the kitchen and ready my gee-whiz-tipsy-and-turned-around act in case I'm about to go out of bounds. Just a panelled hallway. Silver flicker of skirt just rounding the corner. I rush after, taking advantage of the plush hall runner, and nearly barrel into her, yank myself back by my own collar just in time to avoid being seen and creep back a bit from the corner, will she investigate? A pause, a quiet knock, her lisping. It's embarrassing, it's downright shameful, what I will degrade myself to do for a lisping woman, it's like a sickness, it's like I got a button marked STUPID and that's what thumbs it. That lisping mouth full of cool silver sugar slush. I hear the door click and risk a peek—nothing. It's the last door before the corner I'm hid behind; do I risk sneaking up and eavesdropping? Paralyzed by a flash door opening abruptly her startled drawback my bumbling excuses now she knows my face for a snooper I sit tight. Maybe ten minutes later I hear the knob turn and dart back toward the double doors. Phone booth recessed right into the wall I hadn't noticed coming in being fixed as I was on her, in I duck and nothing happens. If she came out, she didn't come this way.

I slip back out and down to the corner—nobody in the hall. Assume she came out. If not, I know where she is. Pad down the runner in the other direction. There's something there to be discovered, practically shouting at me, indistinguishable from the pull of her gravity that draws me in a headlong dive I know I can't stop whatever is going to happen next, whatever it is, it's what this is all about, the next moment. Broom closet. That's all there is here. I have to dree my weird so I yank the door open hoping for a moment of surprise and confusion that will at least momentarily bring the odds closer to level. The door barely clears the jam and stops with a jolt as it hits the edge of my sole; infuriated by this resistance I move my foot and fling the door back with a bang, nearly throw myself down a shaft as black as coal. No broom closet. Nothing but blackness, and a steel pillar. I sure hope nobody heard that door whack open. No other way out—this has to be the door. Nothing I can see in there but the smooth, featureless pillar, rising out of and back into a black hole. The pillar has small streaks of black grease on it. They are floating downward, as if they were melting but they can't be melting because they don't change shape. The pillar is moving. As I watch, the broom closet descends into view, stops. Normal broom closet. One light bulb in the ceiling. Switched on. They leave that switched on?

Get in and shut the door. No buttons, nothing, but then comes the twitch and glide and I guess I'm going up. A gush of nervous and nonsensical sexual excitement like a naked-at-school dream. With a jolt the walls stop moving but the floor keeps going and on a platform I rise to the surface. Stars overhead. Icy, odorless wind. Countless stars, as many lights as there are dark places or nearly. The ceiling with its one light bulb is supported above me on four props, the corners of the broom closet. I step out from under and blink, trying to adjust my eyes. My feet sink into a fine dune. The dust hangs in the air around my ankles. My lungs feel like they're full of helium, lifting my body up. The blood bangs into my head and tingles, not with emotion, something physical. I take a few drunken steps and nearly tumble over some stones. My dim shadow, thrown by the one light bulb, there before me on the black ground. The horizon is alarmingly near. The ground is black.

A little further away now from the platform with its light bulb, the only source of light apart from the stars and an enormous crescent moon, so big it blots out an area of stars bigger than my outstretched hand. A strictly psychological umbilical yokes me to the platform and the lightbulb. Looking down in blind frozen terror I see the stars beneath my feet, through the transparent matter of the planet. The rocks, the dust, the distant mountain cones are all clear as glass; in places reflections appear to be extensions of the reflected object, and the surface of the planet becomes impossible to see. I turn around. Past the bizarrely familiar and out of place platform, with its wooden flooring and prosaic light bulb, towers a huge wall or membrane of what looks like fractured and marbled glass. It resembles a tattered, folio cut book, a warped and swollen book that won't close properly, viewed edgewise. A mile high. The top curving back into darkness, just a few livid horizontal lines, like white foam on invisible night surf. In the other direction, a colossal, angular block, completely dark except for a wan radiance reflecting off the base, which hovers on no support I can see, what must be a hundred feet off the ground at least. The light seeps up one side, showing how it's oddly tilted, and limns one vertical edge. Yeah, and there are black globes, all the same size, sliding up and down the sides.

When I catch sight of her again, striding into view on a kind of pathway I guess, I nearly bust out laughing. Fine, keen. The landscape here is illuminated faintly by a kind of powdered light that ripples sluggishly along the ground in a nearly flat amphitheater with broad, shallow tiers descending to an elliptical floor. Mollusks the size of elephants, with incredibly ornate and elaborate conchlike shells, slink majestically along the tiers or slide along the nearly vertical slopes of the towering sails of black glass which rise like a copse of gargantuan trees to one side. The sails are shaped a bit like meat cleaver blades and axe heads. Two mollusks float up to each other and interact by blowing out arabesques of shell material, which combine and fluctuate through, among other shapes, strictly regular geometrical combinations. It's a tactile-visible language of spontaneous writing, read in conjugations of manipulated angles, arcs, and areas. These giants are intelligent. They learned tool use by gaining mastery over the growth of their shell matter and tissues, forming it into useful shapes. Parts of their anatomies, especially in what I take to be the head and also certain aft parts that might be genitals or maybe organs of elimination, are not entirely solid, but might be composed of some rareified substance analogous to the stuff of the planet itself.

The old man's knowledge ballasts me. He's remembering what he will know, and that's how I get it. Not much point in ducking behind a see-through rock, I just try to keep out of the powdered light and to track the woman, who stands out like a silver needle. She stops, and the ground beneath her trembles and spills upward forming an orifice like a little one-man band shell sluicing inkiness that streams and flutters backward and pastes itself to the outside. Gliding forward, through an impossibly distinct shadow line into the powdered light, the teacher appears, evidently seated on a floating dais. No sunglasses this time. With his eyes exposed, the teacher looks ill and vulnerable. The dazzling white papal robes settle around him on his low seat or maybe he's in the lotus position under there, a brilliant scarlet trail down the middle descending from his bloody chin. He gulps, his lips recede a moment to expose the teeth yellow through the red, blood surges among the teeth, two streamlets round each bend of the exposed jaw and meet precisely in the middle, well and spill down the chin.

She reaches into her tiny reticule and pulls out something that sparkles, a pillbox. With a quick glance at her watch, she opens the pillbox and produces a white snow capsule, leans forward and inserts it into the teacher's mouth. The teacher swallows it. Blood splashes from his mouth in a fan that nearly reaches her. A pancake of blood drops into his lap. Impotence makes his gestures exquisitely gentle. He looks at her steadily. Desperate misery in his eyes. He says something to her in a voice so distorted and eloquent with a horrifyingly controlled torment that I can't listen to it. Even so, I feel it like driving wind that pushes against me and then departs. Unwittingly I shut my eyes. When they open, the teacher is gone, and the woman is coming back up the path toward the platform. In a minute she'll see me. Me, on the planet of the dead, in my scuffed brown shoes and my cheapest of all possible neckties. Everything will depend on my selection of words. Not too fancy or you'll come off like a stuffed shirt not too simple or you'll look simple, and just the right lie. I am confronted with an absolute certainty that I have nothing to say to her. I have nothing but that certainty, stark inside me. I am relying on it. The sheer absurdity of any words in this place knocks them right out of me and the next moment they are back again, all stripped of their urgency and one as good or bad as another. She's here.

"Nice weather ..."

She doesn't stop; advancing toward me, she takes me by my forearm and starts trying to drive me back.

"All right you, come along."

"Just a minute, just a minute!"

I stay put and free my arm.

"I'm no drunk, I'm a respectable journalist—well a journalist anyway. My card."

I hold my card out. She ignores it, eyes on me.

"I was just having a look around is all," I say.

"Improper. Look, mister—"

"—I am—"

"—I neither know nor care to know—"

"—I am looking around—"

"—what you believe you're seeing or—"

"—you expect me to believe you don't know—"

"—where you think you are. You're drunk—"

I shake my head.

"—and you're going, right now."

"You got one weirdo building here."

"Write it up for better madhouses and gardens. Now, will you follow me please?"

"To the ends of the earth, if you like, or whatever planet this is."

"This way."

I stay put and smile.

"I believe I said this way."

I take a few steps toward the amphitheater.

"This way!" she cries. Her voice is so sharp I stop and look back at her. Her face is livid, stiffening into an indignant mask.

"OK, lady, OK," I say. I don't move.

"Do I have to call someone?"

"Call someone."

She's getting plenty sore now.

"You going to keep all this to yourself, is that the idea?" I ask.

I don't know why but for some reason I actually am beginning, no have felt for some time now as if I were drunk. Back at cocktail time I hadn't downed enough to wet a canary's whistle but now it's as if I'd been play acting at being drunk and turned it unwittingly into second nature. Then again, it isn't a bad cover, as long as it goes on being that only.

I gaze out again at the new world of blacks and whites, gulfs of sky, unorientational space, and shore myself in my false drunkenness for protection against the vertigo and panic that paw lightly at me from space. Looking back at her, furious with me, her mouth flat as a razor's edge, this has gone all wrong. I'm past redeeming. But even this stupid, canned conversation is more than I expected to get. And this is the way I've always wanted it. The woman upbraiding me, me standing there sheepish, in trouble. I don't know myself unless I'm in trouble. When the finger beats the air like a conductor's baton and the voice goes shrill and high aah there I am!

"You're what I came to look at," I say honestly.

Her frustration boils over. She rolls her eyes, summoning fresh strength—"Will you leave please!"

"What is this place?"

No answer.

I point to the mollusks.

"What are those things?"

No answer. Eyes fixed on me like she's resorting to amateur hypnotism to get rid of me. I start down the path toward the amphitheater.

"Don't go down there!"

The words spring from her reflexively, I can tell.

"You're sure bossy," I say, without glancing back at her.

I hear her take two steps after me.

"Don't go *down* there!"

This time I turn to face her again. I'd rather be this close to her angry than far away watching her being calm.

"I don't recall signing anything, any paper that said I'd take orders from you. This is a big place you got here and I'm taking a look around."

"You don't know what you're doing."

"Introduce me to the man who does sometime, I'd ask him how he does it."

"He does it by not crashing in where he's not welcome."

"I thought you were going to call someone."

Those lips clamp together again. In the powdered light, her face is like a fawn velvet mask, with blazing, iodined eye whites and glistening black opal irises.

"Is this your place, madame? Are you Astrillia, Queen of the Moon?"

"I'm too busy for this nonsense, that's what I am—"

"Too busy doing which?"

She glares at me. The conclusion of this episode will not be a fade out on a romantic scene.

"Clamsville again, huh? No tipping?"

It's all wrong. In fact I ought to burst out laughing, having as time honored a conversation as this is turning out to be, my head full of vapid thoughts and generally carrying on like a cretin instead of getting my head around an alien world, an alien species right down there not a hundred yards away, intelligent mollusks that are all skin, that excrete living things as waste, that have a language with no possessives, that have a culture centered around taking drugs and creating cyclopean glass calligraphs out of volcanoes, that create artifacts out of something like woven gauze or webbing that is nevertheless as resilient and flexible as steel. Shadows of the dead on the planet. The starlit wandering of the dead abandoning trails of rotting earth and rotting ocean. I should be throwing myself at her feet instead of giving her all this lip.

"All right, if you want to be quiet then listen. If I'm talking to you I'm not poking around in places you don't want me to be."

She folds her arms.

"That's fine. So ... ever since I set eyes on you I can't budge. Not an inch. I don't know what I want or that I want anything, but I have to *see* you. If I could do that without troubling you, if I could be a fly on a wall and just see you ... But that's not how it is."

Am I crazy, or is she starting to warm up? She comes over to me, takes my arm, gently this time, even looks up into my eyes, not by much, because she's pretty tall. I can't smell her perfume because the air is wrong on this planet, in fact we haven't even been listening to each other, just sight reading each other. The sound of our voices doesn't carry right. I'm falling for it even though I know she's just getting rid of me. It's the only way to have this moment of false ease with her. We both know it. Looking down into her eyes I can smell the stink of her rotten body, even in this non-air air, gazing up into my eyes. In her eyes I see the registration as she smells the stink of my own rotten body. Millions of years have passed. We're corpses. All too late. What I reach for in her is a spoiled, decayed life that I could never believe wasn't mine. The apartment building crumbles. Flakes of soot sprinkle down out of the old man's hair. The figures of hope and memory and desire vanish. Death.

UNIT FORTY-THREE
DISENPOETRY

Phantasmagoric poetry is composed by rhetorical dowsing, according to subtle resonances in protolingual ether which tune or detune as each image or each musical effect, or conceptual effect, or micronarrative, or character effect, is walked through. The grammar of this poetry begins when humans are pollinated by astrals, which move from one language-being to another, acquiring and redistributing in the process all manner of lexicalities. The ensuing altered juxtaposition of transposed inflections is an embryo which may flower into a fully developed trope, verse form, etc., if it is exposed to human moods and images in time. When phantasmagoric poetry is read in its own spirit, this attracts astrals which actually become part of the reader's mind, for a while, as much as memory, imagination, emotion, reasoning, etc. The presence of astrals is often perceived in object form, as enigmatic memory or deja vu. Astrals can also be perceived as mental surplus, such as a marked and abrupt increase in thoughtfulness, forgetfulness, intentness, being emotional. At their most subtle, astrals take the form of altogether new mental faculties that defy analysis and labelling. The poem becomes telepathic. Its meaning is as plain as "good morning," but there is no way to explain how this meaning makes its leap. Pages of gibberish are crystal clear. A single line, alone, is a journey that lasts for days and crosses jungle, desert, mountain, lake, city streets, the surface of the moon by the light of a reading lamp.

Read the following passage and see if it changes anything.

UNIT FORTY-THREE READING

Ransoming Hostages

you must be naked to enter the garden
the black moon, a landscape of light, of purest blackness, like a mirror
in a forest
at darkness

medusa destroys those who see her. basilisk destroys those it sees. the medusa is defeated
by the blind. the basilisk is defeated by the invisible.
over there a dresser drawer opens and light pours out as if that drawer were full of
folded angel clothes, in that light you can see the face of the opener, just the astonished
expression,
the hand flashes, creating a black bat that seems to wield the light to and fro, from
open drawers, windows, the lights of stars and files

gestures flash around the empty room
silhouettes flow in and out of each other
I carry their faces with me like bright fiery flags
torturing the living island
I spend so much time admiring their handwriting

the shrubs give off the sherry-like odor of summer
destructine sleep—words form in webs of candied light
a still lake on a pitch black night, like a pool of congealing smoke
invisible suspense

an hour almost seems like a person sometimes
unknown symbolic acts within

rolling her eyes ... she walked right up to me, like a child would—this is *my* creature—

hello, she smiles sheepishly, pressing her upper lip flat with her lower—did you have something to tell me?—yes—she puts a letter or something in his hand, pointing it at him

Tallboys

Vignettes

magic incense

pots of white cream

there on the brown leather sofa seat, a number of small white objects. I investigate. Toenails.

the paradox traps and releases
what treats me as reality

the mountain rains burning cinders

the judicious biting mouth, the house that brutally takes itself

the experiment is designed to overload
the talking wire that runs across the courtyard, the housefront opposite the window plays music for not touching

people getting arrested for their facial expressions

criminalization of translators

the travellers are ghost particles or rays petalled with spring leaves or blossoming with same bright to-be-petals
they treat certain animals as friends or even their own offspring

there was no momentary beginning of life, only a granular intersuffusion of apparent contraries

taking souls away in a napkin

leaning on the bed it speaks a little inchoate word

educate the idol
a whole pavilion of imaginary philosophy
academy of dripping leaves avenues

careful hands careful fingers
boxes his hands all complexity without being lost is held, compressed, sustained, is concentrated, concentration that does not dissipate
constellations new every night, step out to see what this night's contellations would be, sitting on his porch, or perhaps leaning, perhaps standing, perhaps sprawling, in the pipelight and fireflies, sprawling face down to look at the stars with his ass, light turning into rolls of solid froth, rise up in the creases of the mosaic and turn to raised seams of gleaming foam, lava braids settling back in the sinister narcotic billows

become the word you read
centuries of bullshit crumble at its touch, at even the weakest fillet of air from the hem of a coat as someone you don't know turns to go up

a female pan
smiling without malice but like someone bewildered in a pleasant dream

UNIT FORTY-FOUR
THE FORM OF GRAMMATICAL REPRESENTATION

In use throughout this work book, the form of grammatical representation, or FGR, is the grammatical mode reserved for use when describing the workings of grammar, and which is entirely unlike any other of unlanguage's modes. The grammar that you have been reading from the beginning, is unique to this work book, and possibly to other texts on the same subject.

The one exception has been this passage, which is constructed in the mode reserved exclusively for describing the form of grammatical representation, and which is only employed for the purpose of explaining the operation of the form of grammatical representation.

The variations introduced by these modal shifts are very subtle, and will be apparent only to the experienced student. Try to figure out what they are on your own.

UNIT FORTY-FOUR READING

The two men approached the beach. It was night, clear, moonless, stars down to the horizon. The crumbling towers of Varosha were barely-discernible silhouettes. Even the white sand was dim. They pulled the boat up the beach and hid it, paused looking over at the lights of Famagusta.

The first of the two men, Daki, was a guide who'd done this before, and the other was his foreign client. There was nothing strange about him and everything about him was strange. Daki knew how and where to get through the fence and avoid the soldiers. He did not know his client's name or much about his reasons for wanting to enter the forbidden zone and that was as it should be. He had been paid, was due for more after.

Varosha had been sealed by the Turkish military in 1974 and had been rotting in plain view ever since. Now they were inside the corpse. A rampart of luxury hotels lined the shore, their foundations almost laved by the surf. The men moved along in silence, the guide turning now and then to whisper instructions. Each of the towers contained a radio tuned to a computer simulated human voice reciting calmly, a different language in each tower. One was German, one was Greek, one was Turkish, and so on. He couldn't remember which was which. The result was a set of monolinguistic environments. If you entered the building with the Greek radio, everything would go Greek for you, like everything looks red in red light, but that wasn't the reason the radios had been planted there. No one seemed to know the reason. The two men would pause from time to time, and then the mutter of those radios, dully reverberating inside the hotels, reached them.

The client abruptly turned from following his guide and scrambled up a little heap of rubble to survey one of the broad streets beyond. He raised his hands to his face and formed them into a pair of cones, holding them before his eyes like binoculars. Through them he could see the new city, the streetlights shining, the streets filled with teachers, in subfusc and sweaters and neckties and pearls and skirts and t-shirts and costumes, all the teachers of the earth walking to and fro, talking about algebra, rhetoric, listing dates and places, the names of the elements and constellations overhead, harmony, philosophy. Above them, huge grammatical machines made entirely out of language and relationships stalked like tripods or dragons. The client searched for a particular teacher, a head of long unkempt white hair, an ashen face and a shocking scarlet mouth that dripped and splattered.

The guide pulled him down and reproached him nervously. They were not visible from the periphery of the sealed area, but there might be watchers posted inside. He had definitely seen the head and shoulders of men seated at windows during previous visits, although that was by day.

Now this was the difficulty—unlanguage stalks the teacher, becoming for him an inescapable steady doom. He is hounded by grammar machines of phantasmagorica that trap him by blocking meaning channels, forcing his interpretative hand. Whatever may have had some bright possibility inhering within is relentlessly driven and chuted and amputeed until it is bleak and hopeless and puffed up with one agonizing suffocation after another, and contractive adjectives follow conjunctions and pelt down like sleet, shaving the razor down to pounding sleet, an ever narrower, tighter sluice whose sides plainly converge in the distance. A request for a ticket on the train turns into a request for a ticket in the wrong direction, a greeting in the street is received as if it were a serious insult, the language twists in his mouth, the first glimpse of him hatches nigger, faggot, paedo bastard in other minds. Unlanguage can lay it on or hang back, leave the betrayal hanging or seem to forget, but those two lights up on the wall, on the floor, the ceiling, flashing from eyes going by in the hall, never abandon the teacher. He must be punished for daring to teach unlanguage to others. It's one thing to know it, and to be able at last to hear and understand the waves of corpse talk that engulf the earth, crash all around the world like sea froth around a rock in the surf, shimmering flakes and dollops of it tossing all around the worldearth, squawks hums lilts warbles.

I, the foreign client, have just had a look at the timestreet which my sources inform me runs through Varosha. Actually there are several here, but this one I've seen through the lenses of my hands is the one I want.

"Let's go," I say.

Daki leads me through ensorcelled arcades to the street. I pause, and search the cracked pavement.

"What are you looking for?"

"Tracks," I say. "The trail."

"What trail?"

"He was here, and I know his traces—ah!"

There it is, nearly purple in this universe of blue light. This is the bluest night, by the way, I've ever seen. Even Daki's white teeth are pale blue when he shows them, and the blues of his eyes, the blue of his black hair. This blue blood here on the shattered pavement is still wet and sparkling like dew. Spiral out and find the next gout, here it is, now plot the line and follow it from splash to splatter, most of them with little syrupy tendrils like calligraphs, more and more like writing now that I think of it. I chuckle quietly, feeling almost like one of those grammautomatons pursuing him.

"He never stops taking notes, not even for an instant." I say. "His scholarly instincts have deep roots all right."

Following these 'notes,' we travel further inland along the timestreet and into a level of the past, reversing that part of the present and going back in. Varosha seems much bigger, vast, more like Athens than a resort town. Tall buildings surround us like dense forest, and now there is no denying this is a city, a vast one, filled with skyscrapers and huge ingot-shaped buildings. There is a barely audible murmur now, plausibly the noise of a city heard from miles away.

Look behind me. There are the ruins of Varosha and the stars between the towers. The flanks of the nearer buildings look glow painted, and that light becomes slightly more shivering and intense as I watch. The undulating shadows of serpents glide over the walls in schools, so the walls look more like luminous, upright ponds. Serpent shapes appear behind us in the street and trickle in our direction like soldiers. I begin to think that I have thought too much about serpents, and I note in the process that the synonym, which is much more common, and less formal, than the word I have been using, did not only not spring naturally to mind, as is most probable, but I can't even remember it now.

Daki leads us down an alleyway. My footsteps scrape on wet, shining grit. The alley's bricks gleam with rain that didn't fall on me in my starry night. I have fallen behind. Daki is out of sight up ahead. I turn the wrong way, enter an open doorway, surprise two men with glowing eyes who were leaning over a counter reading outspread newspaper and dressed like plainclothes cops. Now they're both straightened up and staring—I take off down the alley, after Daki. Footsteps bang after me, right on me. Banged—used to bang, a long time ago. Panting, I watch the image as my past tenses conjugate away the two men, who flutter in silhouette along the wall, jogging uncomfortably in their confining old clothes, and vanish across the frame's edge. Each time I pull a trick like that I am one trick less, and I don't know how many more I've got. Not all gone, though. I would feel that, I hope.

I find Daki, waiting for me in the ruins of Varosha, by the corner where the old school stands. We press on after a moment's consultation down the timestreet, he believing that we'd only just avoided the notice of a UN watcher or a Turkish soldier. There is blood here, uncoiling like a trampled worm on the ground. The teacher's way. Again a city crowds around us, full of invisible, silent bustle on the other side of the dimensional screen, and towering and massing, seeming to swell and grow heavier.

The two men approach an elongated brutalist pyramid that looks a little like a fantasy spacecraft, complete with hairline detailing and huge orange numbers in microgramma type. They climb directly up the side of the building to a rectangular socket in the white wall, where they force open broad steel doors enamelled in bright orange and marked with a white 2. The doors part without a sound. Inside is darkness and stale air.

The blood trail gives out here, and Daki has never been in this building before. The foreign client reaches for a ball bearing chain that hangs from a suspended light bulb.

"You'll be letting them know we're here," Daki says wearily, "if that goes on."

The other lowers his hand again. Daki checks the time.

Through the doors directly ahead there is an atrium with a skylight far overhead, ringed with color coded tiers. Shreds of clear plastic dangle from the skylight, baffling and mixing with its pale radiance looking like a mammoth jellyfish.

The foreign client checks an impulse to glance at Daki. As they turn left and begin to walk around the orange tier, it suddenly occurs to him he has no idea what he's looking for or what he's doing. Ninety degrees further along the orange tier the walls fold back and the foreign client leads Daki into the room there with feigned confidence. A wall faces the entrance, with gaps to either side. Going around, see, the wall forms the back of a stage shaped like a long tongue covered in big white ceramic tiles. The stage is only slightly elevated and surrounded by consoles that bulge out of the smooth white floor like snowdrifts.

The foreign client examines the consoles. They have stations with sculpted visors and dividers, and each station has a syphon recessed into it. The foreign client finds what strikes him arbitrarily as a suitable looking station area and whips off his glasses, bends to examine the surface from only a few inches away. With his face, he smacks a part of the console where the plastery texture is rubbed smooth and retains almost indiscernible patches of color. He smacks again harder, looks up at Daki who is staring and says,

"I'm fixing it, I'm fixing it."

Another quick blow with his face. The client begins randomly adjusting levers made of clear glass like whiskey bottle necks, and even filled with amber liquid. He is more and more painfully aware of Daki's eyes on him; for some reason I am close to panic simply because he may realize I don't know what I'm doing, but he gets paid so what does he care?

He'll probably run if he realizes I'm crazy, take the boat, leave me here to my own devices. This makes me all the more determined to get these machines working. Like learning a language, you just pick it up and use it, make it work. The controls are simple and the mechanism is highly complex; your own way is more important to the operation than is following directions.

I lean down, put my ear to one of the syphons, in time to hear the word "mustard" very plainly spoken. Scooting two steps over I try the next one. "Ketchup," it says. "Pepper."

It doesn't occur to me that he wouldn't hear anything himself. "Listen," I tell him, trying not to seem strange. Daki comes over and puts an ear to the nearest syphon.

"What did it say?"

"Odos," he says, not understanding.

"Keep listening, make sure you note if it says anything except in Greek."

"What is it?" he asks.

"It can modify the machines made of words that control us. Keep listening."

I tell him to listen mainly to give him something other than my obvious insanity to occupy himself with, and as for me, what could be less important than if I'm insane or how or why, when all that counts is the experiment working, and is an experiment that has to supply its own purpose therefore insane? Of course there is insanity somewhere, of that I'm certain, and that it involves me in some way is equally certain, but whether or not it is confined to me, that is uncertain, that is what with deliberation you must call uncertain.

"Soy sauce," the next syphon says. I am sauce.

"Worcestershire sauce," I call down into the syphon. No answer.

"Mayonnaise," I call next. "Vinegar."

"Aluminum," the machine says quietly.

"Molybdinum," I say.

"Sodium," the machine says.

"Potassium," I say.

"Calcium," the machine says.

"Dressing," I say. "Salad dressing."

"Salt," the machine says.

We're getting somewhere. This is really working.

"Grape jelly," I say.

"Bicarbonate of soda," the machine says.

"Pickle relish," I say.

"Sugar," the machine says.

Daki is talking to his syphon. My estimation of him improves enormously. He is staring over the top of the console onto the stage. The room is unchanged, but my catlike eyes, sharp now that I have my glasses back on, pick out flickerings of light in his pupils, as if he were looking at something flashing, at something like daylight broken in leaves and trembling. Astral machinery. It isn't just a myth. Following his eye I notice a huge dark cloud on the stage, with a lively Latin combo barely visible inside it. Most prominent is a tall thin black man in a tight purple t shirt kind of flocked white and big brown sunglasses playing electric bass short-strapped high up against his chest and with a lot of shoulder action. That's just what I would think of, isn't it, not a surgeon or a revolutionary leader. The music may be faintly audible or just vividly imagined, it doesn't matter, the room brightens with the light of a windowed gallery, a strange rhino like animal, a young woman coming up through a slot in the floor, now standing against white windows, the pang that hooks me through the heart. I know that Daki is seeing something else, bright moments of his own, although this one was never my own, maybe there's some residue of the old man left. The moment the love dart is shot, not even the realization that there is desire, let alone the silhouettes of two bare bodies, silhouettes of the first discovery and the greatest first intimacy, transport of consummation. Consummation is one of the most important brights I've lost; that's old days, that's what I tell myself.

"Peanut butter."

"Lemon juice," the machine says.

"Bread crumbs."

"Butter," the voice answers.

I think Daki gave up on me. I don't know how long it's been since I noticed metal things, a great many of them, attached to the ceiling, mounts in the ceiling, and other mounts coming out of the floor, and it dawned on me then that adjustments to these would help the stage field. The bat flies by listening, and I am like the bat, loathsome, crepuscular, nervous, damaged easily, so I followed my guess and began making the adjustments. The metal things are long hinged arms reinforced with struts, they come to a point at the end, with a ball bearing at the tip, and they, I instinctively guessed this, have to caliper the edges of the field evenly. I didn't check my watch, and I don't own one, so I can only suppose that I blew many hours in this task and that Daki abandoned me meanwhile. He must have tried to reason with me ha ha. I might recall his voice, imprecations, but that could be my imagination. It wouldn't have been like him to leave me without a word, though. He won't tell on me, that's for sure. The field is definitely bigger, brighter, sharper. The second I look at it, all my intensest emotions burst in me. So I don't look at it. All the same, I want to keep it white hot, so I keep running back to yell condiment names into the syphons. It's about the moment I finish fiddling with the last calibrator that I can spare enough attention to realize I am alone and that the serpents of old have entered the pyramid and are gliding like gymnast's ribbons over glowing vertical membranes that appear to be bubbles that jellyfish is blowing outside, that's fine, let it alone. Serpents gathered up in piles, on the floor and on top of the washing machines. Now that I'm alone there's no reason I should keep my clothes on; I'm no more subject to arrest than I would be. I turn from my heap of clothes and throw myself up onto the stage of blinding light.

Now I know what impalement feels like. I'm not even there. This is only a step. I don't know if it's the threshold or the first of many steps. I grab it by the shoulders.

"Do you love me?" I shout accusingly.

The glare changes. It's too hard to get how. Looking at it there's a pain of intensity I didn't think I was capable of like a wafer of insanity across the back of my eyes.

"Get this curse off me!" I scream, losing it.

Over the shoulder I see her again, turning against the window so that her hair spins out like the hem of a skirt and the edge of her face is dusted with light like a crescent moon, and then I see my whole life I lunge for, blundering forward.

I glance to the side and see the room again. There, up on the wall, are the two glows. They sweep down and for a moment I think they'll harbor in the eyesockets of the two cops shouldering toward me but they pass them and drop further heading for the eyesockets of the serpent coiling to strike at me from the top of something as high as my chest. A good sized industrial washing machine. As its mouth opens and its eyes are directed back and away from me the two glows surprise me by illuminating a pair of glistening fangs, a pair of spurting venom sacs that rake my eyes. My eyes explode in pain. Brilliancy becomes dull red gloom and emotion quenched like a song cut off at the climax. Restraining, dragging, talking, etcetera, etcetera, etcetera, etcetera, etcetera, etcetera, etcetera, etcetera, etcetera, etcetra, etcetera, etcetera. ET. CET. TER. A. ET. CET. TER. A. ET. CET. TER. A. ET. CET. TER. A. ET. CET. TER. A.

UNIT ????
THE END TENSE

The end begins anywhere. No unit number can be found. The end unit may occur anywhere in the sequence, and where the end unit is encountered may turn out to be anywhere in the sequence although no less the end for that. The idea to get across here is that the student is being asked to understand the end without reference to serial position, but as a mood only, a mood that can any time overtake, even at the highest numbered unit of the series. The end is brought into an unrelation with the series, which has an impetus of its own.

There is a sharp distinction to be drawn between the end, the closing of the door, and another state of affairs for which there is no good term, typified by petering or ebbing. The end is more positive, definite, and deliberate than petering. Petering simply indicates the exhaustion of motive force, and/or a succumbtion to other related forces. The end is the establishment of an unrelation that is the necessary precondition for beginning. There is no way to begin without first being finished.

Phantasmagoria has no end tense. This tense is not formed by prefixion, medifixion, suffixion, affixion, the employment of particles, by modification of other words, syntactically, or contextually. Instead, one forms no end tense by

UNIT ???? READING

It is said—it is *said*—that I am an inmate of a psychiatric hospital, and

Repeating myself up there, "it is said," was a mistake, but I won't erase it. If I erase it, then it's as good as admitting I take it for granted that repeating those words will make me seem crazy, but I'm not concerned with how I seem, because I'm not trying to put in an appearance. I'm doing something, not trying to do something, that is, not testing; that what I do may be a trial of something is neither here nor there. I certainly am already finished. I don't know exactly what I'm doing, apart from—I almost said, "apart from obeying an obscure impulse to write," but that's a fragment of some nineteenth century stuff that's gotten into me. The impulse isn't obscure, it isn't even an impulse. I am officially putting what I have, in writing, on the other side of the scales of judgement. If I begin by saying that I am an inmate of a psychiatric hospital, then it's because that is what rests, what presses down rather, what shoves the other side of the scales of judgement down all the way, since everyone calls you crazy whether you're crazy every second or only partially or only intermittently. The only ones who are exempt are the ones who more or less always seem normal.

Proving my sanity is something I would like to be able to do, but I am able to do it no better, and no worse, than anyone else. Naturally I have tried this, but the idea of proof here—what is it? Whatever happens to be convincing to my superiors. My habit of referring to them in that way is rightly interpreted by them as defiance, but I think they regard defiance, within what they believe to be well-considered limitations and what I believe to be randomly improvised decisions whose only consistent feature is that they originate with my superiors, to be a potential sign of sanity. Proving my sanity is not really important to me. It isn't important to me at all. If insanity is not a sign that someone can't manage to abase himself as ordered to by the permanent circumstances in which he finds himself, or by living, and therefore a kind of distinction like a disease among hereditary aristocracy, then it can only be humanity, and part of humanity's insanity involves scapegoating some so as to enable the rest to go about their insane business under cover of sanity, like a government that routinely shoots a bunch of haphazardly selected, friendless souls and claims rule of law while going about its habitually criminal business, or business, plain and simple. I just don't want the autobiography of me that they are writing to be the only one. Neither will ever be read by anyone, that isn't the point, I'm just pushing back with my pen against every push of theirs and overwriting their black letters with letters in white ink to achieve neutralization and exhaustion. There is absolutely no need for any conscious intention to spy on someone in order for there to be spying, and there is much too persistent bustle and pointless fussing going on in my near vicinity. How can there possibly be anything left to do? How is it the upkeep of such an empty, minimally-appointed building can demand all this coming and going and scraping on the floor and opening and shutting of drawers and cabinets and closets and rattling of pails and a noise that sounds like dozens of broom and mop handles collapsing in heaps and the loud beaver-tail whallop of a heavy floor covering, a tarp or more likely a thick mat, slapping the floor in the distance and reverberating as if the whole hospital, which is a baffling maze of rooms of all kinds, were acoustically an open hangar? Is this really so very plausible, and is what I put down on paper, ostensibly plausible details and all, any less? Does this building or its staff make me anything I wouldn't be somewhere else?

There's a false plot on offer here about suicide and homelessness etc.

It's a story with easily-anticipated outlines that unwind like creeping tendrils of decay back into the past, shaping it to fit the current situation's needs. The plot is my enemy; it's their plot, the circumstances. That's nothing but a paperweight and not a true story of the truth that only some will be able to live. Life is produced in all kinds of ways and what matters is the ways you do it, which is true ethics in contradistinction to the suffocating false ethics of false necessities of invented blindness. If I am content to stay where I am, it isn't because of whatever is supposed to have happened to someone I am told is myself, happenings so supposedly full of horror that this place is assumed to look, by contrast, like a tranquil haven. In reality I'm content to be here because I don't need to fake sanity while I am here. I hate to generalize, but I wouldn't be surprised if, imagining a genie gave me a God's eye view of the place, that turned out to be the only good thing about this hospital. Or any psychiatric hospital.

*

This will end in what language names "death," and which must, for us as creatures of language, therefore be death. Is death the moment when language is finished with us, or we with it? When I die, do I disappear from existence, or from language? It is impossible, if only for me, to determine whether or not my disappearance from language is my disappearance from existence. My death might be nothing more than the moment in which I separates permanently from me. Death may be the moment one exits the plot and enters an unforeseen level of life. A reader conspires with a book, and pretends along with it that the characters are persons, the plot is a life or lives, in order to use them as doorways and enter into something else, with them as memories.

*

They've just moved me to another part of the hospital. I'm told that they are going to transfer me, but I've heard that before. These assurances come and go, without making much difference. While it would be easy for me to draw up a list of all kinds of nightmarish changes for the worse, I don't feel like it.

I love the bright space that comes before "They've just moved me ..." and that delivers the event to the record. That's just the way it ought to be done. With silence or wind, and light or darkness.

If I set it all down badly, what does it matter, the world needs weak people too, and no one is strong all the time. The world needs bad writers. The silence of countless new voices. I know all about what the world needs; there's no one in the world who knows it better. No one listens to the world the way I do. No proof of that either, but probability of cosmic proportions, so I won't erase it. I only erase misspellings. This is my repetition. My commitment to truth.

It is vitally important that I be sequestrated in the new psychiatric hospital they've just built. The new, state of the art psychiatric hospital, is where I must go.

*

I am admitted to my new domain. A door of blue planks, up and down, with a latch, not a knob. Out through the doorway, which comes to an onionated point, onto a red tiled terrace with frilly white crenelations; the architecture is like a Moroccanesque fantasy wedding cake. A causeway extends from between the crenelations not quite opposite this door, and as I approach it I drink in with soul-inflating pleasure the frightening expanse and vacancy of the intensely blue windswept sky, the intangible wind, and the view. We overlook here a sprawling valley with distant peaks, etched against the sky with uncanny clarity. The valley is banded browns and greens, sulky trees gathered around clearings heaped with stones. Sweeping gracefully up the slope, the silver glitter of the funicular which brings patients, doctors, visitors, and staff up to the hospital from a small terminal in the foothills. The footprint of the funicular is a black circle or scorchmark on the ground. The causeway is straight and narrow between walls that barely reach up past my knees, and it is the upper surface of a steeply sloping, solid white wedge that rises seventy-five feet along the crag the hospital sits on.

The causeway extends perhaps fifty-five feet to a white cone as tall as the crag itself. The top of the cone is a flat circus a hundred and five feet in diameter, with a low wall around the rim, another lower wall within that gives it the appearance of a huge ashtray, and within that there is a circular building with a very shallow spiral roof, like an all-but-flattened conch shell.

I cross the causeway to the circular area quickly, trying to outpace the vertigo that always assaults me in high and exposed places. There are crescent benches molded out of the same albino material as everything else here. Directly before me the building rises. Broad, also nearly-flattened archways fitted with clear glass open it on all sides. There's a door here in the glass.

This is where I am to be quarantined. Over there, to my left, a stairway curves down into a slot in the floor; my living quarters are down below. Before me, a great big table like a giant mushroom, all white and featureless, with a chair. No, two chairs—there's another one on the far side. The table is fixed to the floor on a thick stalk, and seems to be molded all of a piece with the building. There is nothing on the table, which is at least twenty-five feet in circumference, except a big white book, which is closed. It smells like a museum or a library in here; a smell of clean air conditioners and filtered institution air, paste or glue, paper, varnish, paint. It's a smell I've always liked a lot. I imagine that parts of my interior regions must have that smell. The smell is very clean, fresh and antiseptic smelling, sterile, but at the same time it reminds me strangely of the smell that comes out from under fingernails or the sour taste and smell in the mouth a little while after drinking coffee or milk.

I take a quick turn around the room. There are stiff, pushbutton light switches on the walls next to each of the glass doors. The lights are shaped like inverted tulips hanging in a ring from the ceiling, which when turned on throw a halo around the table and a negative halo around that, so that there's a strip of shadow, a black ring, to be traversed between any of the glass doors and the single room's middle area. There are external light switches too, for illuminating the terrace at night. I've just now noticed the few raised planters scattered around the terrace; the soil inside looks very black, speckled with tiny white beads of fertilizer I guess. Growing in the planters are many kinds of small wildflowers and what I guess without much confidence are aloes made of smooth triangles like huge pliable fingernails or naked animal ears. The eaves of the building create a dimple of shade around it.

After this strolling review of my new domain, I sit down at the table and begin to work immediately. Taking my seat I notice the view; the terrace on the far side from the causeway must be subtly lowered in some way, because I can see almost everything from here.

*

I spend every day working with the translation, in colloquy with my idea in whose presence I become the old teacher entranced in senescence and gulping blood. The glory here is so radiant and ethereal by day that the beams chime faintly as they enter through the low archways. Through the arch before me I can distinctly see the remotest of the slough valleys, where the human remains of a colossal mass suicide are visible only as a greyish jumble that seems to smoke with undulating plumes of blowflies. At night, corpse fires burn over there, so that it looks like a village full of lamps or a crowd of giant lizards staring fixedly back in this direction with reflective eyes or densely crowded vigilant constellations, since the horizon often disappears at night. In the blackness, it's easy to imagine the cone is the prow of a massive ship, and the heatless flames up ahead are, I don't know, some kind of ocean lights. Bioluminescent jellyfish.

*

Lights, and in the gloom of the dusk of a day, raise your head. Look around yourself, like an interior full of sharp blackness sliced into the everywhere; whose common motif is abduction by voices for the living self, and the down, down toward the source of the noise acts in conceiving of its own death. The one who speaks is an image, the speaker learning countless spells far worse than loneliness. He can readily step behind such an image, overwhelming his frenzied refusals.

It is already allowing, zeroing in on him, updated. So he marks the place with a slip. They were all meant to die, tucked under his arm. The table, which is covered with idea, the ritual in-front-of-izes itself against them. Realization that he is the victim of the second across books, chasing his shadow just to keep the mob living. He feels the horror of being chosen. Does he own this place, if only because he's not always persecuted for no good reason? Kind of aristocratic, if solitary, way of life, where such outsiders can never expect justice. For fungus or a worm, feasting on the corpse of trust, while a person with a place trusts laboriously, piled up during its lifetime. With other trust, provided that place that he's been reading for a while, and his hand at the edge.

The students form a cult around turns from his work. The library's God. See all of space. Just your bedroom. Secret passages. Grim statuary in phantasmagoria of distinct grammatical monsters. Unliving self that is the ghost the former subself, somewhere in the stacks. The shelves may speak or write as either.

Paces up and down the subtracting self, because the one who speaks is referring as he clears his throat, all because vicarious speaker is not dead. He's disturbing. He scans the ritual whose meaning is impossible to mistake, characters compressed together hard, forcing him to see and accept, the wrong thing heads for his work room with the book. If it is a mistake, why is he terrorized by books laid out neatly in a grid?

The wanderer was not an innocent and has exclusive use of it. It is mercy or nothing, they have no choices, dead city and abandoned wealth. Fallen asleep, his forehead resting on the back students, and teaches the lesson, now and then fits of sleeping come on almost every time and light of his small, toylike lamp along some words, his forehead, his face lined and confused, and the decay, and the iron scent of blood that dribbles words.

*

Let no one say that this asylum is not magnificently well-appointed, let no one say that what I record here is not an accurate description of the asylum I was an inmate of at the time of its writing. My living quarters are magnificently well-appointed. The toilet I use, for example, is the kind that can be flushed again and again without delay. It has no tank at all. The shower, which I use many times a day, comes with a detachable showerhead on a hose, a very unusual appointment in an asylum. The water pressure is good and there is abundant hot water, although I do find it difficult to adjust the temperature. Likewise the kitchen facilities and the sleeping facilities. The recreational facilities not so much.

For me, the palatiality of this asylum solves the problem I've always had, wanting to live in a palace and not wanting to own one, and not wanting to be a part of any kind of system that sustains palaces. No willing part. Included in this latter disinclination is a desire not to be a courtier, a servant, or a functionary, or in any other way to belong to an organization of any description, and that goes for families, plots in novels, countries, classes, and customers. This asylum is like the library in the heart of the abandoned city, or the spacious ruin of which I tenant only a modest fraction, or the isolated outpost. No plot can reach me here. Let no one say this asylum is anything other than what I say it is, likewise for my reasons for being here, likewise about myself, I did not volunteer my face or person for anything, I refuse to volunteer my face, I volunteer myself away from all invitations and turn my face to translation work. I sit over my translation work as long as I can stand it, every day, until I'm too sick of myself to go on. The asylum, or at least this isolation area in it, is probably the environment best suited to prolonging the interval before I get sick of myself, which marks the finish of my working day. When I feel it catching up to me, I take a turn around the room or out on the terrace overlooking the valley, and, observing from the terrace wall the intensely dark blue tiny flowers in the green froth of the outcropping to the west, imagining walking there with insects tossing in my face and besieging me with their plucks, the hollow sound the tramp of my feet makes on the packed earth path, walking there in negative machine, where the ground, as I can see even from my table, is pitch black sour smelling loam, and when sunset gilds one corner of the sky I continue to gaze in imagination from a spot among the rocks on the outcropping as the arriving night turns the valley before me into one unbroken contour of darkness, I find I can go back to the table and work a little while longer, occasionally even several more hours, before the feeling clicks decisively shut around me and that's it.

*

Complete silence prevails here. When I am inside doors, there is no sound apart from my own intermittent racket and the discreet, incessant whirring of the air current. Out of doors, all I ever hear is wind, there having been no other kind of weather since my arrival. Birds and insects I also hear, inattentively, very inattentively. No noises of any kind reach me from the main body of the asylum itself, which is too far away at arm's length. So, I have perfect quiet to bask in, at last, I love it. I say I love it. I say I love it and that's that.

The translation work is doing well, although it would be doing still better if they didn't insist on bringing people to see me every day. I wrote just now of the silence, which permits me to hear distinctly the banging of the blue door behind me and the approach of uncertain footsteps up the causeway behind me, and the mute yawn of the glass door behind me. My visitor typically sits on my right, turned toward me, often with the right arm resting on the table. The chairs here swivel. Each visitor carries a three by five piece of paper folded in half widthwise, which is either handed to me or slid to me across the table. I don't retrieve them if they drop on the floor. Doubling up and outstretching my arm is too painful and embarrassing for me, and I keep this in mind when they reach down and pick the paper back up again, being careful not to gloat. I never drop anything.

The papers usually contain questions and I answer them aloud. I don't know what I tell them; I speak without paying much attention to the words or to the visitors. The details of their personal appearances, I think the plural is correct there even if it is slightly awkward, are not retained in my memory, generally. One woman stands out, because the whites of her eyes were so unusually vivid, were all but phosphorescent, and in what must be a fanciful embroidering of the recollection I discern a thin but distinct lambency on the cheeks and under the brows. She brought a rhetorical question, although I answered it anyway since it was obvious that some answer was called for, otherwise why would she have come? It's impossible that anyone, especially any woman, could have any personal connection to myself. Now I recall that, at the time, I supposed she was a psychologist incognito, bringing with her a question, formulated by a committee of some kind I imagine, intended to elicit from me a seemingly innocent or irrelevant response giving away a weakness or some clue to my inner state that would later be used against me. If that is a vicious assumption, let at least part of the blame fall on them for being secretive.

My answer to her escapes me. As a rule, I received the papers in my right hand as I sat facing forward, the white book in front of me and a small notebook, in which I jotted down my translation in shorthand, to its right. The procedure I'd hit on involved reading the paper by holding it up in front of me so that it came between me and the book, right in the stream of my translation concentration, both to minimize the distraction and to make full use of my faculties in answering. I would read the note, which was never more than one line, seamlessly into my translation, and answer with the second thing that came into my mind. The first thing I would always hold back, although I can't promise that these first things didn't get into the shorthand notebook. Scratching them out later shouldn't be too difficult. I never waste time going back over my notes because I have the feeling that there is a period I have been given to examine the white book, and, the book being enormously thick, and the pages so light and airy, and the columns of type so tightly contracted, I don't think it likely I will come close to finishing. Actually finishing would be a completely disorienting experience that could easily deprive me of my wits permanently anyway.

*

A New Development
  Debating
  Yesterday, or recently, yet another of these.
  I drink a fair amount of coffee over the course of the day, which I brew myself downstairs in the kitchen. I don't know where it comes from, I think there must be a great deal of it stowed in the cupboard because no one ever seems to bring me any food. This means that I am constantly getting up to urinate. And sure enough it seems every time I am downstairs carefully urinating into the bowl I will hear, thanks to the unbroken silence, the clap of the blue door, footsteps on the causeway, the wheeze of the glass door, so that my every interruption evidently is guaranteed to be interrupted as if I were being watched and it were assumed by whoever sends people to me that it's a good time to do so, since I'm breaking off work momentarily to urinate. On this occasion I was again carefully urinating into the bowl when I heard the door clap etc. However, when I, composing myself and as usual trying to wipe the expression of impatience and in fact all expression off my face, climbed out of my living area, I found a man there waiting for me without any paper in his hand and dressed in a blue jumpsuit, open to the waist, exposing a white shirt and necktie, an empty clipboard hanging in his right hand. Then I noticed a group of people on the terrace at the far end of the causeway, and a single person, a large man in a sweater the drab color of mustard, standing opposite them.

The man in the jumpsuit led me along the causeway and motioned to me to stay there, on the causeway, a few feet back from the point at which it joined the terrace. Then he announced the debate topic and we began, the man in the sweater and myself. We argued by turns for a long time. The sun was dazzling but not too hot, and the steady wind made it difficult to hear everything. We both became more and more agitated by the effort of argument and the balks we threw at each other.

I forget the subject and most of what we said, which, at least in my case, was wholly impromptu, as no one had informed me that I would be debating that day, let alone what the debate would be about. I don't say decide, since it seems to me a debate decides nothing apart from who is the abler at getting over. Which of us was the intended beneficiary of this treatment if treatment it was and not just a way to pass the time, I can't say, I'd never seen the other patient before. The end more or less stays with me. I accused him of being unable to think with gaps and instead foaming everything over with "Hegelian mush" and said it is necessary to pin things down in their strict individuality.

"How is pinning things down, as you yourself call it," he insisted, "supposed to be consistent with the relativism that you espouse?"

"It's completely consistent!"

"You call yourself a Deleuzian?" he cried.

"Every deterritorialization is immediately followed by a reterritorialization! It's on the same page in the book! You haven't read it!"

"But that's not a pinning down—!"

"Yes it is!"

"—it's not a pinning down! Pinning down is an Aristotelian argument from—"

"The only question that matters is, 'what is this?'" I said, rapping the banister with the tip of my finger dramatically. "'What is this? What is this?'"

"That is the metaphysical question!" he trumpeted victoriously. "That is essentialist!"

There was some upset then, the group were joining their voices in with considerable animation and I couldn't be sure if they were stirred up by the argument or if there were some distraction, a medical emergency or something.

"I snap—I snap my fingers—" I had difficulty making myself heard over the hubbub of the group, and the rising wind. I was looking to land my barb. "I snap my fingers at your 'essentialismus'!"

There was a brief lull the moment I said this. Do I have anything more? No. Nothing definite or quick enough. The opening closes and he is going on, although now I can't hear him.

"It is a metaphysical question! It is the metaphysical question!" he brays.

"I asked it three times," I say, holding up the number three. "The question is answered by a repetition of the question, not by an essentialist claim, not necessarily by an essentialist claim, but by a repetition."

"That's not an answer!"

"The repetition is the answer. It is the only way to go on from the question."

"The question is itself metaphysical!"

"No it isn't!"

"Yes it is!"

"No it isn't! The answer you are looking for is metaphysical but the question is not yet appropriated to some metaphysics until the answer is given!"

"Your repetition also assumes metaphysics!"

"Now you change the meaning of metaphysics!"

It ended as it started, and I was escorted back along the causeway to the glass door by the man in the blue jumpsuit, largely, I think, because a verbal or manual command to return to where I was before might have seemed like a slight.

A New Development

~~End or Temporary~~

Suspension and Possible End of Debating

In fact, no one has been to see me for days. I am not dissatisfied with this new development because it helps me to settle into the gentle automatism I like on the one hand it's true, I do settle into this with perverse inward expressions of contentment and pleasure because I know it's wrong to escape all feeling, live like a sleepwalker, and that the placidity of my strictly routine and monotonous way of life is a cheat. I ought to be out there getting fucked, but isn't it true that change will find me here just as easily as it will anywhere else—more easily, actually, the more unvarying the pattern the easier it is to disrupt, the more obvious and affecting the disruption is. So I have only retreated to a place where the overall level of change is small enough to be manageable, at the expense of making myself more vulnerable. I imagine that a sailor whose ship is thrown all over the world, at the mercy, more or less, of the ocean, does the opposite but for the same reason:

live in the middle of constant, drastic changes, and change won't mean anything to you anymore either.

New Discovery

I am not awaiting instructions, they are what I am translating:

It seems to me the book before me tells the story of a man who had to be quarantined and specially educated in preparation for a vital journey. He goes nowhere and sees no one in order to prepare him to travel an incredible distance away and meet a person of incalculable importance. Still not sure who this person is. The rank vague too, except that it is supreme supreme supreme. Even so, this person is only a representative of a greater. Not necessarily a greater person, but something greater. Maybe just that: greater.

Since this discovery, have gotten into habit of thinking of self as ambassador, too. Adequate placeholder idea, but could drag along unnoticed assumptions could get in the way of right understanding.

Journey one way.

Translation is training in language at destination.

Persistent association of training in language and destination employing prepositions and elusively antecedented pronouns suggests nonsense idea that translation training is travel to destination or is destination or destiny, difficult to differentiate.

I profit here from my ready way of imposing limits. I've always been past master of raising force fields, drawing separation lines, keeping track of open or closed doors or windows, determining extents and timing things, estimating how much or how little to wait, and so on. If anyone can find the dividing line between the ideas I am trying to translate, or encircle the lot of them and declare them altogether without clear distinctions, it'll be me.

*

Wild excitement.

Constantly deepening excitement.

*

Smelling worse bathing notwithstanding. Sick, definitely. No one comes to the blue door.

Skin dull and lifeless. I look awful. Very sick. Clammy.

No less energy, but no feeling of liveliness. Body feels heavier in fact, much heavier, like lead, but strength seems compensatorially augmented. Thoughts also leaden, though no slower, oppressive dimness, bitter weariness is being imputed to me, less like a mental or physical sensation, more like a dogmatic opinion impervious to reasoning or evidence. Entering into me now there are both this alien opinion and deep excitement like hidden unfolding of electrifying dream. Excitement plainly connected to anticipation of journey, and of meeting. Haunted by worry I am blindly writing gibberish. No retardation in pace nor reduction in volume of work done.

*

Condition worsens. No one comes. Flesh withering. Shiny, sallow patches appearing, like soapy callouses. Joints rusty. Crackle when I move. Abdomen getting pulpy, big discolorations, footprints almost. Sit for hours, total silence, realize no sound even of my breathing, realize not breathing, try to breathe, have to remember how. Stops again the moment I stop concentrating.

Disinclined to move from chair. Work continues faster than ever. Wild excitement, builds. Not mounting. Burrowing. Thrill so intense accompanied by prolonged shudder when I give in and check how much of book translated, much more done than expected. Fierce joy. Overpowering, mute excitement. Nearly ready for journey. I am going to meet the Magus.

*

staring unable not to stare at body valley

Fly clouds still.

going on working Body pieces in pieces small

Change is much advanced.

work without stop no sleep no smearing of white pages although notebook smeared liberally

*

Momentary improvement. Dawn. Brought back by blast of thunder. Watch lightning play over distant mountain. Lightning at dawn, never seen that before.

Asylum might be abandoned.

Not asleep, but not attending to surroundings. I might have lost a hundred years. The power of distraction so great in me. Power of excitement.

Dawn is overcast. Dark. Lights still on. Glass reflection shows corpse propped in chair at table. Can't tell where it is. Can't see it. Invisible. In reflection it has a white book of its own. Only one on the table.

The corpse valley perhaps meant to walk and lie down among them

Can't be trapped in quarantine

Excitement

Magus combines things, words, relations   special way

want to go through all the way

*

I'm in a wheelchair. I can't see who pushes, can't turn my head to look, don't want to, don't know why I don't. I somehow failed to notice until now. I roll through the corridors of the asylum. Very moderate, very even pace. I don't think my body will move. My hands are under the lap robe. A vitality like I've never known is welling up inside me. I feel weightless. Waves of wellbeing from the crown of my head sweep through me. The strands of millions of lives, animal, human, vegetable, are strung across my outline and strummed, making the sounding box of my limbs, my whole body, hum with strength, with superhuman strength, too strong to move, too vibrantly alive to need to. I am starting at last!

On my person, somewhere, the work book is. In that work book, any reader will discover written down in advance what is in store for them. The writing and the reading both together will both predict what will happen, and will cause it to happen also. What will happen will not be exactly as described in the work book. Not these things exactly, not necessarily these things exactly, but, on a certain level, viewed in a certain way, *these things exactly.* None of what appears in the work book has happened, even to me. Those things happened to me, but not in that way. The work book writes itself and dooms its writer.

At last I am going! An elevator ride. Descending, I think. The doors open on a long corridor without windows. We must be deep under the ground. The end of the corridor is dark. There are lights only here, at this end. I am rolled down the corridor. Eager, brimming with life, with incredible excitement, with fantastic strength in every part of me. I am going in there, where, once my eyes get used to the darkness, I will see the most beautiful, the most amazing sights. My body, too, has to accustom itself to my new vitality and power, so that I can move without splitting myself to pieces. I am finally going to meet the Magus. The grading is finished. Look in the box, labelled with your name. You passed.

Michael Cisco is best known for his first novel *The Divinity Student*, winner of the International Horror Writer's Guild Award in 1999. He is an experimental writer with an interest in horror and Lovecraftian fiction. He lives and teaches in New York City.

www.ingramcontent.com/pod-product-compliance
Lightning Source LLC
Chambersburg PA
CBHW081128020726
47505CB00010B/2279